The

Orphan

Daughter

ALSO BY CARI NOGA

Sparrow Migrations

Plover Pilgrimage

Road Biking Michigan

The
Orphan
Daughter

A Novel

Cari Noga

LAKE UNION
PUBLISHING

Text copyright © 2018 by Cari Noga
All rights reserved.

No part of this book may be reproduced, or stored in a retrieval system, or transmitted in any form or by any means, electronic, mechanical, photocopying, recording, or otherwise, without express written permission of the publisher.

Published by Lake Union Publishing, Seattle

www.apub.com

Amazon, the Amazon logo, and Lake Union Publishing are trademarks of Amazon.com, Inc., or its affiliates.

ISBN-13: 9781503901322
ISBN-10: 1503901327

Cover design by David Drummond

Printed in the United States of America

For all the brave souls who dare to become parents.

Prologue
JANE

Kodiak had hunkered under a blizzard for the last two days. The wind was so ferocious I'd gazed at the nautical map on our dining room wall and wondered aloud whether the archipelago the island anchored would rattle apart, its fragments drifting into the Gulf of Alaska and then the northern Pacific. Even across the international date line into tomorrow.

"If it does, we'll go out after 'em," Jim declared, his Coastie pride so assured that I believed him, or at least I would have loved to believe him, especially when he lifted Matt onto his shoulders and paraded around the tiny house with our delighted almost-three-year-old. "A Coastie always delivers."

But the storm abated with no need to call out the Coasties. After two days indoors, I relented and went out with Matt to play on the giant snow mounds. It was colder and windier than I'd thought.

"Ten more minutes, then we go in, OK?" I crossed my arms over my bulging belly, trying to pin down Jim's flapping coat. Maternity snow gear wasn't standard stock at the CGX. Rather than pay for shipping on a special order, I'd worn one of his coats all winter, but the zipper no longer closed.

"Watch me!" Atop one of the mounds, Matt waved a mittened hand, blue to match his hat. I'd knitted both. Another way to stretch Jim's paycheck.

"I'm watching." Inside, my needles now held a pair of booties. Yellow, not tempting fate. We'd know in four more weeks, anyway. As long as the baby was healthy, it didn't matter, I reminded myself. And a brother would be nice for Matt. Still, I wanted a daughter. Amy? Heather? Laura? None of the names we'd discussed sounded quite right.

Matt belly flopped down the path he'd eroded. "I can go fast!"

"Really fast!" I crouched down to grab his icy mitten and haul him to his feet, my chest pressing against my belly. Linda's front door opened, and my neighbor stepped out.

"Jane! Have you been watching?"

"Sure." I nodded at Matt, climbing the snow pile again.

"Not that." Linda shook her head. "The TV. The news." Her words were puffs of white.

My own breath caught, a frozen moment of realization. We all knew the deadline had passed. The Coast Guard was still military, even if civilians didn't realize it.

"He's sending them in. It's on CNN."

My breath finally released in a gusty puff. "Air strikes?"

Linda nodded, and we looked west, toward the base, where Jim and Linda's husband, Adam, were both on duty.

"Come in," Linda said. "I just put a pot of coffee on."

Persuaded with the promise of brownies, Matt ate two before his eyelids closed. I tucked him in on Linda's bed before returning to the TV, where we watched President Bush make promises. Nighttime video of Baghdad followed, a mostly black screen with a sickly yellowish-green glow along the horizon, flashes occasionally erupting above. Then a retired-general talking head, then back to the White House. Repeat.

Matt slept on. The baby was still, too. I'd remember that later. Adam called, said he and Jim had to work late. Linda made dinner, then helped me get Matt back home and into his own bed. On our living room couch, I knitted a few more rows on the yellow booties while the news cycled again, trying to stay awake until Jim got home.

It was after midnight when Matt's cries and an eight-months-pregnant gotta-go-*now* urge woke me, still alone on the couch. Just how truly alone I would remember later, too. No kicking or pushing. Hadn't been all day. Hurriedly I went to the bathroom, not even bothering to turn on a light, eager to soothe Matt. If only I'd turned on the light. If only I'd looked. I'm sure I would have seen the water turning pink. Instead, Jim found me curled up with Matt the next morning. Our son dozed peacefully. The bloodstains on the sheet under me seeped through to the mattress.

January wore on. Baghdad fell. Headlines trumpeted the US victory. Tensions eased on the rest of the base, except for our house, where I unraveled the yellow booties. I gave the needles to Linda when we transferred to the Lower 48 three months later. Houston. Jim said the warm sun would help. He was sure of it.

He was wrong. The cold had penetrated me too deeply. For years, in fact, I longed for a blizzard as wild as the one that shook the islands that time. Even fiercer, one that would have swept Kodiak out to sea, across the international date line, and into tomorrow, so that worst day of my life would never have come.

Chapter 1
LUCY

April 13, 2011, New York City

Phoebe and I walk around on wood-chip trails, looking at wildflowers and listening for birds, so we can fill out the flora and fauna columns on our worksheets. Ms. Kedzie and the other sixth grade teacher said the field trip was to teach us wildlife lessons, but you can see most of the same stuff in Central Park, and Daddy and I go there almost every weekend. Still, I write my list carefully, alphabetizing everything, making sure the columns are even, ten flora and ten fauna, when Mom's text pops up over my Hello Kitty wallpaper.

Landed in LA. Wish us luck! Daddy sends besos. xoxo

"You can get texts out here?" Phoebe says, looking up from her list. It took us an hour to get from the city to the nature center for the field trip.

"Apparently." Mom really wants this meeting with the network to go well, so I start to type back, buena suerte, but all of a sudden Eli Moore and Joel Griffin are standing right next to me.

"Hey! No screens on field trips!" Eli says.

"Go away." I roll my eyes.

"Seriously. Mrs. Williams checked our backpacks, didn't she, Joel? No fair."

"Probably because you're not responsible," Phoebe says.

"Right. Ms. Kedzie didn't check ours," I say.

"Uh-uh. No one's supposed to have them today," Eli declares.

"So give it over!" Before I can stop him, Joel's grabbed my phone.

"Hey! Give it back!"

"Catch!" Joel tosses it to Eli. The two of them break off the path, running through a little strip of woods toward an open, grassy space beyond.

"Come on!" I charge after them.

"Forget it, Lucy. When we tell Ms. Kedzie, they'll get in more trouble," Phoebe says.

But I was sick and tired of them both. They sat behind us on the bus here, and Eli spent the whole trip with his knees up, jabbing my back. Inside, when they showed us the amphibian exhibit, I saw Joel poking at the snapping turtle, teasing the poor thing.

I dodge in between the trees, my Hello Kitty glitter high-tops pounding. The ground's uneven with roots and old logs, not smooth like the trail. Ahead of me Eli trips, sending my phone and dead brown leaves flying.

"Hah!" Serves him right. I close in, but Joel gets there before me and then sprints out of the woods, across the grass. He's fast and turns around to run backward, wiggling my phone, *nyah-nyah-nyah*, which makes me even madder. Deirdre calls things sodding when she doesn't like them. *Sodding crowded subways. Sodding international phone rates.* Sodding boys.

I run faster than ever, lunging after Joel. My fingers brush the bottom of his T-shirt, then grab it. Got him! I lean farther forward, trying to gather in a fistful of fabric, but Joel speeds up, trying to get away, and I'm yanked off balance and falling forward, and it's like the time Mom and Daddy and I saw a home-plate dive when we went to the network family night at Yankee Stadium, except on grass instead of dirt.

When I sit up, my sleeves and leggings have long green stains on them. I can scrape my fingernail through the green gunk on my knee, the smell sweet but too strong. Ms. Kedzie is marching my way, one hand piloting Joel, my phone in the other, her lips in a tight line.

Chapter 2
JANE

April 15, 2011, Old Mission Peninsula, Michigan

Shifting back onto my heels, I admire the row of new green shoots I've uncovered. Garlic grows straight out of the soil, and leaves start forking off the shoot in V formations. It always gives me a good feeling, once I've cleared off the winter mulch, to see those green Vs reaching for the spring sun.

One row cleared, three more to go. I rise, grabbing the old bleacher pad turned kneepad. I used to sit on it at Matt's Little League games. A different rite of spring from a lifetime ago. Turning to the next row, I see Martha's muddy postal car slowing down.

I hold my breath. It's the fourth mailbox since last fall. Plow trucks hit the trifecta this winter, taking one out in December, one in January, and the third in February. That makes this the worst winter, mailbox-wise, since I've lived up north. Now that Jim's gone I'm stuck with replacing them. After the third one sailed into the culvert, I complained at the township office.

"Fact of life around here," said the unsympathetic road supervisor, jamming his hands into the pockets of his Carhartt jacket. "Get a PO box, if you're so tired of it."

I considered it, briefly. But I knew I'd wind up regretting the daily five-mile trip up to the general store that doubles as the post office more than the chore of installing a fourth mailbox, even in the damp gray chill that is February here on the forty-fifth parallel.

Well, just shy of it. The Old Mission Peninsula is a ridge-lined, gnarled eighteen-mile finger of land that slices Lake Michigan's Grand Traverse Bay and pokes right at that imaginary line halfway between the equator and the North Pole. It's a lovely place in summer. Cool lake-effect breezes. Gorgeous views of verdant vineyards and orchards sloping down the hillsides. People don't like it so much in the winter, when the lake-effect breezes drop snow that's measured in feet, sometimes even double-digit feet.

I like it year-round. I live on top of one of the ridges, with a view of a bay on both sides. An aerie just for me. Except for the decimated mailboxes, I like the snow. Like the quiet, the stillness. Like how it further insulates my garlic, nestled under the mulch, my raspberries, my asparagus. Like how it keeps most people away, except for the plow truck drivers and Martha. She'll be careful, I know, but the shoulders are treacherous in early April, spin-your-wheels muddy one day, slip-and-slide frozen the next.

The wind is blowing warm, from the south, and I unzip my own Carhartt as I go to meet her. Actually the jacket was Jim's. It's too big, but I wear it with a couple of sweatshirts underneath.

I pick my way around the potholes in the gravel driveway. Might not be able to get away with letting that go another year. If it's too rough, my tomatoes bump and bruise in the truck. That's not good for Plain Jane's reputation.

My mother used to call me Plain Jane. That was before she married Esteban and Gloria was born. So she wasn't comparing us then. But Gloria turned out to be the pretty one, too.

Muddy ice skims hide several more potholes on the driveway. Martha's still sitting out on the road in her postal car, flashers on. That's unusual. She's not one who likes to chitchat, either. Sometimes I envy her the job. Lots of quiet on the back roads, and a steady paycheck.

"Hey, Jane. Feels a little bit like spring today." Martha's probably fifty, only a few years older than I am, but spending entire days in her car has taken a toll. She's doughy around the middle and pale all year. But she's dependable and has never once taken out the mailbox. She also always has the latest gossip.

"Little bit." I nod, digging my toe into a clump of icy snow. The plow's winter accumulation, thigh high a month ago, has melted to ankle depth, the once-soft white flakes now a crunchy, granular gray.

"Hear about the raid over in Leelanau?" Martha shields her eyes as she looks up at me, so I can't see them.

"A raid? Like for drugs or something?"

"Not drugs. People." Martha reaches over onto her passenger seat and hands me a newspaper. "Immigration."

"ICE busts 12 at Catholic church," the headline reads. "Priest decries raid as 'cruel.'" I squint, but can't read any further without my glasses.

"They came to the Spanish Mass over at St. Pat's and picked 'em up afterward," Martha fills in for me. "Most of them worked late into harvest and were trying to hang on over the winter. Working at the processors, keeping their kids in school."

"There's a crime," I say tartly. "Taking the factory jobs no one else wants. Giving their kids an education."

"And keeping them out of Mexico," Martha adds. "Talk about drugs. It's street warfare down there, the drug cartels and gangs and all. That's what Miguel says, anyway." She adjusts the seat belt around her middle and waves the paper away as I try to hand it back. "Keep it. I've read it. Have a nice weekend."

"You, too," I say automatically, though for me, the only distinguishing feature is that the weekend driver, rather than Martha, will be by. I open the mailbox to check for her leavings. A catalog, junk mail coupons, and three handwritten envelopes, all with local postmarks. Subscriptions, most likely. Nothing that looks like a bill, so I decide to let the garlic wait and open the envelopes instead.

In the house, Sarge meets me at the door, then bolts for the barn. He's an indoor-outdoor cat. Mostly indoors in winter, mostly outdoors in summer. Spring and fall it's a judgment call. Today's the first day he's deemed outside-worthy since last fall. Another good sign.

Sure enough, the envelopes contain three subscriptions to Plain Jane's Community Supported Agriculture. Two are for the standard deal. They pay up front; I deliver a weekly share of whatever the farm produces from June through September. Kind of like a farmers' market delivery service. But the third wants to buy a working share—half off in exchange for coming to work two hours a week all season. The mother says she's eager to expose her kids "to the work ethic of farm life."

Video-game addicts, no doubt. Or permanently glued to their phone or game thing. Great. The county Extension people talked me into offering the working share at the marketing workshop I went to last fall. "By offering an experience as well as a service, you distinguish yourself," the director had said. "Plus, you increase your word-of-mouth exposure exponentially."

Exponentially, all I know is how the work piles up in summer. It's started already, but from May on it just gains speed, like a snowball pushed downhill. It's a lot to handle, but it'll be worse trying to teach someone else to do what would take them twice as long. I do just about everything on the farm, and if I can't, I call Miguel. With his contacts in the migrant community, he can round up someone eager and experienced within twenty-four hours, or he'll do it himself, as well as or better than I can. As I'm pondering the problem, the phone rings.

"May I please speak with Mrs. Jane McArdle?" It's a woman's crisp voice.

"Ummm. Yes. Speaking." When was I last called Mrs. McArdle?

"Thank you. Hold, please," the voice replies.

"Excuse me?" I say. Who puts the person *they* call on hold?

"Mrs. McArdle." Another voice, a man's. "My name is William Langley. I'm an attorney in New York City."

"Yes?" I'm still thinking about the kids in whom I am to magically instill a work ethic this summer.

"It's quite a relief to finally speak with you."

"How's that?" I tune in to William Langley's words. "You're in New York City?" Gloria lives there. She's the host of *Buenos Días, Nueva York*, a Spanish version of the *Today* show, the way she described it.

"Yes, and I've been trying to reach you for the last forty-eight hours. On a matter of some urgency. I've left several messages."

I used to have an answering machine with a light that flashed when there was a message. It finally broke, forcing me to voice mail. But you have to pick up the phone to hear the tone that indicates there's a message. If I don't—and over two days, there's a very good chance I wouldn't—I don't get the message.

"'A matter of some urgency.' And that would be?" I ask.

"It pertains to your niece. Luisa Ortiz," William Langley says.

"My niece?" I blank for a good three seconds. "Lucy?" Gloria's daughter would be my niece, of course.

"Lucy. Yes." He clears his throat. "I'm afraid I'm calling with bad news, Mrs. McArdle. Your sister and her husband passed away in a car accident Wednesday."

Gloria, the pretty one. Always smiling, vivacity spilling over. Her husband, Luis, was an executive at the Spanish-language network that produced her show. Dead? She's nine years younger than I am. How could she be dead?

"It was in California. LA. They were attending network meetings, in talks to begin a West Coast edition of Gloria's show. I'm surprised you haven't heard anything on the news."

I don't watch the news. I don't even have a TV.

"I'm very sorry. I was your sister's family lawyer for several years, and am now the estate's executor. She was a truly vibrant woman. Her fans have crashed the network's servers with messages."

Their world of cameras, attention, and travel was as foreign to me as the language. Gloria sent a fruit basket every Christmas. When had we last even spoken? A twinge of pain surprises me with its force. No more chances now.

"Mrs. McArdle?"

"They were . . . so young. What was it, a drunk driver or something?"

"The police are investigating." The lawyer clears his throat. "I'm sorry to deliver this news by phone. I know you must be in shock. But with a child to consider, I'm afraid we don't have the luxury of time to adjust."

We? We is first person plural. As in, me, I, Jane, am a factor in Lucy's fate.

"Mr. Langley, I'm sorry it was difficult to reach me. You're right, I'm shocked. But I don't know . . . my sister and I . . ." Half sister, actually. A blended family that separated after the end of the short-lived second marriage that forced it into being. Aloud, I say, "It's been several years since I last saw her."

"That's unfortunate." He sighs.

Why should he care that my family drifted apart? Geographically, emotionally . . . what difference could it make now? I gaze out the window at the bed of garlic, all the good feelings gone.

"In their will, your sister and her husband named you Lucy's guardian."

Chapter 3

LUCY

I check Mom's texts again on the bus back to school. One new. **Network sent a limo!** I text back, belatedly. **Buena suerte. Xoxox.**

The trip takes forever. At least I don't have Eli's knees poking me. They put him and Joel on the first bus, right in front of Ms. Kedzie. Mrs. Creighton, our principal, is waiting on the sidewalk when we get back.

"Told you they'd get in trouble," Phoebe says.

But when the bus door opens, Mrs. Creighton and Ms. Kedzie are waiting for *us*. Mrs. Creighton has a fake smile on her face.

"Lucy, would you come with me to my office?"

"Wait, Lucy didn't do anything! It was Joel and Eli," Phoebe says.

"Yeah," I say. "No one told us no phones."

"This isn't about that," Mrs. Creighton says, extending her arm like adults do when they want to swoop you along with them.

"It's not?" I look at Phoebe.

"But we need to get our stuff. It's almost time for the bell," Phoebe says.

"Phoebe, come with me," Ms. Kedzie says. "Lucy, go with Mrs. Creighton."

I follow her into the school, through the steel doors, down the hall. "What's going on?" I ask.

She doesn't answer. Instead she smiles again in that funny way and opens her office door. Sitting there in hard red plastic chairs is a man I don't know with a beard, and Deirdre! What's my au pair doing here?

"Lucy. Sweetheart." She stands up and hugs me. That's funny. She doesn't hug much. English people don't, she says. Her body is shivering, and her eyes are red. What's the matter with her?

"This way." Mrs. Creighton opens another door behind the secretary's desk to her private office. I've never been in here before. "Deirdre, Lucy, please." She pats some chairs. They're soft in here, not hard plastic. Mrs. Creighton sits on the other side of me, instead of behind her desk. Weirder and weirder.

"What's going on?" I look at her desk so I don't have to look at her. She has a square calendar, the kind where you tear off the page each day. It shows "13" in giant numbers. Unease ripples, then subsides. It's not Friday, after all.

"Well, Lucy." Mrs. Creighton clears her throat. "I, uh." She clears it again.

What is it? Why can't she talk?

"I'm—I'm afraid I have some bad news for you." She leans forward, her hands folded. It looks like she's praying.

I look over at Deirdre. She's playing with the zipper on her jacket. "What bad news? What's she talking about?"

When she looks at me, Deirdre's face crumples.

"Your parents went to Los Angeles today—" Mrs. Creighton says.

"I know that," I interrupt. "For meetings about her show."

"Yes. Well, Lucy, the network called your home a few hours ago. Your parents' car was in an accident."

"What?" The limo? My stomach feels like it's dropping. Kind of like it does when Mom tells me she has to go away on a work trip, but faster.

I press the invisible button inside that makes it stop, like an elevator. "I want to talk to them." I'm already reaching for my phone.

"I'm sorry." Mrs. Creighton shakes her head. "It was apparently a high-impact crash. Both your parents were killed."

Killed?

"You mean they're dead?" My fingers lose their grip, and the phone clatters onto the floor.

The second I say "dead," Deirdre starts crying. "Oh, I'm so awfully sorry. I'm so sorry."

Mrs. Creighton stands up and swishes over to Deirdre. They whisper; then Deirdre murmurs, "I'll just be outside, then." As she backs out, the bearded man stands up. It feels like a play: one person goes off the stage, another one comes on. It must be a play. Something unreal. A dream? Did I fall asleep on the school bus?

"Lucy, this is Mr. Meinert. Our school social worker." Mrs. Creighton folds her arms and looks anxious.

"Hello, Lucy." He sits down in Deirdre's chair and pats me on the shoulder. "I'm sorry to meet you under these circumstances. We're all here to help you as much as we can."

I haven't said anything since "dead." The word just keeps echoing in my head—dead, dead, dead, dead. They can't be. They came into my room to say goodbye, super early. Mom was wearing her pink jacket and flats, but I knew she would have heels in her carry-on to change into before the meeting. Now she's dead? She texted me on the field trip, right before Joel took my phone. She can't be dead. I'll text her back. Or even call her. They'll see. I reach into my pocket for my phone again, then remember it fell onto the floor. As I bend down to get it, a whiff of grass from the stain on my knee fills my nose. It's overpowering in its sickly sweetness, and I sit up fast.

"Lucy?" Mr. Meinert crouches low in front of my chair, looking up into my face. "Can you hear us?"

Mrs. Creighton's face looms side by side with his. "Is she in shock?"

I stand up, turning away from them. "I have to talk to them."

"Now, Lucy, that's not—" Mrs. Creighton is shaking her head, but Mr. Meinert puts his hand on her arm. "Go ahead, if that's what you want to do."

"She texted me! While we were on the field trip! It's not true!" I'm hunched over the phone, trying to open the texting window, but my hands are sweaty and shaking. Finally I get the text window open and Mom's last message up. **Network sent a limo!**

So they were in a car. On their way to the meeting. I push the thought away. **Mom! Call me!**

"We'll wait with you," Mr. Meinert says.

I'm squeezing the phone, squeezing so hard, waiting. Finally it says "Delivered" under my message.

"Any reply?" Mr. Meinert asks.

They're probably in the meeting now. And they can't check texts because it's so important.

"I want to go home," I say. Once they're out of the meeting, Mom will reply.

"Certainly. Let's call your au pair, then," Mr. Meinert says.

Deirdre is sitting in the same red plastic chair, dabbing her eyes. "Ms. Needham, we'd like you to take Lucy home now," Mr. Meinert says.

Deirdre jumps up. "Home? By—by ourselves?"

"If you'd like me to come with you—"

"No!" I don't need him. As soon as Mom texts back, I'll be fine.

"Let's follow her lead," Mr. Meinert says quietly, like I'm not supposed to hear. "Does she have a pet, by any chance?"

No reply. Where are they?

"No, no pet," Deirdre says. "Why?"

"They can be quite a comfort, especially to children." He hands her a card. "I'll check in with you tomorrow, but call me anytime, day or night, if you need anything sooner."

"Likewise," says Mrs. Creighton. They all sound like they're talking underwater. Deirdre opens the door. I'm staring at the phone so hard that I trip over the threshold and stumble into the quiet, tiled hallway, almost dropping it again.

"Step on a crack, break your mother's back," someone says in a singsongy voice. I look up and see Joel and Ms. Kedzie, waiting for his turn in the office.

"Joel Griffin! Young man, you just doubled your detention," Ms. Kedzie says. She sounds really mad. "Lucy. I'm so sorry." She pulls me into a hug. "Oh dear, look at your clothes, on top of everything else."

I look down at the green-stained leggings. I rub at them, but the grass smears don't come off. In my head the stupid rhyme echoes. *Step on a crack, break your mother's back.*

Then another voice. *Step on the grass, make her car crash.*

I look down at the phone, but there's no sound and still no reply. Just the last text: Network sent a limo! They were in a car while I was chasing Joel and Eli, and tripping and falling. *Step on the grass, make her car crash,* the voice repeats in my head.

No, that's impossible. But why hasn't Mom replied? I'll text Daddy instead. I try to open a new text window, but my hands are shaking too hard.

"Come on, Lucy. Let's get a cab." Deirdre leads me outside. It takes forever for a taxi to stop, and Mom doesn't text back, and the rhymes keep repeating in my head.

Step on a crack, break your mother's back. Step on the grass, make her car crash.

What did I do?

Chapter 4
JANE

Sun streaming through the window wakes me on Saturday. Sarge is curled into the space behind my knees, a warm, pulsing lump. I keep my eyes shut, clutching the last shreds of the cocoon of sleep, hiding from the memory of the lawyer's call. It felt like a conversation in the movies, up on a screen between actors I don't know, playing characters I'll forget an hour later.

It can't be true. Gloria wouldn't name me as Lucy's guardian. I've only met her daughter twice. She never even asked me! Then again, Gloria had gotten her way pretty much all her life. She might not even think to ask.

"You must be mistaken," I had told William Langley.

"There's no mistake. It's explicit in their will."

Their will. What about my will? If only I'd turned on the light. If only I'd looked. If only the Houston sun had thawed my soul. If only Jim hadn't . . . No. So many if-onlys, none granted.

"There must be someone else. Someone from Luis's family."

"Luis's family members all reside in Mexico. Your sister and her husband were very specific that they wish for Lucy to remain in the

United States. I've been in contact with Luis's family in the last forty-eight hours, and they concur with that arrangement."

They concur, yet no one's even asked me. "Do I have to concur, then, too?"

"You do need to accept guardianship." His voice sounded like he was moving to closing arguments. "Which I certainly hope you will, given that Lucy has no other American blood relatives. I can't imagine Gloria would choose anyone unfit, so pending that formality, Lucy is your child as of Wednesday evening."

I closed my eyes, wishing they could talk to Jim. He could tell them how unfit I am to be a mother. Physically, certainly, since the emergency hysterectomy. Emotionally, twenty years' worth of wounded relationships. As a daughter myself. A sister. A mother, at first so promising, then doubly heartbreaking. A wife. No. The wounds have scabbed over. I can't let anyone pick at them again. The CSA, Plain Jane's, is enough.

"I know this is a shock. I'm sure you'll be relieved to know that Lucy does have an au pair here in New York who's been engaged to provide twenty-four-hour care for the short-term."

An au pair is like a nanny, right? I pictured a prim, severe woman, and sympathy suddenly flickered for Lucy, losing both parents simultaneously. I was too young to remember when the marines in dress blues showed up at the front door of our base housing in Twentynine Palms, but I had Mom. At least until Esteban showed up. Langley continued talking.

"While arrangements are being made, that is. The funeral is set for Tuesday."

In New York? Well, of course. "That's four days away."

"We wanted to give you a few days to absorb the news, and begin to make your own preparations."

My own preparations. My mind reeled, from the farm to-do list that grows longer every day to the strands of yellow yarn unraveled years ago. An illusion of readiness, preparation. Whatever's going to happen will happen.

"A plane ticket, naturally, and whatever else you'll need to have tended to while you're away. I would plan on at least a week. I'll put my assistant back on—she'll take care of all the logistics. Of course, you're welcome to stay with Lucy at her home. It would help with the transition."

Away for a week? Just as the CSA is ramping up for the season. The transition—to a second motherhood? Third, if you count Gloria. Gloria, who's dead. We were talking about plane tickets and logistics, and my little sister is dead.

Sarge rubs against my legs, mewling. His water and food dish are probably empty. Unfit, I want to scream. I am unfit.

Instead I open my eyes. Time to face the day.

I sidle between the bed and the table where my seed plugs are spread, the black squares of soil ingesting every possible minute of sunshine before the biggest south-facing window in the house. In the kitchen I fill Sarge's dishes, start the coffee, then go to my PC. The computer and the dial-up modem are both so old and slow it takes five minutes to download my email. Sure enough, there's a flight confirmation from Delta. Monday, April 18, 1:00 p.m. departure, Traverse City to Detroit to JFK. Another message from the Law Offices of William E. Langley informs me that a driver will meet me at JFK and take me to Gloria's apartment for dinner with him, Lucy, and Deirdre, the au pair.

I close the email window and turn to Google. "Gloria Santiago and Luis Ortiz," I type into the box as Sarge settles at my feet.

Google returns 350,000 results. I click on the first, datelined Los Angeles, which takes me to an AP story about the crash.

"Popular Telemundo host Gloria Santiago and her husband, Luis Ortiz, an executive at the network, were killed Wednesday when their corporate car crashed outside Los Angeles.

"The couple was believed to be en route to meetings with officials at NBC, Telemundo's parent. Unconfirmed reports say the network wanted Santiago, 36, to anchor a West Coast edition of her *Buenos Días, Nueva York* morning show. Ortiz, 44, served as an adviser to his wife. Their driver was injured, as was the driver of a second vehicle, a Los Angeles resident. Local authorities are investigating."

The coffeepot beeps, but I ignore it, riveted by the side-by-side pictures. Gloria looks as vibrant as ever, her curly dark hair seemingly ready to spring off the screen. Luis's dark hair is threaded with gray. So Gloria found somebody else to take care of her. Luis was only a year younger than I am. I wouldn't have put him over forty. I only met him twice, once at their wedding and once at Mom's funeral. Lucy was barely walking then.

I turn back to the search results and find a piece posted on the Telemundo site.

"*Lamentamos informarles,*" screams the headline. In smaller type, "*que la hija de 11 años se queda huérfana después de la tragedia.*"

My Spanish isn't great, but I get the gist. Eleven. Two years older than I was when Gloria was born. Again, sympathy flickers. A rough roll of the dice, no doubt. The headline is above a slide show of Gloria and Luis. I click through the slides. Mostly Gloria, rather. On set in New York. On location during Hurricane Katrina. Receiving a glass trophy at some awards banquet. Luis is in that one, clapping as he stands behind her. Gloria with her arm around a little girl with dark hair who's smiling but looks positively solemn next to Gloria's thousand-watt grin. The *huérfana.* Lucy.

I peer more closely at the screen, waiting to feel something. But our sisterhood became as two-dimensional as the images—no depth, texture wiped away by time. I stand up suddenly, poking Sarge on the floor. He half mews, leaping off to his favorite corner of the blue velvet couch.

Ignoring another beep from the coffeepot, I follow him into the living room, then walk over to the corner bookcase. It's loaded, every shelf stuffed end to end, with more books and envelopes and papers wedged crossways atop the books. The photo albums are on the bottom. I settle cross-legged on the floor and select the ivory one third from the end. The binding cracks as I peel the cover back from the vinyl sleeves.

There we are. Me and Gloria at my high school graduation, San Diego Southwest, class of 1984. Even though it was my graduation, Gloria's the one who shines in the faded print. Her smile looks natural and happy. Mine is forced, my jaw set, one hand clutching the black cap so it wouldn't slide off and we'd have the requisite graduation photo. Right after, Gloria had grabbed the cap off my head and flung it into the air, not bothering to notice where it landed, leaving me to chase it down. That was Gloria, carefree and confident I'd clean up after her. I was eighteen, so she was nine or ten.

Mom must have taken the picture, mustering herself out of her bedroom for the occasion. Esteban was long gone by then. She'd married Gloria's dad when I was eight. She told me later, just before I married Jim and became a Coastie wife, that the best thing about Esteban was that he wasn't in the military.

We moved from Twentynine Palms to San Diego a year after my dad died in Vietnam. Mom got a job in a bank and met Esteban there. He owned a few dry-cleaning stores and visited the bank daily to make deposits. It was good, steady stateside work. He wanted to have a child right away. I remember when she told me, at bedtime one night.

"You're going to have a sister or a brother, Jane."

"When? Why?" I pulled my knees up under my favorite nightshirt, stretching out the rainbow across it. My stomach lurched as I looked at hers. Esteban had already elbowed past me to first place. Evenings of reading aloud together, grocery shopping for our favorite meals, and matinee movies on weekends had disappeared, one by one.

"We want to be a family," my mother said, waving vaguely at the garage where Esteban parked the dry-cleaning van. "Every girl should have a sister, after all. Or a brother."

"I thought we were a family. Already."

"We are. I just meant—you know what I mean, Jane."

I hadn't. But after Gloria was born, I figured it out pretty quickly. It meant Gloria, Mom, and Esteban. I was the outsider, from my different last name to my blond hair and blue eyes to my English-only vocabulary. Suddenly I wonder if Lucy speaks English. She must, if they wanted her to live in the United States. Assumptions, however, have played me for a fool before.

When Esteban left, the factions shifted again. Mom, whose early adoption of the aerobic revolution had failed to keep Esteban interested, simply withdrew except to go to work. Gloria, my half sister biologically, became a de facto half daughter, as I spent high school making meals, meeting her bus, checking her homework, forging Mom's signature on report cards and permission slips.

Like her dad, Gloria was a born charmer. It was easy to fall under her spell. But twice now I'd felt the backlash of charm's fickle hand, the jerk of a hairpin life turn. Freshman year at San Diego City College, when I met the Coastie with the serious blue eyes and a straight, secure path ahead of him, I was all in.

Behind me, Sarge drops lightly from the back of the couch, curling up next to my hip. The sun's passed over his favorite corner, that's why. Clouds are gathering again, masking the early sun.

I shut the album firmly, clapping the covers over the excavated memories, and turn to the present. I'll need someone to check in on Sarge and have Martha hold the mail. Get someone on standby to plow me out in case we get one of those heavy, wet spring snowstorms. Or on the other hand, if it's warm, to bring out my seed plugs, acclimating them from the roost in my bedroom's southern window. Might as well call Miguel. He can check out the driveway while he's at it.

Miguel's phone goes straight to voice mail. I ask him to call back, and poke in the fridge for some yogurt and a muffin. As I swallow the last of my stand-up breakfast, I see his dirty white truck coming up my driveway, arm hanging out the window, even though it's not yet broken forty-five degrees.

"*¡Hola*, Jane!" He sticks his head in my back door. "*¿Cómo estás?*"

"*Hola*, Miguel." I smile, ignoring the how-are-you. "Thanks for coming so quickly."

"I was in the neighborhood, down at Nelson's. You heard he's putting in hops this year?"

"Nope." English is my first language and Miguel's second, yet like Martha, when it comes to peninsula gossip, he is far more fluent. Nelson's decision doesn't surprise me, though. Seems like a new brewpub opens every month in Traverse City.

"Ripping out his oldest cherry trees and converting five acres." Miguel shakes his head.

"When's the last time you had a *cerveza*?" I ask.

"*Anoche,*" he says immediately.

"Last night, OK. And when's the last time you ate a cherry pie?"

Miguel pauses, ruminating, running his hand over his bristly black hair he keeps crew-cut short. Like Matt, but by choice, not edict. He grins.

"Aha. Point made. I can't keep up with you entrepreneurs. *Mañana, mañana*, always tomorrow you're thinking about."

He's right. And that habit goes back to the night in my San Diego bedroom when I learned Gloria was on her way. My ability to live in the present vanished because for the first time, I was worried about what tomorrow might bring.

"Speaking of tomorrow, what's going to happen with the group that got picked up over in Leelanau?"

His grin disappears. "Looks like they'll all be sent back."

"Families, too?"

He shrugs. "If they want to stay, the timing might work, coming into the season. But most of the time, they go back, too. Want to keep the family together." He shakes his head, running his hands over his hair again. This time it looks like he's trying to pull out the short strands. "I wish I could make them see. Mexico is so bad right now. What's more important, staying together or staying alive?"

"It's that dangerous?" I ask skeptically. Overnight I've come to resent Luis's unknown family south of the border, absolved of any obligation to Lucy.

"*Sí.* This group is probably headed to Ciudad Juárez. Three cartels are fighting for the smuggling routes. Thousands dead."

"Thousands?"

"*Sí.*" Miguel nods, holds his hand over his heart. "And now, *el presidente* has brought in the military."

"That's a good thing, right?"

"I hope so. But there is so much corruption. Government, police, too. If you don't want to die, you join a gang."

"Has that happened to your family, Miguel?"

He shakes his head. "No. They are not in a large city. But I worry. *Mi hermano*, I worry all the time they will try to recruit my brother. And my little sister."

"Gangs recruit girls, too?"

"Not for the business. But they are, how do you say it, collateral goods. Kidnapped as trophies, as hostages, or for prostitution." His jaw sets. "Ana Maria's *quinceañera* is next year. She needs to stay safe. Stay in school. I pay for her school. It's better than nothing, but it's not safe like here." He folds his arms, staring out my window.

"Well." I want to put Miguel back to his easygoing self. "I'll be out of town starting Monday for at least a week. Can you backfill the potholes on my driveway, and check in on Sarge while you're at it? If it's warm enough, take the seeds out, too?"

"*Claro*, of course, Jane. You can count on me." He relaxes.

Miguel's sister stays with me all afternoon. *Safe like here.* The lawyer said Lucy's Mexican relatives wanted her to stay in the US, too. Maybe they are thinking of Lucy's welfare, after all. *La huérfana.* Gloria's *hija.* *Mi*—what was the word for niece? I go back to the computer.

Sobrina. Lucy *es mi sobrina,* the translation site tells me. And legally, according to Langley, my child. What's the word for child? As I type, the crosswinds of memory collide. Esteban's long-faded voice in our San Diego backyard. A nurse in an antiseptic Alaskan hospital corridor, where Jim's Coast Guard path led us. Where I learned that it wasn't charm that was fickle, but life itself.

Niña. I yank my hands back, as if the keyboard scalded me.

Chapter 5
LUCY

"Can I come in?" Mr. Langley asks through my bedroom door.

I blink a few times, staring out the window from my bed. After the field trip, I climbed in here and haven't gotten out since except to go to the bathroom. Deirdre brings me food on trays. I hear her and Mr. Langley talking. They seem in a hurry, but nothing's happening. They walk around talking on their phones; then they talk to each other; then they call other people.

Now it's afternoon, and getting gray and cloudy. Lying with my head on my pillow, all the buildings look like they're growing sideways.

"Lucy?" He knocks again.

"It's not locked."

He opens it and stands there, not saying anything.

"What?" I roll over. His shiny black shoes are almost buried in my shaggy pink rug. Shaggy like uncut grass. *Step on a—*

"Can I sit down?" He points to the foot of the bed.

I shrug.

The mattress bounces when he sits. Sometimes Daddy made it do that on purpose, to make me laugh. But Mr. Langley's a lot fatter than Daddy and does it just by sitting.

"I want to talk about your parents' memorial service."

My stomach starts doing its elevator drop.

"I've gone ahead and scheduled it for Tuesday. They left fairly detailed instructions, but I wondered if there's anything you'd like to include."

"Like what?" I've never been to a funeral, or a memorial service.

"Oh, it could be a lot of things. Playing a song that was special. Writing something to read out loud. Sharing any kind of special memory."

"Would I have to get up and talk?"

"Not if you don't want to."

I stare out the window, thinking about it.

"Like this, for instance." Mr. Langley heaves himself upright and takes a picture from my desk. It's of me and Mom and Daddy at Disney World, with Mickey Mouse in front of the Magic Kingdom. "This looks like a good memory."

It was. Because of Mom's TV show, we got our own guide and didn't have to wait in line for the rides or anything.

"Or this one." He picks up another photo, of us at the Rockefeller Center ice rink. That was just before last Christmas. Phoebe took it. Mom was really working. She just came down from her office for a few minutes. She didn't even skate, but you can't tell from the picture. Daddy and Phoebe and I had fun, though.

"You've got a lot of nice pictures here," he says, looking around the room. "Maybe we could display them somehow."

"You mean take them?" I sit up, grabbing both frames from him. "No."

"Not permanently. I was just thinking of reproducing them. Picture's worth a thousand words. Maybe on a larger scale, mounted on easels—"

"They're mine. You can't take them."

"Oh." He looks disappointed. "So is there anything you would like to have at the service?"

Mom and Daddy, I think. *Just Mom and Daddy.*

Later, though, I decide pictures are what I want to show, after all. Trips, holidays, birthdays. They're digital, so I don't have to give them up. I can scan the Disney one. Then I'll put them all into a slide show, like we did at school in New Media class, with music. Almost like a video.

Lying on my bed, I find the school slide show on my phone. It's all about New York and how we represent the city's diversity, Ms. Kedzie told us. We all took pictures of our neighborhoods, places that were important to us, and the show goes through them while that old song "New York, New York" plays. It ends with a little bit of video, our whole class doing a kick line to the song.

For my picture, me and Daddy went to one of our favorite bodegas in Sunset Park. They would always give me a piece of candy and tell Daddy, *"Señor, tiene una hija muy bonita."* He would smile and say, *"Gracias."* Then when it was the two of us, he would tell me that yes, I was pretty, but not to forget that it was important to be smart, too.

That day it was raining, and I'm standing under the striped red-and-yellow awning that covered up the outdoor shelves, trying not to get wet. Daddy was getting wet, I remember. He was trying to hold a big umbrella and take the picture at the same time, but the umbrella kept falling. I was laughing, and that's when he took the picture. My mouth is kind of open, but otherwise it's a good picture.

That was the last time we went there. Some boys hanging out at the subway called me *bonita* when we left, but Daddy didn't say *gracias* to them. He put his arm around me and made sure he was between me and them as we walked past. Under his breath I heard him say that *barrio* was getting kind of rough.

The shelves were full of baskets of all different kinds of peppers. We bought some and made chiles rellenos that night. Daddy wore his long white apron that said *el cocinero*, the chef. Deirdre was out, so when Mom got home we all ate dinner together, just the three of us. It was still raining, and the raindrops spattered the dark window outside, and it was bright and warm inside.

Remembering that makes me feel good enough to get out of bed. At my computer I open the pictures folder, but the bodega picture isn't there. Wait, since Daddy took it, it must be on his computer, on the desk in their bedroom.

Next to the computer is a wedding photo of him and Mom, one of me when I was a baby, and this year's school picture, all in frames. I lay the wedding and baby photos down on the desk, to take to my room and scan. I need more old pictures like that, ones that probably aren't on the computer. I guess I'll need even older ones, too, of Daddy growing up in Mexico, Mom in San Diego. But thinking of them there, in other places, is scary. Where am I going to grow up? We don't have family here in New York. Will Deirdre stay? I've never had an au pair more than a year. When they met at the network in Miami, Daddy was already, like, thirty. Daddy said he knew two things when she walked into the studio: she was going to be a star, and he was going to marry her. "Then you came along, and all three of us lived happily ever after," he would tell me.

All three of us. Tears rise. I blink hard and bite my lip. For a second I want to run back to my room and crawl under my covers. Hide from the grown-ups and their phones and plans and happily ever after.

The computer beeps, all powered up. Even if it's not happy, there is going to be an after. After Tuesday. Instead of opening the pictures folder, I click on the contacts and start scrolling through to *O, Ortiz.* There's a bunch of names and numbers, all starting with 52—that's Mexico's country code, Daddy told me. His sister, Aunt Bonita, still lives there. She has a daughter a little older than me, too. Her name's Gabriella, I think. We only visited once, a long time ago. A couple of names have email addresses, too. Bonita Ortiz has both an email address and a phone number. Are they coming to the memorial service? What about Mom's family? She had a sister, too. I can't remember her name. I look under *S* for Santiago, but there's no one listed. Nobody's told me anything about what's going to happen. All of a sudden I feel exhausted, but I don't think I can make it to my room. I flop down on Mom and Daddy's bed instead, crawling under the covers on Mom's side. There's another picture on the nightstand, of me when I was about three, sitting in her anchor chair on set. When I was little I loved to sit in her chair and spin. When I got too dizzy, Mom would stop the chair and hold me until the room stopped spinning. The tears fall.

"Lucy?" A woman's voice. Mom? Am I dreaming?

"Let's just let her sleep." A man's voice. Was I dreaming all this time? Am I finally waking up, with Mom and Daddy coming home? My eyelids flutter open. But it's Deirdre, not Mom, sitting next to me, and Mr. Langley in the doorway. My stomach elevator starts to creak.

"Why aren't you sleeping in your own room, Lucy?" Deirdre frowns. "I'm not so sure it's a good idea," she tells Mr. Langley, like I can't hear her.

"I was making my memorial video. He told me to. And then I just got tired . . ."

"I'll take care of it, Deirdre, thank you. If you would give us some privacy, please . . ."

"Of course." Deirdre's still frowning, but she backs out of the room.

"So." Mr. Langley closes the door behind her and sits down on the bench at the foot of the bed. "I have some news."

I lie back down. It feels so cozy here in their bed. I turn to look at the nightstand, to see the picture again.

"I was able to reach your aunt Jane today. Your mother's sister."

I close my eyes, imagining spinning in the chair, Mom's smiling face and everything in the studio blurring.

"She'll be here Monday, to attend the funeral and get reacquainted with you."

The huge weather map on the wall, the coffee mugs on the desk for Mom and her guests.

"And then, after the funeral, you'll move to Michigan to live with her."

Wait, what did he say? I turn over, the studio vanished, to look at him. "Michigan? Why?"

"Your parents named her your guardian."

"Guard—what?"

"I know it's a lot to absorb right now, but it's best that you know there's a plan. This is what your parents wanted for you." He stands up. "Try to get some more sleep. It's probably the best thing."

When he leaves, I don't have to close my eyes for everything to be spinning.

Chapter 6

JANE

"Ladies and gentlemen, on behalf of Delta Airlines, we'd like to be the first to welcome you to New York. Passengers making connections will find departure information from the representative at the gate or on the boards throughout the terminal. If New York is your final destination, we wish you a pleasant stay here in the Big Apple."

There probably isn't a real apple tree on the island of Manhattan, yet it's the Big Apple. *La Gran Manzana,* as bilingual Lucy would also say. That was one bit of relief: Langley told me Gloria spoke to her in English and Luis in Spanish. The au pair speaks English.

As I follow the signs to ground transport, I notice uniforms everywhere—whites, blues, khakis, camo. I think of Matt, on the other side of the Atlantic. We last talked on his birthday, in February. Not so long ago, for a mother and her enlisted twenty-three-year-old son. Having a son join the military might upset other mothers, but I'm relieved he's found a place for himself in the army. And stationed in Germany I know he's safe, at least relatively safe. He's a medic, mostly doing transport. The distance is a dam against my guilt and regrets, too. Twenty-year-old regrets, now. Half my life. Or maybe double my life, the way it feels. Despite Jim's assurances, the move to Houston hadn't helped. Though the subtropical weather there was the opposite of Alaska's cold, dark bleakness, the year-round sameness was just as oppressive. It mirrored the dullness I felt inside, too, despite going through the motions of motherhood. A singular stupor set in, inuring me to all but the lonely ache for what we buried on Kodiak. I'd take Matt to the playground but furtively watch the little girls and brother-sister duos, berating myself for what I could no longer give him. Yet the hysterectomy offered relief, too; at least there was no further risk of damage to heart and soul. Back then, my marriage didn't occur to me. Nor did the possibility that Gloria would get the daughter I was denied.

Near an escalator a man is talking on his phone and holding a cardboard sign: "McArdle." Seeing my name, I hesitate. If only there were someone else. If only Gloria and Luis's car hadn't crashed. If only our blended family hadn't separated, like oil and water.

The driver hangs up and scans the room, catching my eye. With a lift of his eyebrows and a nod of my head, I'm committed. I follow him outside, where the air, thick with diesel exhaust and surprisingly cold for April, gags me.

Through the square of glass in the silent cab, the sharp gray-and-black geometry of the city looms above me, so different from the organic greens and blues that unfurl from my windows at home. The peninsula will be another country to Lucy.

Her apartment building is a few blocks from Central Park, Langley told me. Already, amid all this concrete, I'm feeling like a dried-out sponge. I plan to walk to the park tomorrow. Grass, trees, open space. I need my daily dose.

The driver unloads my bag and approaches a doorman. "McArdle. Fourteen A. She's expected."

Expected. As if this were all planned and arranged like any normal family visit, rather than a tragedy that's altered the axis of two lives. My heart is pounding.

With military precision, the doorman nods and opens the door. In the lobby he summons a luggage cart with a snap of his fingers. He jabs the button to the elevator, whose doors open instantly, then escorts me to 14A and departs. All without a word.

A twentyish brunette wearing an I-love-New-York sweatshirt opens the door.

"You must be Mrs. McArdle. I'm Deirdre, Lucy's au pair," she says in a British accent, holding out her hand.

So much for the prim matron. I shake her hand automatically. "Call me Jane."

"Mr. Langley was hoping to be here to meet you, but he's been delayed, so I'll show you your room first."

I follow her down a hall. "Where's Lucy?" My mouth is dry.

"I'll be leaving to pick her up from school directly," Deirdre says. "She usually has tae kwon do after school Mondays, but under the circumstances . . ."

My pulse slows with relief at another reprieve, dwelling on Deirdre's words. *Circum*, from the Latin, round, just like the circles I've been going in since Langley called. Now I imagine our circumstances as a Venn diagram overlaid on a map. Lucy, *la huérfana*, orphaned in New York, at the center of one circle. Me in Michigan at the center of another. Our edges barely overlapping, somewhere over Lake Erie, maybe. Until five days ago, when the circles started sliding toward each other, like tectonic plates.

"I'm kind of surprised she's even at school," I say.

"The social worker suggested that a neutral environment could be helpful. She's only been there since lunch—for an appointment with him and to see her best friend."

A neutral environment. As opposed to home, which is certainly charged with my arrival. Not to mention Gloria and Luis's absence. Tectonic might understate our circumstances, actually.

Deirdre opens a door to a tiny bedroom. "I hope it's to your liking. After you're settled in, you can wait for Mr. Langley in the living room."

I set my suitcase on the zebra-striped rug and sit on the bed, which is covered in a bright-red spread. It's one of those beds that have a dozen different pillows arranged on top. I touch a beaded one tentatively. Why would you put all those beads on a pillow? At home I have flannel pillowcases on regular pillows and a green quilt that I got on sale after Jim departed. That was one thing I wanted brand new. The old one was still perfectly fine, so I gave it to Goodwill. I don't have a rug, just bare wooden floorboards. Makes it easier to sweep when one of the seed trays spills.

In the living room the wood floor makes me feel better, even if it does have a fussy parquet pattern. Langley never shows up, though. When the door opens again, it's Deirdre, accompanied by a slight figure who hesitates behind her. The hair is what I notice first, two thick braids of dark hair brushing her shoulders. Her face is tilted down. She's wearing jeans, silver glitter high-tops, and a purple hooded sweatshirt with neon peace signs.

"Lucy, you remember your aunt Jane," Deirdre says. She steps to the side.

She couldn't remember me; she was barely walking. "Hi, Lucy." My voice sounds forcibly cheery. I step forward with my arms open. "You've grown up a lot."

"Hi." She crosses her arms, keeping her head low, not looking at me.

"Well." Deirdre looks from me to her as my arms fall back to my sides. "Mr. Langley apologizes. He got held up at the office but will be here for dinner. At six thirty."

"OK," I say.

"I'll let you two get reacquainted, then." Deirdre backs out. I stifle an impulse to run after her, since it's just after five and dinner feels about a hundred years away. "I'm sorry about your mom, Lucy. I mean, about your parents," I amend.

"Everyone is." She goes to the window and stares out, her breath fogging the glass.

"How are you feeling?"

She shrugs, reaching for the end of her braid and twirling it around her finger. I can see her features better now—sharp and pale. I don't see Gloria's sparkle and verve anywhere.

Both her parents just died, I remind myself. I walk to the window and look out, too. Central Park is visible in the distance. Just the view of the green rectangle is comforting.

"That's Central Park, right?"

She nods, trailing her finger through the circle of condensation she's creating on the window, drawing a lopsided heart.

"Maybe we can take a walk there together later."

The line she's drawing stops. She shrugs again.

"No rush. Tomorrow's fine."

"Tomorrow's the funeral."

"Right." I wince. "Well, Wednesday, then. I'm going to be here until the weekend."

"And then what?" She turns away from the window and looks directly at me for the first time. Her jaw reminds me of Miguel's in my kitchen.

"I—I think we're going to figure that out this week."

Her shoulders relax for a moment.

"I don't have to go live with you?"

Shit. Is it good the feeling's mutual? Something we have in common?

"Let's try not to decide anything now, OK? Just get to know each other better."

She bites her lip and looks away again, down at her sparkly high-tops. I pull the photos out of my bag and lay them on a table.

"I brought some pictures of your mom when she was a little girl."
I went through all the albums and tried to find a good sample. Trips to
the beach, holidays, birthdays. After she blew out the candles, Gloria
always told everyone what she wished for, even though I told her not
to. She usually got it anyway. I bet Gloria and Luis pretty much granted
Lucy's wishes, too.

"Yeah?" She turns to face me again.

"She's around your age in this one." I point to the graduation picture. As Lucy moves toward me, I see that the heart she's drawn in the
condensation is disappearing into droplets of water, bleeding there on
the glass.

Chapter 7
LUCY

Mr. Langley's finally here. While he and Aunt Jane talk, I take her pictures back to my room, eight altogether, to scan and add to the slide show. Mom's the oldest in the graduation one on top, about the same age as me. There's a birthday picture where I count six candles on her cake. Aunt Jane's sitting off to the side. A back-to-school picture with both of them standing in front of a tree. A Christmas picture on Santa's lap, and a summer picture at the beach. Aunt Jane's in that one, too, kneeling next to Mom in the sand. Three baby pictures, one with Mom propped up, one crawling, one standing up, holding on to an ugly light-green couch. Even in the baby pictures, she has lots of curly hair. Mine has always been dark and thick like hers, but never curly. Sometimes she curled it for me, like for school pictures or a special occasion, but the curls never even lasted all day. It's so thick that it's hard for me to do anything except put it in a ponytail. Phoebe did the braids in Mr. Meinert's office today. We liked to do each other's hair. Plus, then I didn't have to look at her.

I spread out the pictures with Aunt Jane next to my laptop. Mom looks the same in all of them, just like I remember, huge smile and hair springing wildly from her head, no matter what she's wearing or how old she is. Aunt Jane looks happiest in the one at the beach. She's smiling in the graduation one, but it doesn't look real. In the birthday and back-to-school one, she's barely even smiling.

She wasn't today, either. And the clothes she was wearing were so ugly. Jeans, a green fleece vest, a long-sleeve T-shirt. All faded, like her grayish-blond hair and pale skin and blue eyes. One knee even had a green stain on it. I couldn't stop looking at it. "What's that?" I asked, pointing.

"What's what?" She didn't even notice anything.

"On your knee."

She rubbed at it.

"Must be a grass stain. I'm afraid I don't have a very fashionable wardrobe. I'm a plain Jane." She laughed, a loud, barking sound that made me flinch. "Sorry. Inside joke. That's the name of my business, too. Plain Jane's."

"Oh." I didn't know she had a business. Not that I want to know. Especially if it means wearing stained, dirty clothes. I threw away the leggings I tore on the field trip as soon as I got home and scrubbed off the grass stain on my knee, but I couldn't stop the rhyme in my head. *Step on a crack, break your mother's back. Step on the grass, make her car crash.* Now Aunt Jane wants me to go to Central Park. Hah.

I turn to the computer and open the slide show. Mom's wearing bright colors in almost all the pictures. Hot pink, turquoise, bright green. Shiny necklaces. Red lipstick. Her dark hair bounces to her shoulders and is almost as wide.

I pull my braid over my shoulder and twirl the end, looking down at my lap—my arms in the sleeves of a deep-purple sweatshirt, my jeans shot through with glittery threads, my striped socks. People always said I look like her, even with straight hair. But I feel like Aunt Jane looks. Like I could just fade away.

Chapter 8
JANE

The funeral is private. The network's organized a memorial event, too, but Tuesday's service, held at a funeral home, is limited to a few dozen of Gloria and Luis's closest friends and colleagues, Lucy, Langley, Deirdre, and me.

"No one from Luis's family?" I ask Langley.

He shakes his head. "His father is dead, and his mother's in poor health. I don't know much about his siblings. His sister told me they don't have the documents to make an international trip."

Thankfully, Luis and Gloria stipulated cremation, so there are no caskets. You can't escape the funeral feeling, though, with the rows of folding chairs and flower arrangements all over the place. A slide show plays on a big screen, rotating pictures of Gloria, Luis, and Lucy. A Spanish song plays, a sad, slow one, as the pictures peel back the years. A wedding picture, white satin and lace, whiter teeth in giant smiles. Heads together over champagne glasses at an outdoor table, a palm tree visible behind them. Holding a newborn Lucy wearing one of those pink-and-blue striped knit hospital caps, the same exact kind I got for Matt. They didn't give me anything in Alaska. Not a chance to hold her.

Only prescribed consolation that chided more than comforted. "After all, you still have your son," the doctor said.

I stare at the pink face that isn't even discernably female. Gloria called me from the hospital, the first year I ran Plain Jane's. I knew she was expecting, of course, but they hadn't found out it was a girl. I managed to keep it together while I congratulated her. Then I escaped to the tomato rows, where neither Jim nor Matt would come looking, and wept for hours. My daughter was buried on Kodiak while Gloria held hers in her arms. With Lucy, my sister changed everything then, as she has again now.

After that, the pictures are less familiar. In front of a Christmas tree. With Lucy at age three or four, the Statue of Liberty looming over them in the background. All three of them are dressed up. Lucy's holding a small American flag.

"That was Luis's citizenship day." Langley's at my elbow.

"He wasn't already? He and Gloria met in Miami. At the network."

Langley nods. "He'd been in the States for years at that point, ever since he attended the University of Texas."

"But he hadn't become a citizen?"

Langley shakes his head. "He was proud of his heritage and didn't want to renounce Mexican citizenship. He tried for years to get a dual application approved."

The music has changed, something instrumental but happier than the Spanish song. It's familiar, but I can't place it. On the screen the pictures churn toward the present. A birthday party, the cake adorned with five candles, Gloria and Luis on either side of Lucy, each flashing five fingers. Disney World, Lucy on Luis's shoulders, Mickey Mouse in the middle, Gloria on the other side, the Magic Kingdom castle behind them. Reigning over a perfect family. The unfairness of it rises from deep in my gut, just like in the tomato rows on Lucy's birthday. *I* was the responsible older sister who did what she was supposed to do. A thirty-year-old memory rises up, Gloria pestering me at my desk.

"Janey, play with me."

"I've got homework to do, Gloria." Mom was meeting Esteban for dinner, and I was stuck babysitting, as usual.

"Play with me! Mama said!" She stuck out her lip. Over her T-shirt she wore a fancy purple dress, one of the left-behinds at the dry cleaners that Esteban brought home for her.

"I did. You wanted to play dress-up. I pinned up the straps so you won't trip."

She shook her head. "Play hide-and-seek."

I tried to ignore her, but she shook my elbow, breaking the pencil lead.

"Gloria! All right, fine. You go hide. I'll count. One, two, three . . ." I tried to stretch out the counting as long as I could, squeezing in a couple of math problems before ready-or-not, but she always got what she wanted. Right up to and including the ideal, idolizing husband. Jim and I were good at the beginning. After Alaska I even took solace in the stasis we fell into, rationalizing that at least nothing was getting worse.

"Finally, a few years after Lucy was born, he gave up," Langley continues. "'I have an American family, so I will be, too,' he decided."

"Hmm." The picture changes again, to what looks like formal network portraits of Gloria and Luis. Luis and Lucy in the kitchen, wearing monogrammed aprons. Ice-skating outdoors. I study Luis's expression, his smile crinkling his face all the way up to his dark eyes. He did what I never could despite three chances: assimilate. Sister, wife, mother, they all felt like roles handed to me. I tried to embrace wife and mother; look how that wound up. Only Plain Jane's feels natural, a role I've made my own. Can I do Aunt Jane any better?

Then the full-screen picture suddenly shrinks down to a tiny square surrounded by white space. I see myself in my high school graduation gown, next to Gloria.

"That's the picture I gave Lucy! I wanted her to see her mom at her age. How did it get up there?"

"Lucy must have added it," Langley says.

"Added it to what?"

"She put this slide show together."

"The whole thing? With the music and everything?"

He nods.

"It looks so professional. She's only eleven!" I scan the room for Lucy, standing with another little girl whose parents are talking to Deirdre. "Where did she learn how?"

"She's got a media production class at school."

"But she did this at home, right?"

Langley nods. "The technology's pretty accessible these days. You wouldn't believe what they can do on a phone. Don't forget the genes, either. Lucy was the daughter of two talented people."

A man in a black suit coughs a few times, quieting the room's buzz. "If you'll all find a seat, please, we'd like to begin the service."

Lucy sits between Langley and Deirdre, in the front row. Unsure where I belong, I sit on the end of the row, leaving a few seats between me and Deirdre. I watch Lucy more than the service. She keeps her head bent, her hair a curtain on both sides. If she cries, I don't see it. In my head I keep humming the song from the slide show, the one whose name I still can't remember.

Chapter 9

LUCY

Wednesday I don't have anything to do. Aunt Jane wants to take me to Central Park later, but I'm not going anywhere near grass. She's meeting with Mr. Langley first, though, in Mom and Daddy's bedroom, where the desk and computer are. Deirdre has the morning off, so she can't keep me from listening. Luckily the door's open a crack.

". . . payout of both life insurance policies, and the various retirement funds, there will be money from the sale of the apartment. It all goes into a trust for Lucy until she's twenty-one. The income the trust generates will be sent to you for her care until then."

Twenty-one? I have to live in Michigan for ten whole *years*?

Aunt Jane nods. She's sitting on the bench at the end of the bed, facing Mr. Langley at the desk.

"We won't know that amount for sure until the apartment sells. Still, I'm estimating about eighty thousand dollars annually."

"Eighty thousand dollars? Are you kidding?" Her voice is shocked. It sounds like a lot of money to me, too. But sell the apartment? Someone else will live here? In our house?

"Again, depending on the price of the apartment, we expect the trust to be valued at approximately four million dollars. Assuming two percent investment growth—being conservative, of course—that's eighty thousand dollars per year."

Million!? I can't hear what Aunt Jane says next.

"Do you have a financial planner or investment adviser?"

She shakes her head. "Just an accountant who does my CSA taxes. Maybe she knows someone."

CSA? What does that mean?

"Well, that's a start. I wouldn't go cold-calling, if you can avoid it." Mr. Langley leans forward. "With this much money all at once, you could attract an unsavory sort."

Aunt Jane says something else I can't hear.

"The trust will distribute annually. So this first payment may take a while. January, perhaps. Any more financial questions?"

She shakes her head.

"Moving on, then. Medical history. We'll have all of Lucy's medical records transferred when you've chosen a doctor. I'll review it, but I don't recall anything remarkable."

A doctor in Michigan. No more Dr. Muñoz.

"On the school front, we've arranged for you to meet with Lucy's teacher tomorrow. She's in sixth grade, as you know, and I've confirmed that the teacher intends to pass her through to seventh next year. Academically she appears to be on the front end of the middle of the pack. You know about her interest and abilities in media production."

Pretty and smart. My stomach elevator stops sinking for a minute, and I feel a little burst of pride. Aunt Jane glances at her watch.

"The last thing is personal effects," Langley says. "Your sister of course wanted Lucy to have her special jewelry, including her wedding and engagement rings." He stands up and takes off the picture that hides the wall safe. Mom kept her fancy jewelry for awards dinners in there. Earrings and bracelets and necklaces. I loved how everything sparkled. Sometimes she would let me fasten the clasp of her necklace.

I get all those diamonds? Excitement flashes for a second, making me feel more mixed-up.

"You're giving them to me now? How will I get them back home?" Aunt Jane says, not taking the gray velvet bag Mr. Langley's holding out.

"Carry them with you on the plane. It's safest to keep items like this with you when traveling. When you get home you might want to rent a safety deposit box, but you wouldn't want to ship it."

She looks in the bag and takes something out.

"That bracelet was Luis's gift to Gloria when Lucy was born, and is to be presented to her on her eighteenth birthday. There's a special note in the will."

"All right."

"It's a nod to the Beatles song, you know."

"Song?"

"It was in the slide show yesterday." He hums a few notes.

Tears rise, hot in my eyes. Daddy used to sing it to me all the time. Aunt Jane shakes her head.

"'Lucy in the Sky with Diamonds'?" Mr. Langley raises his eyebrows.

"Oh, right." Aunt Jane puts the bag on the desk.

"Only now it's Luis and Gloria in the sky. With the diamond left here on Earth." Mr. Langley sighs.

"You mean Lucy," Aunt Jane says after a second.

"Yes. I know you haven't seen it since you've been here, but she sparkles, Jane. She's a vivacious, curious, beautiful girl. She was Gloria and Luis's pride and joy."

The tears are dribbling down my cheeks, and my stomach elevator feels like it's hit the basement. I can hear Daddy's voice, singing.

"I know some people would probably say they both worked too much, but nurturing Lucy was the most important thing in their lives. I just hope that will continue to be the case when she moves to Michigan with you."

"What are you talking about?" Aunt Jane's voice gets louder.

"In New York, Lucy is exposed to a dynamic, multicultural world. It's the cultural capital of the country, with museums and music and theater and universities. You know she's bilingual. She's had au pairs from three or four countries. She takes tae kwon do twice a week, piano lessons weekly, and rotates between swimming, cooking, and art classes at the Y."

"Unlike a rinky-dink town in flyover country, halfway to the North Pole?" Now I can hear her fine.

"I didn't say that."

"But you meant it."

"I was only thinking out loud about a best-case scenario."

"In a best-case scenario, either Gloria or Luis would have crawled out of that car crash."

Step on a crack, break your mother's back. Step on the grass, make her car crash. I squeeze my eyes shut as the hot tears come faster.

"I'm talking about you moving to New York to live with Lucy," Mr. Langley says.

"What?"

What? My eyes pop open. Is he serious?

"It would allow Lucy to retain some stability. Her home, her school."

"Absolutely not. Out of the question." Aunt Jane sounds really mad now.

"May I ask why? You don't have deep roots in Michigan."

"Who are you to measure my roots?"

"You and Gloria grew up in San Diego. After you married into the Coast Guard, you relocated several times."

"How do you—"

"Your son's in the military, stationed overseas. Your husband d—"

"You've been investigating me?" Aunt Jane is practically yelling.

"You're surprised? That's part of my job."

"Well, I have a job, too. One that requires me to live in Michigan." Her hands are curled up into fists.

"Plain Jane's CSA."

CSA again. And that name, Plain Jane's, that she said the first day. But what does it mean?

"I don't sit in front of a television camera, Mr. Langley. I don't negotiate contracts worth millions. But the CSA is mine, and I'm not giving it up. And in order to run it, I need land. Farmland, specifically. Land you can grow things on. The kind of land that's in short supply in New York City."

"But why do you need to make a living farming? We've discussed the trust income that will be coming to you. If the apartment were retained, we'd have to have a more aggressive investment strategy, but . . ."

"Why do I need to make a living farming?" Aunt Jane flings her hands in the air. "Look, I'm trying to do the right thing, but I don't need to explain myself to you. I don't need to justify my life." She stalks toward the door. Toward me. "I need some air."

I duck into my room across the hall, my heart racing like a train coming into the station. I'm supposed to go live on a *farm*?

Chapter 10

JANE

How dare he.

Anger seethes from my body, almost a visible presence, it feels like. I'm outside the apartment building with no idea how I got here— whether anyone else was on the elevator or whether the mute doorman opened the door. Instinctively I aim north, for Central Park, down Fifty-Sixth Street and then up Eighth Avenue, glimpsing the green as I turn the corner. I walk faster, past a bus stop, a hot-dog cart, a homeless guy. I almost run, tunnel vision trained only on that green.

For the next hour, I walk off my anger, feeling my body settle back into something like its usual cadence and rhythms. Central Park has no vegetable beds, no curving hillside views. The water is a tiny pond compared to Lake Michigan. But there is green.

Ahead a bigger knot of people is gathered. A street performer, someone hawking their juggling or strumming for a little cash. But as I get closer, there's no apparent entertainment. No musicians, no magicians, no mimes. Nothing to see until I'm literally almost on top of it, a black-and-white mosaic circle, inlaid in the asphalt path. Yellow forsythia branches lie on top of it.

Seized with a sensation of trespass, I step back and notice letters in the center. I walk around to read them right side up.

"Imagine," it says. The forsythia branches have been arranged to form a giant peace sign, with three radiating below the *G* and a single branch laid on top of it. Votive candles in glass jars flicker around the word.

A young Japanese woman with a shock of magenta in her hair approaches me with a camera.

"Take picture?"

I nod, automatically holding out my hand. She beckons a young man. More yellow forsythia branches stick out the top of the backpack he leaves on a bench. Instead of standing, they lie down on the mosaic, faces propped on their elbows, feet in the air.

"Make sure to get peace sign," the woman instructs me.

I nod, firing off a bunch of shots before handing back the camera. She scrolls through the shots eagerly, showing one to her boyfriend.

"That's pretty, what you did with the flowers," I say. Forsythia is one of my favorites, a harbinger of spring.

They smile, pleased. "We came from Tokyo to do it," the man says, pushing up thick-framed glasses.

"All the way from Tokyo?"

The woman nods. "We are dreamers, too." She puts the lens cap on the camera and hangs it around her neck. "He was hero. She was so beautiful. Thank you for picture."

They return to the bench with the backpack, where they drape around each other, one earbud apiece from a shared iPod.

I look back at the mosaic, pieces starting to click into place, like coins dropping into a newspaper machine. The Beatles again. John Lennon lived near Central Park, didn't he? Langley's humming echoes in my head, and the lyrics tangle with the blur of changes over the last week. Imagine Lucy in the sky, flying to Michigan. Imagine a plain Jane hauling home diamonds. Imagine living for today . . .

Today. Soothed by the walk, the green, awe of the couple traveling thousands of miles to create their tribute, I step back to admire it and let myself imagine living for today. Just today, not yesterday or yesteryear. No if-onlys, no regrets, no resentments. Free from the shadows of marriage and motherhood misfortune, free to live in the present, with Lucy. *Mi sobrina. Mi*—the word rises again, unspoken—*niña.*

A pigeon flaps in front of me, snatching one of the forsythia branches, ruining the peace symbol. I notice a plaque that says the mosaic is indeed a memorial to Lennon. This part of the park, called Strawberry Fields, was his and Yoko Ono's favorite place.

Hardly a place for real strawberries. Far too shady, my farmer's mind says. And just like that, I'm homesick. Intensely, wholeheartedly homesick, and instead of going forward, I only want to go back. Back to my plots that await tilling. Back to the knobby hills and the views of the bays. Back to my potholed driveway. Back to my bedroom and stand-in greenhouse, with barely room to walk between the bed and the seed plugs. Back to Miguel, always willing and able to help out. Back to Martha and the CSA subscriptions she brings to my mailbox. Even back to my work-share customer family who won't have a clue what to do. Because at least they want to be there. The rest belong there, like me. As for Lucy in the sky with diamonds, I hope she's comfortable with her feet flat on the earth.

Chapter 11
LUCY

Friday afternoon Mr. Langley knocks on my door again.

"How have you been getting on with your aunt?"

I shrug, my shoulders poking out from under the bed covers for the first time all day.

"Are you feeling at all reconciled to moving to Michigan to live with her?"

Sitting up, I shake my head, hard. "I want to stay here."

"I wish that could happen."

"She could move here." *Like you said.* I look at the pink rug, watching him through my eyelashes, tears starting to well.

Mr. Langley's feet shift, and he sighs. "That's not going to happen, Lucy."

"Why not?" Why didn't Mom and Daddy make that part of the will?

"It's just the way it is. But I have a compromise plan. Can I sit down?"

I shrug again. He'll tell me. He lowers himself on the bed, making the mattress bounce.

"You'll live here through the end of the school year with Deirdre. This way you have more time to adapt to the situation."

He says it like it's a sure thing or something. I pull my hair back into a ponytail, thinking about it. Deirdre is OK. Sometimes I wish she had a boyfriend here, like Caitlin, my last au pair, so she'd pay a little less attention to me. I'm not a kid anymore. But anything that puts off moving to a farm is a good thing.

"Then what?"

"Then in June, you move to Michigan to live with your aunt."

The tears rise up again, hot and angry.

"Can't you find someone else? What about Daddy's family?"

"Lucy, I'm sorry. I wish I could. But your mother had no other family. And your father's family is all in Mexico."

He keeps saying that. So what? I'm still their family. Sometimes I wonder if Mr. Langley even told Daddy's family about the car crash, since none of them came to the funeral.

"I know it's hard to understand. But there are laws. They can't just leave Mexico to come take care of you."

"I could go there." I sniff loudly, trying to keep the tears from leaking. One slides past my nose anyway.

"Now, how would that be any better than moving to your aunt Jane's?" He pats my hand and hands me a tissue.

"They don't live on a farm," I say. Not that I remember, anyway. I was only a baby. And there's Gabriella. A cousin.

"No. Lucy, I'm sorry. But moving to Mexico is not a good idea. It's not going to happen."

So it's not that it's impossible. It's that he thinks it's not a good idea. Well, my ideas count, too. I'm eleven years old, almost twelve. And now I have two months to figure out how to make it happen.

That night, after Deirdre thinks I'm asleep, I sneak into my parents' room. I log on to the computer and go back to Bonita Ortiz in the contacts. My aunt Beautiful. I fantasize about calling her.

"*Hola. Soy* Lucy Ortiz. Can I speak to *Tía* Boni—?"

"Lucy? *¿Luisa? ¡Gracias a Dios!* We have been so worried." Her voice gets faster and faster. "We heard about the car accident. It's awful, poor Luis, *mi hermano* . . . but we were so worried about what would happen to you. No one called to tell us anything."

"The lawyer said you can't do anything because you live in Mexico."

"Do nothing? *¿Por mi sobrina?*" Her voice would get self-righteous. "Just try to stop me. You are family. We belong together. We will be together. *Juntos pronto.*"

Together soon. I can hear her so clearly. But it's too late to call now, so I'll email her.

> Dear Aunt Bonita—This is your niece Lucy in New
> York City. You heard about Daddy and my mom,
> right? They say I have to go live with another aunt.
> I don't want to. Please, can I come live with you?
> Write back soon.

I sign it, "Love, Lucy," hit "Send," and watch it disappear on the screen. Will she be able to read English? I should have written in Spanish! No, she'll be able to read it. I wish I remembered what she looked like. Besides beautiful. I know she'll be beautiful, like Mom, with her bright, white smile and her curly hair and all her pretty clothes and jewelry and shoes that she let me try on.

I leave the desk for the walk-in closet. Mom's closet. It's giant. It even has a foldout stepladder that slides around the room on this little track so you can get to the things on the top shelves and racks. With all her TV clothes, she needed a lot of space. She would sometimes send me up that ladder. "Lucy, can you bring down my navy-and-white spectator pumps? Find the scarf I bought on our trip to Majorca? Be a dear and grab the box of summer purses?"

I loved looking through it all as I searched for whatever she wanted. And Mom always knew what she wanted. I've been in Deirdre's room, too. "I don't have anything to wear," she'll say, staring into her closet. Though in her accent it sounds more like—ware-uh. "Oh dear, I don't have anything to ware-uh." Sometimes she'll ask me, "How do you like this sweater"—sweat-uh—"with these jeans, Lucy? Should I wear boots with this skirt, or flats?"

Mom would never do that. I'd find what she wanted, and she'd say, "Thank you, sweetie," and put it on, knowing exactly how it should go. And she was always right. When she was done dressing, I'd look at her reflection in the full-length mirror. "Mom, you look beautiful," I always told her.

The night before the accident, I watched her pack. "Travel clothes," she said about the pink jacket and lacy white blouse and black pants that she chose, because they wouldn't wrinkle much. "I'll miss you, Lucy," she told me, putting her arm around me. "Hey, we match."

We stood side by side, right in front of her mirror. I was wearing my Venice Beach T-shirt from our vacation last year. She was wearing her hoodie. If I look again, hard, maybe I can see her.

The mirror is full length and freestanding. You can spin and tilt it, too. All I see is me, wearing my fleece peace pajama bottoms and the Venice Beach T-shirt. I keep forgetting to put it in the wash. My hair is hanging in my face. I push it away and step closer to the mirror, tilting it toward me, staring so hard, trying to see again how we stood there, how our arms brushed, how she wrapped hers around my shoulder and held me close against her side. I squint into the mirror, trying to make myself see double. Just one more glimpse together. One more.

From the desk something beeps. Aunt Bonita's reply! I rush back to the computer. A pop-up window is on the screen.

Message undeliverable. No known account.

Chapter 12

JANE

"Lucy. Lucy. What in the world got into you, sleeping in your mum's closet?" I follow Deirdre's voice into Gloria and Luis's bedroom. She's kneeling in the closet, shaking Lucy by the shoulder.

"Wake up, Lucy."

Lucy, curled into a ball on the floor, opens her eyes.

"Your aunt's leaving today, remember? She wanted to say goodbye," Deirdre says.

Lucy nods stiffly, rubbing her arms, sitting up slowly.

"You're freezing. What were you thinking, sleeping on the floor like that?" Deirdre opens a few drawers and finds a hoodie. It says Venice Beach, just like Lucy's T-shirt. "Put this on."

Watching Deirdre act so motherly, my brain starts to chant. *Unfit.* I drown it out by talking to Lucy.

"So, I guess this is goodbye for now." I clear my throat. "I'll call you in a few days, OK?"

Lucy nods, crossing her arms. The too-long sleeves cover up her hands.

"And I'll see you in June for your first peek at Michigan." Tentatively I reach out with one arm and wrap it around her shoulders, a half hug.

I see us reflected in the full-length mirror, me in my jeans and fleece vest, Lucy's dark hair against my shoulder. Tucked into me like that, enveloped in Gloria's too-large hoodie, she looks younger, vulnerable. Cautiously I rub her back.

But she pulls away, turning her back on our dual reflection. "I'm hungry, Deirdre."

In the cab, I exhale genuinely for the first time in a week, a gust of guilty relief. On the way back to JFK, I vacillate between damning myself for not trying harder with Lucy and feeling relieved about the two-month respite. Langley's proposal that she finish the school year in New York was a life raft. Especially since it's two months of spring. For the CSA it's my critical season, but even before, it's always been my favorite. Everything offers promise in spring. Except for Mom's funeral, I haven't been in a church in years. But when the waist-high snowbanks finally melt, when the crocus and forsythia blossom, something in me can conceive of the concept of benevolence freely bestowed.

I remember the Japanese tourists and their forsythia branches. Imagine, indeed. Imagine coming all that way to create their ephemeral tribute. Imagine—how does it go? The tune plays in my head, then segues into the slide show song, "Lucy in the Sky." Does Lucy imagine Gloria and Luis are in heaven, watching over her, their diamond left on Earth? *If you are, what in the world were you thinking?* I ask the cab ceiling.

Aboard the plane, I shove the bulging briefcase Langley's assistant packed with Lucy's files and the gray velvet bag of jewelry in the overhead compartment, out of sight. As the plane rises above the clouds, obscuring the city, a sense of lightness swells up, like a fishing bobber riding a wave. I'm going home. Back to the farm, to my Old Mission aerie, to Plain Jane's. Plain as in everyone else stripped away. Gloria and the reins she's managed to control even in death. Lucy and her enormous needs. Away. To the familiar and simple life that I created for myself.

We only stayed in Houston a few years. Moving to Michigan was what actually started to lift my stupor. I'd never lived anyplace where all four seasons were experienced equally. The rhythm of it, the even pace, was soothing. The contrasts between seasons underscored the best of each: spring's delicate promise, summer's verdant fulfillment, autumn's warm colors and crisp nights, winter's austerity. It also made Plain Jane's possible. Old Mission was full of farmers, and most had their own roadside stands. I signed Matt up for Little League and Jim as an assistant coach. During their long evenings at games, I'd go for walks and observe. One of the neighbors clued me in that our place was well suited for a garden.

"Raspberries, rhubarb, asparagus. Somebody had a garden around here once, and not a shabby one, either," was Sally Martin's assessment after her first visit. "If we clean up these raspberries, you could have a few pies yet this summer."

That was the start. I froze the raspberries we didn't eat that first summer. All winter, opening each pint felt like a gift. We cleaned up the rhubarb and asparagus beds, too. Next spring I harvested that and planted my first garden, a salsa one, to supply Sally. She and her husband, Don, ran a stand May to October.

Spending the days outside, alone, and in charge suited me. Peppers here. Tomatoes there. Cilantro here. A domain all my own, where I could keep everything orderly. Nothing changed unless I made it happen. Not to mention balm for the grief and guilt I still lugged, five years on from Alaska. In the soil, I saw that what I nurtured could truly flourish. Any mistakes were for a season, not a lifetime.

Sally and Don introduced me to the CSA business model, too, and proposed a partnership. I considered it, but got cold feet. It seemed too much to promise. Plus Jim suggested that maybe I should show up at Matt's baseball games.

So I went to the games and expanded my garden instead. The third summer, I added strawberries, salad greens, potatoes, peas, beans, carrots, cukes, squash, tomatoes, and zucchini. And I kept records. Which tomato varieties fared the best, which greens made the crispest salads, which potatoes were the most flavorful.

By year four I was growing far more than we could eat and asked Jim to help me build a roadside stand. We had an ideal location, right on the main road to the lighthouse.

"It's pretty busy at the station. We're down a few guys. I'll help in the fall, OK?"

That summed up our marriage by then. Polite, civil, but always putting each other off. Sally introduced me to Miguel, only a few years older than Matt and eager for any work. He had the stand built three days after we met. Solid, sturdy, painted a cheerful red. He built the compost bin next. There were always odd jobs I couldn't get to, and work at the station never seemed to relent for Jim, that fall or next.

The local foodie scene took off. "Farm-to-table" became all the rage in restaurants. The flow of farm-stand customers grew. Matt started high school and added basketball to baseball. Parents weren't asked to coach anymore. Jim spent more time at the station.

Then one February day, Sally called, late. "A stroke, they think. We're in the ER."

Her eyes were red, but her voice was steady when she came out to the waiting room. "The doctor said he'll need months of rehab and who knows how much function and strength he'll regain."

"Oh, Sally. I'm so sorry."

"I want you to take our CSA customers."

I protested, but she wouldn't take my no this time. And Plain Jane's was born. Since then I've hung on, through the recession and despite losing Jim's day-job income. Matt graduated and left for the army, a mission fulfilled, if not accomplished.

Now there's Lucy. Another chance at a daughter, an optimist might say. Or a person of faith, neither of which I am. Still, was it right to leave her there for two months? Should I have moved to New York? I could bring Sarge. My customers would miss me, at least some, but they'd find another CSA. Miguel would find work. Langley was right: the only thing tying me to Old Mission is me. If I uproot again, Lucy doesn't have to.

Then again, why deny that her life has changed forever? Isn't that the first stage of grief, one she has to move on from? A fresh start might be best.

The plane banks, then emerges through the clouds. The grids of the suburban Detroit streets, my layover city, appear.

"Ladies and gentlemen, we are beginning our descent and should arrive on time. Those of you with connecting flights will find departure gate information in the terminal," the flight attendant says.

The contradictions in the language strike me. *Departure information in the terminal.* Beginnings come from endings. All you can do is try to hang on to everything so it doesn't get lost along the way.

Chapter 13
LUCY

An hour after the cab leaves, Aunt Jane seems like a ghost. The funeral feels like a dream, too. It seems like a regular Saturday morning, one where both Daddy and Mom are at the studio. For a second I want to believe that—that I could go there, sit in Mom's anchor chair, and spin like I did when I was little, but spinning backward, rewinding the days until I get back to that day, and the field trip, and I'd let stupid Eli and Joel run away with my phone and not go anywhere near the grass.

Deirdre comes in with her travel coffee mug. "Right, Lucy, you'll come with me on the errands this morning, OK?" One of her questions that isn't.

"I want to stay home." I push away the pretending. I'm not a little kid. I can't rewind the days, and I don't have many more left in New York. I want to get back into Daddy's computer and Mom's closet. There are boxes of family stuff behind the clothes on the top shelves. One might have more information about Daddy's family.

"We'll leave in ten minutes, then." Deirdre's checking her phone, not listening.

"But—" Before I finish, I change my mind about arguing. I know she doesn't like me in their room, so better to keep my plans a secret.

"So we're going to drop off your winter coat at the dry cleaner's, pick up more multivitamins at the pharmacy, and get a few items at the grocery." Deirdre talks briskly as we head down the elevator.

At the dry cleaner, Mrs. Kim is there as usual. "Mees Deedree. Mees Lucy. Lots for you today."

Deirdre looks confused. "I wasn't planning to pick anything up. Just this coat of Lucy's to drop off."

"Suits for Mrs. Santiago and Mr. Ortiz. Many. No one here for two weeks." She pushes the button that makes the hanger rack spin. Just like I imagined doing on Mom's chair.

"Oh dear." Deirdre looks at me. "I never thought—I suppose they don't get the news, either in English or Spanish."

Abruptly, the rack stops spinning. All the clothes swing violently. Mrs. Kim unhooks two navy men's suits and one charcoal gray. Daddy wore the gray one with a light-purple shirt. Whenever he did, I always tried to wear purple, too, so Mom would smile at us together. I can see her smile now. *Mi guapo esposo,* she'd tell Daddy. My handsome husband. *Mi hermosa hija.* My beautiful daughter. *Mi preciosa familia.* My precious family—all gone now. The clothes are like costumes for a family that used to be.

Four or five of her outfits hanging next to Daddy's suits, each wrapped in its plastic sheath. An emerald-green dress that she wore with a cropped black blazer. A houndstooth jacket and skirt with a pink sheath underneath. Deirdre throws up her hands as it piles up. "We can't even carry all that home."

"One hundred seventy-two," Mrs. Kim announces. Deirdre goes paler. "I didn't bring that much with me."

"Problem?" Mrs. Kim asks, turning her head between us.

"Well, yes. Rather so," Deirdre says, her words halting. "You see, last week, Lucy's parents—"

"Died," I say, looking straight at Mrs. Kim. "In a car accident."

"Car accident?" Mrs. Kim looks uncertainly between us.

I open my arms wide, then crash my fist into my other palm. Mrs. Kim's eyebrows fly up her forehead.

"Quite. Yes, Lucy's—Lucy's pretty much summed it up there. So we don't need the clothes, Mrs. Kim," Deirdre says. "If you wanted to sell them yourself, in fact . . ."

"Sell them?" I turn to her.

Mrs. Kim's face puzzles, then clears. "We keep?"

Deirdre nods.

"Wait a minute," I say, but Mrs. Kim is talking louder.

"OK. Next Wednesday for Mees Lucy jacket, OK?"

"OK!" Deirdre pilots me out of the store. "Thank you."

On the sidewalk, I hear Mrs. Kim hollering in Korean to someone. I turn on Deirdre in English.

"What do you think you're doing?"

"What do you mean?"

"The clothes!"

"What about them?"

"You shouldn't have given them away!" Tears, angry and sad, spring to my eyes. They may be costumes now, but they're mine.

She looks surprised. "You wanted to keep them?"

"Yes!" I sniffle and swipe my arm against my nose.

"But why? Whatever would you do with them?"

I have no idea. I already feel a little babyish, sniffling and yelling on the street. "All my parents' stuff is mine now. I just want to keep them."

"Lucy, that's not practical. You're moving, you—"

"I don't care! They're mine! Just leave them alone, OK? Leave me alone." I start running down the street.

"Lucy, wait!"

There's a bus stop down the block. I'll take the bus home and get money, then come back and pick up the clothes.

"Wait, Lucy!"

I can run faster than Deirdre. I get to the little shelter at the stop and look down the street. No bus. I look the other way. I can see Deirdre jog-walking down the street, slow in her boots with the pointy toes and heels. Come on, bus. Still nothing in sight. I look back. Deirdre's getting closer. I slump down on the bench in the shelter, hoping the man waiting in a wheelchair shields me. I'm still wearing Mom's hoodie, and it's cold. I pull up the hood, then my knees, and squeeze them tight against my chest, trying to gather myself in as small as I can. I sniffle against my knees, turn my head back to check for the bus, and that's when I see her.

Her blinding white smile. Her curly dark hair out to her shoulders. Her crossed arms inside black-and-white-checked jacket sleeves, the same one Deirdre just left at the dry cleaner.

Mom, standing there life-size, smiling at me. Words are stacked up against her body, from her shoulder to her hip.

A VOICE OF TRUST
BEST LATINA ANCHOR, NY MARKET, 2008, 2009, 2010
GLORIA SANTIAGO-ORTIZ
CHANNEL 10, 7–9 A.M. WEEKDAYS
¡NO LA PIERDAS!

Behind Mom's picture, plastered to the bus shelter, the bus stops and opens its doors. The man in the wheelchair gets on. I don't. At first I don't think I can breathe. Then my chest starts heaving as I stare at that picture, locked in. The bus glides on. From the other direction Deirdre arrives, panting. "Lucy! You mustn't run off like that. If I can't trust you—"

She bends down to touch my shoulder. "You're shaking. What—"

Then, from the corner of my eye I see her look where I'm looking. At the ad. At Mom. Her mouth falls open. "Lucy. Sweetheart. I'm so sorry."

¡No la pierdas!

Don't miss her. Oh, but I do.

Chapter 14

JANE

Miguel did a great job on the driveway, barely a bounce from road to house. At home Sarge is glad to see me, or me and my key, more like it. He's out the door as soon as I'm in, bounding for the barn. Ready for a mouse after a week of cat food. I drop the heavy Lucy briefcase on the black-and-white-checkerboard kitchen floor and head to the fridge myself. Stark on the nearly bare shelves are yogurt, an apple, and a hunk of my favorite sourdough from Bay Bread. I eat standing up, gorging myself on everything that I've been homesick for this last week. The white cabinets that line the two walls, the counters that become an assembly line on CSA delivery eves. The double-basin iron sink that still holds my green Extension coffee mug with a leftover swallow. Above the sink, the kitchen window with what the Realtors call a "seasonal" view of West Bay, which I'll lose all but a slice of when the leaves fill in next month, but for now stretches blue and peaceful to the Leelanau Peninsula.

My gaze shortens, sweeping from the bay to the precious swath of west-facing land between the house and the rear property line. These are the beds that need tilling and tending, the real strawberry fields. And garlic, salad greens, and rhubarb and everything else that follows, asparagus to zucchini. I drop my spoon into the coffee mug and toss the apple core into the compost. Time to get to work.

My spring to-do list is short: prep and plant. But it's deceptively simple. To everything there is indeed a season, and that season is spring. Making my farm plan—everything from spacing out the distance between plants and rows to what goes with what and where to put the succession plantings so I've got a steady supply of lettuce and carrots and beans all summer long. Prepping the beds, installing the pea trellises. Pulling off the winter mulch. Then, when it gets warmer, this time of year, bringing the seed plugs I started in January out to the sun to acclimate, then back indoors for the chilly evenings.

That was one of Miguel's to-dos. I'll bet they've grown an inch, at least. Heading to my makeshift bedroom greenhouse, my toe bumps the briefcase, tipping it over. The catch bursts, spilling papers and files onto the black and white squares.

"Damn it." I scoop them up, trying to keep the papers in the manila folders that Langley's assistant neatly labeled: medical records, school records, insurance policies, bank and miscellaneous financial, car accident, apartment. Where to store all this? I keep meaning to turn Matt's old room into a home office, get the computer out of the kitchen, into a place where I could fit a filing cabinet and get better organized. Whenever I've tried to start, though, something seems to get in my way.

Matt's room feels like a tomb. The rolltop desk is closed, as are the blinds, casting everything into dimness. The blue plaid bedspread is tucked in smoothly and neatly, belying how it regularly hung askew whether Matt's gangly frame was under it or not. The walls still bear his army poster and framed basketball and baseball team photos. The bookshelf is grounded by two and a half shelves of the Encyclopaedia Britannica that we hauled here from Houston. A year or two later the Internet rendered it obsolete. The rest of the shelves are crammed with more souvenirs of bygone boyhood: yearbooks, trophies, and medals from his years playing sports. Maybe it's less of a tomb than a shrine, of sorts, a monument that I did try, which was more than my mom did after Esteban. I made an effort.

I slide up the rolltop desk cover and pile the folders on the smooth wood, then hesitate with the gray velvet bag. Not the safety deposit box Langley advised, but for now it will do. I push it behind the folders and tug the top back down. It catches a few times, but I manage to close it completely. There. No one would be the wiser.

The thought echoes as I stand with my hand on the doorknob. The thing is, no one else matters. Just me. Maybe I was never meant to convert Matt's room to a home office. Maybe it was destined to stage an encore mother act, with Lucy. Once Matt left home, the raw edges did dull a bit. With an empty nest I could more easily forget that it was only ever half-full. I look around, imagining the walls cleared of the army poster and sports photos, a fresh coat of paint, the shelves bare and ready for girlish paraphernalia, the blinds open to let sunshine stream in.

But it was also after Matt was gone that Jim dropped the divorce bombshell, shattering my illusion about our marriage's state of benign neglect.

"Matt's grown up and on his own, after all. It'll give us both a fresh start," he'd said. He meant a fresh start for *him*. With Kate. And her daughter.

The daughter. That hurt the most, him recouping what first drove a wedge between us. He'd been seeing Kate for a whole year when he finally told me. She worked in IT, and they met when her company was hired to install some new software at the base. It was love at first click, or something. He'd been offered a transfer to Clearwater, Florida, and wanted to take her with him. Take *them* with him.

Even if we'd lost the intimacy, I had thought our marriage was at least still honest. I knew the planting, blossom, and fruit emergence date for every single tomato plant I'd grown for the last three years. But for a whole year, I hadn't known my husband was having an affair. It hurt, like Jim had picked at the scabs Plain Jane's had helped heal. Can I risk that again?

I close Matt's door and my mind to the picture of the room retrofitted for Lucy. Outside, I stab my shovel into the depths of the compost pile, which hasn't had a good turn since Thanksgiving. Dig, lift, flip. Dig, lift, flip. Dig—and then my rhythm is abruptly halted, the shovel still sinking in where the slatted two-by-four sides should have stopped it, halfway burying the handle.

Two rotted-out boards on the back of the bin are responsible. I give the whole thing a once-over, shaking it vigorously. Several boards are loose, and one corner sags. It's been ten years—probably should be replaced altogether. On the other hand, two new boards and pounding a few nails would be faster and cheaper. As I dither over the choice, Miguel's truck pulls in.

"*Bueno, ¿sí?*" He hands me my spare house key while nodding toward the smooth driveway.

"You did a great job. What do I owe you?"

"One fifty."

"Really?" Supplies had to be at least fifty.

"*Sí.*"

"Let me get my checkbook." Leaving the shovel stuck in the compost, we walk back to the house. Miguel's truck is full of bundled stacks of newspapers. "What are you doing with all these?"

"Delivering up to the store."

"Another job?" Besides being a 24-7 on-call handyman and farm laborer for anyone in Grand Traverse or Leelanau Counties, Miguel already drives a school bus route.

He nods. I don't push it. You do what you have to do. The story of our lives, me a hollowed-out mother, dutifully following Coast Guard orders, Miguel the lone American in his family, born to Mexican migrant parents while they were in the US. One day he came home from high school to an empty house.

"Deported," Martha had told me, solemnly. "His sister still had her Dora backpack on."

Lonely and frightened, he had to be, but I've never heard a word of resentment. Instead, he parlayed good humor, bilingualism, and connections with the migrants into a liaison role that makes him virtually indispensable around here. I've seen him on the school bus route, and he's just as good natured there, too, waiting for kids running late, waving and smiling to any passing vehicle. Now running newspapers out to the end of the peninsula. Inside the house, I scribble out a check for two hundred dollars.

Outside he glances at it and frowns. "Too much."

"Go ahead. Take it."

He shakes his head. "Only what's fair. No charity." He waves the check at me, trying to give it back.

I keep my hands in my pockets. "You fed Sarge and kept an eye on the place all week, too."

He shakes his head again. "That was helping *una amiga.*"

He looks upset. No good deed. Shit.

"Then consider it an advance on my next job. Since I already wrote it. All right?"

He hesitates.

"Please. In fact, I've already got one. Gotta rebuild the compost bin. Boards are rotted out." I jerk my thumb over my shoulder. "Use that for some two-by-fours. After you get it built, you can let me know how much more I owe."

His face relaxes and he folds the check into his pocket. "OK. I'll go measure."

Chapter 15
LUCY

I don't talk to Deirdre again until we pass Midtown Pets and I have to stop and look in the window. I love dogs and cats, but especially kittens. Daddy's allergic, so we can't have one.

Daddy's allergic. *Daddy was allergic.* I forget, and when I remember, it feels like it's happening all over again, everything going just fine and then Mrs. Creighton calls me to her office and everything stops with a jerk, like the dry-cleaning rack, and there I hang, swinging wildly. Deirdre keeps walking ahead, pulling the little foldable cart.

"Deirdre, wait. Can we go in?" I call her back.

"Oh, Lucy, we've got all the shopping with us." She turns around.

She's got a cat at home in London, though. "Please? They're so cute. Look at that little gray one there. What's your cat's name again?"

She's already smiling. Or maybe she just feels guilty about before, in the bus-stop shelter. "OK. Just for a minute."

It smells in the shop, and it's kind of noisy, but I don't mind. On the back side of the cages stacked in the window, I can get close, even put my fingers up to the cage of that little gray kitten. She sniffs my fingers and mews, arching her back against the cage.

"Looks like she likes you," Deirdre says.

"Can we take her home, Deirdre, please?"

"Oh, Lucy, no. You're leaving in two months."

"I could take her with me. I'm going to live on a farm, remember? Farms have all kinds of animals. Please?"

Deirdre starts to shake her head. No! She can't say no! I never wanted anything this bad. Desperately I search for a reason. "Mr. Meinert said a pet would help me, right?"

That scores. Deirdre sighs. "Well, if you're going to get a kitten, we should go to a rescue organization, not buy one."

It sounds like she's going to say yes, but I like that little gray kitten so much. I look back at her, lapping up water in her dish, then at Deirdre.

"Can we go today?"

She looks at her phone and nods. "Let's take the food home, and then we'll see what we can find."

While she's putting away the food, I go online.

"Deirdre, look! The Humane Society's on Fifty-Ninth. It's so close."

She looks over my shoulder. "Fifty-Ninth and Second. All right. But we have to call your aunt first. Make sure it's OK."

"It'll be fine! It's a farm, right?"

"You never know. What if she's allergic, too? I'll just call now."

Aunt Jane doesn't answer.

"All right, then. Let's have a little lunch," Deirdre says.

I look at the pictures of the dogs and cats while we eat. "I don't see many kittens."

"A kitten would be a lot of work. You'd have to train it and all. An adult cat, one that's trained, might be easier."

I want a kitten. Something cute and cuddly and little. Something to take care of, that I'll take care of forever and ever.

It's one o'clock, and Aunt Jane hasn't called back. One fifteen. One twenty-five. One thirty.

"Deirdre, they close at four! And they're not open Sundays. Please, can we just go now?"

She sighs and looks at her silent phone again. "All right, then. It is a farm, like you say."

At the Humane Society they don't let us see the animals right away. I sprawl on a chair while Deirdre fills out a questionnaire with about a million questions. "'Any pets already in the household?' No. 'Any experience with pets?' No. 'Any children?' Yes. 'Pet preference?'"

"Kitten!" I interject.

"'Are you willing to pay licensing fees and have your pet spayed or neutered?' Yes." Deirdre checks the last box. Finally!

"Can we see them now?" I jump up, following her back to the counter.

"Well, that was quick," says the lady there, whose name tag says she's Aliyah, from Brooklyn. "So you're looking for a cat today?" She has the musical voice of someone from Jamaica, or the DR, blond dreads and cat-eye-shaped glasses.

"A kitten," I say before Deirdre can say anything, and then I hold my breath. If I don't breathe before she answers, they'll have a kitten.

"Hmmm. Well, we don't always have kitties, but you're in luck. Today we do have a litter."

It worked! I let out my breath in a whoosh, and we follow Aliyah past rows of stacked cages, around a corner, and down a hall. All the way at the back, next to an exit door, is a cage with four kittens mewling and tumbling around. I drop down to my knees.

"Oh, Deirdre, look—they're adorable!" I watch them bat at each other. "How old are they?"

"About six weeks. Something must have happened to the mother. Someone brought them in two weeks ago, skin and bones and freezing. Two didn't make it." Aliyah lowers her voice, intending to tell only Deirdre the last part, but I hear her. Something happened to the mother—what about the father? Poor kitties, left all by themselves.

"Dear me," Deirdre says. "Are they all right now, then?"

"Right as rain. See any you like, young lady?"

"That one." I point at one with patchwork fur. Yellow and white and gray, too. It sits a little bit apart from the other three, washing its face. "Is it a boy or a girl?"

"Girl." Aliyah unlatches the cage and hands her to me.

I stand perfectly still, afraid I'll startle her. She's tense, too. I can feel her body throbbing and her tiny claws through Mom's hoodie, but otherwise she holds herself rigid. She's so tiny! I stroke her soft back. *I'll keep you safe now.*

"She still has her claws?" Deirdre asks.

"Generally we leave at least their front claws. It's much more humane. And if there's any chance she might become an outdoor cat, she'll need them."

I flinch when she says "outdoor." *Step on the grass, make her car crash.* I'll keep her inside, where we'll both be safe together. "Does she have a name?"

Aliyah shakes her head, the blond dreads waving. "The honor's all yours."

She's latching the cage and walking down the hall, talking to Deirdre about cages and bottle-feeding and training. It's happening! I have a kitten. She's relaxing a little in my arms, too. Until I start walking away from the cage. She starts mewling again, pushing herself up on my forearm, trying to peek over my shoulder. Behind me, the mewling from the cage gets louder, too.

Her paws knead a rhythm on my chest, like she's trying to climb up it. Aliyah and Deirdre have turned the corner.

I turn back to the cage, letting her sniff between the wire squares. The ones inside jump and paw at the cage. Now that she can see them, my kitten seems more content. She settles back down in my arms, head on her paws.

"I'm glad you got to say goodbye," I whisper into her white ear.

"What are you going to name her?" Deirdre asks as we walk along Fifty-Ninth.

"I don't know yet. It's got to be just right."

"Not just Kitty, then?"

"Uh-uh." I shake my head as we turn down Lexington. We walked over, but carrying the cage and all, Deirdre wants to take the subway.

"Funny how different it feels over here," Deirdre says. "We're not all that far from home."

"Uh-huh." At least it's still New York. Imagine how Michigan will feel. Her name should remind me of the city, I decide. She's going to be my ambassador. To the foreign land of Michigan.

We go downstairs, into the station at Fifty-Ninth and Lex. Lex. I turn the word around in my head, liking the sound of it. It doesn't sound girlish, though. Lexie? That does. Lexie. It reminds me of Daddy, too. He went to school in Texas and joked about being Tex-Mex, from both sides of the border. Yes, Lexie.

At home, Lexie stays asleep in her cage even after she's inside.

"Probably worn-out from the trip. Everything so strange all of a sudden," Deirdre says. "Let's just let her sleep. I could use a little lie-down myself."

"Go ahead." A chance to get back in Mom and Daddy's room! Being in there, I can't get surprised by that awful, jerky feeling of remembering they're gone. Maybe I can find out more about Daddy's family, too, so I don't have to go to Michigan.

"What, the au pair napping while the child runs wild?" Deirdre shakes her head.

"I don't run wild. I'll just watch TV."

"I know. You're a good girl, Lucy. It's just—" Deirdre yawns before she even finishes.

"It's fine." Please! "Lexie will keep me company."

"I'll just stretch out here on the couch with you."

Ten minutes into some cooking show, Deirdre is sound asleep. I slide off the couch, take Lexie's cage, and tiptoe down the hall.

Inside my parents' room I waver. Back to Daddy's desk and computer? Or Mom's closet?

The closet, I decide. Up on the top shelf, there's stuff that I've never seen moved, let alone opened. Three boxes labeled GS-O. Gloria Santiago-Ortiz, Mom's initials. Two with Daddy's: LO, the same as mine. I pick his to start with. It's not too heavy. I get it down the ladder and open the flaps.

Photos. In albums, in envelopes, loose in the box. They're older—mostly square instead of rectangle, the color faded. There's Daddy, in between a woman and a man. He's a lot younger, with a dark-brown mustache. It looks funny. He has his arm around the woman, not Mom. Is she Aunt Bonita?

The other man is standing a little bit separate from them. Who's he? He's got a mustache, too. All three of them have dark hair and big smiles. I wish Daddy had talked more about his family. They're standing outside someplace in the picture. Where they grew up in Mexico?

I dig back into the box. The newest-looking thing is a stack of envelopes wrapped in a rubber band. Inside the top one is a handwritten letter and a school picture of a girl who looks a little older than me, wearing a uniform. There's another picture of the same girl holding a soccer ball. That one's a normal picture, a rectangle. The girl isn't smiling. In the corner it says, "Aug. 2010."

I frown at the swoops and swirls of the letters. I speak Spanish pretty well, but reading, especially something handwritten, is way harder. It is from Aunt Bonita, wishing us a merry Christmas. Her daughter, Graciela, is twelve in the picture, she says. Graciela, that's my cousin's name. Not Gabriella. I didn't know she was so close to my age.

"Lucy? Lucy, where are you?" Deirdre is calling from the kitchen. I throw everything back into the box and push it behind some clothes before she walks in. With a cousin so close to my age, why didn't we visit more?

"Here again?" She frowns. "I don't think this is healthy, Lucy."

But I have to stay here. I have to find more about Graciela, *mi prima*. About the rest of Daddy's family in Mexico. My family in Mexico. I cross my arms.

"How would you know?" I ask, remembering something else from the first day. "Mr. Meinert said to follow my lead."

That was a good one. She hesitates.

"All right," she finally says. "A half hour. And I'm calling Phoebe's mother about a playdate."

Lexie woke up when Deirdre came in and is mewling inside her cage. I let her out. She starts playing with the photos, batting them around with her paws.

"No, Lexie, no." I gather up more of Graciela, or at least a girl playing soccer. She's got boobs. I look at my flat chest, then back at some more letters, but I can't read much. Aunt Bonita sounds worried about money, and someone whose name I can't read. The only recent pictures are of Graciela, so I can't figure it out that way.

Lexie is still walking over everything, so I put it all back in the box and go to the computer.

"Gloria Ortiz car crash," I type into Google.

There are thousands and thousands of stories, in English and Spanish, too. I hold my breath on the first couple I click, afraid of some new detail. After three or four, though, I figure out they're practically the same story. Two dead. Driver injured. Investigation ongoing. Interstate 405 closed for hours. Even the same pictures of Mom and Daddy. I click one more story, and suddenly there's a new picture. Of the car. Crashed in all along the passenger side, with fire coming out the back. *"El coche de la muerte,"* the headline says. I gasp and squeeze my eyes shut, but it's too late.

"Lucy! Time's up!"

"OK." I close the window, but I can't unsee that picture.

That night I dream of cats, of soccer players, of Mexico. Soccer players in bright-red jerseys chasing cats. Soccer players kicking balls at a piñata, like I had for my birthday when I was five. The piñata crashing to the ground, grass smears all over it. Then a car crashing silently, bursting into flames, and a cat meowing loudly. I wake up with a gasp, and it's Lexie, meowing next to my ear.

It's eight thirty. The rest of the house is quiet. I pet Lexie, trying to slow my racing heart down to her speed. Is it too early to call Aunt Bonita? I wrote down her number, before, when I sent the email. It's scarier to call, but I have to try.

I tiptoe to the door and peek out. Deirdre's is closed, and it's dark under the door. Lexie jumps off my bed and leaps over to the door, mewling.

"Shhhh, Lexie!" I close it quickly and tiptoe back to my phone on the nightstand. I push all the numbers, and then it rings, and then a man's voice starts talking.

"This call requires an international service plan. Please contact your cell phone provider for further information." There's a pause, and the message repeats. "This call requires an international service plan. Please contact—"

I hang up, tears prickling my eyes. Am I just doomed to live on a farm in Michigan?

Now I wish I had a Facebook account. You're supposed to be thirteen. I won't even be twelve till August, but I know some kids in my class have them already. I never much wanted one, but maybe I can find Graciela that way.

It only takes about two minutes to set up my own account. I type her name into the search bar, hoping it's Ortiz. I feel a flash of despair after I click. Aren't there, like, a bajillion people on Facebook? What are the chances?

But it comes back with a list. "Are you looking for Graciela Ortiz in San Juan, Puerto Rico; in Phoenix, Arizona; in Puerto Plata, Dominican Republic; in San Diego, California; in Chihuahua, Mexico?" I choose Mexico.

It's a girl who looks about the right age. Lots of pictures of her dressed up. She's got bigger boobs than in the pictures in Daddy's boxes. It says she likes soccer and movies and pop music. Her "about" information says her birthday is March 14. So she just turned thirteen, actually.

I lean back in the chair, and Lexie jumps onto my lap. I pet her, trying to decide what to do.

"Lucy?" Deirdre knocks on the door "Are you up?"

"Uh, almost. Give me a couple minutes." I click on "Message" and type quickly. "Hi, I think you're my cousin. My name is Lucy Santiago-Ortiz and my dad is Luis Ortiz. I live in New York City. I'm trying to find my family because both my mom and dad died last week. Please write back."

I close the window and pick up Lexie. My stomach elevator is shaking. "Coming," I say to Deirdre before she can call again.

Chapter 16

JANE

Errands. I fill up at the cheap gas station and replenish the fridge at the grocery store. At the box store I pick up lumber for the new pea trellises and a patch kit for my irrigation lines. It'll be another month yet before I can test and inspect, but I'll have to do it eventually.

Back at home I realize I forgot to buy cat food, which I do need now. Damn. Can't concentrate, can't focus. Questions about Lucy infest my mind like weeds in July. How much like Gloria is she? How resilient? Do I need to arrange for any counseling or therapy? How will she get to school? How am I going to manage the money? How am I going to juggle the CSA and taking care of her?

I suppose I should call Matt. Let him know what's going on. I calculate the time difference. He's six hours ahead and usually works an early shift. So I should probably try around three o'clock his time, nine o'clock mine. Tomorrow, then.

It's raining the next morning when I dial the long series of digits that goes straight to voice mail.

"Hi, Matt, it's Mom. Just calling to—" To what? To tell him I'm basically a parent again? That I've got another chance at the daughter I never had, while the son I had suffered for it? The idea startles me, emerging fully formed from the wisps of memory, wish and regret that have fluttered since Langley's first call. Could Lucy really fill that void? "Just calling with some news. Call when you have a chance."

I hang up and sit with the phone on my lap, thinking back, way back. To Kodiak, before the void was even a fissure. The nautical map on the wall of our cramped but cozy base housing, wind howling outside, Jim parading around with Matt laughing on his shoulders. Taking the pregnancy test on one of Alaska's eternal summer evenings, creeping in to tell Jim in the bedroom that we'd darkened by hanging sleeping bags over the windows. Our small wedding, Jim in his spotless white uniform, sweeping me up and down the steps of the courthouse to a cab that took us to one of San Diego's fanciest hotels, where they upgraded us because Jim was a Coastie.

If only.

The phone rings, the long string of digits blinking back on the screen.

"Hi, Mom."

"Matt!" I'm flummoxed, now that he's the one reaching out. "Can you talk now?"

"Yeah, I was with the CO when you called. I'm off duty now, don't have to be anywhere till eighteen hundred."

I haven't heard military vocabulary in years, but it comes back in a rush.

"So what's up?" Matt says.

"Some news." I hesitate. "Do you remember your aunt Gloria?" I can't recall when Matt last saw her.

"The one who sent the oranges?"

"Right." Wherever Jim's orders took us, Mom and Gloria sent a fruit basket every Christmas. "Some San Diego sunshine," the cards said. Gloria kept up the tradition wherever she moved to. In Miami, where she lived for most of Matt's years at home, it was all oranges. Especially after I started Plain Jane's, their annual December arrival only underscored our different lives. Alien up north, the oranges would sit on the table, silently screaming of the food miles they'd racked up.

"Mom? You still there?"

"Yep. Sorry." I blink, the vision of the oranges vanishing. "Well. Gloria and her husband, your uncle Luis, they were in a car accident last week." I hesitate, counting back. "No, almost two weeks ago, really." This is one of those strange occasions when time seems to both race and stand still. Has it already been two weeks? Can it be only two weeks, with forever stretching ahead?

"Was it—"

"They were both killed."

"Jesus." I hear a sound kind of like whistling. "Sorry, Mom."

"Thanks. It's, it's been hard to wrap my head around." I grope for the right words. "We hadn't seen each other in years."

"She was pretty young, right?"

"Thirty-six." I take a deep breath. "And she had a daughter. Your cousin, Lucy. She's eleven."

"Eleven—Jesus." I hear a sigh over the line. "What's going to happen to her?"

"She'll be moving here to live with me. That's the real news. Gloria named me her guardian." I hear myself say the words, yet I still can't believe the impact they wield.

"Wow."

In the silence that follows, I analyze Matt's single syllable. Is it "wow," wistful, as in, poor Lucy? Is it "wow," incredulous, as in, what was Gloria thinking? Is it "wow," filler, as in, not interested? His life will go on unaffected, after all, six hours and four thousand miles away.

"It's like having a kid all over again," he says finally.

It *is* having a kid all over again. Maybe the third time will be the charm, like they say. I lost my daughter. Grief and guilt carved a gulf between the mother I wanted to be and Matt. With Lucy, I could get it right.

There it is again. That unbidden desire for another chance. Another bite at the apple. But my apple orchard here hasn't been tended in years. Back by the rear property line, it's bearing but overgrown. I had plans to get it in shape—prune the trees, fertilize, and add apples to the Plain Jane's menu. After Jim, that got buried by a landslide of other priorities and expenses. Now it's too late. Or is it? I walk down the hall, peeking in Matt's door. Her room in New York was pink. But at eleven, going on twelve, that might be too juvenile. Maybe a shade of blue? Or a bright green?

"Mom? Still there? Mom?"

"Yeah. Yes. Sorry, lots to think about lately."

"Uh-huh." He pauses. "Well, that means you'll be sticking around home for a while, right?"

"Yeah. I mean, I'd be staying here anyway, what with the season starting." Why would he even ask?

"Right." He clears his throat. "I've got some news, too. I met someone."

"You met—someone? Like, a girlfriend?" Matt didn't date much in high school. He went out with friends in bunches but never seemed to pair off.

He laughs. "Yeah. Like a girlfriend. She's over here, too."

"In the army?"

"Yeah."

"Is that OK, to date someone?"

"We're the same rank, so yeah, it's OK."

"Well then, I'm happy for you. That's great." I feel more like Matt's coworker than mother, fumbling for the right words. "Tell me more about her."

"She's from Georgia. A little farm. Kind of like me. She's been here about a year. She's an MP."

"What's her name?"

"Allison."

Matt sounds happy. A girl from a farm. I feel a little bit proud, like I somehow influenced it.

"We've both got leave coming up next month. We're going to head back to the States, to her family's. I was hoping maybe you could come down there for a couple days."

His voice sounds hopeful. But next month? May? Dismay, more like. I shake my head. "Oh, Matt, I wish I could, but that's not a good time. Especially not this year."

He sighs. "Dad said you'd say that, but I still—"

"Could the two of you visit up—Dad? You've talked to him?" I swallow the lump in my throat, realizing the answer. Clearwater's driving distance from Georgia. Two sets of parents for one visit if they go to Georgia.

"Yeah." The conversation lags now, the silence stretching. Damn it. Damn it. Maybe I could get Miguel to look after things again, get away for just a day or two. But would Jim and Kate be there, too? Matt wouldn't arrange for us to come at the exact same time, would he?

"Well, when you know the dates for sure, let me know. I'll see if I can work something out." The expected words leave my mouth, but who am I kidding? May is the mad sprint. May is a frenzy of last-minute everything: plant, cover, sign up. May does not negotiate. I get thirty-one days to set the stage for the growing season. Painting bedrooms isn't on the list, either. Even if Miguel could manage things, a trip to Georgia would mean a plane ticket not in my budget.

"I'm really sorry, Matt. If only—"

"Mom, it's OK. If it doesn't work out, you'll meet Allison another time. You've got the farm, and now getting ready for Lucy and all. I understand."

There's the truth in words, and the truth underneath the words. Probably Matt does understand. He was around more than Jim to see how things worked with Plain Jane's. But it's also true that if I don't meet his first girlfriend, and Jim and Kate do, I'll be falling short. Again.

From Kodiak to Houston to Traverse City and now Georgia, my track record of maternal failures zigzags across the continent, and now aims right at Lucy.

86

Chapter 17
LUCY

I'm eating breakfast slowly. One Lucky Charm at a time. Because after breakfast I leave for school, and I don't want to go to school. Every day at school is one less day here and one more closer to moving to Michigan. I still haven't heard from Graciela yet, and now it's already May and Deirdre keeps talking about me moving.

She's buzzing around the kitchen, pouring coffee, buttering toast, checking her phone. Lexie meows and jumps onto my lap, out of her way. I pet her absently, concentrating on my bowl. First I eat a heart, then a shooting star, then a clover and a horseshoe. Then a blue moon, then a rainbow—wait, are the rainbows all gone? I stir around the bowl.

"Right, so, Lucy, I've got my appointment at the embassy this afternoon. Straighten out some things with my visa. If you need me, I'll have my phone, but I won't be able to pick you up or come to school between one and three," she says.

There's a rainbow! I spoon it up. "OK." Now a balloon marshmallow.

"Do you think you'll be all right today, then?" She peers at me over her coffee cup.

"I think so." I've called her to pick me up early from school a few times. When I say I feel sad or upset, everybody feels sorry for me and lets me do what I want, including leaving school. Lots of the time I do it on Thursdays, so I can skip seeing Mr. Meinert. His questions give me that jerky feeling of finding out all over again. Today's Wednesday, though, and now I'm spooning my Lucky Charms faster. They really are lucky today. If Deirdre is out this afternoon, I can get into Mom and Daddy's closet. She's like a shadow, never leaving me alone long enough to get back to the boxes and find out more about Aunt Bonita and Daddy's brother and the rest his family. I try to stay awake until after she's asleep, but it never works. I take a long swallow of orange juice and finish my toast in two big bites. "Done."

"Looks like you found a bit of appetite this morning. That's good." Deirdre smiles. She pushes my lunch box across the table. "Ready to go?"

"Righto," I say, adopting my pretend British accent.

She laughs. "Lucy, you seem almost your old self this morning." My old self, the girl who had two parents. The girl from the slide show, at the Statue of Liberty and the ice rink and Disney World. The girl smiling at the mirror, with Mom. The girl in the picture at the bodega on the rainy day, laughing at Daddy getting wet. And I do feel sad.

At school, when Ms. Kedzie says good morning, I make sure my voice sounds sad. When she calls on me, I pretend to be distracted and not hear her. At recess I go to the swings alone but just sit, away from Phoebe, dragging my feet on the pavement, instead of swinging.

As everyone's lining up for lunch, I make my move. "Can I go see Mr. Meinert? I don't feel so good today."

"Of course, Lucy." Ms. Kedzie's voice goes all sympathetic. "Take all the time you need. You can catch up later."

"Thanks." I smile a tiny, brave smile. Almost there. I make sure to stop at my locker on the way to the office, getting my backpack with my subway pass.

In the office, the secretary says Mr. Meinert's away at a meeting. Uh-oh. Every other time he's seen me immediately.

"He'll be back by one. You can wait in his office."

By one I want to be home. "Can you call him or something? I really feel like I just want to go home."

"Hmm. He's not on school property. I'll call Mrs. Creighton."

Mrs. Creighton comes out, her mouth smiling but her eyes worried.

"What's the problem, Lucy?"

"I'm just not feeling so good today."

"Not feeling so good, like sick? Or sad?"

"Sad."

"And you want to go home?"

I nod.

"All right. I'll just call your au pair, then, and—"

"No! I mean, it's fine. You don't have to call her."

"That's our policy, Lucy. She has to come pick you up."

"But I take the train home alone after school." *Be sad, not mad.* I slump in my chair, catching a sympathetic look from the secretary as she leaves with a stack of papers.

"It's still school hours now. We're responsible for you. It's different."

"All right." I sigh. "Don't bother. I know she can't come this afternoon. She's busy."

"Busy?" Mrs. Creighton frowns. "I'll check if Mr. Meinert can get back here sooner."

I stare at the ceiling after she leaves. It's twelve thirty. It'll take me a half hour to get home. I'm losing my chance.

Wait. I'm leaving this school. Getting in trouble won't matter. I don't have to hang around. I can just go.

My heart thuds. I sit up and look around. I can hear the copier down the hall, probably where the secretary went. Just down the hall, out the front door, down the street to the subway.

It's easy. It's exciting to be out of school at lunchtime. The trains aren't so crowded, so I can sit down. I watch the funeral slide show again and a new video I made of Lexie, playing with a crumpled-up piece of paper. At our building Edward doesn't say anything, just opens the door for me. I unlock the door and lean against it. The pounding in my chest eases. I did it!

It's after one o'clock already, but I have another plan. I'll move the boxes to my room, where Deirdre won't interrupt me. I have plenty of space in my closet. I don't know why I didn't think of that before.

Lexie meows and follows as I tiptoe into Mom and Daddy's room, through the bedroom, into the closet. There are the five boxes, two marked with Daddy's initials, three with Mom's. Grabbing the top one to take to my room, I see my reflection with the stack of boxes. I stare into the mirror hard, trying to see me and Mom together—the old-self Lucy. But I just see me and the boxes.

I'm headed back for the last one when I hear voices from the kitchen. Deirdre's home early! No, wait, there's two voices. A man's and a woman's. And the woman doesn't have an English accent. The man's voice is Mr. Langley's. What's he doing here now? Who's she? Stay and listen? Go get the last box? The box wins. I tiptoe down the wood hall and back into the closet and grab it.

After I've hidden it with the others, I slip out, flattening myself against the wall where the hall opens to the front foyer. Lexie meows. I pick her up and shush her, stroking her back.

". . . should go for at least two point five, based on the neighbor-hood comps." The woman's voice, her heels clicking. "Midtown loca-tion, views of the park, four bedrooms . . . it needs some updating, but still, highly marketable."

"Good." Mr. Langley. "I'd like it on the market by July 1."

"Absolutely. The sooner the better." The heel clicking stops. They're almost in the foyer.

"Well, we do have to consider the daughter. She'll be here until school ends in mid-June."

"Hmmm." The woman taps her foot. "That doesn't give us much time. You'll dispose of the furnishings?"

"Yes, at an estate sale. After Lucy moves out, of course. We don't want to disrupt her environment prematurely."

Their voices are getting louder. My heart is thudding again. They're going to sell our apartment. And all our furniture. My stomach elevator is plunging, and I slide to the floor, a cry escaping. Lexie meows, too.

"What's that?" The lady's voice.

"Is someone home? Deirdre?" It's Mr. Langley, getting closer. Who cares if I get caught now? "Deirdre?"

They're both in the foyer. The lady's carrying a legal pad and writing notes. Mr. Langley strides across the shiny tile. "Lucy! What are you doing home from school? Are you sick?"

I shake my head, crying now as he crouches down next to me.

"Where's Deirdre?"

I shrug.

"They let you just come home from school by yourself?" He's reaching for his phone. Who is he calling? Deirdre or school?

The lady clears her throat. "Perhaps we should arrange to complete the walk-through later, then, Bill?"

He looks up, the phone already at his ear. "Yes, sorry, Vicki. This is unexpected, obviously. I'll call you later."

"Fine." But she's looking past us, down the hall, toward the open bedroom doors. She doesn't want to leave. I run down the hall, banging Mom and Daddy's bedroom door shut, then my own. Deirdre's is already closed.

"Go away! Get out of my house!"

"Lucy!" Mr. Langley sounds reproachful. How dare he?

"You, too!" I turn on him. Lexie meows and jumps out of my arms.

"Oh dear." The lady looks shocked and backs away. Her heels slide, and she teeters, dropping her notebook before she catches her balance. I can read some of her notes: "Kitchen: Cabinets OK. New counters? Living room: Buff floors, remove drapes. CAT ODOR!!"

Mr. Langley puts away his phone. He never talked to anyone. He picks up her notebook and opens the front door. "Again, I apologize,

Vicki. I'll call you as soon as I can." He closes it almost in her face, then turns to me. His face is sad now.

"I'm sorry you saw that, Lucy. I expected you would be at school, so—"

My chest is heaving again. "You're going to sell it? My house?"

"After you move, what would be the point of keeping it?"

"It's my house!"

Mr. Langley sighs. "Lucy—"

His phone rings. He looks at the screen. "Thank God." He pushes a button. "Deirdre? It's Bill Langley. I'm at the apartment. Lucy's here, too."

Even over the phone, I hear Deirdre's screech. "Lucy? She's supposed to be at school!"

"Yes, she surprised me, too. I was here with the agent, doing a prelisting walk-through. She overheard us, and now she's quite upset. How soon can you be here?"

He listens, then nods. "All right. I'll stay until then." He hangs up. "Deirdre's on her way."

I figured that out already. I don't say anything, just stare at him, my fists balled up. I hate him. First he makes me go live with Aunt Jane in Michigan. Now he's selling my apartment. And Deirdre was in on it.

"Lucy, I'm sorry. I wish I could change things."

"Then don't sell it!"

He sighs again. "It doesn't make any sense to keep it."

"I don't care!" I stamp my foot. "Go away. Just go away and leave me alone!" I run down the hall to my bedroom, slam the door, and reach under the pillow for Mom's Venice Beach hoodie. I scrub the sleeve against my hot, wet face and flop down on my bed, reaching for my phone and earbuds. I swipe Hello Kitty's paws. The screen looks different. On top of the blue Facebook square is a little red number one. I touch the square. One new message. *"¡Hola, prima!"*

Graciela has written back!

Chapter 18

JANE

I pace in front of the fireplace that serves as the airport passenger rendezvous, glancing at my watch every ten seconds. Lucy's plane is late, and my biggest plot of strawberries needed to be picked yesterday. I tried to check the flight information online but gave up because the computer was so slow. Could have picked at least another row. Well, Lucy can help. She'll settle in faster if she's busy. Not much beats a Michigan strawberry, either. I'll make some shortcake later. A welcome-to-Michigan treat.

It's still hard to believe that this is it, I'm taking her home today, although the specter of her arrival has encroached closer and closer since Langley's phone call about the furniture a week ago.

"Lucy has some items she'd like to keep from the apartment. I've arranged to have them shipped."

"What kind of items?"

"Smaller furniture pieces. A chair from her bedroom. Some electronics—her video-game system."

"A video-game system? I don't even have a TV."

"Deirdre tells me she rarely actually plays it. I think it's a symbolic statement. The school social worker says it's entirely normal to want to preserve things that are sentimental or familiar."

I got that, though from the opposite purpose, like the new quilt to excise Jim from the bedroom. Hmm. I surveyed my small living room, wondering how much symbolism could fit. Rather than Matt's room, I've decided Lucy's going to sleep upstairs, in what would have been the guest room if we'd ever had guests. There's a bed and dresser and enough space for her chair and a desk, for homework. Whatever doesn't fit, we can always store in the barn.

"There's more you should know, Jane." Langley's tone got more serious. "Lucy's been acting out lately."

"Acting out how?"

"She recently left school on her own, without permission. When she discovered that the apartment was to be sold, there was a rather heated encounter with the real estate agent."

If I found out I was losing my home, I'd respond heatedly, too. In fact, I did, though Langley's probably forgotten the conversation when he suggested I move to New York.

"While they're not typical of her behavior, both incidents are within the bounds of normal grieving for a child, the school social worker says. They may even be evidence that she's moving forward, from the denial stage to anger."

"Hmmm," I said, out loud this time. Was I still angry at Gloria and Luis? What comes after anger, for both of us?

"I'm telling you so you can be prepared. He's suggested that arranging a counselor may be helpful."

"All right."

"Would there be a professional in your area that can handle pediatric counseling?"

There it was again. The condescension. Traverse City is not New York City, but it's not the back forty, either.

"I'll ask around."

"Good. On legal matters, I've received the official police report on the car accident. The limo driver's been found culpable, which gives you grounds to make a claim on Lucy's behalf."

"What grounds?" Just then a blue car had pulled into my driveway. My work-share customers, the Livingston family, here for their first day.

"I'm sorry, I've got to go now. Do whatever you think best." He was the attorney, after all.

"Ladies and gentlemen, your attention please. Flight Four Forty-Two from Detroit is now approaching gate two. Passengers will be disembarking momentarily."

Here we go with the rest of our lives. I stare down the hallway, heart thumping, searching for the dark-haired, moved-beyond-denial-to-anger child with the glittery high-tops.

No. She wears flip-flops, and a hooded sweatshirt that looks huge on her, the sleeves covering up her hands. White earbuds form a Y under her chin. She's looking all over except at me. Trailing her is a uniformed flight attendant, carrying something that looks like a cage. What in the world? I step into their path.

"Hi, Lucy. Welcome to Michigan." Awkwardly I wave, and then reach out to hug her. I catch a snatch of music from the earbuds. I feel a tremor—is that the music, or anxiety? She steps back before I can decide.

"Jane McArdle?" The flight attendant sets down the cage and glances at a paper. "ID? All right, then, we're all set," she says as I show her my license. "You two have a nice day!" She flashes a blank smile and disappears.

Lucy's still not looking at me. Other passengers stream around our trio, like water around river rapids.

"Um, what's in the cage?" It's draped, but looks just like Sarge's. She doesn't answer.

"Lucy?" I say it louder. "Can you take the earbuds out, please?"

With a sigh, she pulls one out.

"What's in the cage?"

She looks at it like she's never seen it before. "This is Lexie. My kitten."

"You didn't have a kitten before."

She shakes her head. "Daddy was allergic, so I couldn't."

"So you got her—after?"

"From the Humane Society." She pushes up the too-long sleeve, then picks up the cage. "Mr. Meinert thought it would be a good idea for me to have a pet."

"Who's Mr. Meinert?"

"The school social worker."

First shipping five hundred pounds of furniture, then bringing a cat halfway across the country. What other suggestions did Mr. Meinert offer?

"Your crate arrived yesterday." It was quite a bit bigger than Langley had implied, a five by eight that arrived on a semi. But there was plenty of room in the barn. They lifted it off with a forklift.

"You didn't unpack it, did you?" She sounds anxious.

"Not yet. It's in the barn, ready and waiting for you. Now, did you check anything?"

Fifteen minutes later, we're each wheeling a suitcase through the terminal doors, into the parking lot. Lucy's kept her earbuds out, but barely said a word. I've heard some scrabbling inside the cage, but the kitten's been quiet, too. It's a tense quiet, though, not peaceful. We're both walking on eggshells.

At my farm truck I wince. I'd planned to stop at the car wash but ran out of time. It's pretty filthy, mud caking the back tires and the underpanel.

She's got to get used to it. Why not start now? retorts my anticonscience, the voice clamoring to go finish the strawberries. I heft the suitcases into the back.

Lucy doesn't say anything, just opens the door on her side. She ducks her head into the back, but there isn't much to see—junk mail, a beat-up just-in-case blanket I keep there, jumper cables. She glances at me.

"Uh, where do I sit?"

I point at the passenger seat. "Right here."

"The front?"

"Mm-hm." What's the problem?

"OK. It's just—I've never sat in the front seat before."

"Never?"

"Uh-uh."

Belatedly, I wonder if she's tall enough to sit in the front seat. They're supposed to be some age or height or weight. Frustration rises as I try to remember. I never thought I'd need to remember.

I leave my window halfway down after I pay at the exit booth. It's a beautiful summer day, and equilibrium, if only geographic, is just forty minutes away. I glance over the cage between us, trying to remember the script I followed when Matt sat on the passenger side.

"How was the rest of the school year?"

"Fine."

"Mr. Langley sent me your report card. You did well, especially considering—"

"Considering what?"

"Well, the accident and all."

"My parents died. Why can't anyone just say that?"

Her voice is flat, no tremble or break.

"Sorry. You're right." So she is past the denial stage. "Before school starts here we'll go and take a tour. Meet with the teachers. Help you ease into the new year."

She shrugs. "They must have had a new kid before. It's no big deal."

"Yes, but the point is for them to learn about you. What you've studied already. It sounds like some kind of video or film class would be good for you."

"It's called New Media." She snorts. "Like they'd have that at a school for farm kids."

I let it pass. Defensiveness, I understand. "Not everybody farms here."

She looks at me.

"Most don't, actually." I wave my hand out the window. Exhibit A, Traverse City's sprawl. A mall, car dealerships, a Burger King, gas stations, quickie oil-change places. "They just like to live in the country."

"Why?"

I can't help laughing. "For the peace and quiet."

"Really?" She shakes her head.

The sprawl extends only a couple of miles, thankfully. After several more miles of silence, we come to the gateway view. It's the point where peninsula folks feel truly at home. Up a small hill, over the top, and *voilà*. East Bay comes into view first, on the right. Then West Bay on the left, the land undulating down to the water. It's beautiful in all seasons, but this early summer time, new green leaves with all their promise, is when it's most serene.

"This is the place where I always feel I've come home," I tell Lucy, rolling down my window the rest of the way.

No reply. Fair enough. If someone tried to convince me that the Brooklyn Bridge signaled home, I'd be skeptical, too.

I continue north, through the twisting turns, each mile punctuated by a sign proclaiming the business that's "adopted" it, cleaning up the roadside litter a couple of times a year in exchange for their name on a sign. That was another one of the Extension agent's recommendations for Plain Jane's at the marketing workshop last fall. "Free, year-round exposure that will resonate with the environmentally, socially conscious people who are your most likely customers—and happen to be driving right toward your farm. It's a win-win-win!"

She was probably right, but I never signed up. Just as well. With all the new customers this season, plus Lucy, when would I have time to actually clean up the highway?

"How much farther?" Lucy says after ten miles of silence. Her voice is small now, the affected defensiveness vanished.

"Another few miles."

"I haven't seen any stores. Or restaurants. Or offices."

"There aren't many. The peninsula is mostly residential."

"The people who want to live in the country."

"Right."

"Plus one who doesn't," she says, almost to herself, settling her earbuds in again.

Chapter 19

LUCY

Beyond the window is nothing but green. OK, some blue, on the edges. The sky and the water. But in between, all green. Rows of trees with dark-green leaves. Huge fields with rows and rows of what look like fences, with something a lighter shade of green climbing up. Houses with giant green squares in front of them. Grass.

It runs along both sides of the road, too. Aunt Jane feels most at home here—and now it's supposed to be mine? My stomach elevator is dropping, like from the twentieth floor. The wind rushing in the window is loud and cold. I put my earbuds back in and pull up the hood and pull on the strings of Mom's Venice Beach hoodie, cocooning my head.

Aunt Jane drives on and on. It seems like hours since we left the airport. Inside her cage, Lexie starts meowing. She gets that I'm scared. I'm sure she is, too. *Step on a crack, break your mother's back. Step on the grass, make her car crash.* Lexie's all I have left. What could happen to her if I do the wrong thing again?

I knew a farm would be bad, but not this bad. How am I going to stand it until July, when Graciela's boarding school gets out and she can talk to Aunt Bonita about me moving there? She only can go online on weekends because her school is really strict about the Internet. That's why it took her so long to write back on Facebook.

Aunt Jane slows down. Are we getting close, finally? She's turning left, onto a rocky kind of driveway cut through more grass. It's bumpy and dusty, little clouds puffing out from under the tires as we roll along. There's a white house up ahead, on my side. It has a stone porch and a big tree in front, the branches reaching toward her house.

My house. Our house. That I can never go in. Between the truck and the side door is all grass. A mile or a block or the length of the school hallway. It doesn't matter. It's grass.

"So, here we are." Aunt Jane opens her door and jumps down onto it! She turns back to me and pastes on a smile. "We'll get you settled in upstairs, then I'll show you around outside. I bet you never picked strawberries before!"

Nope. Won't today, either. She's rolled both suitcases up to the side door when she notices I'm not behind her.

"Lucy?"

I slide down, my fingers curling tight around the bars on Lexie's cage.

"Lucy? What's the matter?" Through the closed window her voice is muffled.

"I can't get out." I shake my head.

"Why not? Is that door stuck?" She yanks on the handle on her side. When it swings open I can see the grass just one long step away. There are even some taller, weedy-looking things brushing the step up to the door. I suck in my breath and scoot away, toward the steering wheel.

"There. Sometimes it sticks. We'll be using it more now, though. It'll loosen up." She turns around. As if that's that.

I wait until she's inside, then reach over and slam the door shut again, pushing down the lock. One thousand one. One thousand two. One thousand three. She reappears, hands on her hips this time.

"What in the world is going on?" The door is muffling her voice again, making her sound like she's underwater, like Mr. Meinert and Deirdre did in the school office. I wish one of them were here. Anyone to help me.

I clutch Lexie's cage. "I can't get out," I say again.

"Look, I know it's hard. It's different. But you have to give it a chance here—"

"It's not that," I interrupt.

"Eventually, though—" She pauses. "Then what?"

"The grass."

"What about it?"

"I can't walk on it."

She looks down at the ground, then back at me.

"What do you mean?"

"I can't walk on it. I won't. It's—I, I, I just can't."

"Can't walk on this? Grass?" She pulls up a handful, letting it fall from her fingers. She looks at me, questions all over her face.

"Fine. Don't believe me. I'll just stay here, then." But it's hot in here, and I'm thirsty, and I'm starting to have to go to the bathroom. I press my knees together under the cage and pull the hood off my head.

"Stay in the truck? Lucy, I've got hours of work ahead. Come on, now. Be reasonable." She reaches for the door handle, with the same hand that picked the grass, then realizes I've locked it.

"Open the door, Lucy!" She rattles it.

"Uh-uh!" I scoot over more and huddle behind Lexie's cage.

"I've got customers expecting strawberries this week. It's going to rain later. I need some cooperation."

I don't know what she's talking about. Strawberries? Rain? Who cares?

"Go! I'm not stopping you. Just leave me alone."

She flings her hands into the air. "I can't let you just stay—" Her hands fall down, and suddenly she turns and stalks across the grass to the house. It takes her eight steps to get inside.

I breathe shakily. Lexie's meowing again, and I pull off the drape over the cage so I can look at her instead of all the green. I'm not all alone, after all. And I'm safe locked in the car.

All of a sudden there's a creak and whoosh of air. Aunt Jane's back, a key in her hand.

"Ahhh! You scared me." I grab for the door, but she's standing in the opening, blocking me.

"What if I give you a piggyback ride inside?" Her voice is loud now, with the door open.

I start to shake my head.

"Just listen. You climb onto my back. I'll carry you across the grass, over to the door. There's a little concrete threshold, see?"

I look over her shoulder, at the tiny gray square in front of the door.

"I'll put you down there."

I really do have to go to the bathroom.

"You won't trip? I won't fall?"

She shakes her head.

"What about Lexie?"

"I'll come back for her."

I stare at the green gap between the car door and the house. It's the only way.

"OK."

Aunt Jane swings the door wide, then backs up into the open space. "Wrap your legs around my waist."

I close my eyes so I don't see the grass. It's only eight steps. Lexie meows again.

"OK, now hold on to my shoulders," she says. "I'll walk on the count of three. One, two, three."

She lifts me out of the truck. Daddy used to give me piggyback rides. I imagine he's carrying me down Fifty-Sixth Street, to visit Mom at the studio. We're both laughing. I can see the picture so clearly it feels like I can touch it.

"Ow. We're here. Let go. That hurts."

I open my eyes. There are fingernail marks where I gripped her arms, but we made it! We're on the concrete square. Aunt Jane opens the door, breathing a little hard. I slide off her back, stepping onto the concrete, then through the door onto a black-and-white checked floor. A cat brushes my legs.

"You have a cat, too?"

"Meet Sarge. I guess I don't have to worry that you're allergic."

"Do you think he'll like having Lexie to play with?"

"Actually, I'm worried about that. Sarge is pretty used to ruling the roost."

"He wouldn't hurt her, would he?" He's a lot bigger than Lexie.

"I hope not. Might as well find out. I'll bring her in."

"Wait, I have to go to the bathroom."

The bathroom has pink and white square tiles, and the sink seems really low. At least nothing is green. When I come back out, Sarge is sitting on a blue couch, licking himself. Aunt Jane is waiting by the open kitchen door.

"Be right back," she says.

When they come in, Lexie's little nose is pushed against the cage bars, and she's mewling like crazy. As soon as Sarge sees her, his tail swells and his back arches. He hisses. Lexie backs up to the farthest corner, hunkering down as small as she can. I grab the cage just as Sarge leaps at it.

"¡Gato malo! Bad kitty!" I stamp my foot. Sarge backs up, then hisses again. "We should have stayed in the truck."

"Oh, dear God," Aunt Jane says. "Take her upstairs. Your room's up there." She opens the door again and pushes Sarge outside with her foot. "I'll be up in a minute."

I run up the stairs and slam the door. Aunt Jane has a cat! A killer cat. The door falls open. I bang it again. It swings open. I lean back against it, my arms wrapped around Lexie's cage.

I can't believe it. She never said she had a cat!

Well, I have to keep Lexie safe. That's first. I look around the tiny room. It has little half walls on the side and a sloping ceiling. Like an attic. There's a little desk and a chair. I jam the chair under the doorknob. There, that will keep it shut. I survey the room. What else could hurt her?

The one window is open. It looks out over the porch roof. That big tree shades the yard and the porch. If Sarge is an outdoor cat, too, he can climb up there and crawl down the thick branch that practically makes a runway to the window. I slam the window shut.

I put Lexie's cage on the bed and unlatch it. She's still huddled in the back, next to an empty food dish, her nose twitching like crazy. That mean old cat has probably marked the whole house. Well, not this room. Not anymore.

"It's OK, Lexie. Come here, kitty. You're safe now."

There's a knock on the door. Aunt Jane tries to open it, but the chair stops her. "Lucy? What's going on now?" She rattles the doorknob.

I move the chair, and the door falls open. She stands there looking uncertain.

"So you found your room."

I nod.

"Are you hungry?"

I shake my head, then remember Lexie's empty bowl. "But Lexie probably is."

"You can give her some of Sarge's food. It's in the mudroom, where we came in."

Well, that's one good thing about him being here. I follow her downstairs where she shows me the cat food, then clears her throat.

"I guess you probably don't want to pick strawberries with me."

"Uh-uh."

"Have you always been, um, afraid of grass?"

I'm not afraid of grass, exactly. Just of stepping on it. But how can I explain that?

"Because no one told me that, and—"

"Go on. We'll be fine inside."

"Well . . ." She looks like she wants to go but thinks she should stay.

"I'm serious. We'll be fine inside. As long as he's not." I nudge Sarge's dish with my foot.

"OK. I'll keep Sarge out there with me." She puts on a weird hat. It looks like a baseball cap, with these two flaps hanging from the back, down past her shoulders. "I'll check on you in a bit, then."

I scoop Lexie's bowl full, almost finishing off the bag. So there. I let her use his litter box, too. After she eats we go back upstairs. It feels kind of like a tree house. It is getting hot with the window shut, so I turn on the ceiling fan while Lexie sniffs in all the corners. It doesn't take long. There's a twin bed. At home I had a queen. The half walls are paneled and white, and the slanty walls and ceiling are painted a light blue. The front wall with the window and the back wall are covered with flowered wallpaper. I put my iPad on the desk and open the drawers of the tall white dresser. All empty, ready for my clothes. I'll put the mirror next to that. There's not much room for the papasan chair now, but if I move the desk—

Wait. Where's my stuff? The furniture, my fuzzy pink rug, the five boxes from the closet. Aunt Jane said the crate got here. Where did she say it was? The—uh-oh.

I go back into the hall, to the window that overlooks the driveway. The barn is beyond the truck. In between is more green. Three, maybe four times as much as the eight steps to the house. The tears come hot, like the rest of the upstairs. Through them, blurry, I can see Aunt Jane's hat moving around in another giant green rectangle.

Lexie meows, rubbing against my ankle. I snatch her up and crumple onto the bed, my stomach crashing down to the basement again, and I can't find the elevator button to make it stop.

Chapter 20
JANE

Does Lucy have a phobia? I've never heard of a fear of grass. Some city affliction? Or triggered by Gloria's and Luis's deaths? Why didn't Langley or Deirdre mention it? Most of all, how is she going to cope here? Musing over the mystery slows me down. I've picked less than half the strawberries when Miguel's truck swings into the driveway.

"*Las fresas.* My favorite," he says.

"Try one." I wave at the bucket. "What brings you by?"

He bites one off and tosses the stem. "Came to see if you could use any help."

"Now?" I sit back on my heels. Rain's held off so far, but the western sky is darkening. Haven't heard a peep from Lucy.

"I've got someone new. Came up to work with his cousin, but cherries aren't ready yet."

I stand up and stretch out my back and gaze at the truck. Someone's sitting in the passenger seat. My stomach rumbles. I skipped lunch to pick up Lucy. I should check on her, too.

"All right. Good timing. I want to finish up these before the rain hits." I wave at the two remaining rows and the empty bucket.

"Juan!" Miguel yells at the truck, waving him over. They talk in Spanish, faster than I can follow. Juan turns to me, smiling one of those smiles so full of gratitude I feel guilty, knowing what I'll pay him.

"Are you sticking around or coming back?" I ask Miguel.

"Stick around. Help him get started."

"All right." I step over the rows with the full bucket. "Just let me know when you're done."

Child and kitten have deserted the kitchen and entire downstairs. Leaving the berries next to the sink, I call upstairs. "Lucy? Everything OK? Lucy?"

No answer. Frowning, I climb up, ducking my head under the low ceiling where the old stairs make a ninety-degree turn. "Lucy?"

Her door is not quite shut. She's asleep, earbuds on and phone by her side. The screen is dark, but I'd bet a bucket of strawberries she was playing that funeral slide show. So much for being past denial. Lexie's curled up by her feet. The sweatshirt she was wearing is hanging on the chair. Though the room's warm, an impulse compels me to drape it over her, resting my hand on her back as it rises and falls. She stirs, and I yank my hand back. Sleep is probably the best thing for her.

Back in the kitchen, I put the stopper in the drain and fill the sink to wash the berries, then open the cupboards, hoping there's enough quart-size containers leftover from last week. This is really happening. A living, breathing child is under my roof. Not just a child, a girl. *Una niña.* My head spins with memories. A fierce blizzard. But not on Kodiak this time. Matt's older, nine or ten, sleeping, and it's here, on Old Mission, a snow day. I slipped into his room to turn off the alarm so he could sleep in, tucking the blue plaid bedspread over his shoulders, just like I did with Lucy's sweatshirt.

"I need to get my stuff."

Lucy's voice startles me from the reverie, just as I've filled the last container. I peer over my shoulder at her, standing on the stairs, holding her cat.

"Ummm—your stuff?"

She nods.

What's she talking about? "We brought in your suitcases." Actually, I did.

"I mean from my crate. Out there." She points toward the barn.

"Your crate? Oh, right!" I glance at the clock. After four already? Juan and Miguel will fill up the sink again any minute. Then there's the rest of this week's share to prepare, greens to pick, measure, wash. Then make dinner, including that shortcake. "Tomorrow, OK?"

"But I need it tonight!"

I try to put myself in her place, remembering how I felt in the cab in New York. This is another country to Lucy. Maybe another planet. A familiar pillow or chair might help a lot. And maybe if I opened the crate for her, it would be incentive to walk on the grass, in order to get her things back to the house. I should confront this fear or phobia or whatever it is head-on, not let it fester.

"OK. Walk out there with me, and we'll bring it in," I say.

"I can't! I told you." She's near tears.

"Lucy—"

A knock on the door breaks our standoff. I wave Miguel and Juan in, their buckets transformed into red pyramids. A second before the door closes, Sarge bounds in behind and leaps at Lucy and Lexie.

"¡Gato malo!" Lucy shrieks again, backing away.

Miguel and Juan look stunned; by her Spanish or by Sarge, I'm not sure. Not another scene! "Lucy, take Lexie back upstairs. Miguel, get Sarge out of here. Juan, bring me those strawberries," I snap.

They stand frozen for another moment, then move all at once. Miguel grabs a hissing Sarge in a fast, smooth motion and opens the door. Lucy disappears. Juan dumps the strawberries in the sink and exits, muttering something about more. A moment after the door closes behind him, Miguel returns.

"That's one mad *gato*." Long scratches line his arms.

"Sorry about that."

Miguel shrugs. "His territory."

"I've got bandages and rubbing alcohol. Down the hall." I lead him to the bathroom.

"Is it safe?" Lucy calls.

"It's safe," I say wearily.

She pads downstairs, still holding Lexie, on her guard.

"Who were they?"

"Miguel and Juan."

"They live here, too?"

I shake my head. "Miguel works for me now and then, around the farm. Today he brought Juan."

"Hola," Miguel says, emerging from the bathroom, smiling despite the scarlet scratch marks. "Is your *gato* OK?"

She looks down at Lexie and seems to relax. She nods.

"Sorry I let Sarge in. I didn't expect another cat, or—"

"Not your fault," I say. I haven't told anyone but Matt about Lucy's arrival, and I didn't know about Lexie myself. "This is my niece, Lucy," I say. "Lucy, this is Miguel Esquivale."

"Con mucho gusto, Lucy. ¿Hablas español?"

Lucy nods.

"¿Cómo se llama tu gato?" He scratches between Lexie's ears.

"Lexie," Lucy says.

"Con mucho gusto, Lexie," Miguel says, reaching out as if to shake a paw. I catch the tiniest smile from Lucy before she confronts me again.

"I need to get my stuff tonight."

"Tomorrow, Lucy, I promise."

"But I need it!" Now her lip trembles.

I set the consequence, I have to follow through.

"Can I help?" Miguel says.

"Yes!" Lucy's face lights up. "I need my stuff from the crate in the barn."

"Miguel, that's kind of you to offer, but—"

"Let's go take a look, then. *¿Vamos?*" He steps toward the door and cocks his head toward Lucy.

Her face darkens. She takes a step back.

Miguel looks from her to me, his eyebrows lifted.

I give up. "I'll walk you out to the barn."

"Not without me!" Lucy wails.

"He'll just check it out first. Make sure I've got the right tools to open it," I tell her.

She hesitates. "You won't open it without me?"

Miguel shakes his head. "On my sister's honor."

"OK." Lucy sits down on the blue velvet couch, Lexie in her lap. "I'll wait."

Outside, Juan is moving methodically along the strawberry row, nearly to the end. The risk of the rain seems to be past again.

"So you probably wonder what that's all about."

Miguel shrugs.

"Aren't you going to ask?"

He shakes his head. "Jane, you are a private person."

He's right, but the Lucy invasion has drained the energy required to keep my fences up. I suddenly feel so worn-out I can barely walk, let alone explain everything that's happened since April and how I'm now the guardian of a child who apparently has a grass phobia, of all unheard of things. I've been up since five o'clock working, and there are at least four more hours before I can think of sitting down, let alone going to bed. Besides the strawberries there's lettuce, rhubarb, and greens to wash and bag and snap peas to measure. And Lucy's welcome shortcake to bake.

"Lucy's afraid of grass," I say abruptly. "That's why she didn't want to come outside."

"Afraid?" We're at the threshold to the barn door. Miguel squats to pick a handful of the grass that grows clumpy here. "Of this?"

"She wouldn't get out of the truck this afternoon, when we got back from the airport. I had to carry her into the house piggyback."

"Afraid of grass. *Pero, ¿por qué?*" He says it almost to himself.

"I don't know why. The lawyer never mentioned it."

"Lawyer?"

"My sister's. Lucy's mother's. She and her husband died in April, in a car accident."

"Dios mío." Miguel shakes his head.

"She named me Lucy's guardian. Lucy's moved here to live with me." The story spills out now. "This crate"—I elbow the side—"has all the worldly goods she brought with her from New York."

"New York? New York City?" Miguel says, walking around the crate.

"That's where I was this spring, when you fixed the driveway."

"Dios mío," he says again. "First no parents. Now no *casa*. I have a crowbar in my truck," he says, heading back toward the house.

No *casa*. The magnitude of the two words settles heavily. Plain Jane's is my world, especially since Jim left. I trot after him. "OK. What are you going to do?"

"Open the crate."

"But the grass . . ." My voice trails off. "She said don't do it without her."

"I can give piggyback rides, too." Miguel's rummaging in the box in the bed of his truck. Seeing a pile of newspapers, I wince. He was probably up even earlier than me. He thrusts a crowbar and a hammer into my hands. At the side door, he steps into the kitchen.

Lucy's there in a moment but keeps away from the door. "Can you open it?" She looks hopeful but wary.

"Absolutely. Piggyback ride to the barn?"

Joy breaks over her face. "What about Lexie?"

"Put her back in her cage," I say quickly. No more catfights today, please, God.

"Climb aboard." Miguel crouches down when Lucy returns minus Lexie.

In the barn, Lucy slides off his back and runs up to the crate, her joyful scream cracking the thick heat of the barn. "It's here! *¡Eso es!* My crate! Open it, please, please, *ábrelo!*"

Miguel pries the crowbar under one side, working his way down to one corner, around the other side. Lucy bounces on her toes, her hands clasped together. Miguel turns another corner, up the third side.

"You've almost got it! Almost!" She's not taking her eyes off the thing. With a grunt Miguel loosens the last side and lifts off the cover.

A padded blue blanket crumples to the floor. Inside, everything is swathed in similar padding. Lucy tries to peel back a corner. Something creaks as it shifts inside.

"Hold on. We have to do this the right way." Miguel goes to the barn door. "Juan! *¡Ven aquí!*"

He looks up and, without hesitating, stands and heads our way.

"Wait. He's—" I say.

Miguel shakes his head. "Strawberries can wait. She cannot."

"Excuse me?" But even as I object, I simultaneously realize my maternal instincts haven't improved, even with six years of rest.

"*Lo siento*, Jane." Miguel bows his head for a moment. "I'm sorry. But she cannot wait."

Lucy's watching him with a hero-worship gaze. She's barely looked me in the eye. He and Juan start talking a mile a minute in Spanish, gesturing, touching the blankets. Together they lift down a box and set it on the barn floor. Lucy flies to it, unwrapping the blanket. "Winter clothes," she reads on a label, disappointment obvious. "Keep looking!"

More boxes follow. More clothes, computer, a PlayStation. Lucy gets increasingly restless with each revelation. What in the world is she waiting for? Miguel extracts a long, flat piece.

"My mirror," Lucy says. "My mirror, my mirror!" She pulls off the protective blanket. Indeed, it's a full-length mirror in a wooden frame, set into kind of a pedestal.

That's what she had to have tonight? There's a mirror in the bathroom. Even a full-length one on the back of my bedroom door. I shake my head, the weariness returning.

"I'll just head back to the house, then." Might as well get back to work, since my presence seems superfluous. Just like when Gloria was born. Like mother, like daughter.

I'm washing lettuce when Miguel opens the door, the mirror under his arm. He props it in the living room and turns to leave.

"Lucy's room is upstairs."

"You can take it up later. We just want to get everything across the grass while it's still light."

"Both of you?" I see Juan heading this way, his arms full.

"*Sí.*" He holds the door for Juan, then jogs back to the barn. Lucy hands him a big wicker half-circle thing. Juan leaves his boxes and departs again. My living room is turning into a warehouse.

Back and forth they go, a half-dozen times before Miguel brings Lucy herself, on piggyback again. Above his shoulder, Lucy's face is relaxed, almost happy.

"*Buenas noches, linda.*" Miguel pats her shoulder after she slides off.

"*Buenas noches. Gracias,*" Lucy says. With another little shriek, she bounds into the living room to review her inventory.

"I'll walk you out," I say, grabbing my wallet. I hand Juan a twenty-dollar bill. I try to pay Miguel, too, but he shakes his head. "Take it. You worked for more than an hour bringing all that stuff in."

"*No es trabajo.*"

"It wasn't work? Then what was it?"

He doesn't answer for a long minute, placing his tools back in the box, climbing into the driver's seat. Did he hear me? Then, a moment before he starts the engine, he answers. One word.

"Duty."

Chapter 21
LUCY

"When do the buses come?" I ask Aunt Jane at breakfast. I finally have my room the way I want it, with the mirror and papasan chair and nightstand and lamps moved upstairs, the picture of Mom and Daddy and me at Disney on the nightstand, and my fuzzy pink rug on the floor. The mirror and chair were too heavy for me to carry alone, so Aunt Jane helped, but otherwise I did it myself. I have a food and water dish for Lexie, too. Aunt Jane said the litter box had to stay downstairs, in the room she calls the mudroom. Otherwise, Lexie's safe from Sarge.

But now there's nothing to do. No-thhhing. It is so boring here. No TV at all and barely any Internet. I tried to go online with my iPad, edit some videos I started in New Media class, and check Facebook for messages from Graciela, but it disconnects after, like, two minutes. So I didn't even bother to set up my computer. Miguel and Juan haven't come back; nobody comes except for a lady who delivers the mail. She does it in her car, instead of walking, and leaves it in the mailbox at the road that I can't walk to. Sometimes people slow down near this wooden stand thing by the road, too, but then when they see there's nothing there, they speed off again. Aunt Jane said she used to sell her vegetables there. I guess she stopped because she's so busy with other stuff. She always says she never has time. I don't get it. She says people like to live in the country because of the slower pace, but she keeps complaining about being behind.

So I have nothing to do, and I'm so lonely, stuck in the house, surrounded by grass, everywhere. From every window, that's all I see. It's like being a prisoner, almost in solitary confinement like we learned about in social studies, except for Lexie. *Gracias a Dios* for Lexie. She's saving my life.

If I can take the bus into town, though, I could explore. Maybe go to a movie. Aunt Jane said there's a downtown. Downtowns have sidewalks, so it will be OK.

"When do the buses come?" I ask again because Aunt Jane hasn't answered. She's writing a list or checking things off or something.

"Buses?" She says it like she's never heard of one. "We don't have regular bus routes out here."

"I've seen buses go by."

"Yes, but it doesn't work like you think. People make special arrangements."

"Why?"

"There's not enough people living out here for a bus to come on the chance somebody's waiting to go somewhere. It's not efficient."

"Then how does it work?" I tap my spoon against my cereal bowl.

"You have to call and make an appointment for the bus to pick you up. More like a taxi, I guess." She sticks her pencil behind her ear and pours more coffee.

Actually, for taxis you just go out on the street and wait, too. "So how am I supposed to go anywhere?"

"Where do you want to go?"

"Anywhere! To see the town. A movie. Anywhere besides here. I'm so bored. There's nothing to do."

Aunt Jane sighs. "Well, I'd have to drive you, I guess."

And she doesn't have time. "I know, I know. You're too busy."

"I'm sorry, Lucy. This is the time of year when I simply have to work. Make hay while the sun shines, you know?"

I shake my head.

"It means as long as there's daylight, there are things to do. Your mom had to work a lot, too, right?"

That was different. My neck prickles. Mom had an important job, on TV. I stand up, leaving my dishes on the table, which I know bugs her. "Never mind."

Upstairs I put my earbuds in and flop onto the bed that I just got out of half an hour ago. Lexie meows, and I unlatch her cage. I make her stay in it if I'm not with her. Sarge mostly stays outside, but you never know. With her lying on my chest, I open the funeral slide show again. The weight of her body breathing against mine and the sound of her purring feels good. I know the pictures by heart now, and that feels good, too, to see Mom's and Daddy's faces.

At the Statue of Liberty picture, Lexie jumps off my chest, heading for the door. Time to do her business.

"Don't you go down there without me." I pull out the earbuds and follow her.

While she's busy I turn my phone to video and wander around the house. Maybe I'll send it to Phoebe so she can see where I'm living now. Except there's not much to see. The only room I haven't been in is the other downstairs bedroom, the one Aunt Jane said was her son's, who's in the army now.

The door creaks, making my stomach jump, even though I know Aunt Jane is out in her garden and will be all morning, probably. Lexie brushes my legs as she darts in and up onto the bed, making me jump again. This is my house, too, now, right? So why shouldn't I be in here? Still I tiptoe over to the window and lift one of the blind slats, aiming the phone at Aunt Jane wearing that weird white hat with the flaps. Some of the plants are as high as her waist, so when she walks around, it looks like she has no legs. Creepy.

117

I'm opposite the door now, on the other side of the bed. Lexie's in the middle of the blue plaid bedspread, washing her face, the only noise or movement in the whole still, quiet room. I've got lots of videos of her, so I turn it off and just look around. Another kid lived here. Even if he was a boy and even if it was a long time ago and even if he didn't hate grass, he did it. It's only been a few days, and I don't know how I'm going to make it. Maybe he left clues.

In the corner there's a giant covered desk that matches the night-stand, both dark-brown, heavy wood. A tall bookshelf, dark wood, too, and a closet, the door open a little bit. I push it closed and sidle around the bed to the bookcase.

The top shelf is filled with trophies. Most of them have little gold or silver baseball players on the top, tiny bats stuck to their shoulders. I brush the dust off the plaque on one. "American Legion Youth Baseball, 1997." There're some medals hanging around the trophies, blue and red ribbons with the medals lying flat on the shelf, or dangling below.

ALL-CITY CROSS COUNTRY MEET, 2002, 2003, 2004.
CHERRY CAPITAL 2-MILE CHAMPION, 2004

Some plaques for basketball with later dates.

MHSAA CLASS A DISTRICT CHAMPIONS, 2004, 2005

Two and a half of the shelves are filled with a set of books, all black with gold letters. The pages have gold edges, too. Each one has a letter of the alphabet on the spine. "Aa–An" is the first one, then "Ao–Be," then "Bi–Ch." I tug that one out—they're crammed in tight. Encyclopaedia Britannica, world edition. It makes a cracking sound when I open it. *Step on a crack, break your mother's back.* Quickly, I close it.

There's a bunch of other matching books with blue covers. The Hardy Boys, they all say. Some yearbooks. I plop down with them on the bed next to Lexie, who meows and digs her claws into the bedspread.

"Stop it. No, Lexie." I pat her. She rolls over to have her belly rubbed. "Be a good girl."

"Trojans 2004–05, Traverse City Central High School," it says in gold letters on the cover, like the encyclopedias. Inside, the first page has a picture of the school. It's so small! Just one story, brick with a flagpole in front. Around the picture are signatures and notes. "Semper fi!" underlined a bunch of times. "GO ARMY" in all capital letters, like the poster that's over the desk. "Matt, it's been nice knowing ya. Good luck with Uncle Sam. Xoxox, Lindsey." "It's been a fun four years. See you at the reunion! Kelly," who's drawn a little heart. Some other boys have just signed their names, Dylan and Caleb and some others I can't read. A few other people drew flags.

I never knew a soldier before. At home, at the September 11 memorial, they were always around in their camouflage uniforms. Sometimes at the airport. But I never talked to one. Does he bring his guns home when he visits? Does he still sleep in this room? Aunt Jane said he was twenty-three. Only a year older than Deirdre. She's probably back in London now. She was trying to get another au pair job but had to go back home first for her visa. She didn't want to. *Sodding suburbs,* she said when I asked why, sighing. *So boring.* She should see this place.

I flip through the yearbook. Lots of pictures show kids outside, on sports fields, sitting at picnic tables. Since the pictures are black-and-white, the grass looks gray, but it's still grass. Prickly and cold and lethal and all. Tentatively I brush my finger over the picture. Just that makes me shiver, and involuntarily I clap the yearbook shut. Lexie startles, jumping off the bed over to the desk chair. I follow her. The desk has a bumpy cover with two little knobs, one at each end. I fiddle with the knobs, and the cover starts to slide up. Cool. You could hide whatever you wanted in here. Except it gets stuck. Something underneath is jamming the cover. I slide it back down and then up again, rattling the knobs, trying to coax it past the stuck spot. There, I've got it up a little farther.

In the hall I hear voices. A man's. Is Miguel here? Quickly I slide the cover back down, right to where it got stuck, then slip out the door, down the hall to the kitchen. Miguel and Aunt Jane are both there.

"*¡Buenos días! ¿Cómo estás?*" He's smiling. I smile back. He's the nicest person in Michigan so far. "Brought you dinner." He taps a bag on the table. "You like tamales, *¿sí?*"

The word sounds so good. Like home, with Daddy at the stove, wearing his *el cocinero* apron, smiling while he stirred and Mexican music on the CD player. I nod, afraid I'll cry if I try to talk.

"*Excelente.* There's plenty for two. *Y arroz*, some chips—"

"When do you find time to cook?" Aunt Jane says.

"I didn't." He shakes his head. "Señora López did."

"Who's she?"

"The best Mexican cook on Old Mission." Miguel grins. "Every weekend we meet for soccer games at the park. *Las mujeres* all bring food. There's always some left over."

Just like we'd take leftovers to Mom's office for lunch on Sundays, all three of us eating at the anchor desk on set. I blink fiercely, before any tears fall. I guess Mom did work a lot. Still not as much as Aunt Jane. And I had Daddy.

"That's very kind," Aunt Jane says.

"It's a big party," he says, turning to me. "Maybe you can come to the next one."

I look down at the kitchen floor, making sure one foot is squarely in a black tile, and the other in a white. *Step on a crack, break your mother's back. Step on the grass, make her car crash.* Soccer's played on grass.

"What do you think? The games are *muy divertido*."

I shrug. Aunt Jane's watching me.

"Jane says you're bored."

"A little, I guess."

"A little, you guess?" Aunt Jane raises her eyebrows.

I look down again. I can't go to a soccer game.

"Tell you what. Juan's wife, Esperanza? She is lonely, too. It's her first summer up here. She doesn't know anyone. I could bring her out, tomorrow maybe, and you could take the bus into town together. Maybe see a movie."

That sounds fun. Esperanza. Hope. If she's Juan's wife, she's probably older than Deirdre but younger than Mom.

"Oh, I don't know about that." Aunt Jane frowns. "A stranger?"

"She is very responsible, Jane. She should meet you, too," Miguel says. "She is trying to build her own business. She makes jewelry, Mexican jewelry. She and her sister, back in Mexico. *Muy hermosa.*"

"I don't wear any jewelry," Aunt Jane says, holding out bare wrists, shaking her hair behind naked earlobes.

"I mean about the business part. You know about all that. You could tell her where to sell it. And Lucy could help her practice English."

"I want to go. Come on, Aunt Jane." Anything, anyone, is better than another day stuck here.

Aunt Jane sighs. "Is she legal?"

"Of course." But Miguel looks unsure, too.

"Bring her over tomorrow and we'll see."

Chapter 22
JANE

After Miguel leaves I head back outside. A dark patch of soil over in the lettuce section catches the corner of my eye. The drip irrigation's on an overnight timer that should have shut it off at 5:00 a.m. By now the soil should be back to its uniform sandy gray.

Must have gotten kinked or blocked somehow. Crouching down, I inspect the length of plastic hose all along the row. No visible problems. But when I flip the switch to test it, rather than the efficient, steady drip, the water spurts up at the wet spot in a wasteful, geyser-like spray.

I flip the switch off again, then stoop over the dark patch of soil, groping for the line. My back sends up a mild protest. Something's been nibbling at the line. Damn it. I can patch it, but those never hold for long. More important, all the plants past the hole missed last night's watering, and today promises to be a scorcher, unseasonably hot for late June.

Instinctively I check the angle of the sun. The lettuce is still in shade. I could get in an hour or so with my old sprinklers. Delivery day was yesterday, meaning everything's got to last another week. Withering from heat or ripening too soon means wasted food and unhappy customers. Even though riding out the ups and downs of a real farm is supposed to be part of the CSA experience, I've always been leery of testing that tolerance.

For the hundredth time, I wish for a walk-in cooler. I could pick early and keep everything fresh until delivery day. But that remains on the wish list, part of the whole washing and packing assembly line that always seems out of Plain Jane's reach.

Maybe next season, a voice whispers. *You'll have the estate money.*

That's Lucy's money. It's for her benefit. I locate the old rotating sprinkler in the shed and screw it onto the hose.

If you can work more efficiently, that does benefit her, the voice argues. *Less rushing around. More time. You could take her to that movie, instead of Esperanza.*

Or maybe hire Esperanza to do the picking and packing tomorrow, and take Lucy to the movie yourself. The flip side of the idea springs up out of nowhere. On its heels, a dozen "buts" clamor. Esperanza doesn't know my systems, where I keep everything, how I like it done. She wants to learn English, and Lucy can help her better than I can. Lucy's already expecting her to go along and won't want me instead. And at the core of it all, a guilty truth: I'd rather work on Plain Jane's.

Hauling the sprinkler down to the dry end of the lettuce plot, I imagine my guilty thoughts spinning out of my head just like the water. Now to patch the irrigation line. I affix it carefully, with my soil-blackened fingers and adhesive, tacking on a prayer.

I wait until evening to turn it back on, cutting the volume by half to keep the pressure down on the hose. I'll leave it on longer to make up. I look back at the house. It's so strange to see a light on upstairs now, evidence of another inhabitant, even if she does mostly hibernate. Lucy didn't say much at dinner, but she did eat, gobbling up Señora López's tamales and rice. I added a jar of salsa I canned last year and a bowl of strawberries, which Lucy ate most of. Sitting there together reminded me so much of me and Gloria, back in high school. Déjà vu all over again. I thought about asking about the grass phobia, whether she had ever seen a counselor or tried to overcome it, but the movie plan seems to have mollified her, at least for the time being, and I didn't want to spoil the détente. No Sarge or Lexie confrontations, even. I guess that's progress.

The next morning, though, I go out to a failed patch. The geyser is more of a burble today since it was turned on so low. Another hot, dry forecast and another lost night of moisture. This section won't make it another five days. The only solution is a Saturday farmers' market day, sell what I have before it's no longer saleable. So I'll get to show Lucy Traverse City, after all.

Chapter 23
LUCY

Esperanza Ramirez does wear a lot of jewelry, especially bracelets and big, dangly earrings. She seems quiet, but maybe she just doesn't speak much English. "Papers," she says, showing Aunt Jane something.

"Good." Aunt Jane looks relieved.

"The bus will come at nine thirty," Miguel tells Jane. "I've got to take Juan over to a job."

"All right." Aunt Jane seems preoccupied, as usual. "That sounds fine."

As soon as they've gone, she stands up and grabs her flap hat.

"I'll see you two this afternoon, after lunch?"

"¿Después de comer?" I translate for Esperanza.

"Sí." She nods.

The kitchen's quiet. Esperanza looks over at Sarge's food dish on the floor. "¿Tienes un gato?"

"That's my aunt's cat. Mine's upstairs." That reminds me, I'd better make sure Lexie's safe in her cage. "I'll be right back."

I look all over before I finally find her on the hall windowsill, looking out. "Don't get any ideas," I say, taking her back to my room, where the *M* encyclopedia volume from Matt's room lies on my bed, open to the Mexico entry. Reading the encyclopedias is something to do, and the climate section was really good news. "Much of Mexico, especially the northern regions, has a dry climate with infrequent rainfall." So not much grass! I was right when I told Mr. Langley it would be better than here.

"Lucy!" Esperanza calls upstairs. *"El bus."*

"Coming!" I close the book to finish later and get Lexie safe in her cage. She meows and scratches at the bars. She's doing that more and more.

Downstairs, Esperanza isn't in the kitchen. She's not in the living room or bathroom, either. Where did she go? Then the side door opens.

"Lucy? *¡Venga!*" She's waving me over from outside, pointing at the road with her other arm. *"¡El bus está aquí!"*

I look through the living room window and see it, one of the funny white short buses they have here, pulled over on the road, the front yard between us.

Step on a crack, break your mother's back. Step on the grass, make her car crash. I can't walk out there.

She's already dead, a voice inside me whispers. Make the bus crash, then. With us on it.

Leaving Lexie all by herself, for Sarge to have for lunch or something. No way.

"Lucy?" Esperanza's back inside now, frowning at me.

"I can't," I tell her, then remember. *"No puedo."*

"No te entiendo," she says, shaking her head.

No one understands. *"Simplemente no puedo.* I just can't. I'll have to stay here," I say.

Behind Esperanza, Aunt Jane's face appears, looking tired even though it's morning. "Grass again, right?"

I nod.

She sighs. "I'll ask the driver to pull in."

The driver opens the door, and I watch Aunt Jane talk, pointing back to the house. The bus doesn't move. She points back again, then stands with her hands on her hips.

The door closes, and the bus starts to move down the road. Esperanza rouses, as if to try to stop it, but then the back lights start flashing and the bus is slowly backing down Aunt Jane's driveway. Aunt Jane follows it and waves to the driver, a bald man who looks pretty mad, and comes back in the kitchen.

"Doorstep service."

"Actually, the door's on the wrong side," I tell her, looking at the floor.

She doesn't say anything. I hear a loud exhale, then some muttering.

"All right, then. In for a penny, in for a pound," she says, turning around. "Climb on."

I straddle her back. She does it better this time, not so wobbly. Esperanza follows, not saying anything.

On the bus steps I slide down. The whole bus is empty. Esperanza sits down next to me. The bus driver looks curiously at us in the rear-view mirror.

"Downtown? State Theatre?"

"Yes," I say, watching Aunt Jane's face as the bus moves. She still looks tired, but something else, too. Resigned? Resentful?

I prop my phone next to the window, filming the endless green. Phoebe will never believe it if I don't show her. That's all there is, the whole drive to town, except when we pass a police car with its flashers on, the officer outside, standing next to the car he pulled over. Esperanza slides down in her seat, even though there's no way he could have seen her.

Downtown isn't much. A couple of blocks of stores. No skyscrapers. No newsstands. People walk around drinking coffee from paper cups and looking at their phones. They're all wearing shorts and T-shirts. No one's dressed for work or really going anywhere, just wandering around. Some people have dogs on leashes.

But I'm safe from grass at least. There're trees and flowerpots, but the trees are boxed into little squares cut in the concrete and the plants into baskets hanging from streetlights.

The theater marquee says *"Mr. Popper's Penguins"* at ten thirty. That's it? One movie in this whole city? Esperanza looks at me and shrugs.

I guess it is, and since it doesn't start for half an hour, we buy the tickets and walk around, too. Across the street is a kind of plaza. Some kids a little older than me are skateboarding. Another little group is bunched next to the bike rack, talking. They're all white. Other than that, it's the most normal-looking thing I've seen since I came to Michigan. I watch one girl who has her nose and eyebrow pierced. She's laughing at some boy. She looks about Graciela's age. I still don't know if she's sent any more messages on Facebook.

"Uh-oh. I smell bacon," I hear the boy say.

I follow his gaze to a police officer, coming from the other side of the plaza.

"Break it up, kids. No skateboarding here, you know that."

"*Vamos*, Lucy." Esperanza pulls at my arm. She's acting nervous again, like on the bus when we passed the police car. "*Tengo calor.* Let's go in, where it's air-conditioned."

I let her pull me into the theater. "How come you get so nervous when you see a police officer?" I ask once we're sitting.

She looks at me but doesn't answer. I ask again, in Spanish. "I thought you had a visa or whatever."

"It's always better not to attract attention."

I think of Mom. Her bright clothes and her huge bright smile. Her life-size picture on the bus-stop shelter. The plan for the West Coast edition of her show, so the whole country could see her. Now not even I can. My stomach tightens.

"Why?"

She shrugs. "It's the way it is for us."

"For Miguel, too?" He doesn't seem like Esperanza and Juan. He's loud; he's always in front. She shakes her head.

"Miguel is an American."

"He is?"

"*Sí*. Born here. *Tiene suerte*," she says.

"Lucky how?"

"His parents were migrants. They came up here to work in the orchards every summer. *Las cerezas, las manzanas*. One year, Miguel was born on their way home. In Texas."

Where Daddy went to school. So Miguel's Tex-Mex, too.

"How do you know all that?"

"Our families are friends in Mexico."

"Wait. He lives here, but his family lives in Mexico?"

"*Sí. Fue terrible.*" She shakes her head.

"What was terrible?"

"*Los deportaron*. All but Miguel."

"Deported?" It sounds like a story Mom would tell on the news, not something that would happen to anybody I know.

She nods. "A long time ago. There were three *niños* by then, Miguel, Ana Maria, and Jorge. Back and forth they went, every year, until one year their parents decided, why not stay?"

"And they did?"

Esperanza nods. "For a long time, *no hubo problemas*. Miguel's mama wrote mine, so proud her children were in school. Learning English." She sighs and shakes her head again.

"What happened?"

"Immigration came for his parents while they were at school. Then they waited for the school bus. *Su hermana*, Ana Maria, was only nine years old."

Younger than me. But she had her parents. Poor Miguel. All by himself. Just like me. Tears rise.

I rest my head on the back of the seat, hoping they won't trickle out. The black theater ceiling is covered with bright white lights, like a starry sky. I think of the Spanish song I put in the slide show for the funeral. *"Abrázame muy fuerte"* by Juan Gabriel. Daddy used to always sing it to me. I picked it because he said it was our song. It means hold me tightly. I can't translate it all, but it's about loving somebody more than anything else. My favorite lines were the ones about every star in the sky saying "I love you." I remember after Daddy sang it to me at bedtime, he'd point out the window and say, *Hay miles de millones de estrellas, niña.*

Billions of stars. Billions of I-love-yous. I brush away a leaking tear. Esperanza, still talking about Miguel and his family, doesn't notice.

"They took them across the border, to Ciudad Juárez, and dumped them." Her voice is quietly mad. "*El padre*, he found work washing dishes. Miguel and a priest from *el Norte* found the rest of them locked in a filthy hotel room. They were there for weeks, *las ventanas, las puertas*, all locked."

Windows and doors locked for weeks? "Why?"

"Ciudad Juárez, it is not safe. Many criminals. Drugs, gangs." She shakes her head, pressing her lips together. "Miguel brought enough money to get them back to our village. Ana Maria, all she had was her Dora school backpack."

I look down at my flip-flops, Hello Kitty's face peeking back at me between my toes.

"Now, in the country, they are safe, but Miguel has to work very hard to support them."

"At Aunt Jane's."

"*Sí*, her farm and others. Plus he drives the school bus, delivers newspapers . . . *no hay trabajo en México.*"

"Oh." Why isn't there any work? "Is that why you and Juan came here?"

"*Sí.*" She nods. "But it is harder now. Papers, all that."

"Maybe that's why my cousin can't come to see me. She lives in Mexico." That's what Mr. Langley said. I didn't believe him, but if Esperanza's story is true, maybe he wasn't lying.

Esperanza nods. "Miguel's family cannot come see him. They have a lifetime ban because of the deportation."

I think about that. Would it be worse if Mom and Daddy were alive but I couldn't see them? The theater lights are starting to dim.

"He can visit them, *claro*. He will go back for Ana Maria's *quinceañera*," Esperanza says.

Then the lights go out all the way, and I can let the tears come as the star ceiling sparkles with I-love-yous that I can't reach.

Chapter 24
JANE

Saturday. Farmers' market day. I check in with the market master. Since I'm not a regular, I have to settle for one of the secondary spots, which isn't shaded, nor do I have a canopy. It's clouding up, though. I tie on the carpenter's apron that I filled with change last night and set out my price list. Strawberries, six dollars per quart. Zesty mixed greens, washed, five dollars a bag. Mild mixed greens, washed, five dollars a bag. Rhubarb, two dollars a bunch. That's everything. I prepped it all last night, while Lucy was at the computer in the kitchen.

"This Internet is so slow!" She pounded her fist on the desk, then stood up abruptly, Sarge yowling as her chair almost squashed his tail. "I can't load anything."

More complaints. She's been here less than a week and it's been all complaints. I plumb down deep, trying to tap into more sympathy. I know it's rough, moving so soon after a death. Oh, how well I know. I try to cut her slack, like arranging that movie trip with Esperanza, but she keeps reeling it in. The grass. Sarge. The crate in the barn. That she can't go anywhere. Now the Internet.

"High-speed service is expensive." With effort, I kept my voice neutral.

"I have money! Mr. Langley said."

He talked to her about money? Well, I know she was aware of the apartment selling. A sixth grader could certainly figure it out. "You will, but it's not accessible yet."

She sighed, pacing back and forth like a caged animal. In a way she is, refusing to go outside. She keeps her earbuds on a lot, curled up with Lexie on her bed.

"What's that?" she asked, pointing to the leafy green-and-pink variegated stalks that darken to curved fuchsia ends, where they snapped off at the soil line.

"Rhubarb."

She touched a stalk tentatively.

"Ever tasted it?"

She shook her head.

"Want to try?"

"No, thanks."

"Go on. Just try it." I snapped a stalk in half, handing her the pinker, sweeter end. She nibbled, then made a face. "Yuck."

"Too bitter?"

"People eat this?" She stares at the stalk like it's infectious.

"Most people cook or bake with it. Usually they add something. Strawberry-rhubarb jelly, apple-rhubarb pie. Maybe"—I had a brainstorm—"maybe even salsa."

"Ewww." She tried to hand it back to me.

"Put it in here." I held out the ice bucket I turned into my countertop compost container, half-full of coffee grounds and eggshells.

"What's that for?"

"Compost."

She looked at me blankly. So much to learn, so much she doesn't get. I changed the subject.

"Plan to get up early tomorrow. We're going into town for the farmers' market."

"How early?"

"Five a.m."

"Five?" She was incredulous. "No one gets up that early."

"Farmers do," I told her. "Sorry. They've got free wireless down-town, so you can get online there. Or you can sleep in the truck. But there's no getting out of it."

She took my words literally. She hasn't stepped out of the truck, even though the market is set up on an asphalt parking lot. Not so much as a toe has touched grass yet, as far as I know. In the cab I see her hunched over the iPad.

Customers are starting to arrive. "Your strawberries fresh?" asks a middle-aged man wearing a Mackinac Island sweatshirt.

"Picked 'em yesterday," I say as brightly as I can.

"Then I'll take two." He hands me a twenty-dollar bill. With effort, I put Lucy out of my mind and settle down to business.

An Amish family is set up across from me. In between customers I watch them, as covertly as I can. The oldest girl looks about Lucy's age, but plain and severe in her long dress and apron, her brown hair captured in braids. Like Lucy's was the first day, in New York, but hasn't been since. No Hello Kitty in sight. Nor did she spend the last evening complaining about the slow Internet. I count three other younger kids, two boys and a girl. The mother is pregnant with a fifth. I wonder whether the balance will tip in favor of boys or girls. Or will it change at all? She looks far enough along. She's done it before. That's what I thought, too.

Even not counting a baby, that's already six people in the house-hold. How do they navigate so many relationships? Parent and child, brother and sister, brother and brother, sister and sister. Husband and wife. I was so drained by the one that ended before it even started. Maybe relationships are an exponential kind of strength. The more you have, the stronger each grows. If I'd carried our daughter out of Alaska, how would life have been different? As a family of four, would we have been stronger—a solid square instead of a tipsy triangle? If Jim weren't in Florida starting over, would I resent Lucy's arrival less? Is it all a vicious circle, with only myself to blame? My body denied Matt a sister, my grief the mother he deserved, and drove Jim to the warmth and comfort of another woman's arms.

By eleven the salad greens are gone and I'm down to just a few quarts of strawberries. Mostly rhubarb remains. Lucy's tastes weren't so far off the mark. I survey the Amish family again. A lot of bakery items have left their table. Maybe I can arrange a barter.

"Morning." I address the girl Lucy's age. "Could I talk to one of your parents about a trade?"

At first the mother is cool toward the idea, but then the youngest girl sees the strawberries.

"Please, Mama?"

"She can try one," I say. "You all can."

The children crowd around, eager and hopeful, but waiting for approval. When the mother finally nods, they each carefully choose one, then wait for her to eat hers first.

"Quite good," she says after holding it in her mouth for a moment. "Will you take a dozen eggs and a loaf of bread?"

"Certainly." I push the produce over while she summons the Lucy girl to fetch a bag.

"Looks like you have your hands full," I say to fill the silence.

The mother lifts her blue eyes to me. She's young. Probably not even thirty.

"Yes. Full of blessings." She smiles, spreading one hand over her expectant belly, gathering her children close to her with the other. "And may God bless you."

Her words don't make me flinch like they usually would. The apron's full of cash. Lucy's been occupied with the iPad. With the clouds most of the morning, the plot with the still-broken irrigation line shouldn't be too dry. It's been a good morning. Maybe even a blessed morning. I keep one bunch of rhubarb after all. I'll look for a salsa recipe at home.

Chapter 25
LUCY

For the first time since I got here, the little circle connection thing spins and actually connects when I go to Facebook! Graciela left a message last Saturday morning: "Are you there? How are you?" Then time-stamped in the afternoon, "Lucy? *¿Dónde estás?*"

I reply. "I'm here! I hate it. It's boring and the Internet doesn't work. But today I am someplace with Internet until twelve o'clock. Write as soon as you get this!!"

I click "Send" and look at the clock. Almost six, or almost five for Graciela. Way too early. But Saturdays are when she gets to go online, and Aunt Jane said we would be here all morning, so we should be able to talk.

I rest my head against the window. It's too early to try Phoebe. And later her mom will probably make her go to temple. She doesn't like to, but she can't do anything about it, especially since her bat mitzvah is next year. I wonder if I'll be invited? Probably not. She'll have forgotten all about me. She might have already, even.

I'm afraid I might forget Mom and Daddy, too. So I keep watching the slide show. I know it by heart now, the Disney World photo, then the Statue of Liberty photo, then ice-skating, then their wedding. And the music, "Lucy in the Sky with Diamonds" and *"Abrázame muy fuerte."*

I put the earbuds on and zip up Mom's Venice Beach hoodie. It's already completely light out, another weird thing about Michigan. It stays light so late, almost to ten o'clock, and then it's morning really early. Aunt Jane said it's because we're on the edge of the time zone, and she'll get a shade for my window. It makes it hard for me to fall asleep, but I don't know if it's being light or that it's so quiet or what. Here there's traffic from the road and people talking and I'm really tired, so it's easy to drift off to sleep.

A funny noise wakes me. Kind of like an alarm clock, but I've never heard it before. For a second I don't remember anything about Michigan or Aunt Jane and I'm terrified, not knowing where I am. Then there's the awful jerk of remembering, everything all at once, and then the same sound. From the iPad. I touch the screen, and there's a reply from Graciela: "I'm here, can you talk?"

She's there! My cousin is there right now! I touch the chat box, feeling like I'm touching her, and type back. "Yes!"

Below my finger, more words appear in Spanish.

"I can only talk for a minute. Only two hours of Internet today."

"Why?"

"Exams. Have to study." She adds a face with a tongue sticking out.

She has exams still? I've been out of school for almost a month.

"Two more weeks and I go home. I can talk to Mama then." This time there's a smiley face.

Finally! My stomach does its elevator thing, but it's going up this time.

"Your school is so long there," I reply.

"Way too long! You'll have to go, too, if you move here." She sends a winking smiley face.

School's better than sitting around alone all day. As long as I could bring Lexie. Do allergies run in families? Would Aunt Bonita be allergic, too?

"Are you allergic to cats? Or your mom?"

"No. Why?"

I look for a picture of Lexie, then send her one.

"So cuuute!!! But you couldn't bring her to school. *Las mascotas están prohibidas.*"

No Internet, now no pets. My stomach elevator stops going up.

"Mama would take care of her."

But she's my kitty. I stare at the screen.

"How come you go to boarding school?"

"Mama says it's better than school at home. No boys."

"Who cares about boys?"

"She does. But maybe, if we were together, she would say it's OK."

"You think?"

"She always talks about family. *'Es muy importante.'*"

I hope so. Family is important. Daddy always said so. So why didn't we visit more often? Why didn't they come see us? Graciela seems so nice. Maybe if we had always known each other and visited and stuff, she wouldn't be at boarding school. And I wouldn't be stuck here. My stomach elevator starts dropping. I can picture Daddy's face, smiling as usual. But instead of feeling sad, I'm angry.

"I have to go now. But in two weeks I'll have Internet all the time."

Not me.

"But keep trying, OK? Even if I'm not here?"

"OK. *¡Hasta luego!*"

Wait. I should give her my phone number. Aunt Bonita could call internationally, I bet. Or my address. Both. But the screen tells me Graciela is gone. Sighing, I turn around to check for Aunt Jane in her booth.

She's gone, too. Where could she be? The back of the truck was full of stuff when we left, and now there's just empty crates and boxes. Guess I have to look. Thank goodness this is a parking lot. I slide to the comforting gray pavement and sidle alongside the truck. I can see her table now, empty. In front of it is the biggest crowd I've seen since the airport, streaming in both directions. Just like that day at the movies, they're all white, all wearing T-shirts and shorts. Some are pushing strollers or holding little kids. They're all smiling and happy.

Then a mom bends over to pick up a baby, and in the space behind her, I see Aunt Jane, talking to a lady wearing these weird old-fashioned clothes. A long dark-blue dress with an apron over it and a white cloth covering her hair. She has some kids with her. The older girl is dressed the same way, her hair in super long braids that hang below the white cap. The younger girl has braids, but they're not covered. *Did her sister do them, like Phoebe used to for me?* My stomach elevator starts to creak, but then Aunt Jane turns around and spots me.

"Sold out. I'm ready to go," she says, coming over with a bag.

There're two boys, too. They have these straps hooked to their pants that go over their shoulders, instead of a belt. Daddy once wore something like that with a tux for an awards show. I can't remember what he called them. They look like their pants would fall down without them; they're both really skinny. Their shirts have buttons and collars, not T-shirts like everyone else is wearing. The older boy has a hat on, too, made of straw.

"Did you find what you were looking for online?"

"Kind of." I can't stop staring at the family. Why are they wearing those old clothes? "Why did you go over there?"

"Over where?"

"There." I point. "To talk to them."

"Oh. To arrange a barter."

"A what?"

"A trade. Some of my stuff for some of theirs."

139

"Why are they dressed old fashioned like that?" That boy's hat. Straw is like dried-up grass, isn't it? My nose crinkles.

"They're Amish. They practice a religion that requires them to dress that way."

"Oh."

"You saw all kinds of different cultures and languages and clothes in New York, right?" Aunt Jane's voice sounds like a lecture is coming.

I shrug.

"Well, this is one of the Midwest's. Amish people dress plainly and simply. Men grow beards. To varying degrees, they don't accept or use modern technology."

Huh. "I guess we have something in common after all, since I can't even get online at your house." As Aunt Jane's jaw drops, I put my earbuds back in and climb in the truck.

Chapter 26
JANE

It's work-share day. I straighten up and survey the Livingston crew. Jared disappeared inside more than fifteen minutes ago. His brother, I can't remember his name, has earbuds in and is singing more than weeding. Now Paul, the husband, is talking on his cell phone, his back to us. The word *coach* marches across his shoulder blades.

Rebecca is doggedly weeding along. One out of four. I sigh. The Extension people did not address how to instill discipline in the ranks of the working-share customers, especially difficult since enforcement of the "working" aspect crosses with the chief customer relations commandment: the customer is always right.

Pausing to drink from her water bottle, Rebecca catches my eye and seems to read my mind. "Paul!" When he turns, she pantomimes hanging up the phone with one hand, the other on her hip.

He frowns and flashes her a hand. Five minutes. I see her read his lips and back off, hands falling to her sides.

"I apologize. A work call. He'll be through momentarily," she says. "I'll go and fetch Jared from indoors now."

Jared's and Lucy's heads are visible through the kitchen window, not watching us, but engaged in something together.

"It's all right. Looks like he's with my niece. If he can break through to her, I'll credit him five rows of weeding." Again I tried to persuade Lucy to come out today, on the grounds that she could meet someone her age. Again, she refused. The grass fear gets more entrenched by the day.

Rebecca relaxes her ramrod stance slightly. "How old is she?"

"She's . . . um . . . going into seventh grade." I dodge a direct answer. When *is* her birthday? It must be on one of those papers I put in Matt's desk.

"Jared will be in seventh this year, too. He just turned twelve."

I nod, accepting the information. These exchanges of biographical details always puzzle me, have since Matt was a baby. Why did someone else pushing the next swing care how old he was or if he'd walked yet or gotten a tooth yet or started preschool? They were also unpleasant reminders, since I couldn't help but answer, silently, *He's twenty-three. Lives in Germany, stationed over there. She would have been twenty. Lives—well, never mind.*

"She's visiting, then?"

"Actually, no. She lives here. With me."

"Oh." Rebecca turns to face me fully, surprise evident. "Is she at East Middle?"

"No. I, um, I haven't enrolled her in school yet."

"Oh." She pauses. My first-person answers plus her own curiosity minus her instinctive Midwestern reserve have presented her with a riddle. I sense Rebecca doesn't like riddles.

"It's a recent development," I fill in. "She moved here from New York City last month." I take a deep breath. "After her parents died."

"Oh my goodness, I'm so sorry. How sad." The reserve kicks in again, and she changes the subject. She shades her eyes and looks over at her husband. "We lived in New York for a couple years after we got married. It was glamorous then. Paul worked on Wall Street. I was at a law firm in the twin towers. But when we decided to have a family, we moved back home."

Paul's walking over now, putting his phone in his pocket. He taps the other son on the shoulder and gives him a high five. The son grins and goes back to his weeding with more energy.

"Sorry. Second quarter's closing, something crashed, Tina couldn't run the reports." He speaks more to Rebecca than to me.

"Fine. It's straightened out now, then?"

"Yep." Paul nods, swabbing at his forehead with his T-shirt sleeve. The front bears the community soccer organization's logo. I wonder if coaching, like the work share, was another Rebecca idea, and if so, whether Paul offered suggestions for family activities, too. Jim either went along, like with Little League, or begged off, as with Plain Jane's, but rarely initiated anything together.

"So you used to work on Wall Street?" I haven't looked for a financial adviser to handle Lucy's estate. Might as well ask a few questions.

He looks surprised and glances at Rebecca. "You tell her that?"

"It just came up in conversation," Rebecca says. "I'm going to help Jason now."

Jason, that's the other son's name.

"Yes, a hundred years ago, I worked on Wall Street," Paul says as Rebecca heads for Jason's row.

"And now?"

"I run my own wealth management firm in Traverse City. Livingston Partners LLC at your service." He doffs an imaginary cap.

"Wealth management, huh?"

He grimaces. "Marketing speak. There're no partners, either. I'm the only one. Well, there's my secretary. Tina."

I laugh out loud. I like his forthrightness. Someone I could trust.

"Plain Jane's should hire your consultant. I could use some marketing advice."

"Well, she's right there." Paul nods at his wife.

"Rebecca's your marketing consultant? She said she worked at a law firm."

"She did, back in New York. But this town's overrun with lawyers. After we moved, it took her a year to find a job at a quarter the salary. When Jared was born she decided to stay home, do the marketing gig on the side."

"I see." Rebecca's made Jason take off his earbuds, but his body language says he's not listening to her.

"We'd better get back at it," I say to Paul. "Next time I'm in town, though, I'd like to stop by your office. I expect to need some financial advice by the end of the year."

"You bet. Anytime." He looks interested. "Strawberry prices at a record high this year?"

"Not exactly."

"Rebecca could probably help you make that happen." He sweeps his arm across the farm. "Grown pesticide-free in hand-tilled soil . . ."

And for what seems like the first time since Lucy arrived, I'm laughing again.

Chapter 27
LUCY

I'm in the kitchen with Lexie when a kid bursts in the door. He's about my age, reaching into his pocket and whistling.

"Oh, hey." He stops short. "I was looking for the bathroom?"

"Down the hall." I jerk my thumb over my shoulder.

"Thanks."

Lexie brushes up against me as he passes. Outside, Aunt Jane's talking to a woman. A man and another kid are kneeling a little way away. The toilet flushes and water runs. The kid comes out holding a Nintendo DS.

"Is that your family?"

"Yeah."

"What are they doing?"

"Weeding. Again." He rolls his eyes. "We always weed. So boring. And so hot."

"Want a drink?" I open the fridge. "There's some juice. And lemonade."

"Lemonade?"

I pour two glasses. "Why do you come to weed my aunt's garden?"

He rolls his eyes again. "It was my mom's idea."

"Why?"

"She thinks we're, like, spoiled or something. She says, 'You boys need to know how a hard day's work feels.'"

"Oh." It sounded weird. Days could be hard anywhere. On location, Mom sometimes worked eighteen hours a day. What's so special about a garden? "Do you, like, get paid?"

He shakes his head.

"Bummer."

"Yeah." He looks at me kind of sideways. "So, Jane's your aunt?"

I nod.

"Where do you live?"

"Here." I pick up Lexie so I can feel the reassuring vibrations of her heartbeat. That's the first time I've said it. I live here, at Aunt Jane's, in Michigan. I'm not a New Yorker anymore. I don't live with Mom and Daddy anymore. I'm still their daughter, but it doesn't feel like that means anything anymore. I pet Lexie a little faster.

"What grade are you in?"

"Going into seventh."

"Me, too. Are you going to East Middle School?"

"I don't know." Talking about school starts my stomach elevator dropping.

"Jared!" A loud voice interrupts. "Where have you been? I hope not playing that DS, young man."

Jared's mom comes into the kitchen, her hands on her hips. She's tall and thin and has the same brown hair as Jared. Coming in the door, she looks mad, but her face changes as soon as she sees me. Maybe she's bipolar or schizophrenic or has split personality disorder or something, like I read about in the encyclopedias in Matt's room. I've gotten about halfway through them now. She looks normal, but if she signs up to work outdoors, in the dirt, when it's hot and smelly, for free, then she's got to be a little bit crazy. Still, I'm relieved for the interruption.

"Well, hello! You must be Lucy."

146

"Uh-huh."

"I'm Jared's mother. We're work-share customers of your aunt's. But Jared here is not doing his share, so I came to check on him." She holds out her hand. "The game."

"We were just talking, Mom. I swear."

"Yeah. We were just talking," I chime in.

"Lucy's going to be in seventh grade this year, too," Jared says.

"How nice. Now, Jared, it's time to come back outside."

"Awww, Mom. It's so hot out there. And I'm so bored."

"Outside. And the DS."

"Hey, you wanna play?" Jared turns to me.

I don't really like video games, but I'm bored, too, stuck in this house, reading encyclopedias. I shrug. "OK."

"Very considerate, Jared," his mom says, shepherding him to the door. "Bye now, Lucy."

"Hey, Mom? How come she's not outside helping?"

The door closes on Jared's question.

I fool around with the game for a half hour or so before Jared knocks on the door.

"We're leaving now."

I hand it back.

"We'll be back next week. Maybe you can borrow it again," he says.

"OK. Whatever." I shrug.

He steps off the little concrete threshold, backing toward his car. "See you later," he says before he gets in.

Their car is really small and quiet. It turns onto the road like the bus did, toward Traverse City. Aunt Jane isn't around anywhere. I size up the little square of gray concrete where Jared was standing. It's just like the sidewalks in New York. Through the open door the warm sun bakes my face. It's nice. Tentatively I step onto the concrete.

The heat feels even better now. A little sticky, too, like summers in New York. I hold the screen door open because I'd have to step off the square for it to swing closed. To see the bay I look back through the screen. It is pretty, with a few sailboats and the green hills rising around it.

I feel a movement behind my legs. It's not the breeze; there's no wind at all. Just a quick, soft brush, gone the next instant. Then another. I look down. Sarge, going outside as usual. And Lexie behind him. *Lexie!*

I stoop to catch her, but she's too fast, my fingers barely brushing her tail before she's off the concrete square, darting after Sarge toward the garden. "Lexie! Come back!"

Involuntarily I take a step toward her, before I yank my foot back onto the concrete. I can see Aunt Jane now, carrying a basket in each hand.

"Aunt Jane! Lexie's running away! She ran out with Sarge!"

She plunks down the baskets, full of red berries but not strawberries, next to the door, her hands in her dirty garden gloves. She's got that weird hat on too—with the strips hanging down in the back that she says keeps her neck from getting sunburned.

"Go get her! Please, go find her for me."

"Chase a cat? Oh, Lucy. Not now. Deliveries tomorrow. If she's with Sarge, she'll be fine."

"No, please! Please go find her. Lexie's never been outside before!" I'm crying.

"She'll be fine. She's still got her claws, right? Put her food and water right here at the door. She'll come back when she's hungry, I promise you." Aunt Jane reaches out to squeeze my elbow.

"No, no, please, you have to find her now!" I can barely gasp the words out. My heart feels like it's going to burn through my chest, but I'm cold all over, too. On tiptoe at the edge of the concrete square, holding on to the door, I lean out, pleading to the grass and the sky and the world. "Lexie! Lexie! Come back! Please, please come back!"

"All right." I hear a deep sigh. "All right. I'll go look."

"Oh, thank you." I gulp down a sob. "Thank you."

"Maybe while I'm at it, I'll find a weed—or two or three or ten—that Jared missed." She pats my shoulder with her garden-gloved hand, then squeezes my elbow again. "Try not to worry. I'm sure she'll be back."

She strides across the gravel strips of the driveway, then the grassy section between it and the garden. She steps into a row between what I know now are the tomatoes and the beans. Faintly, I can hear her calling. "Lexie, Lexie. Here, kitty. Here, kitty, kitty."

Snuffling, I wipe my nose with my sleeve. *Put her food at the door.* I bring the dishes down from my room and fill both the food and the water bowls. Opening the door again, I set it outside on the gravel, right at the edge of the concrete. Actually, it would probably be better to set it right inside. So Lexie can see it but would have to come in to eat. I look for something to prop open the door.

Aunt Jane's basket. I stretch to reach the wire handle. Too far. In the kitchen I find the broom, then lean back outside to jab the broomstick under the basket handle. I drag it across the gravel and wedge it against the open screen door. It's heavier than I thought, and a couple of raspberries roll out, and the dust my dragging raises coats them with a light-brown powder.

Then I wait. And wait. And wait. I try to braid my hair but give up after I mess up crossing the sections, like always. Finally, for something to do, I pick up the fallen raspberries and take them to the sink. I've seen Aunt Jane just eat them whole. Cautiously I rinse them off and pop one into my mouth.

Biting into it, I taste a burst of sweet. It's bright and warm, like the sun is trapped in the skin. If Daddy were eating them with me, he would have done that thing he did when he really liked something, pinch his fingers together and kiss them.

Back at the door, I watch Aunt Jane's hat moving around in the garden. She's not saying "here, kitty, kitty" anymore.

"Did you find her?" I yell.

I guess she can't hear me. She doesn't answer, anyway. I sit on the floor, next to the bowl of cat food, and pull up my knees and cross my arms around them, holding myself together. When did Lexie eat last? She must be hungry by now! She's never been outside except in her cage. Will she try and eat the raspberries and all the stuff growing out there? Is that OK, or will it make her sick? *Lexie, Lexie, Lexie. I remember how you climbed up on my shoulder, crying the day I took you home from the Humane Society. I know how you felt losing your family, Lexie. But you love me now, and you won't leave me alone here, will you? Will you, Lexie?* I pick at the scab from an old scratch on my arm, drawing fresh blood. *If you just come back, I'll never complain about you scratching me again.*

"Lucy?" Aunt Jane's in the doorway, her foot almost on top of Lexie's dish.

"Don't step on it!" I jerk the dish out of the way.

Aunt Jane screams. "You scared me to death. What are you doing, sitting on the floor?" Her hand, still in the garden glove, is over her heart. Her T-shirt is wet.

"Watching for Lexie. Is it raining?"

Aunt Jane nods. "She'll come in soon."

"What if she doesn't?" I lean out the door. There's so much sky here, and it darkens so fast when thunderstorms come up. I kind of like them at night, when it's already dark. They cool down the weather so it's comfortable to wrap up in a blanket with Lexie and sit at the window, watching the lightning over the water, listening to the thunder. During the day I don't like them so much. Especially when Lexie's out in it.

Aunt Jane hesitates. Then, "She will," she says, not looking at me. "I'm going to change. Then we'll have lunch."

Lunch is one of Aunt Jane's weird ones, of whatever's ready in the garden. Today it's a big salad with some turkey and cheese and raspberries on top. I never ate fruit on salad before. Lexie doesn't come back. Sarge approaches her dish a few times. I shoo him away. So Lexie got away from him, too! Now she's completely alone out there. The rain stops at two o'clock. She's still gone. Aunt Jane puts on her hat to go back outside.

"Why don't you look with me? She's more likely to come to you."

"I'm going to make a lost poster," I say, ignoring her question. I know she's right, and I want to—I want to be able to run outside and scoop up Lexie and keep her safe forever and ever. But I can't take the risk.

Aunt Jane sighs and leaves, stepping carefully around the dish this time. I find my phone and start scrolling through the photos of Lexie, all the way back from when I got her at the Humane Society. She was so small! There's Phoebe holding her, and there she is curled up on my old bed. I need something more recent. There she is, stretched out on the windowsill in the hall. That's the best, since it shows all her markings. I'll give the poster to Martha and ask her to put copies in the neighbors' mailboxes. I'll—

"Meow."

"Lexie!" I drop the phone and rush to the door. She sits right down at her dish and plops her face in it. I crouch down and stroke her head to tail. She's not wet, so she must have found some place to hide. I start crying again. The door is still propped open, and I see something on the concrete square. A mouse. Dead.

I stifle my shriek. She might get scared and run away again. Instead of trying to shut the screen door, I leave the raspberries where they are and push Lexie farther into the kitchen so I can shut the regular door. She meows again, but she's too hungry to be indignant. When she's done eating she crawls up on my lap and falls asleep.

"Reunited?" Aunt Jane comes in with the raspberries.

"How did you know?" I've moved us to the blue velvet couch. The house is stifling now that the door's shut, and Lexie's hot on top of my thigh, but I'm not going to budge her.

"The mouse." Aunt Jane scratches behind Lexie's ears. I feel her body burrow toward the touch.

"Why would she bring it here?"

"To show it off. It's like a trophy."

"Ewww."

She shrugs. "Just the way it is."

My leg is starting to fall asleep. Maybe I will move Lexie for a minute. I slide her to the couch. She stirs but doesn't wake up.

Aunt Jane's washing her hands at the kitchen sink. "So Lexie's safe and sound. How are you doing?"

"I'm fine." Tomorrow's CSA delivery day. "Are you going to use the little baskets?"

"What?"

"The little baskets, you know, that you put them into. The square ones." I point at the cupboard where I've see them.

"Oh. You mean the quart containers. Actually, these go in pints. They're over here."

She opens another cupboard and takes out a stack of containers. I start scooping the washed raspberries into them. "You need forty-seven, right?"

"Um, right. Thanks." I feel her watching me. "How did you know I had forty-seven customers?"

"I heard you once." I shrug. "I never ate berries like these."

"No?"

"Uh-uh."

"That's a travesty." She pops one into her mouth.

I shrug again. "Just the way it is."

She laughs. "What did you think?"

"Better than the rhubarb."

"Maybe I'll make a farm girl out of you yet."

I stiffen, a handful of raspberries frozen in transition.

"Moving on is hard, I know," she says. "But this fear of grass, of being outside, it really is time to try to overcome that. I know you felt helpless today, and it doesn't—"

"Come on, Lexie," I say loudly, cutting her off. I drop the raspberries in the container. "I'm going up to my room now."

"Lucy—" she says, but I'm already up the stairs with Lexie in my arms.

Chapter 28
JANE

In July, the days are races against clock and heat. I set my alarm to beat the sunrise and head straight outside, savoring the solace, sights, and sensations of the farm: the pink horizon, the precise angles and lines of my vegetable beds, the dewy morning grass that reveals my footprints. Lucy still hasn't touched it. Today I'll start looking for a therapist. I'm no closer to an answer than the day she arrived, whether she's always been afraid, or if there was a trigger like the car accident. The other day she shut me down cold again, even after Lexie came back. And she wouldn't come out to help look. Right there, that tells me this goes pretty deep. She loves that cat more than anything but couldn't take a single step to help her.

I work steadily for two hours before my growling stomach sends me back inside for breakfast. Shedding my garden gloves on the counter to brew the coffee, I use the brew time to sort a stack of accumulated mail. Extension newsletter, full of articles on how to maximize my non-existent marketing program. Recycle. Junk mail, postcards for carpet cleaning when the carpet's been gone for five years. Recycle. A postcard with the latest Internet and cable promotion. Recycle. Glossy restaurant coupons. Recycle.

Wait. I pull the postcard back out. Introductory offer, high-speed Internet for $39.99 per month for one year, plus free installation. Forty dollars a month would be doable, I think. Once the estate money comes in, definitely. Lucy's birthday is next month. I checked the files in the desk after Rebecca's question. This could be her present. Normally I'm as anti-screen as Rebecca, but Lucy needs something to watch besides that funeral slide show. Plus when she starts school, they'll probably have to do research, for reports and things. I dial the 800 number for installation.

Birthday gift, check. Spurred on by the accomplishment and my first cup of coffee, I decide to tackle the therapy. From the drop-down list of specialties on the Blue Cross website, I check both "Social Worker, Pediatric" and "Psychological Counseling, Pediatric" and then type in the zip code. Filtering by in-network takes it down to four in alphabetical order. The first has an office in the Grand Traverse Commons, the former state psychiatric hospital that's being redeveloped into a residential-retail-office complex. Hmm. Irony or omen? Back in the nineteenth century, that whole place was a working farm, complete with fields, barns, and cows in the stalls. Patients worked as part of their treatment. I dial the number.

"Good morning, Sarah Fischer."

"Good morning." I glance at the clock: 8:05 a.m. and no secretary. With two words, Sarah Fischer's earned two points. "I'm interested in arranging therapy for my eleven-year-old niece."

"I'd love to help," she says after listening to my summary. "My recommendation would be exposure therapy."

She explains that she would try to desensitize Lucy's fear gradually, first by looking at grass with her, then touching, then walking on it. If the real thing is too overwhelming, they start a step backward, with pictures.

"It sounds time consuming," I say. School starts in about six weeks, and she needs to be able to walk to the road to catch the bus. They're not going to pull into the driveway.

"It can be. However, it's also a very effective tool for overcoming fears and anxiety that can manifest from a variety of causes—whether it's grief, upheaval from the move, a true phobia, or some combination."

"I see."

"Your niece has been dealt a pretty tough hand, Ms. McArdle. Long-term, that cause has to be isolated and treated, but in the meantime exposure helps overcome what's interfering with her daily life."

"All right. When's your first available appointment?"

More than two weeks away, as it turns out. Still, I take it. Besides being an early bird and a sole proprietor, Sarah Fischer conveyed an inspiring confidence. After we hang up, I swallow the last of my coffee and pull my garden gloves back on over my calloused palms. *A pretty tough hand.* Stepping outside, into the July humidity, I dredge up the memory of a Houston scene. The first, worst, anniversary. At breakfast, I'd told Jim what day it was, and he barely blinked. "It's best to move on, Jane," he'd said as Matt ran into the kitchen. "Get your tricycle, buddy," he'd told him. "Your mom needs to get outside."

I'd gone, following as Matt pedaled. If I understood Sarah correctly, that was exposure. To my child, to the duties of mothering. And I kept it up, for years after. Cub Scouts, Little League, school sports, birthday parties, I ticked off the boxes. Exposure after exposure. And what I also knew is a fact drilled into everyone who sets foot on the US Coast Guard Air Station in Kodiak, Alaska, in base orientation: you can die of exposure.

Chapter 29
LUCY

It thunderstorms off and on all week. Aunt Jane's in and out all the time, trying to fit in her work. I'm afraid Lexie's going to escape again, so I keep the doors shut and locked, too. This makes Aunt Jane mad.

"I come up to the house with my arms full, and you've locked the door!"

"Maybe you should use a wagon or something."

"That's not the point."

I turn away.

"This fear of grass is making you irrational. We need to figure out a way that you can overcome it. I've made an appointment with a counselor."

I think back to the field trip. Chasing Joel and Eli and falling on the grass. Mom's text. *Step on a crack, break your mother's back. Step on the grass, make her car crash.* What could happen to Lexie? She's all I have left. A counselor can't make me do anything.

"The sun's out again," I tell Aunt Jane. "You'd better get out there. Two more days till delivery, right?"

But the rain is back before dinner and goes on all evening. Aunt Jane sits in front of the computer, working on her records, she says, since she can't go back outside to work. By the time I go to bed, it's pounding the windows. Thunder is rumbling, lightning crackling, wind roaring. I film some of it, then fall asleep with Lexie at my feet. A huge boom of thunder jerks me awake at 3:19 a.m. The rain is louder than ever. I scoop Lexie up and clutch her to my chest, waiting for my heart to slow down. There's another crash of thunder, and the green 3:19 blinks off to black.

Not just the clock. My whole room. Totally black, scary black. All I can see are Lexie's yellow eyes. I pull the quilt around my shoulders.

"Lucy!" Aunt Jane is calling from downstairs. "Lucy, are you OK?" A flashlight beam bobs into my room. Along the walls the shadows of the trees whip back and forth.

I'm finally happy to see her, especially when she hands me another flashlight. Lexie immediately goes nuts, trying to bat away the beam of light, meowing as her paws keep missing.

"The power went out."

"I know."

"What a storm." She looks out the window. "Thank goodness I got all the raspberries picked. They'd be beaten into the ground tomorrow." She yawns. "Well, if you're OK, then I'll head back to bed."

I never said I was OK. I'm scared. But she's halfway down the stairs already when it thunders again, the loudest yet. Except it's not thunder. It's a tree branch! The old maple in the front yard punches a hole in the window glass, and the smashing seems to go on forever. I aim my flashlight at the end of the bed. The branch knocked over my mirror, too! It's facedown on the floor. Did it break?

"Aunt Jane!" I screech. The rain is blowing inside. *Please, don't let the mirror be broken.* I lean over the edge of the bed, trying to lift the corner. It's so heavy. My room isn't just cool now; it's freezing. As I lift the mirror, there's another tinkling crash as the glass falls out. No!

"Watch the glass!" Aunt Jane is back. "Shit. Come downstairs. Do you have slippers?"

I shake my head. I want to pick up some of the mirror glass, just one piece, but she grabs my hand and my quilt, too, and pulls me downstairs.

"You can sleep in here," she says, opening Matt's door. "We'll deal with the window in the morning."

I haven't been in here except to get encyclopedias since the first week. The blinds are still open a little, and the desk cover is cracked just where I left it. I lie down, pulling my own quilt tighter around me. Mom's mirror is broken. I'll never be able to picture us together again. Beyond the blinds there's a flash of light. Aunt Jane goes to the window and gasps.

"What? What's going on?" I jump off the bed.

"The downed power line. It's still live. See it sparking out there?"

I can see something arching and arcing into the air, throwing off sparks, between us inside and her parked truck. It looks like a possessed Fourth of July sparkler.

"We can't stay inside," Aunt Jane says, grabbing my hand, pulling me away from the window. "I just filled up yesterday. If that line hits the gas tank . . ."

I remember the fire in the pictures of the car crash I saw online, and scream.

"I'm sorry! I'm sorry. I didn't mean to scare you." Aunt Jane crouches down to look me in the eye. "Stay calm. We're going to be OK."

I nod, still seeing that picture.

"The side door's too close to the truck. We'll have to go out the front door, then go around to the barn. I'll call the power company from there."

"Can you carry me that far?" *In the dark? In the rain?* I silently ask.

"I will. It's the only way. It's far enough and there's no power there to worry about." She goes to the living room and tugs open the front door. I've never seen it open. It's still pouring.

"Got a jacket?" Aunt Jane is putting on her own.

"It's upstairs." Mom's hoodie is still under my pillow. Suddenly a pair of headlights swings down the driveway.

"Who on earth—" Aunt Jane stares as the truck approaches the house.

"It's Miguel!" I say.

"Must be on his newspaper route. He can't go near that power line!" She pulls up the hood of her jacket and runs outside. She points toward the house, and Miguel follows her.

"*Venga*, Lucy. Jump up here." He leans against the arm of the couch. I climb up on the cushions and perch on his rain-spattered back, just like the first day.

"Ready?" Aunt Jane's standing holding the door open.

"*Sí*. You lead with the flashlight. *¡Vámanos!*"

He jogs out into the blackness. Now it actually feels chilly. The rain is slowing down, and the clouds are starting to part, showing the moon, more than half but less than full, and the stars! So many more than outside my New York bedroom.

"This way. Watch your step." Aunt Jane is ahead. "Hurry. Let's get her where it's dry."

"*Espera*, Jane. Shine the flashlight over there," Miguel says, shifting me up, pointing with his head toward the house.

Aunt Jane points the flashlight at the ground, then follows it up. The line is dropping off a post on the roof.

"Look, part of the line is on your roof. We'll have to call someone pronto. It could start a fire."

"At least it's soaked through." She shakes her head. My teeth are starting to chatter.

"Come on, let's get her to the barn. Are you OK, Lucy?"

I'm exhausted. My room has a hole in it. Mom's mirror is shattered. It's July yet my teeth are chattering, so hard I can't even say no.

Aunt Jane pushes open the old barn door. I haven't been in here since the first day, to unpack the crate.

Miguel crouches down, and I slide off cautiously. My feet hit the hard concrete floor. Ahhh. It's stuffy and warm and safe here.

"Go on, now, Miguel. Finish your deliveries," Aunt Jane says, taking off her jacket and draping it over my shoulders. "We'll be fine."

"Call in that line. Where's the other end?"

"It connects to the line that runs along the back of the property. The main one that runs up and down the peninsula." She nods vaguely. "Probably where the outage occurred."

"I'll let you know what I find out." Miguel gives me a hug. I watch him climb into the truck, his lights disappearing down the road. Something bumps my leg, and I look down. Sarge. I don't know how he got out here. Was he even inside when the tree crashed into the window? Wait.

"Lexie! She's still inside!"

Aunt Jane's face falls.

"She must still be in my room! Go back, please!"

"She'll be OK, Lucy. We closed the doors, remember? She can't run out and get hurt." Aunt Jane squeezes my hand. "When it's daylight I'll go back and get her."

"But Miguel said the house could catch on fire! The truck could explode! And there's all the broken glass in my room. Please, don't leave her in there!" I'm crying.

"OK. OK. Easy." Aunt Jane squats down next to me. "I'll go get her."

"Really?" I stare.

"Be right back." She runs back over, up the porch, and in the front door.

I stare at the house, trembling even huddled inside Aunt Jane's jacket. Lexie, Lexie, Lexie. It seems like Sarge understands something is wrong. He stays with me, rubbing against my leg.

Hours pass. At least it feels that long. I wish Miguel hadn't left. It's starting to get a little bit light now. The blackness has faded to deep

161

blue. The rain has stopped. The power line isn't swishing and sparking in the air anymore. Nothing is moving. Where are they? How could I have forgotten Lexie?

Then the door opens, and Aunt Jane is jogging back to the barn, one arm folded against her chest. She's smiling. The next moment Lexie is in my arms, purring and nuzzling and safe.

"You found her!" I burrow my face in her fur. "Thank you, Aunt Jane. Thank you!"

"You're welcome." Aunt Jane picks up Sarge. "What a night."

I look up at the lightening sky. The stars that say I love you are fading. But everything I love is safe and sound, in the barn.

Chapter 30
JANE

Midmorning, a power-company truck comes to assist with the live line. I go out to meet him, leaving Lucy dozing in the barn. I folded a stack of those padded blankets from her furniture crate into a modified mattress, and she conked out under my jacket. My first daylight look at the damage leaves my heart pounding. The tree branch, a hefty primary limb, pokes through Lucy's window, aimed right where her bed sits.

"Storm was pretty bad. Knocked a lot of main lines down," the guy confirms. "Monday, probably, before we can get back out here to hook you up."

They're barely out the driveway when another truck bumps up. "Mel's Tree Service," the car door reads. "On call 24-7, reasonable rates, insured."

"Got a call about a tree?" asks the bald driver, Mel, presumably.

I raise my eyebrows and point to the house.

"All right. We'll take care of it. You want us to clean it up while we're at it?"

"What do you mean?"

"Make a clean cut, then seal it."

"Seal it?"

"Latex sealant. Keeps the bugs and disease out."

I wince. I'm not officially organic, but I try to keep as green as I can.

"This time of year, might help save the tree."

I shake my head. "I'll take the risk."

"Suit yourself."

It takes almost an hour to get it off the roof. "Where you want it?" Mel hollers.

"Out of here."

"Haul-away's extra."

"How much?"

"This size . . . all the way back to town . . ." He pauses, sizing it up. "A hundred bucks."

I wince again. Reasonable rates, my foot.

"Can't use it for firewood?"

"No fireplace." I rub my temples, thinking. Well, I could put firewood bundles in next week's CSA. The shares are for whatever the farm produces, right? This week, Plain Jane's has produced a bumper crop of firewood.

"Maybe I can, after all. How much to cut it up?"

He looks at the tree again. "Fifty."

Miguel could find me someone for twenty-five. "Just leave it."

He shrugs and climbs back in the truck.

"Might want to get someone out to take a look at your roof," Mel says as he turns the ignition. "That branch pulled off a couple layers of shingles. It's down to the weather wrap by that window."

He guns the engine and is gone.

On call, reasonable rates, insured, and bearer of bad tidings. I look up at the window, at the jagged glass sticking out of the frame, then think of Lucy in the barn. It could have been worse. Reaching for the phone in my pocket, I dial Miguel.

"*No hay problema.* I'll call Juan. He needs work. Cherry season is over."

"Aunt Jane!" I turn to the barn. Lucy's awake and waving from the door.

"What?" I holler back.

"I have to go to the bathroom!"

Another piggyback ride, which comes with the bonus of scratches on my neck and face from Lexie. Lucy refuses to leave her in the barn in case she runs away again. She's probably right to worry. After her two tastes of freedom, Lexie is no longer a docile house kitten. She fights Lucy the whole way, and my face is collateral damage.

"Sorry, Aunt Jane," Lucy says when I deposit both of them on the concrete square.

Last night she was scared. Now she looks contrite, and only about eight years old. A memory suddenly whooshes up, of a tearful Matt confessing to losing a new baseball glove. I swallow hard and clear my throat.

"Don't go in your room. The window's full of broken glass. Miguel's bringing someone to fix it." I swipe hair out of my eyes. Lexie's scratches sting as the sweat from my forehead seeps into them.

"I won't." She hesitates. "Are you going back outside?"

"I—well." I am hungry. Coffee would be a godsend, but there's no power. "Let's see what we can find to eat."

"OK." She smiles a little. "I'm hungry."

Miguel's truck pulls in while we're eating, Juan in the passenger seat.

"So, firewood today, *¿sí?*" Behind Miguel at the door, Juan heads to the tree with a chainsaw and an ax. "And I'll measure the window—" His words stop as he looks me up and down. "Your face. *¿Qué pasa?*"

"What?" I look at myself in the side-view mirror. The scratches are across my forehead and down my cheeks. My T-shirt is ripped, too, and another scratch follows the tear along my collarbone. I didn't even notice that, underneath the sweat and dirt.

"Lexie." I shrug.

He nods.

"I don't know what to do. I thought by now that she'd be over this, this grass phobia, or whatever it is." I swing my arm, taking in the scene.

"Time. She needs more time. Be patient."

She's got about five weeks. That's when she'll have to leave the house for school. Maybe Sarah Fischer will get a cancellation. I open the side door. "It's the only room upstairs," I say, waving him inside with his tape measure.

Miguel bounds up the steps with his usual energy. Outside, the chainsaw revs as I wash up in the bathroom. Steps. Time. Patience. Gradual exposure. I wrench off the faucet and run back outside.

"Stop, Juan!" What's the word in Spanish? I can't remember, but as I run over I slash my finger across my neck. "Stop!"

The noise stills. I reach for the saw.

"I have an idea!"

Juan was cutting it into logs, each about two feet long. I slice what amounts to a disc off the tree limb, only a couple of inches thick. Then another, and a third. Juan looks at me, puzzled. Miguel comes back outside.

"*¿Qué pasa?*" he says, looking between Juan and me.

"Look." I slice off two more, then lay out all five in a row. I step onto the first, then the second, then the third, fourth, fifth.

"Stepping stones," Miguel says, grinning. Stepping stumps, really.

"Exactly! We can make a path of these for Lucy, from the house across the grass."

To the driveway. To the barn. To the road, even, where the school bus will stop! But will Lucy be willing? I hand the saw back to Juan. "Cut enough to get to the driveway, and we'll give it a try."

The three of us line up ten of the wood discs from the concrete threshold at the side door to the matted rectangle of dead grass that marks where I park.

"*Bueno.* Now let's see if it works," Miguel says.

Please, please, let it work. I call for Lucy, who steps onto her three-by-three concrete square. Is her nine square feet of the world about to exponentially increase? What if she rejects them, just because it's my idea? "Show her, Miguel."

He looks surprised, but obliges, stepping onto the first circle. "*Mira*, Lucy." Then the next. He looks over his shoulder. Lucy's face reveals nothing. He goes the rest of the way, opens the door to the truck, and climbs in.

"Your turn," he calls back. Lucy hasn't moved a muscle. "*¿Conmigo?*" He goes back to the concrete square and holds out his hand. "*Está bien*, Lucy. You're safe."

Slowly, Lucy takes his hand. She lifts one foot—in the same Hello Kitty glitter flip-flops she wore when she arrived—and places it on the first circle.

One foot left behind on pavement, one striding forward. She glances at Miguel, who nods. Carefully, she brings the other flip-flop to stand beside its mate.

My breath rushes out in a gust. Miguel grins at her. Lucy smiles back, then takes another step. And another. Then she's swinging each foot in front of the other, not needing to pause together. Miguel is opening the truck door, and she's up in the cab, all by herself! She did it!

Even Juan, who has no idea what's going on, smiles. Miguel whoops, holding up his hand. Lucy smacks her palm against his in a high five. "*Fantástico*, eh, Jane?"

I don't say anything at first. Instead, I go over to the concrete square and wait.

Miguel offers his hand again, but she doesn't take it. Lightly, her eyes holding mine, she jumps onto the first circle. Then she's crossing back over them, one, two, three, and standing next to me on the concrete square, a little smile lighting her face. Following Miguel's lead, I hold up my hands, and she slaps them, a double high five. High ten.

Chapter 31
LUCY

It's Tuesday, the day Jared and his family come. I'm watching for them from the barn, with my iPad.

A line of tree trunk dots connects the house to the barn. There weren't enough from the branch that fell on the house, but Aunt Jane told Juan to go around and cut up some of the dead trees. Then she laid them out to the mailbox, to the shed with all her tools, and to here, where I can log on to someone else's wireless connection, some neighbor who doesn't know how to make their network private. Since we don't have power back yet, it's doubly good. The window's not fixed yet, either, so I'm still sleeping in Matt's room.

I go to Facebook. I haven't contacted Graciela since I tried at the farmers' market right after I got here, more than a month ago. She'll be done with boarding school and home with regular Internet. Her latest post shows a picture of her with Aunt Bonita, their arms around each other. *"¡Vacaciones de verano al fin!"* it says. It looks like summer vacation; she's wearing a bathing suit, and she's definitely got boobs. But she's thirteen. Will I look like that when I'm thirteen?

Aunt Bonita looks like Daddy. She's wearing sunglasses on top of her head and the same kind of smile that crinkles up her cheeks. She seems older, though, and I thought she was younger. Under the sunglasses her hair shows gray. Is that from worrying about the boys at school? In that letter I found in Daddy's box, she was worried about someone. If I were there, Graciela and I would watch out for—

"Hey, you've got an iPad. Cool."

I jump. Jared's standing in front of me.

"You scared me!"

"Sorry."

"I didn't hear your car." I look out the barn door.

"It's a Prius. They're really quiet."

He's looking at the Facebook page. "You know Spanish?"

"Yeah."

"Jared!" His mom is standing in the driveway, her hands on her hips. "Jane's ready for us now."

He rolls his eyes. "Wanna come?"

"Uh-uh." I shake my head.

"How come?"

"I, uh, sunburn really easily."

He looks skeptical.

"We tried it once. I got really sick, and Aunt Jane said I didn't have to anymore." He can't prove I'm lying, anyway.

"Oh."

"Jared! Now!"

"See you later." He pauses a moment. *"Adiós."*

"Adiós."

He goes out, kind of kicking at the grass with each step. I feel sorry for him.

I check Facebook again. Graciela's still not online. I switch over to the camera. My phone is almost full with all the videos I've made, but there's lots of room on the iPad.

I aim it out the barn door, at Jared and his family in the garden, and zoom in on them. Jared's brother and his dad are kneeling side by side in front of a row of dark-green leaves. His dad laughs, loud. Like Daddy did. I can't imagine Daddy dirty in a garden, wearing shorts and a baseball cap like Mr. Livingston, though. He always wore suits and black or brown shiny shoes, never tennis shoes. On the weekends he would wear khaki pants. Maybe a short-sleeve shirt in summer, like now. When he cooked, he always wore the long white *el cocinero* apron, to cover his clothes.

But even if he doesn't look like Daddy, Mr. Livingston acts like Daddy. He laughs and puts his arm around Jason and smiles, and even though I can see four other people, Aunt Jane and Jared and Jason and their mom, Mr. Livingston fills up the whole iPad. Missing Daddy fills up my whole heart. I look up at the blue sky that hides the I-love-you stars. I wish I could see them, because then it would be nighttime, the Livingstons would be gone, and I wouldn't have to watch anyone else's family together.

Now Aunt Jane is talking to Jared's mom. She nods and they all look over at me. I wish I could read lips. Now Jared is getting bigger, and bigger, and bigger. He's walking toward me. I stop recording.

"What are you doing?"

"You're done already?" I say, ignoring his question.

"Jane said I could keep you company. Tell you about school."

School. Here. My stomach gets that funny feeling. I don't want to think about anything else new. "Won't your mom make you come back?"

He shrugs. "Jane's the boss, she always says."

"Huh."

"I like Jane," he continues. "I don't like farming, but she's cool."

"She's cool?" I think about the cool people I know. Tomas, the weatherman at Mom's station. Alan, my swim teacher at the Y. Graciela, maybe. Not Aunt Jane.

He nods. "She doesn't stand over me all the time, telling me what to do."

"Try living with her." Aunt Jane isn't bossy, I guess. But she isn't much of anything—not nice, not mean. Not strict, not nosy. Not motherish.

"She said we could get some lemonade. If you want."

I hesitate, then remember the stepping stumps. I can do it now. "OK."

Jared walks alongside the circles back to the house. I watch him sideways, looking at his feet. He doesn't even notice the grass.

"So it's middle school, and you change teachers for every class."

"We did that at my old school. That's no big deal." I shrug.

"Every class?"

"Not every class, I guess." Ms. Kedzie was my main teacher, but I had different teachers for French, art, and New Media.

"And you get to pick some classes. Electives."

"We did that, too."

"Like what?"

"New Media."

"New Media?" He says it like the words aren't English. "What's that?"

"It was, like, a little bit of English and a little bit of computers and a little bit of art."

"All in one class?"

I nod as we go into the house. "We made stuff, like a class blog."

"Yeah?" Jared leans his elbows on the counter, sounding interested.

"We had a poetry contest and a photography contest. We put the winners on the blog. We made a video." The "New York, New York" video. I pour lemonade into two glasses.

"Cool." Jared sounds impressed.

I shrug. It didn't seem cool then; it just was. "What's your favorite subject?"

He takes a long drink. "It was recess. In elementary school."

"That's not a subject."

"It's my favorite, though. We had a zip line on the playground." He finishes the lemonade and wipes his mouth with the back of his hand.

"Huh." The school playground. It's probably grass. But he's talking about his old school.

"Yeah. And there's a big hill that goes down from the parking lot. In the winter, we went sledding."

"I've never been sledding."

"Never?" Jared's mouth falls open, and his eyes bug out. "New York sure is different."

"Meow." Lexie and Sarge arrive in the kitchen together and sit down in front of the door. Ever since Lexie followed him out, Sarge tolerates her a lot better.

"You've got cats." Jared sounds envious. "My mom's allergic."

"So was my dad." I say it without thinking.

"Your dad?"

"Never mind." I can't believe I mentioned him. Daddy and Mom are private, only for me to remember. I feel like the turtle we saw on our field trip. If you left him alone, you could see his head and he walked around. But when someone poked at him or picked him up, he pulled in his head and legs.

"My mom said your dad died," Jared says. "Your mom, too."

"I said, never mind." How did Mrs. Livingston know?

Sarge swipes a paw at the door and meows louder. So does Lexie.

"Looks like they want to go out," Jared says, moving toward the door.

"No!" I jump in front of him, blocking it. "Not Lexie. She's an indoor cat." I scoop her up. "Now you can open it."

Jared cracks the door, and Sarge darts through it. Lexie wriggles frantically in my arms, but I hold her tight.

"Close it now!"

Jared does and I let Lexie drop, but not before she's scratched my arm. A red line springs up on my skin.

"Ouch! Bad kit—" Wait. I said I wouldn't complain. I grit my teeth.

"What's the big deal? Why can't she go outside?" Jared follows me down the hall to the bathroom.

"She just can't. She's from the city." I wash off the cut. It really stings.

"So?"

"So she'd be scared outside."

"Doesn't look like it." Jared points to Lexie, who's plopped back in front of the door and is mewing as loud as she can.

"What if something got her? A raccoon or a skunk or—" I don't know, but there must be more animals around here. I peel the papers off a Band-Aid and lay it over the cut. I'll need at least three more to cover it.

"Looks like she can take care of herself," Jared says, nodding at my arm.

"Forget it, OK? She's my cat and she stays inside." I glare at him.

"OK, OK. Jeez," Jared says, backing up toward the kitchen. "I'm gonna go back outside."

"Wait! Don't open the door!" I run back down the hall, but it's too late. Lexie's gone again, leaving me stinging and alone.

I prop the door open and do the food-dish thing. Jared and his family leave. He doesn't come and say goodbye. Like I care, anyway. When Aunt Jane comes in, she's holding my iPad.

"Oh, thanks." I grab it.

"You should be more careful where you leave it," she says.

"I just forgot."

"OK." She looks at me for a long minute. "So you have a Facebook account?"

Did she see Graciela's messages? Does she know I want to run away to Mexico?

"Aren't you kind of young?"

She didn't see. I shrug. "Everyone does."

Or saw and didn't read. Or read and doesn't care. That's probably it.

She sighs. "Well, I guess if it's done, it's done. Just be careful about who you make friends with online." She puts her hat back on and heads for the door. Out to the garden. Again. Then she turns around.

"Juan's coming by later with new glass for your window. You can sleep upstairs again tonight."

I wonder if the mirror glass got swept up with the window glass. Probably. Nothing left of the mirror at all. And yes, Aunt Jane would probably actually be glad if I moved. *Step on a crack, break your mother's back. Step on the grass, make her car crash. Move to Mexico, Aunt Jane's happy to see you go.* Briefly, her smiling face as we did the double high five flashes in my head, but I push it away.

Juan shows up by himself instead of with Miguel, driving a beat-up old car that spews black smoke. He's smiling for the first time.

"Compré un auto," he tells me. *"Amo los Estados Unidos."*

He bought a car, so he loves the United States? Doesn't he have one in Mexico?

He shakes his head. *"No hay trabajo in México. Sí no hay trabajo, no hay dinero."*

No work, no money. Just like Esperanza said. But Graciela and her family have money. I'm sure of it. How else can she go to boarding school?

He carries the new pane of glass upstairs. I go into Matt's room to get my quilt and pillow and phone. Lexie still hasn't come back. I flop onto the bed with the "Bi–Ch" encyclopedia. Maybe the cat section will tell me how to lure Lexie back.

But it doesn't. I'm so tired of being alone! Now Jared won't be back for another week, and he's mad at me, anyway. Maybe I should have been nicer, but he was asking about Daddy. I can't talk about him. Or Mom. Like the turtle, I'm only safe in my shell, even if it's lonely inside.

The desk cover is still cracked the way I left it the first time I came in here. Idly I jiggle the knobs, trying to unstick it. It slides up a bit, then gets stuck on the right side. It's open enough now that my hand slides underneath, though. I feel a stack of papers and push it to the left, then jiggle the knobs again. Almost. I slip my hand underneath again and push the papers over more. The cover slides freely now, disappearing into the top of the desk. I did it!

Underneath are a bunch of folders with typed labels. Automatically I read them. Medical records, school records, insurance policies, bank and miscellaneous financial, car accident, apartment.

School records? Apartment? Aunt Jane doesn't go to school or have an apartment.

And then, tucked behind the folders, I see it. The bag, the gray velvet jewelry bag with the drawstring top that I watched Mr. Langley give Aunt Jane through the crack in the door.

"Lucy? *¡Ya he terminado!*" Juan's voice accompanies his footsteps down the stairs from my room.

All done, and just in time, too.

The gray velvet bag tucks neatly into my hand. Upstairs I hide it in my middle dresser drawer, in between two winter sweaters.

Chapter 32

JANE

It's been almost a week since the storm, and I still haven't filed an insurance claim on the roof repair. The big question is whether it'll be worth it. I doubled the deductible to twenty-five hundred dollars after Jim left, and I had to cut costs by any means necessary.

But when I pick up the phone to call in the claim, the message tone beeps, and William Langley's formal voice fills my ear. "Mrs. McArdle, William Langley in New York. I have some news on the apartment. Please call at your earliest convenience."

That could be good news for my roof repair bill. Of course, the money's to be spent on Lucy's behalf, but since the gash in the roof is right over her room, I'd say fixing it qualifies.

"Mrs. McArdle," he says, after the same cool assistant connects me.

"Jane, remember?" Mrs. McArdle hasn't existed for five years.

"Yes. Well. Jane, then. How is Lucy?"

"She's fine."

"Settling in well?"

I sit down at the kitchen counter, contemplating the question. Didn't voluntarily leave the house for weeks except on piggyback. She still spends hours with her earbuds and phone. On the other hand, she and Jared seem to have hit it off. She's showing a faint interest in the farm, even if she won't admit it. Lexie's runaway attempts illustrate acclimation, and now the stepping stumps have empowered Lucy. Going out to the barn today was a huge step.

"There's been some adjustment, but I think she's making progress."

"Good. Very good. That's the most important thing, after all."

His last words raise an antenna. "After all" is a justification.

"Every girl should have a sister, after all."

"After all, you still have your son."

"Matt's grown up and on his own, after all."

"You have news about the apartment?" I say.

"Yes. The apartment has sold."

"That's wonderful!" I sit more upright, unknown weight sliding off my shoulders. Roof repair, therapy for Lucy.

"However, in the process of arranging the closing, I discovered unknown financial obligations."

The antenna flickers up on my unease meter. "What do you mean, exactly?"

"A second mortgage. A rather substantial one, taken out more recently." He pauses. "One that the proceeds from the apartment were insufficient to cover."

"You mean they were—" I search for the word, trying to remember it from all the housing-crisis stories on NPR a year or two ago. "Underwater?"

"That's correct. The estate, however, was also in possession of the payout of the life insurance policies, both the network's and their personal ones. Those assets have offset the debt."

Why can't he speak plain English? "The life insurance paid off the second mortgage."

"Yes."

"And how much is left for Lucy?"

"Unfortunately, very little." He clears his throat. "Actually, the jewelry that Gloria bequeathed directly to her daughter constitutes her largest asset from the estate."

"The jewelry I brought back in April? That's all that's left?"

"If it wasn't already in your possession, I believe that, too, could have been lost."

In other words, Mrs. McArdle, things could be worse. After all.

Chapter 33
LUCY

It's CSA delivery day, and Aunt Jane brings back six of her bins.

"I just don't understand. If you know you're going on vacation, why wouldn't you arrange for someone else to pick it up? Such a waste."

"What happened?"

She keeps talking to herself like she hasn't heard me. "I should raise prices next year. Clearly, people don't value what they're getting."

"What don't they value? What's the matter?"

"Six no-shows today. I waited an extra hour, but either they're out of town or just forgot."

I look at the piles of stuff. Tomatoes and onions, carrots and cucumbers. I recognize a lot more than I used to, but I still don't know what the long green things and big purple blob things are.

"Now it will all just go to waste. I don't have time to do market this weekend."

"Why don't you put it out on that stand?" Every day cars slow down as they drive past, then speed off again. There're lots of stands like it on this road. Some are just a table with a money jar. Aunt Jane's is a lot fancier, with a counter and some shelves. I can see into it from my window. I don't know why she doesn't use it.

"I suppose I could." She sounds doubtful. "I haven't used that stand in two years."

"I could do it."

"You?" Her eyebrows climb up her forehead.

"Yeah!" The stepping stumps go out to the mailbox. The farm stand is right next to it, practically. I could sit out there and sell the things, like that Amish girl at the farmers' market. Earn money for a plane ticket to Mexico! Plus it would be something to do. I'm so, so, so bored. All of a sudden I really want to. "Please, Aunt Jane? Please, please?"

"Well, OK. Actually, I think that's a great idea. But we'll have to clean it off first. I'm sure it's filthy. Full of spiderwebs."

"Spiderwebs?" I pause. *Step on a crack, break your mother's back. Step on a spiderweb*—Nothing. "OK. How do I do that?"

"How do you clean?" She shakes her head as she disappears into the mudroom, returning with a yellow bucket, but she's smiling, too. "Soap and water. Fill that up at the sink."

Water splashes out of the bucket as I lug it along the stepping stumps, plus an armful of old towels. At the farm stand I hesitate because it's a long step from the stump to the platform part of the stand. I swing the bucket up first, then jump. The stand shakes a little when I land, but I feel safe. There's a slanty roof built over the platform, and some shelves under the counter. The back panel is painted red to match the counter, with white letters that say "Plain Jane's Produce." It's like a solid wooden boat, floating on the sea of grass.

"Here." Aunt Jane's voice behind me makes me jump. "Start with this." She hands me a broom. "That'll knock most of the cobwebs down."

I poke the broom into the back corners and sweep it across the white letters. It looks better right away. I jab it under the counter to sweep the shelves. It hits something that I drag to the front.

"Hey, what're these?" I lift a bunch of flat pieces of wood onto the counter. "Peppers, tomatoes, onions," I read as I turn them right side up. There's lots and lots, each with a word that looks like it's sort of burned into the board, with hooks sticking out the bottom and these little wire loops on top.

"The old signs," Aunt Jane says in kind of a dreamy voice. "Matt made these in Scouts. I forgot all about them." She traces her finger into the grooves of the *T* and *O* on the tomato sign, then takes the pepper sign and slides the loops of that onto the hooks of the tomato sign. "They hang below the mailbox, see?"

"Cool!" The signs hook together into kind of a ladder listing everything so that people driving by can see. I never noticed before that the mailbox post has its own set of hooks. "What do we have for today?"

"Tomatoes and peppers and cilantro. Those will probably be the most popular. People can make salsa," she says, sorting through the signs. "And eggplant and zucchini."

"What are those?"

"Those purple and green things you were looking at inside." She laughs. "Now get busy cleaning. Look, here's a customer already." A car is slowing, its turn signal blinking.

"Told you." I feel triumphant. "Oh, wait, it's just Jared." The quiet car is the giveaway. Most people drive noisy trucks like Aunt Jane's, but theirs hardly makes any noise at all. "Why are they back?" They were already here this week.

"Rebecc—er, Mrs. Livingston said she'd like to come more often. It's just her and Jared today. He can be your assistant." Aunt Jane waves as Mrs. Livingston stops the car and Jared gets out. I haven't seen him since he let Lexie out, and I pretend I'm busy with the broom.

"New project today," Aunt Jane says. "Jared, come with me to the house. I've got an old price list somewhere. When you're all set up, hang up the signs."

"Good to see you back in the realm of roadside commerce, Jane!" Mrs. Livingston says, laughing extra hard the way she does. "That's how

I first discovered Plain Jane's, you know. We were on our way to the lighthouse and I saw . . ." then I can't hear them anymore.

I clean the whole stand while Jared hauls out the six bins nobody picked up. The bucket water is practically black. I walk out to the last stepping stump and carefully hook up the sign.

"Good work," says Aunt Jane, bringing out a piece of paper and something that looks like another towel. She stands back and looks it all over. "Does this ever bring back memories."

"What kind?"

"Oh, good ones. You know, the good old days, when I had just started Plain Jane's." She nods at the mailbox. "Matt made me those signs as a Christmas present. Miguel built it. Everything was so exciting, my own business."

Exciting? Now Aunt Jane just seems worn-out and tired all the time. What happened?

She hands the towel thing to me. It's what she was wearing at the farmers' market that time we went, basically a pocket you tie around your waist. "Here's your change apron. There's not much, so ask people for small bills."

I have to cross the strings behind me and then tie them in front because they're so long.

"These prices are from three years ago, so add a dollar to everything," she adds, tapping the paper. "I think you're all set."

After she leaves, it gets quiet.

"Is Lexie OK?" Jared finally says.

"She's fine. You can just play on your DS. I don't need any help." I don't want to talk about why Lexie has to stay inside.

"I didn't bring it today."

"Oh." Figures. "Well, let's set everything out, then." I grab two handfuls of tomatoes from the first bin and pile them on the counter. One starts to roll off, toward the front. Jared catches it before it drops to the grass.

"Thanks." We make a pile of each thing, emptying three of the bins before we run out of space. I try to arrange them nicely, remembering how they set out things in baskets at the bodega. When we're all done I take a picture with my phone, admiring the bright colors.

"Want me to take a picture of you?" Jared says, reaching for the phone.

Of me? He walks in front of the stand, still not paying any attention to the grass. "Smile."

A minivan pulls over. Our first customer! Excitement flashes. Like Aunt Jane must have felt.

"Your tomatoes look fabulous. How much?" says the lady driver.

Aunt Jane's list says three for two dollars. "A dollar each," I tell her.

"What a deal. I'll take eight." She hands me ten dollars. "Keep the change."

Keep the change? Darn, I don't have anything to put them in, either. "Jared, go find some bags."

While we're waiting, I carefully put the ten-dollar bill and all the money I started with in the apron's right pocket. Then I take two dollars and move them to the left pocket.

Before the minivan's out of sight, two more cars have pulled over. They buy tomatoes and cilantro and zucchini and tell me to keep the change, too. Jared's unloading the other bins as fast as I'm waiting on customers. Every time, I put the money they give me into the right pocket and stuff the extra change into the left pocket.

When Mrs. Livingston comes out carrying two glasses of lemonade, we've sold all the tomatoes, peppers, cilantro, and eggplant, and only a few onions and zucchini are left. I can feel the rolled-up bills wadded into both pockets of the apron.

"Nearly sold out. You two make a good team," she says, handing us the glasses.

"Can I do this every week, Mom?" Jared says.

"Better than weeding, huh?"

"Way better." He nods, gulping his lemonade.

"Lucy, was he a good assistant?"

"Yeah." I have to admit it. Lots of people had questions, how to get to the lighthouse and restaurants and wineries and beaches. I didn't know but Jared did. I didn't realize anything besides the lighthouse was close by. It might be fun to go to a beach one day. No grass there.

"Well, we'll have to see what Jane says. We've got to get going now, though, Jared. Your brother's got a dentist appointment."

"Oh." He actually sounds disappointed. I follow them back to the house, sticking to the stepping stumps and fingering the money in the left apron pocket, trying to guess how much is in there. We had at least twenty customers, and almost all of them told me to keep the change. Mostly bills and a few coins. And it's mine.

I wave goodbye as their car glides away and then go inside, up to my room, to count all the money from the left pocket: $22.50. I fold it up and slip it into the gray velvet bag with Mom's jewelry, hidden with my sweaters. I'll need a lot more for a plane ticket, but I'm finally on my way to Mexico! I grab my phone to send Graciela a message. When I unlock it, though, there's the picture Jared took. The "Plain Jane's Produce" sign is behind me and all the vegetables arranged in front, bright and colorful, just like I'd hoped. The sun's shining down on everything, all bright and colorful like a calendar picture, almost. And I'm smiling.

Chapter 34

JANE

After lunch I count the money from the apron. Seventy-five dollars in little more than an hour. Not bad. Pretty good, really, considering the food would have otherwise gone to waste. Best of all is that Lucy initiated it. Two weeks ago she never would have tried something like this, but she actually seemed to enjoy it. Another good memory for the stand. I set aside five dollars for her, humming to myself.

With her and Jared occupied, I had a chance to talk to Rebecca about the news from New York, too.

"You mentioned you were a lawyer once," I said as we left Jared and Lucy at the stand.

"Once, yes. A lifetime ago." She gazed up at the cloudless blue sky. "At least it feels that way. Why do you ask?"

"I got a call from the lawyer handling Lucy's estate last week."

"Oh?" She looked at me sideways as she pulled on her gloves, automatically like she does now.

"It wasn't good news." I handed her a weeding fork. "Tomatoes today."

"I'm happy to listen." She cocked her head to the side, waiting.

"Well, when I was out there for the funeral, he told me Lucy would have a substantial estate once my sister's apartment sold."

"Define substantial."

"Four million dollars. That included all the investments and insurance policies and estimated apartment proceeds."

"That's substantial, for an eleven-year-old." Rebecca nodded.

"It was all supposed to go into a trust for Lucy until she turns twenty-one."

Rebecca nodded again. "And you're the designated trustee?"

"Exactly." Relieved that she was familiar with the process, I started talking faster. "He told me that the trust would be invested conservatively and that I could expect about eighty thousand dollars in annual income for Lucy."

"Hmm." Rebecca's eyes narrowed.

"Then last week he called to say that the apartment had sold. And they found a second, unknown mortgage on it. A 'sizable' one, he called it."

Rebecca's eyebrows rose, but she stayed silent.

"Basically, paying off that mortgage drained the estate. The sale price wasn't enough. Between insurance policies and investments, it's covered, but there's nothing left for Lucy."

"Nothing?" Rebecca echoed, a note of incredulity in her voice.

"That's what he said, except for some special jewelry of Gloria's. I brought that back with me in April, after the funeral. It's probably worth a few thousand, tops."

Rebecca exhaled. "He told you all this in a phone call? Have you received any paperwork, anything to corroborate this story?"

I shook my head. "He said I would, but nothing's come yet."

"Jane, you need a lawyer. ASAP." She stood up, her body literally overshadowing me in the tomato row.

"That's where I thought you'd come in." I paused and sat back on my heels.

"I'm happy to offer advice, but I haven't practiced in years, and I never handled probate. You need someone experienced. Preferably someone licensed in New York."

"Someone I can't afford, you mean." I turned back to the tomatoes. "What's a Manhattan lawyer run? Five hundred bucks an hour?"

She hesitated. "I don't think you can afford not to. You're talking Lucy's entire future here."

Which is exactly what I didn't want anymore! These big-stakes decisions, someone else's fate in my unreliable hands. Small stakes, or at least limited stakes, that's what I want now, limited to affecting me, myself, and I. This tomato variety or that one. To water today or hold out for rain tonight. Not the future of an eleven-year-old. I remember the big Amish family at the farmers' market, wondering if one relationship strengthened others. Maybe, but they're also all at risk if one cracks, the unpredictable fissures inevitably finding and rupturing weak points.

"I've still got some contacts in New York. I could find someone who would do a phone consultation, at least, with no obligation."

"I can't ask you to do that, Rebecca."

"You're not asking. I'm offering."

"Say I do it. Then what? They do the consultation, tell me I'm screwed. I've just wasted time."

"You don't know that. It's just due diligence. Like you do here, right? Researching the best varieties, all that."

I didn't say anything.

"At least let me talk to Paul about it. He still goes to New York a couple times a year. He may even know someone who knows this lawyer. What'd you say his name was again?"

That very afternoon, Martha delivers an oversize envelope with the return address, "Law Offices of William E. Langley." Inside there's half a dozen packets, most of them thick, held together with binder clips. Closing documents from the apartment sale. Insurance policies.

Investment statements. At the bottom is a heavy envelope, embossed with a gold seal: "Los Angeles County, California, Official Records."

Los Angeles County? I open it up.

"Certificate of Death," it says in ornate script. "Luis Alejandro Ortiz, male, age 44. Cause of death, primary: Blunt-force cranial trauma. Secondary: Internal bleeding. Date of death: April 13, 2011. Place of death: Scene of car accident."

Underneath his is Gloria's. "Gloria Santiago-Ortiz, female, age 36." Same causes, same date. Under place of death, though, it lists UCLA Medical Center.

On paper the words are so clinical, but their grisly implication sends a shiver through me. Gloria *did* crawl out of that car crash. Extracted, more likely. But she lived beyond the initial impact, which is not what Langley told either me or Lucy. I can understand why he told her the instant-death story, but why me? What other discrepancies would show up if someone checked things out? I call Rebecca and leave a message that if she or Paul can turn up a New York lawyer who would do a phone consultation, I'd like to talk to them.

I'll wait for expert guidance before I wade into the rest of it. I shove everything back into the big envelope and take it into Matt's room, where everything Lucy-related has sat since April. I add the envelope to the stack of folders under the rolltop. There. Out of sight, out of mind.

Except it isn't. All afternoon, I find myself thinking about Gloria. In my memories, something's always moving—her hair bouncing, mouth smiling, stride pounding. It's hard to imagine her even asleep, let alone passive and prone on an ambulance gurney. Was she conscious? Did she know Luis had already died? Did she realize her own death was near? Was she agonizing for Lucy? Was she remembering the second mortgage, excoriating herself for leaving her daughter bankrupt? Did she feel grief, loss, or pain? Was there ever any hope of saving her, or was the ambulance really a hearse? As it carried Gloria away, I imagine Lucy, on the other side of the country, oblivious to what was about to upend her world. And me, in the middle. Another Venn diagram, three circles converging this time.

The questions needle me into the evening, until I fall into a fitful sleep. A nightmare wakes me at five fifteen. It's still completely dark. We're definitely on the downslope to the equinox. Sitting up, I try to quell my pounding heart, grasping for the fragmented details. Something lost. Or stolen? A dream, or those questions about Gloria, still nagging? Propelled by the dregs of the dream, I cross the hall to Matt's room and open the desk.

Lucy's jewelry is gone.

Chapter 35
LUCY

Two customers called Aunt Jane to tell her to hold their deliveries this week, and there are three no-shows. I'm already at the stand with the money apron tied around my waist when Jared arrives.

"A pair of entrepreneurs, aren't they?" Mrs. Livingston says to Aunt Jane.

"Never too early to learn what it means to earn," she replies. "Jared, there's one more bushel basket of tomatoes by the house."

The first customer pulls up just as they leave. "Keep the change," the man says. This week I wear shorts with pockets so I can slip the change right into my own pocket. Using the neighbor's Internet, I sent Graciela a message that I'd found a way to get the money for a plane ticket to Mexico.

"Did you ask your mom about me moving there yet?" I typed.

She didn't answer, just sent back a bunch of smiley faces and this: *"Siempre quise una hermana."*

I never wanted a sister, but if it means getting a mother and father back, I'll take one.

"Ugh." Jared returns, lugging a giant basket full of tomatoes. A few spill out as he sets it down, rolling toward the road.

"Watch it! If they get bruised, people don't want them." He's put the basket on the scrubby gravel spot between the stand and the last stepping stump. The tomatoes rolled onto the grass, beyond where I can reach them. "Pick those up."

"You pick them up." He flops down on the grass and closes his eyes. "I carried them all the way here. I'm tired."

"You spilled them." I cross my arms. Another car is slowing down.

"So what." He keeps his eyes closed.

"Another car's coming. Come on. Get up," I hiss. "It looks bad."

"Jeez." He sits up and shades his eyes as he looks at me. "You're not Jane. You can't boss me around—"

"Shhhh!" The car doors are closing. It's a white Mercedes. A man comes out the driver's side, talking on his phone, and a lady in wedge sandals comes out the passenger door. She scoops up the spilled tomatoes as she approaches.

"What is this, a yellow-brick road?" she trills, lifting her sunglasses on top of her head. With her other hand she's swinging a giant straw bag with a skinny loaf of bread sticking out. She looks kind of like Mom did when we went on vacation, even though she's blond. A perfect sundress and sandals with straps wrapping around her ankles. Sparkly earrings and bracelets, a big diamond wedding ring on her finger. I haven't seen anyone that dressed up in Michigan. My own T-shirt and shorts are wrinkled. I stand up straighter and brush away a stray cat hair.

"Everything looks luscious. Just what we need for our picnic." She plops the tomatoes on the counter. "Fresh picked, I presume."

"Uh-huh," I say.

"Well, let's see, we're here through Sunday. There's the picnic, then salad for the dinner Friday. I'll need at least four and—oooh, bruschetta! Steven, we could make a divine bruschetta, couldn't we? Steven?"

The man is still standing by the car, talking on his phone. The woman sighs, then repastes her smile as she turns back to me. "Let's make it eight tomatoes, some of your garlic, some parsley, and two onions."

"That'll be fifteen dollars." I put everything in a bag.

"Steven. The young lady needs fifteen dollars." Her voice is sharp again. "Steven!"

He turns around, reaching for his wallet while he keeps talking, and hands me a twenty-dollar bill.

"Let me get you your change." I reach into my pocket.

"Oh, keep the change, dear," the lady says, tucking her hand into the crook of his elbow, tugging him back to the car. "Steven, for God's sake, we're on vacation. Can't you put the damn phone—" And the doors slam, the engine starts, and they're gone.

Five dollars! The most anyone's told me to keep. I turn away from Jared, trying to slide the money in my own pocket so he doesn't notice. I wore Mom's Venice Beach sweatshirt, too, which is long enough to cover the pockets.

"Fudgies," says Jared from the grass.

"Huh?"

"Those people. Fudgies." He stands up and waves his hand in the direction of the white car. "That's what we call tourists."

"How come?"

"They like to buy fudge." He stands next to me and leans onto the counter.

"They bought tomatoes. And garlic and onions."

"They're still fudgies. They had Illinois license plates. Probably from Chicago."

"So?" A few blades of grass have fallen off his shorts, onto the floor of the stand.

"You're, like, kind of one, too," he says, tipping his head back.

"Me? I never ate fudge."

"It mostly means somebody who's not from around here."

Oh. Well. That's for sure.

192

The

"Someday you'll be permafudge, though. Like us."

"Huh?"

"That's people who moved here from someplace else."

"Uh-uh." I shake my head emphatically. "I'm going to live in Mexico." The words come out of my mouth before I can stop them.

"No way." Jared's mouth falls open. "Mexico?"

"Yes way. My dad's family lives there." Another car is coming. "Never mind."

We're busy with customers for the next half hour. It feels good to have told him, even by accident, like it's a real plan, not just a wish or an idea. I manage to brush the fallen blades of grass off the floor with my shoe. Good thing I wore my high-tops today instead of flip-flops.

"Does Jane know?" Jared says as a minivan pulls away, headed to the lighthouse, giving us a break.

"Not yet." Not till I'm there. Carefully I slide the two-dollar change the lady told me to keep into my pocket. "I haven't got it all figured out, exactly. So don't, like, tell your mom or dad or anything."

"I won't." He looks kind of insulted.

"Good."

It's quiet for a second. I finger the money in my pocket. I have more than last week, maybe even thirty dollars in there. And if Aunt Jane gives me another five dollars, that's almost sixty dollars—

"How are you going to get there?"

"On a plane. Duh."

"Do you get an allowance?"

I shake my head. "But Aunt Jane paid me to do this last week."

"She did? That's not fair! I helped."

"But you're the work-share people, remember? It's your job."

"Still. It's not fair. How much?"

"Five dollars."

"Five dollars?" He laughs. "It's going to take you forever. A plane ticket to Mexico is, like, a thousand dollars."

"You're lying." I haven't looked online yet.

"Uh-huh." He shakes his head. "It's super expensive to fly from Traverse City."

"How do you know?"

"My dad is always complaining about it. When he has to travel for work, he goes to Grand Rapids. He always calls the airlines pirates. So never mind. Keep the five dollars." He laughs. "You'll need it."

Chapter 36
JANE

We're on our way to Paul's office. Rebecca said we should talk in person about finding a lawyer, but other things, too, apparently. I gave her the envelope from Langley last week, when Jared and Lucy ran the stand again. "Paul's done the due diligence" is how she put it when she called.

The bag of jewelry, however, is still missing. I scoured Matt's room, but it's simply vanished. I feel awful. I must have moved it later in the spring and just forgotten where. It'll turn up. It has to. At least Lucy is unaware. How could I explain misplacing all she has left of Gloria?

Paul's office is at the Grand Traverse Commons, just like Sarah Fischer's. Conveniently, he was available before our long-awaited appointment with her, so Lucy's coming, too. I told her she could hang out with Jared. I didn't say anything about Sarah or her plan for exposure therapy, but I've thought about it plenty. Coast Guard orientation aside, does that mean all throughout Matt's childhood, what I considered going through the motions—tricycle follower, Cub Scout den mom, baseball-game watcher—was actually the *right* thing to do?

I pass a cement mixer for the third time. The Commons redevelopment is well underway, except for signage. I've seen two backhoes, a cement mixer, a couple of dump trucks, and at least two dozen pallets of the signature pale-yellow bricks used in all the buildings, but I can't find any street signs.

"What's the address?" Lucy pulls her earbuds out.

"It's 500 Red Drive. Maybe I should call."

"Nah." She's pushing buttons on her phone. She looks up and out the window. "Turn right here."

"We already went that way once."

"Google Maps knows everything. Just turn."

She navigates me expertly to a small parking lot, where I recognize the Livingstons' Prius, and jumps onto the asphalt without hesitation. It can be so easy. Are we figuring this out?

Jared's in the reception room, playing with his iPad. "You brought yours, right? Dad's in there," he tells me, flicking his thumb toward another door.

"Good to see you, Jane." Paul stands up to shake hands. He doesn't look as different as I expected. The TBAYS T-shirt and shorts have been replaced with a button-up and khakis, but it's still several degrees of formality away from the pinstripes and tie I envisioned. "Have a seat. Rebecca got held up, but she'll be here any minute."

I sit down on a couch underneath a framed diploma. He's got an MBA from Northwestern. Across the room I see a membership in the association of Certified Financial Planners and another from the local chamber of commerce.

"All the bona fides on display, I see."

He smiles. "My decorator will be glad you noticed."

"Rebecca?"

"The one and only. They're supposed to foster an atmosphere of trust."

Hmm. "Well, if I didn't already trust you, I wouldn't be here."

"Right. Well, let's get to it, then." He holds up the envelope with all the documents. "Rebecca can tell you more about your legal options going forward. I checked into the financial transactions and did a little digging on Lucy's parents. Luis especially turned out to have some interesting history." He taps a stack of papers.

"Good news or bad news?"

"Let's start with the good," he says. "By and large, everything appears aboveboard."

"Meaning what, exactly?"

"No tax evasions, no shell accounts in other names. Nothing bogus or fishy about the transactions themselves."

"Then there is nothing left? Langley was telling the truth?" My stomach feels like an empty pit. If that's the good news, what's the bad?

There's a knock. "Sorry I'm late," Rebecca says. Through the open door I glimpse Lucy and Jared, huddled over their iPads, before it clicks closed again.

"Let's back up." Paul puts on a pair of glasses and reads from a sheet on the top of the stack. "The financial hole started in 2009. Luis made a large withdrawal from his 401(k) that year. In"—he shuffles some more papers—"August."

Almost two years ago. "How large?"

"Fifty thousand." Paul looks at me over the top of his glasses. "But by taking it before retirement age, he would have been subject to both taxes and early withdrawal penalties. That could have increased the eventual cost to more than sixty thousand dollars."

"OK, but that's still a lot less than four million."

"Right. Like I said, this was the start of the hole." Paul clears his throat. "Shortly after that withdrawal, Luis started regularly transferring money to an account in Mexico."

Mexico? "I thought you said there was nothing fishy."

"It's perfectly legal to transfer funds internationally," Rebecca says. "The money was deposited in a bank account belonging to Bonita Ortiz, Luis's younger sister."

Be nice to have a brother like that. Or a sister. Not that I'd have taken money from Gloria.

Paul continues. "The electronic deposits started at the rate of five thousand dollars per month in August and continued through January 2010. Then in February it jumped up to six thousand, and then to eighty-five hundred in March."

"And then it was gone," I say, doing the math. What could Luis's sister have spent fifty thousand dollars on, give or take, in eight months?

"Correct. Luis then withdrew the balance of his 401(k), another twenty-five thousand. That, too, went to Bonita Ortiz in Mexico, minus fees and penalties. Two ten thousand-dollar deposits were made in May and July 2010."

"Good grief." I stare at them. "Did Gloria know about this?"

"We don't know," Paul says. "It was an individual account. He wouldn't have had to reveal anything."

"But what comes next would have been a joint decision," Rebecca says.

"The second mortgage?"

"Right." Paul nods. "Taken in September of last year, against the equity in their Fifty-Sixth Street apartment. For five hundred thousand dollars."

"Half a million dollars?" I echo.

"Manhattan real estate," Rebecca says.

"Did that go to Mexico, too?"

"About half of it did." Paul flips through the papers again. "Between September and their deaths this past April, Luis sent two hundred fifty thousand dollars to his sister's account in Mexico."

"So is there two hundred fifty thousand somewhere for Lucy?" A swell of hope inflates me.

"Unfortunately, no." Paul looks directly at me again. "The apartment assessment seems to have been inflated. It didn't sell for nearly enough to pay off the second and original mortgages. They had some credit card debt, too."

"An inflated assessment is aboveboard?"

"Well, not exactly, but unfortunately, it's all too typical." Paul takes off his glasses. "Inflated values basically caused the housing crisis. And living on credit cards is practically the American way."

"So that's where the life insurance payouts went."

"Yes, and Gloria's 401(k), which wasn't much to speak of. In fact it looks like some of the creditors are still waiting in line."

Good Lord. Could an eleven-year-old wind up holding her parents' IOU? I try to digest it all. "Is that everything?"

"Not quite." Rebecca holds up a form that wasn't copied straight. The words "State of California" tilt toward the top of the paper. "The driver of the other vehicle in the car crash sued the limo company and the driver."

"Police are investigating," I remember reading online the morning after the crash. "Was he drunk?"

Rebecca nods. "Langley opted to join the suit on Lucy's behalf. For the time being. But as guardian, you could bring your own claim, too."

A conversation fragment surfaces. *Grounds for you to make a claim.* International bank transfers, underwater mortgage, credit card debt. Now a lawsuit. I rub my temples. Not even big-stakes decisions, these are megastakes. Mega Millions, that state lottery game. With odds probably as bad as the lottery's. "With creditors still waiting in line, if I sued, would Lucy get the money?"

Paul and Rebecca exchange a look. "There's a lot of factors—" Rebecca says.

"I think we're done," I say, standing up. File a lawsuit for Visa and Mastercard's sake? Try to keep up with legal minutia from two thousand miles away? No thanks. Our appointment with Sarah is in ten minutes, anyway. Rebecca jumps up, her hand on the door.

"You should look through the documents yourself. Think about it. You've got time. Paul, do you have everything back together?"

"Almost." He taps the stack of papers he was reading from against the desk, squaring it up and securing it with a binder clip. As he slides it into Langley's original envelope, something flutters from the stack. Rebecca and I both stoop to catch it, but she plucks what turns out to be an envelope from the floor.

"UCLA Medical Center," she says, reading the imprinted return address. "I don't remember seeing this before."

"Neither do I," Paul says.

"That's where Gloria was taken after the accident. Probably a bill."

Get in line, UCLA. I jam it in the larger envelope with everything else.

Chapter 37

LUCY

"Look," Jared says, tipping his iPad toward me as soon as the door closes on the grown-ups.

He's on an airline reservation website. Departure airport, TVC, that's Traverse City, I remember from my luggage tags coming here. Arrival airport, MEX. Round-trip cost, $849. My stomach elevator drops.

"Told you."

He doesn't sound mean, but it still hurts. How could it cost that much? Wait.

"Let me see that again." I look at the screen. "That's round trip. I only want to go one way."

"Oh, right!" Jared clicks a couple of times, and the figures change: $789.

"That's it?" I cross my arms and flop back on the couch, staring at the ceiling. I'm screwed. And stuck.

"My dad has miles with Delta." Jared's voice is below me now. He's sitting on the floor with the iPad. "Look."

Sitting up I look over his shoulder. He's logged in to his dad's Delta account. One hundred eighty thousand miles of credit.

"You could use that."

"Thanks." It is nice of him to offer. "But, um, then your dad would know."

"He never uses them up. Mom's always saying he wastes them."

"Jared." He doesn't get it. I try to speak patiently. "It's not that he would know we used the miles. He would know where I'm going."

"Wait. You're still not telling Jane?"

"Uh-uh." I shake my head.

"How come?"

"Just because." The thing is, I don't really know why. Part of me thinks Aunt Jane would be glad, but another part thinks she would try to stop me, since me living here was part of the will. Once, with Andrea, two au pairs before Deirdre, I wanted to stay longer at the zoo and hid from her when it was time to leave. The security people found me in the underground room, watching the penguins in their tank. Daddy was super mad, even though they found me in, like, an hour. What would he and Mom think about me running away from Aunt Jane? But I hate it. Well, running the farm stand was kind of cool, and with the stepping stumps I can leave the house now. Still. They'd never even visited before they decided to stick me here. They didn't know what a farm was like. Plus in Mexico I have a cousin my own age. *Familia.*

"But when you, like, go, she'll figure it out."

"By then I'll be in Mexico, with my other aunt and my cousin. It'll be too late." I say it more confidently than I feel. Graciela still hasn't said whether Aunt Bonita will let me live there. What if she says I can't?

Jared shakes his head. "How are you going to fly? They won't let a kid on alone."

"You can pay to go by yourself." Like the flight attendant who walked me to the Traverse City flight, carrying Lexie's cage. An unaccompanied-minor fee, I think it was called. Wait, could I take Lexie with me?

"So you need even more money, then."

Ugh. He's right.

"And how are you even going to get to the airport without Jane—"

"I don't know! I told you I haven't figured it all out yet."

"Haven't figured hardly anything, seems like."

"And I didn't ask you to, like, be my travel agent or anything." I wave my hand at the iPad.

"Jeez. Excuse me for living." He looks hurt.

The door handle turns, and the voices on the other side get louder. I think I hear my name.

"Close those websites," I hiss at Jared. It *was* nice of him to want to help. "Sorry. Look. I'll tell you more next time you're at my house."

He shuts down the sites just as the three grown-ups come through the door.

"Ready, Lucy?" Aunt Jane says in the fake-positive *Let's go!* kind of voice she uses when she wants me to do something. Out of the parking lot, she turns the wrong way.

"You were supposed to go left," I say.

"We've got one other stop to make."

"Where?"

She hesitates for a second. "To see someone."

"Who?"

"A—a therapist."

"A *what*?"

"A therapist. A social worker."

"Why?"

"To help you get over your grass phobia."

"I don't need any help!" I feel like the turtle again, just as he was picked up, his legs flailing before he pulled them into his shell. "The stepping stumps are fine."

"They've helped, yes. Now it's time for you to take the next step." She turns into a driveway. She doesn't seem to have any problem finding her way around now.

"Says who?"

"Come on, Lucy. You have to admit life's going to be a little confining if you won't walk on grass."

I cross my arms. The rhymes are running through my head. *Step on a crack, break your mother's back. Step on the grass, make her car crash.* I would have been fine if we'd stayed in New York. Or if I go to Mexico. *Much of Mexico, especially the northern regions, has a dry climate with infrequent rainfall.* I mean, when I go to Mexico.

She parks and turns off the engine. "Just try it once. Please."

I hesitate. She went after Lexie. Twice. But that was different—Lexie was really gone. She tricked me into coming here! I'll bet this trip wasn't about financial stuff at all.

"Uh-uh." I shake my head. "You just wasted your time," I add, the ultimate Aunt Jane sin, and put my earbuds in.

Still, I can hear her sigh. "Fine. I'm going in anyway, to cancel the appointment."

Her door opens, then bangs shut. I stare out the window, thinking about the $789 ticket and Graciela's school in the country. In the north, in the dry climate. I'll bet it's on Facebook. Maybe I can find some pictures. I lift the cover on my iPad. They probably have Wi-Fi all through here. Aunt Jane's door opens again.

"Hello, Lucy."

It's not Aunt Jane's voice. My head jerks up, and an earbud falls out. A lady with gray hair like a grandma is standing in the open door, looking at me across the seat, but I never saw a grandma who looked like this. She's got glasses hanging around her neck on a beaded chain and this long, flowy purple dress on.

"I'm Sarah Fischer," she says, putting on her glasses and peering in the car at me. "Your aunt tells me you don't want to come to my office. I came to see if I could help you reconsider."

I shake my head, putting my earbud back in. I'm not saying a word.

"It's an asphalt parking lot." She taps her foot on it. "And the side-walk goes straight to the door." She cocks her head in a question.

I shake my head again. I'm staring straight out the front window, but I can see her from the corner of my eye. Aunt Jane's standing there, too, holding a white plastic bag that she didn't have before.

Sarah waits for longer than I expect. "All right, then, not today. Maybe we can try another time."

"I'm not coming back here again," I say.

Aunt Jane sighs. "Sorry to have bothered you."

"Not at all." Sarah takes off her glasses. "Call if I can be of help in the future."

She walks down the sidewalk while Aunt Jane opens the back door and puts the white bag in the back seat. Usually she just throws stuff over the front seat into the back. Why's she being careful with this? What's inside?

I stare out the window, wondering, until Aunt Jane pulls into a gas station. Twisting around, I keep my head low as I tug the bag along the seat, toward me. It has a drawstring top that's twisted and tucked underneath whatever's inside, something heavy. Aunt Jane's still busy with the pump. Quickly I work it open. It smells funny, too, a wet, outdoorsy smell. I peer into the opening.

Grass! A big hunk, sitting in a black tray, like a takeout container. I can't help but screech as I snatch my hand back and hunker against my door, as far away as I can get.

"What's the matter?" Aunt Jane's face is in the window.

"You have grass in there!" I point at the back seat.

Aunt Jane's gaze follows my finger. I pulled on the bag when I jerked back, and now it's balancing on the edge of the back seat, almost tipping. She opens the door and rearranges it like it was.

"It's called sod."

"Sod?" What kind of a word is that? "What's it for?"

"Usually, people make lawns out of it."

"Why do you have it?"

"I asked Sarah if we could take it home. The idea is that you touch it—"

"What!"

"Just for a few seconds at first. Then longer and longer. By controlling the time and circumstances, it's supposed to help you learn to control your grass fear."

"No way." I am not touching that thing. At least the name fits. I can hear Deirdre. *Sodding rain. Sodding traffic.*

Aunt Jane opens her mouth, but just then the gas pump makes that thunk sound, all filled up. She shuts her mouth and turns to hang the nozzle back up.

Sodding farms. Sodding aunts. All the way home I keep my earbuds on and my gaze out the window, ignoring that sodding sod in the back seat.

Chapter 38
JANE

East Middle School is brand new. It looks like a jail, all solid cinder-block walls with a strip of glass-block windows. There's grass around, but sidewalks lead from parking lot to door. As I pull into a spot, I don't see a playground. Maybe they don't get recess in middle school. I hope not, after the therapy fiasco. Lucy hasn't touched the sod, not even the bag, which has been sitting in the mudroom for nearly a week. Probably all dried out by now. I should return the tray part to Sarah.

She didn't seem surprised Lucy refused to go in. Said a lot of people were hesitant about therapy. I have to admit I get that. Before we left Alaska, the doctor wanted me to see a therapist. I made excuses. No babysitter for Matt, needing to pack up for Jim's transfer. *I'm fine, don't worry.* But the real reason was that I was afraid. Pain and guilt I under-stood. Deserved, really. I was *supposed* to feel bad. What's worse than a mother losing her own child? So how could I trust a process that was supposed to make me feel better?

The secretary is writing on a whiteboard, back to the door, but her head swivels as I open it. "Good morning! How can I help you?"

"I'd like to enroll a new student."

"Wonderful!" She finishes her sentence—"Find Local Difference lunch source"—and turns to a filing cabinet. She glances inside a folder and then hands it to me. "We'll need all the forms filled out completely, plus a copy of the birth certificate and immunization record before the first day of school September 6. And what grade will the new student be entering?" She's opened another folder and looks at me expectantly.

"Um, seventh. She's turning twelve next week," I say.

"Very good. We'll look forward to meeting—" She makes a note inside her folder and then looks up at me, eyebrows raised. I feel like I missed a cue.

"Excuse me?"

"Her name?"

Oh. "Lucy. Lucy Ortiz."

"Lucy." She writes it in the folder, then holds out her hand. "I'm Mrs. Montgomery, the principal."

I shake her hand, feeling confused again. "I thought you were—"

"The secretary. Of course." She shrugs. "No full-time secretarial help till two weeks before school."

A DIY principal. I feel more at ease.

"And you are Mrs. Or—"

"Uh, no. McArdle. Jane McArdle. I'm Lucy's aunt."

"I see." The principal hesitates. "It is district policy that enrollments are accepted only from parents or guardians."

"That's me. Her guardian. She moved here to live with me in June, after her parents died."

"Oh dear. I'm so sorry." She shakes her head, then gestures to a chair. "Do you have time? I'd love to find out a bit more about Lucy. That's a tough situation."

Tough. The same way Sarah described it. As I recount the events since April, that seems pretty accurate. Mrs. Montgomery seems to agree, shaking her head at all the appropriate intervals.

"What a tragedy. Kids are resilient, though. Getting back to a school routine will be a huge help, I'm sure."

I nod.

"Has she been able to make any new friends? Peers are so critical in these situations."

"There's one boy, Jared Livingston. I believe he's going to be in seventh grade, too."

"I'll check and see what I can do about arranging for them to share a few classes." She makes a note. "I think we can give Lucy a very strong fresh start. Anything else you can think of?"

"There is one more thing." I hesitate. The grass phobia sounds so ridiculous. Just then her phone rings.

"I'm sorry, it's the main district office. I've got to take this."

While she talks I peruse the folder. A sample schedule reveals that, indeed, there is no recess in middle school. Policy booklets. Forms galore. I start to fill one out but get stumped on the second page, the blank for a backup emergency contact person. Esperanza? She'll be going back to Mexico soon. Miguel drives the school bus. Rebecca? I've only known her three months. Is my pool really so shallow? Closing the folder, my gaze falls on the to-do list on the whiteboard. Besides finding the Local Difference lunch source—interesting—there's "install security camera software," "review bus routes," and "set up media lab." A countdown figure says Mrs. Montgomery has twenty-five days to get it all done.

Media lab. That sounds like the class Lucy mentioned when she arrived, New Media. Where they made videos and stuff. I feel a little surge of triumph. So there, William Langley. Little old Traverse City can match the curriculum of her New York school. Plus she'll have some classes with Jared. A new routine, with some familiarity. A strong fresh start, like Mrs. Montgomery said.

Then maybe I shouldn't reveal the grass phobia, after all. It just saddles Lucy with the expectation she can't get over it. She sees how

Lexie's adjusted. She's doing the stepping stumps herself, and the farm stand. She won't go to see Sarah, but with no recess, there's no imminent need to worry about it at school.

"We'll check in next week, then," Mrs. Montgomery says into the phone, and hangs up. "I apologize, that took longer than I expected."

"It's fine," I say.

"So, you were saying there was one more thing?"

"Yes." I take a deep breath. "Tell me about this local lunch program source you're looking for?"

Chapter 39
LUCY

On my birthday I wake up to Lexie pawing my pillow and the sun streaming in my window. The rest of the house is quiet. Just like always.

I'm twelve years old today. On my other birthdays, Daddy would burst into the room early. "*¡Feliz cumpleaños!* A birthday should be celebrated all day!" he'd say, handing over flowers or balloons or a doughnut with a candle in it.

Mom was at work in the morning. But Daddy would have her show on while he made breakfast, and she always wished me a happy birthday on the air.

"*Hoy es un día especial en mi casa,*" she would tell the weatherman, Tomas.

"A special day? *¡Díganos, Gloria!*"

"*Hoy es el cumpleaños de mi hija.*"

"Your daughter's birthday? *¡Fantástico! ¡Feliz cumpelaños, Lucy! ¿Cuántos años tiene?*"

Siete, ocho, nueve, diez, once. I remember back at least that far. Last year Daddy's breakfast was chocolate-chip pancakes. Each pancake had eleven chocolate chips.

I carry Lexie downstairs. No flowers, no balloons, no chocolate-chip pancakes. Even though I knew there wouldn't be, even though the empty house looks exactly like it always does, it feels worse today, like I could vanish into the vacant kitchen and no one would even notice. If no one counts the years, do they count at all?

Through the window, Aunt Jane's hat is moving around the garden, bent over the rows. She stands to stretch. Catching sight of me, she waves, then flashes her garden-gloved hand twice. Ten minutes? That's new. Usually she stays out there all morning. Before it gets hotter than she likes.

A pan of blueberry muffins is on the counter. Lexie jumps up to sniff. "Shoo, Lexie." I take one and pour myself a glass of juice. They're delicious, so much sweeter than the ones I remember buying at the deli. Almost as sweet as the chocolate-chip pancakes.

"Morning!" Aunt Jane comes in, smiling, hanging up her hat. Morning is her favorite time. It's when she's most relaxed, anyway. Maybe it's because she hasn't fallen behind yet.

"Morning," I say, like always, like it's any other day.

"Happy birthday!"

She remembered! "Thanks."

"Did you see the card?" She points over to the computer. A card with my name is propped on the keyboard. I didn't notice that before. Opening it, I read, "Happy birthday," above a cat holding a bunch of balloons. On the inside it reads, "Hope your day is just purr-fect." Below that, Aunt Jane has written "Log in!" and a little smiley face.

"Go on, do it." She seems excited.

I type the login and password. The little wheely thing spins. Then the Google search page pops up, in seconds instead of minutes. No buzzing or whirring noises from the computer, either. It stays quiet. I look at Aunt Jane.

"I upgraded to high speed!" she says. "Now you can use your iPad inside, or the computer, and it won't take forever. You can watch videos—"

"That's my birthday present?" I interrupt.

"What? Well, um, yes." Her smiles wavers. "I thought you would like it. You spend so much time in the barn. And I've vowed that this fall I'm finally going to work on a website for Plain Jane's. So it'll be useful for me, too." She pauses. "Do you like it?"

"Yeah. I just, uh, wasn't sure." Because everyone else already has high-speed Internet because it's normal, not because of a birthday! Because a birthday present is something special for the birthday person, not something that's useful for other people!

"Oh. OK. Well then. Good." She clears her throat. "I planned a little party for tonight, too. We're meeting Miguel and the Livingstons at Osorio's. I'll make a cake, and we can come back here for dessert. What do you think?"

Osorio's has pretty good Mexican food. Esperanza took me there once. But I always got to pick the restaurant for my birthday dinner. I would wear a new birthday outfit. Daddy would tell me I looked beautiful, so grown up, that he couldn't believe how big I was getting, and make a big deal out of opening the taxi door for me.

The ding of a text message jars me out of my reverie. It's Phoebe! I haven't heard from her since a postcard the first week I got here.

Happy birthday! Can you Skype?

I guess I can, now that the Internet actually works.

"Go ahead," Aunt Jane says. "I'll start the cake."

I carry Lexie up to my room and put the chair in front of the door so she can't get out. She meows and looks at me over her shoulder pitifully.

It's so good to see Phoebe. She's sitting on her bed, her hair in two frizzy pigtails, surrounded by about a hundred stuffed animals.

"Lucy!" She grins and reaches out toward me, as if to touch through the screen. "Happy birthday!"

"Thanks." I can remember exactly what it was like to sit in her room, the window that looked out on Ninth Avenue, talking about school, watching videos, playing around with making our own. I miss that so much, it feels inside like it does when Lexie accidentally claws me.

"I miss you," she says, like she can read my mind.

"Me, too."

"I wanted to call, or text, but my parents kept saying no. That I had to let you get used to living with your aunt."

"It's hopeless." I sigh. Lexie is meowing and batting the door. No, Lexie, you're staying with me on my birthday.

"What's it like? It's country there, right? Is it really that bad?"

"Guess what she got me for my birthday?"

Phoebe shrugs. "Books? Gross clothes?"

I shake my head. "High-speed Internet."

She looks confused. "That's a birthday present?"

"She thinks it is."

"She didn't just already, you know—"

"Have it? Nope. And that's not all." All the flaws and injustices of Old Mission come pouring out. "We're, like, twenty miles away from the nearest teeny little town. There's only two movie theaters. I always have to ask for a ride, and since she's always working in her garden, I hardly ever get to go."

"What about buses? Or trains?" Phoebe's eyes grow wide.

"There's some buses, but they work weird. You have to call them, they don't run on a schedule."

"So then you're just, like, stuck at home all day?"

"Pretty much." Lexie keeps meowing and batting the door. She wants to get out, too. Fine. I open the door, and she darts into the hall.

"Oh wow, Lucy." She sinks back into her stuffed animals for a minute, then sits up, excited. "But guess what, my mom says that you can come visit us sometime!"

"Yeah?" Being back in Phoebe's room, lying on her bed, watching videos, just hanging out *together* sounds so good. "When?"

"Winter break, she said."

"That's not for a long time."

"Yeah." She looks down at her hands. "Are there *any* other kids around?"

I start to shake my head, then remember Jared. "Well, one. He comes out here with his family. To work in the garden."

"A boy?" She sits up on her bed. Her shirt slides down her shoulder a little bit, showing a thin pink strap. A bra?

"What's his name? How old is he?"

"Jared. He's going into seventh, too." When did Phoebe start wearing a bra?

"He comes to work? Why?"

"His mom makes him. His whole family. It's for some kind of deal on the vegetable deliveries Aunt Jane does. I don't get it, exactly."

"What's he like? Is he cute?"

Cute? He's just—Jared. "I don't know."

"Do you have to work, too?"

I shake my head. "Well, sometimes I help her get the stuff ready. Wash it, divide it up. She delivers it to the customers once a week."

"They don't just go to the grocery store?" She tugs her shirt over the pink strap.

I feel dumb, talking about this. Who cares? "I don't know. I told you, I don't really get it."

"Sorry. I just—I want to know what's going on. I wish you hadn't moved away. I've been so bored all summer."

"Yeah." We stare at each other for a minute.

"At least school starts in a week," she says. "I'm going to have Mr. Glass for homeroom this year."

"A man teacher. Weird," I say.

"Do you know your teacher?"

I shake my head. "School doesn't start until September." Almost three weeks.

She starts to answer, but then I hear a knock and her mom's voice. "Phoebe? It's time to go!"

"Just a second. I'm talking to Lucy. It's her birthday."

"Lucy! Happy birthday, dear. How are you doing?" Mrs. Solomon's face peers into the camera suddenly, covering up Phoebe's. She has big boobs. Maybe that's why Phoebe already needs a bra.

"Hi, Mrs. Solomon. Thanks. I'm fine."

"Mom, move back. I can't see," Phoebe says.

"Oh, I'm so glad you're adjusting, dear. It's been so hot in the city this summer. It's probably much more pleasant there, with the water and the fresh air." She moves out of view. "A couple more minutes, Phoebe, and then we have to go."

"'K, Mom."

"Bye-bye, Lucy," she says, waving a hand back in front of the camera. "Have a wonderful birthday!"

"Thanks. Bye," I say as the door closes.

Phoebe shakes her head. "Sorry."

"No, that's OK. It was kind of nice to see her." She acted more motherly in thirty seconds than Aunt Jane has, ever. "Where are you going?"

"School shopping. We got the list." She waves a piece of paper.

I can see our school's name on the top. No, Phoebe's school. Not mine anymore. My throat squeezes tight, and my stomach elevator starts falling. "Oh."

"I wish you could move back, Lucy."

I feel like I could cry right there, but Lexie suddenly comes back, climbing into my lap.

"Is that Lexie? Wow, she's gotten so big!"

As I'm scratching behind her ears, my stomach elevator stops. "I know."

I see her look to her door and frown. "Mom's yelling. I better go. Happy birthday, OK?"

"Thanks. Bye." How am I supposed to make my own birthday happy, I wonder as Phoebe's face shrinks to her Skype icon, a picture of her skating at Rockefeller Center that time we went, her pigtails sticking out below a hat with a huge pom-pom. I'm only twelve, but it feels like that picture was a hundred years ago.

Chapter 40
JANE

In the fridge I rummage for the carrots I picked just last night. My specialty, carrot cake. Preheat the oven to 350, and then from memory I pull the ingredients. Butter, white sugar, brown sugar, hardened in the canister since I used it last—what, at Christmas? Sugar doesn't go bad, though. Eggs. The kitchen computer screen is black, back in sleep mode, the birthday card lying facedown next to it. Lucy was underwhelmed by the Internet gift, that's for sure.

I set out the cream cheese to soften for the frosting, then root out my old mixer. A wedding gift, speaking of gifts. The outlet is loose, and the plug slips out a few times, but otherwise it works fine at twenty-four years old. Make do, that's what I always did, and should have with the Internet. Should have asked Rebecca what to get her, or Esperanza. My maternal instincts backfire again. I never was good at gift giving, but what's funny now is I feel as disappointed as Lucy looked.

Vigorously I slather my old layer cake pans with shortening and pour the batter in. Haven't used these in years, since Matt's last birthday at home, probably.

My eyes shut involuntarily, blocking the gloom-tinted memories. Matt's birthday is February 4, just two weeks after the Alaska anniversary. I couldn't say stillbirth, not even to myself, the two syllables packing double cruelty. *Still* as in motionless, what I failed to notice in the hours before. And *still* as in always. Forever. As soon as New Year's passed, the dread would start.

Grief stalked me after the anniversary date, too. Matt had already passed walking and talking, but every new milestone—riding a tricycle, first day of preschool, first lost tooth—was marked with a shadow, mourning for what I'd miss with my daughter. Poor Matt.

I shake myself. Don't go there. Not today. There's the party to get through yet. I slide the pans in the oven and set the timer on my watch. Forty-five minutes. Enough time to scout out the old apple trees along the back of the property, where the power line fell.

There are eight hundred kids at East Middle School, and the district got a pilot grant to serve them local produce once a week. Mrs. Montgomery estimates a quarter to half of them will try the Local Difference items, which are served Wednesdays. The menu's written a month out, though, so I need to let her know what I'll have now. Carrots and potatoes, yes. Probably some squash and tomatoes. Broccoli. But apples are what she really wants. The trees haven't been tended in years, but they're still bearing. Bearing at least two hundred apples a week through October, that's what I hope.

I follow the stepping stump path to the barn, then cut across on the verboten grass. This could be a godsend. Lucy's window is fixed, but the twenty-five-hundred-dollar deductible on my homeowner's is haunting me now, a tarp battened down with two-by-fours is all that's covering the damaged part of the roof. The adjuster estimated fourteen hundred dollars. I've got about one thousand in my savings account. The tarp will do for another month, end of September at the outside. It's got to be done before then, so a little extra cash flow from the school would be perfect. It's not going to replace eighty thousand dollars in interest income, but I couldn't really fathom that much money, anyway.

What kind of debts could Gloria and Luis have had that would gobble up the entire estate? Deirdre seemed like a luxury, but Lucy told me she always had an au pair. So they must have budgeted for her.

Still, who am I to preach about poor financial planning? Before Jim left, it was in my Plain Jane's plan to get the apple trees pruned and back into managed production. Never got around to it. A half-million-dollar second mortgage, a twenty-five-hundred-dollar insurance deductible. It's just a matter of scale, and timing, too. Bad timing on the Internet service, but it's too late now.

The apples look better than I'd hoped, though a little small. There's a few weeks yet before picking. They could bulk up, especially if I thin out some of the leaves, let the light get in better. I snap one off and take a bite. A little tart, but again, it's early. I count along the branch. Just two or three of the trees would serve Lucy's school. Mrs. Montgomery gave me the food service director's card. Munching my apple, I head back to the house to make a call.

In the kitchen, the papers from school have gotten mixed up with the legal packet I reviewed with the Livingstons. Lexie was probably prowling up on the counter again. As I paw through the pile for the business card, the envelope with the UCLA Medical Center logo flutters out of Paul's clipped stacks.

I didn't notice before, but it's hand addressed to the family of Gloria Santiago-Ortiz. Maybe not a bill. What else could it be? Lifting the flap, I pull out two sheets of lined notepaper. The first has just three handwritten sentences:

"This letter was dictated by Gloria Santiago-Ortiz during her transport to UCLA Medical Center on April 13, 2011. I am enclosing it with her hospital records. My sympathies."

It's signed only, "LA County EMT."

The second sheet is covered front and back in the same handwriting. After the first word, I can hear Gloria's voice.

Janey—
They won't tell me about Luis. I think he's already dead.
If I go, you get Lucy. I'm sorry. I should have told you. I
couldn't. Take care of her. You will, won't you?

The next part is in blue ink, like the EMT stopped, then started writing with a different pen. Was Gloria at her end, begging him to go on?

You were such a devoted mother. I was afraid. I'm
sorry. Too late now. Forgive me. Just take care of our baby.
Watch out for Nando. His family must not—

The end. Did the ambulance arrive and the EMT need to rush her out? Or did he drop first the black, then the blue pen as Gloria coded on the gurney?

I read it again. My chest and head feel like the bay in November, a roiling tumult of waves. The handwriting swims off the page, the loops and swirls of the letters like the mesh of a net, dragging me under.

Why couldn't she tell me they picked me as Lucy's guardian? Why did they pick me? *I'm sorry. Forgive me.* So she felt guilty, too. But for what? Afraid of what? Who's Nando? Why should I watch out for him? Is it even a him?

I imagine her face, her amends recorded, entrusting me. *You will, won't you? Devoted mother.* She never knew the truth, how guilt was my puppeteer, putting me through the motions with Matt. How my grief transformed to resentment upon Lucy's birth, trapping me. I thought I was *supposed* to feel bad, because until now, I never thought anything could be worse than a mother losing a child.

There is, and Lucy knows it: a child losing her mother.

Chapter 41
LUCY

At my birthday dinner, Jared sits across from me. Is he cute? He has brown hair and freckles. He's not skinny, not fat. He's dressed up a little bit—he always wears T-shirts, but tonight he has on a shirt with a collar. But he still seems just like Jared. I stop thinking about it and listen to Miguel, who's next to me and ordering for all of us in Spanish, joking with the waitress, who looks kind of like Mom. Not as pretty, but dark curly hair and a big smile.

"*Voy en primavera,*" he tells her.

"*¿Toma fotografías?*"

"*Claro, me encantan las fotografías, ¡tomo muchas!*"

"*Gracias, Miguel.*" She smiles and pats him on the shoulder.

Why does she want him to take pictures? Where is he going in spring? I ask after she leaves.

Miguel smiles. "Home."

"Home—you mean to Mexico?" My breath quickens.

He nods. "For my sister's *quinceañera*."

Like Esperanza said! Could Miguel be my way to Mexico? "Why does she want you to take pictures?"

"Her daughter is turning fifteen in two years. She wants to give her a traditional *quinceañera*, so she wants to see pictures of one."

I'll be fifteen in three years. I bet Aunt Jane never even heard of a *quinceañera*, let alone is planning for it. She's sitting on my other side, talking excitedly to Jared's mom, about some heirloom thing. A tomato. An heirloom tomato would be dried up or rotten, wouldn't it? What's to get excited about?

"Would the birthday girl like her gifts now, or after dessert?" Jared's dad is talking to me. Gifts?

"Now, please."

He hands over a big purple gift bag with curly ribbon on the handles and sparkly tissue paper sticking out of it. This looks more like the kind of present Daddy would have given me.

Inside is a beach towel, a green hooded sweatshirt that says, "Lake Michigan: Unsalted," and an iTunes gift card. I've seen Jared wearing one of those sweatshirts—his is blue. The towel is covered with peace symbols and flip-flops. I probably wouldn't have picked them out myself, but they're not bad. With the new Internet, I can use the iTunes card, too.

"Thanks." I pull on the sweatshirt since it's kind of cold in the restaurant. I couldn't find Mom's hoodie before we left. I put the gift card in the front pocket.

"You're welcome. You look like a local," Mrs. Livingston says, nodding.

Like a local? Is that permafudge, like Jared said? I grip the gift card so tight the edge cuts into my palm. This is not home.

"Now mine," Miguel says quickly, handing me a small silver box with a bow.

Inside are three delicate beaded bracelets. They're so pretty, bright red, yellow, blue, and green glass beads on silver wire.

"Esperanza makes them," Miguel says. "I told her I needed something special."

"They're beautiful," I tell him, sliding them on my wrist.

"They certainly are," Jared's mother says, reaching for my hand, lifting my wrist up close. "Something to keep in mind for someone else's birthday," she says, raising her eyebrows at Jared's dad. "Does she sell them anywhere?"

"A few places, I think. The taco stand in Cedar. At a winery. I'll find out," Miguel says.

Maybe we could sell them at the farm stand. That fudgie lady, she would have bought a whole armful. Under the table I spin the bracelets around my wrist. They look like a birthday present. Something pretty. Something special, not useful. *"Gracias,"* I manage to say, though my throat is tightening like it did this morning with Phoebe.

"Feliz cumpleaños." He leans over and brushes a kiss on one cheek, then the other. Like Daddy did sometimes.

"¿Qué es esto? ¿Una fiesta de cumpleaños?" The waitress is back with chips and salsa, scolding Miguel for not telling her we're celebrating a birthday. *"¿Cuántos años tiene?"*

"Doce." I tell her I'm turning twelve before Miguel can answer.

"¿Hablas español?" Her eyebrows lift.

"Sí." I nod.

"¡Fantástico! ¿Cómo te llamas, niña?"

Next to me Aunt Jane's elbow jerks and she drops a chip, spilling salsa on her shirt.

"Lucy."

She smiles. *"Me llamo Raquel."* For birthdays, dessert is free." She sounds like Mrs. Solomon this morning, all warm and smiley and motherly.

"Oh, I made a cake," Aunt Jane says, looking up from dabbing her shirt. "We'll have dessert at home."

I saw her baking it. A carrot cake. "It's the carrots that are growing like rabbits, not the other way around," she told me, smiling at her oh-so-not-funny joke. "This will help use them up." A useful birthday cake, even! She didn't even ask if I liked carrot cake.

"I want to have dessert here," I say.

The table goes quiet. Jared's dad clears his throat.

"Why not two desserts? What's a birthday for, anyway?"

"*¡Qué bueno!*" Miguel laughs. Mrs. Livingston, who looked nervous, does, too. So does Raquel. Aunt Jane forces a smile.

"Two desserts it is, then."

Dinner is delicious. I have enchiladas and try all three salsas. The cake is a gooey, yummy chocolate. Raquel presents it with a pink candle and starts singing "Happy Birthday." Closing my eyes, I blow it out and make my wish: to move to Mexico.

It's a little weird being the only one eating dessert. The table quiets again, until Miguel starts telling a long story about one of his birthdays. When we leave, I ask if I can ride with the Livingstons.

"Well. If they've got room. I guess it's all right." Aunt Jane looks deflated, and I feel glad.

At home they all sing again. Aunt Jane bought a number-twelve candle. It's pretty babyish, but at least it's special for me. I make the same wish. She serves the cake with vanilla ice cream. It does taste good, the frosting especially. Everybody seems to eat really fast, and all the adults say no thanks to coffee.

"Paul, Jared, we should be on our way," Mrs. Livingston says. "We'll see you Tuesday," she tells Aunt Jane. She hugs me. "Happy birthday." She hesitates for a minute. "I know you've had a tough year. I hope this is the start of a better one."

"Thanks." I hope so, too, but not the way she's thinking. "Thank you for the presents, too."

"Bye, Lucy. Happy birthday." Standing by the door, Jared kind of waves.

"Time for me to go, too, *bonita. Feliz cumpleaños,*" Miguel says, picking me up in a bear hug.

"Thank you for the bracelets. I really like them."

"*De nada.*" He sets me down. "I'll be sure to tell Esperanza, too."

It's just me and Aunt Jane. I yawn loudly. "I'm pretty tired. I think I'll go to bed, too. Come on, Lexie."

"All right. Good night, then. And happy birthday." Aunt Jane looks kind of sad, standing there in her shirt with the salsa stain still visible, all the dirty dishes and the little bit of cake left over. She gave Miguel a big piece to take home, so there's not much left.

Where is Lexie? "Here, kitty, kitty, kitty."

"I'm sorry about making the Internet service your present, Lucy."

My stomach elevator starts creaking.

"I should have asked you what you'd like. And how you'd want to celebrate. I guess I'm just not very good at this."

My hands clench each other. The birthday card is still lying next to the computer. Purr-fect. Hah.

"It's been so long since I had a child in the house. And this time of year is just so hectic. But I should have tried harder for your birthday. So I'm sorry."

"It's OK." I shrug. Why do I feel guilty on my birthday? But all of a sudden I feel bad about eating the cake at Osorio's and riding home with the Livingstons. "That was a pretty good cake. I liked the frosting," I tell her.

"It's cream cheese," she says.

"Uh-huh." Lexie finally brushes by my legs. I stoop to pick her up quickly, before she can run away. "Well, good night."

"Good night, Lucy. Sweet dreams."

She's never said anything like that. In my room I jam the chair under the door so Lexie can't go find Sarge in the night, and flop down on my bed with the iPad. Might as well use my useful birthday present. It is nice not to have to go out to the barn.

I check my Facebook account. Now I'm only lying about my age by one year. There's the little red number that shows a new message. I click on it—from Graciela! It takes me a second to understand, since it's in Spanish, which I haven't seen written for a couple of months now.

"Lucy. I asked and asked, but Mama says you can't come live with us. *Lo siento.* I'm sorry."

Chapter 42
JANE

Rebecca's invited Lucy to go to the beach with them. Invited us, actually, but a day at the beach is something I can't afford in August. Miguel took her into town, and I'll tack errands onto the pickup trip. We need kitty litter again. It's Lucy's job to take care of the cats, and I have to admit she keeps the litter box cleaner than I did. We go through that stuff three times as fast as I did with only Sarge. Then I'll stop at the bank to see about a business loan, to put in some new apple trees for the farm-to-school program. Miguel told me about some new dwarf varieties, trees that bear heavier and sooner. The food service director still hasn't called back, but if the bank can turn it around quickly, I could get them in yet this fall.

Do I really want to put myself in debt again? Jim and I were always conservative. We got a fifteen-year mortgage on this place and only had four years to go when he left. Either he felt guilty enough not to ask me to put the house up for sale or he was just in too big a hurry to get to Florida with her. *Them.* At any rate, he abandoned the equity. With Matt in the army we divided his intended college account, which I earmarked strictly for the payments. Last year I got the deed.

Fresher still is Gloria and Luis's financial spiral, precipitated by the second mortgage. But no, this is different. Not just a loan, but an investment. In Plain Jane's, in a local business. In *my* local business. I'm arguing half to convince myself, half to practice for the loan officer. But first stop is delivering the sod tray back to Sarah Fischer.

The door to her inner office is open, and she's sitting at a desk strewn with papers, glasses perched on her nose.

"Well, hello again, Jane." Sarah smiles a surprised welcome, taking off her glasses so they dangle on that beaded chain.

"Brought this back." I hold up the tray. She looks puzzled for a second, then clarity dawns and she takes it.

"Did it help?"

I shake my head. "She wouldn't go near it."

Sarah nods. "I expected as much. For a first visit it was a lot to ask of her, even here."

I shrug. "We tried."

She nods again and taps the tray with her finger, like a tambourine. "You know, you really didn't need to return this."

"It was no trouble. I was in town, anyway."

"I see." She seems to be waiting for me to go on.

"It's part of the ethic of farm life. Always return what you borrow."

"A good motto." Sarah smiles. "Remind me what you do again?"

"I run a CSA. A community supported agriculture."

"That's right. Basically a small farm?"

I nod.

"Which creates the problem for Lucy."

I nod again, then consider. Well, is that the truth? Lucy arrived afraid of grass.

There's another pause, like she's waiting for me to say more. "I'm sure you've got a busy schedule, so I'll let you get to it."

"No clients today. Paperwork catch-up," Sarah says. "If you'd like to talk more, I'm happy to listen."

"Me? What would I have to talk about?" Even as I ask, I'm remembering the doctor in Alaska.

"Lucy, for starters. Taking on guardianship is quite a stressor. Add in that she's moved long-distance and a phobia on top of that . . ." Sarah's voice trails off.

Which did come first, the fear or the farm? The chicken or the egg? Does it matter? I'm due to meet the loan officer at the bank in twenty minutes, though.

"I can't today. But I'll think about it."

As unproductive as the bank meeting is, I should have stayed at Sarah's office. Or even gone with Lucy and the Livingstons to the beach. Fifteen years as a customer didn't mean squat when it came to a business loan. He didn't shut the door completely—"Let us know when you hear back from the school district"—but his skepticism was plain.

The pet superstore is my last stop before collecting Lucy. I stack two of the megasize kitty-litter bags in the bed of the truck. The meeting stank, but at least the mudroom won't.

Chapter 43
LUCY

Aunt Jane appears in the bathroom doorway as I'm brushing my teeth. "Midweek farmers' market tomorrow morning."

Ugh. I spit out the toothpaste. "Do I have to get up at five?"

She shakes her head. "Esperanza's coming to take you school shopping."

"She is?" I love school shopping day. Daddy takes me in the morning for supplies—folders and notebooks and pencils and pens, a new backpack, a lunchbox. Then we meet Mom for lunch, after she's off the air. Usually in one of the Midtown office towers whose floor-to-ceiling windows give a view of the whole city. "A new school year, Lucy. The world is at your feet!" Daddy would say. Then he goes back to the station, and Mom takes me for clothes and shoes. At home Deirdre helps put all the clothes away and has me write my name in all the folders and notebooks and pack the backpack for the first day.

Daddy and Mom are dead. Deirdre is somebody else's au pair. None of that is going to happen this year. I gulp hard.

"I'll leave you some money and the list. Rinse the sink," Aunt Jane says, turning on the faucet. "After the market, I'll meet you at the store and take you over to school for your orientation."

"I don't need an orientation." I look up, into the bathroom mirror.

"It's required," Aunt Jane says to my reflection.

"Wait. Is it really orientation?" She could be trying to get me back to that therapist. With her sodding sod.

"Yes. It's really orientation."

"How do I know?" I turn to face her.

"You'll just have to trust me." She clears her throat. "Good night, then."

I wait until she's gone and look up into the mirror again to see myself, alone there in the glass.

I don't hear Aunt Jane leave the next morning. When I go downstairs there's a sheet of paper and two bills under the salt and pepper shakers. Forty dollars? I can't get school supplies for forty dollars! Probably not even a backpack. I look at the paper.

Traverse City Area Public Schools Middle School Supplies

Ruled composition books—5 (college ruled, perfect bound or perforated, not spiral)

Three-ring binder with pocket—1

Ballpoint pens—blue or black ink—4

Pencils—No. 2—6

Combination lock

?—Backpack—no wheels

?—Insulated lunch container (for students not purchasing hot lunch) + cold pack

Recommended:

Calculator

Dictionary

The question marks are handwritten, not typed. Then I notice something else on the table. Aunt Jane has left this little sack thing there. She brought drinks in it to the farmers' market that time I went with her. Is she asking if I can use that for a lunch box? And my old backpack?

I always got a new lunch box and a backpack, every year. That's part of going back to school. How come she only gave me forty dollars? I have plenty of money, Mr. Langley said. Maybe it hasn't started coming yet? He did say it could take a while. Still. I guess it's too late to ask about it for today. Absently I pet Lexie, who's rubbing up against my leg. I have a calculator and a dictionary on my phone, so I won't need those, but what about clothes and shoes?

Don't you have clothes and shoes? What about those boxes in the barn? I can hear Aunt Jane's voice now.

Sarge comes in the kitchen, too, meowing. Their dishes must be empty. I fill up both food and water and take a blueberry muffin for myself. A loud car interrupts my eating and stewing. Juan's driving the same beat-up blue car he was so proud of before. Esperanza's next to him. It's not spewing the black smoke, though. He pulls up where Aunt Jane usually parks, right next to the row of stepping stumps.

"¡Hola!" Esperanza smiles when I open the door. She's dressed up in a white outfit with ruffles on the skirt and sleeves and colored stitches around the ruffles. *"¿Estás lista?"*

"Yeah, I'm ready." Juan's still in the car with the motor running. "We're not taking the bus?"

"No iremos en bus. Nunca más." She shakes her head and smiles even bigger. *"¡Tenemos un coche!"*

"I know. I just thought . . . Juan would have to work. And we'd take the bus, like before."

"Work this afternoon," she says. "This morning, we all shop."

I hesitate. Aunt Jane didn't say anything about driving with them. Juan waves. He's wearing a seat belt. Through the open window I can hear Spanish music. The car only has two doors, but where he's parked I could get in the back seat using the stepping stumps.

"OK. Hang on." I go back into the kitchen and get the list and money.

Esperanza's crossed her arms and is tapping her foot on the concrete square, but her smile returns when she sees me. *"¡Vamos!"*

How come she's so happy? Outside she has to move her seat forward so I can fit into the back. I never rode in a car like this. Back here I can see how Esperanza sits close to the middle, resting her hand on Juan's leg. When he stops at the road, they kiss before he turns right, toward Traverse City.

Esperanza looks over her shoulder. *"¡Hoy es un día muy importante!"* she tells me, with another huge smile.

"English, *querida*, English," Juan says.

Why does Juan care if Esperanza speaks English? She blushes and nods. "Today is . . . an important day. Very important!"

"How come?"

"I—get—my *anillo*—*¿cómo se dice?*" she says to Juan.

"Wedding ring," he says.

"I—get—my wedding ring today!" Esperanza says triumphantly.

"You're getting married? Is that why you're all dressed up?" I look at my shorts and T-shirt.

She laughs and shakes her head. *"Estamos casados*—we are married," she corrects herself before Juan does, "already. But we had no money for a ring." She beams at Juan. "Now I am truly an—*esposa?*"

"Wife," Juan says. He turns down the music and reaches over to pat her leg. "Didn't I tell you? First a car. Now a ring. Next, our own house."

"*Y un niño,*" Esperanza adds.

"You're going to have a baby? And a house? Here?"

"This is a great country," Juan says. The same thing he told me when he came to fix my window. I get that they can make money here. But it's not home. How can they be so happy?

"No baby now," Esperanza says, as Juan turns into a parking lot. "But soon. *Tendrás que esperar un poco.*" She giggles.

"A-1 Buyers," the store sign says. "Pawn, buy, sell. Best terms in TC!" There're lights on inside, but when Juan pulls the door, it doesn't open. He looks at his phone. "Ten more minutes."

Esperanza sighs, then shrugs, putting her arm around me. "Ten minutes? *No importa.* After this, we get your things, Lucy."

"It's fine." I shrug. School shopping in Traverse City is going to be a letdown, so I'm in no hurry.

A woman with dyed red hair comes to the door, smiling as she unlocks it. "Today's the big day, right? I can open early for that. Hi, honey." She smiles at me as we all troop in. "Your daughter?"

My hair stands on end. Nobody's done that. Mr. Livingston acts like Daddy, and the fudgie lady customer at the farm stand dressed like Mom, and Raquel looks like Mom. But nobody has mistaken me as belonging to any of them. It makes me feel good, for a second.

"No." Esperanza smiles, following Juan to a glass case in back. "*Una amiga.*"

Just like Lexie darting out the door, the good feeling escapes, and I feel lonely again.

"Well, nice to meet you, honey." She unlocks the counter and reaches inside. She's older than I thought. I can see gray under the red when she bends her head. "Fifty more and it's all yours."

Juan nods and digs into his pocket, pulling out some folded bills. He hands them to the lady, who counts it quickly and smiles. "Put it on her finger, then!"

My stomach feels kind of funny as I watch Esperanza, smiling and crying now, as Juan picks up her left hand and slides the ring on her finger. He puts his hands on her face and kisses her. I can see her hands on his back. It's two rings, actually, a gold wedding band and a diamond ring. The diamond is a lot smaller than Mom's. Smaller than any of the diamond jewelry in the gray velvet bag. Fifty *more*, the lady said. So Juan already paid some. How much?

"Amor," sighs the red-haired lady, patting her hand on her chest. "One for him next? I've got a nice man's ring for only one hundred!"

Juan shakes his head.

"Now, a house," Esperanza declares.

"The American dream." The woman smiles. "Good luck, kids!"

I follow them out, feeling like my face must be green. The American dream! Esperanza and Juan are getting everything they want. And my Mexican dream is a crushed birthday wish.

Chapter 44
JANE

Meijer's parking lot is packed, as usual. As planned, I head to the café and spot Juan first. He's not working? He, Esperanza, and Lucy all have soda cups and are sharing a giant bag of orange popcorn. A bag rests at Lucy's feet.

"Hi," I say. There are only three chairs at the table, which leaves me standing awkwardly. Juan and Esperanza seem extra cuddly, his arm around her shoulder, her hand on his thigh. "Ready to go?" I reach into my purse for my wallet, but Esperanza shakes her head. "Today was a celebration!"

Of what? I start to ask, but Juan stands up, and I see the BATA bus pulling up next to the rows of shopping carts.

"Good timing," I say as we step outside. But Juan and Esperanza walk past the shopping carts, heading to the parking lot, too.

"They have their own car now," Lucy says.

"They do?" They drove Lucy themselves?

Juan nods, pride obvious on his face as we reach my truck.

"*Adiós*, Lucy!" Esperanza waves her hand, the one not threaded through Juan's arm. Her bracelets and rings flash in the sunlight.

"Bye," Lucy says. "Thanks for the snack."

"De nada." She smiles and then snuggles her head onto Juan's shoulder as they walk down the row.

"They bought the popcorn? I definitely should have paid her." I turn around, scanning the lot for them.

"It's no big deal. Like she said, we were celebrating."

"Celebrating what?"

"Juan bought Esperanza's wedding ring." She says this without looking at me. "We picked it up before we came here."

"Picked it up where?" *Please, say a jewelry store over at the mall.* I start the engine.

"Some store. A-1 Buyers, I think it was called." She shrugs and puts in her earbuds.

They took Lucy to a pawnshop? In their own car? When the trip was supposed to be school shopping via BATA? I never said they couldn't, but still, it rankles. A twelve-year-old at a pawnshop? And what kind of car could Juan possibly afford? Does he have a driver's license? Insurance? As I head out of the parking lot, I see. A navy-blue two-door Toyota Camry. Probably flipped its odometer twice, but the exterior doesn't look that bad, newer than my truck, in fact. Juan's been here barely two months, and according to Miguel, it's been an average season, at best. How could he have enough disposable income to buy a car?

Esperanza's opening her door as we pass. She waves again, her jewelry sparkling. Again, something rankles about the whole morning. Rankles as in rank. Off, not right. Something's just not right about it all. But that could just as well be my guilt over not taking her to begin with. I glance over at Lucy, lost in her music, then once more in the rearview mirror.

And as Esperanza closes the door, it dawns on me with the abruptness of awakening postnightmare, with the crushing deadweight of a fallen tree, with a truth that pierces like shards of glass, how Juan could afford a car and a wedding ring for his wife.

Chapter 45

LUCY

I wait for the school bus on the stepping stump next to the empty farm stand. It's shady, and goose bumps pop up on my arms. At home it was always so hot for the first few weeks of school. I shift my old backpack stuffed with the new school supplies and look down. The grass has grown up around the stumps, and some long pieces bend over toward my feet. Inside my Hello Kitty high-tops, I curl my toes. The shoes are almost too small. But Aunt Jane was right about the rest of my clothes. The jeans and shirts and underwear from the boxes in the barn all still fit just fine. I think about Graciela's bathing suit picture and the pink strap under Phoebe's shirt. I'll probably be the only seventh grader who doesn't need a bra.

"So, big day," Aunt Jane says. She's wearing her usual jeans and green fleece, her hands cupping her coffee mug.

Huge day. Major day. Terrifying day. "I guess." And I guess she doesn't take first-day pictures. We always took one at home and one at school. Like the birthday breakfast and school shopping, another tradition taken away. The goose bumps are really bad now, and I rub my arms, but at the same time my armpits are sweating. Did I put on deodorant?

"Cold?" Aunt Jane asks. "I'll get you a sweatshirt." She turns to go back to the house. Lexie's and Sarge's heads are together in the front window.

"It's fine."

"Lucy, you're shivering. Don't be silly." She jogs off toward the house. Lexie's and Sarge's heads disappear. Going to stake out the door. Sure enough, when Aunt Jane opens it, they both dart out, toward the barn. It's happened so many times that I know she'll come back, but it still makes me both scared and jealous to see Lexie running out the door, over the grass, following Sarge wherever.

"Sorry." Aunt Jane hands me a sweatshirt, the green Lake Michigan one Mrs. Livingston gave me for my birthday.

I let the backpack slide down and pull it over my head, wondering what happened to Mom's Venice Beach one. I haven't seen it in, like, forever. Wondering and with everything dark for a second, I lose my balance and sway on the stepping stump, feeling the edge instead of the flat part. When I poke my head through, my right foot is balanced on the stump's edge, the long grass brushing the white tip and the glittery side.

"Here it comes," Aunt Jane says as I yank my feet side by side again. Even though I'm warmer with the sweatshirt, I'm shaking, my body vibrating like the noisy bus engine. *Step on a crack, break your mother's back. Step on the grass*—make the bus crash? The door opens, and in the driver's seat is—Miguel?

"*¡Buenos días!*"

"You're a bus driver, too?" I'm confused and glad to see him. My legs steady as I grab the backpack and step toward him, onto the last stepping stump.

"*Sí.*" He grins and holds up his ID.

"Bye, Lucy. Have a good day," Aunt Jane says behind me.

I turn around. She's smiling, too. "Did you know?"

She nods. "Well, I was hoping. We didn't want to tell you in case it turned out Miguel couldn't get this route."

I stand there on the last stepping stump. I can't get from it to the bus step. There's too much in between, grass and weeds and gravel, not the yard but not the road, either. My legs start wobbling again. Miguel is watching me and Aunt Jane, and all the kids on the bus, probably, too.

In a second he's out of the driver's seat. "*Mira*, Lucy." With the toe of his boot, he lifts up the stepping stump behind me, the one I was just standing on, and drops it in front of me, bridging the gap to the bus. It's a long step, but I can do it.

"*Bien.*" Miguel pats my hand as he slides back into his seat and pulls the lever to close the door. And then it's just us. I'm the first kid on, so no one saw. I sit on the same side as Miguel, right behind him.

The bus only stops a few times on the peninsula, but after we get into Traverse City, it stops a lot. Miguel says hi to everyone in his loud, cheery voice. Most of the kids say hi back, but not very loud or happy. At one of the last stops, after three girls and two boys get on, just as he's about to shut the door, a mom leans in, her foot on the step.

"You're the new driver?"

"*Sí,*" Miguel says, smiling. "Miguel Esquivale, at your service."

"What happened to Mrs. Hale?"

"Señora Hale has another route this year," Miguel says.

The mom's wearing one of those "Lake Michigan: Unsalted" sweatshirts like mine, only red. She crosses her arms over it. "She drove this route for the last three years."

Miguel nods.

"She knew all the kids. She was always on time. Even in winter."

Miguel nods again. "Very important. In fact, it's time for me to go. If you don't mind?" He tugs on the lever that closes the door. It doesn't touch the mom, but she jumps back as if she got squashed. I see her turn to another mother at the bus stop who has her arms crossed, too.

"What's she so mad about?" I ask as Miguel pulls away.

He doesn't say anything for a few minutes and then shrugs. *"No importa.* I'm used to it."

"Used to what?" But the bus is stopping again, and a whole bunch more kids climb on. A girl sits next to me, so we can't talk anymore.

When we finally get to the school, there's a bunch of buses ahead of ours. A couple of kids stand up and start shoving each other in the aisle, but Miguel looks up in the rearview mirror.

"No horsing around on my bus, boys," he says. He's not yelling, but you can tell he means it. He sounds like he did the first day, when he told Aunt Jane he was going to open my crate.

The boys stop, but don't sit down. They're the ones who got on at the stop where the mom wanted the old driver.

"Sit down," Miguel says in the same voice.

Everyone is watching the boys now. One sits, but the other one stands for a few more seconds, watching Miguel.

"Come on, Pete." Another kid yanks his arm, and finally, he sits.

"Excelente," Miguel says.

The bus in front of us moves. We're next in line. Miguel opens the door. My stomach elevator drops about ten floors. He smiles at me.

"Hasta pronto, linda," he says, winking, as I get off. See you this afternoon. So he'll drive the bus back, too.

On the sidewalk there's a ton of kids yelling and waving and pushing past me in all directions. Everybody seems to be meeting someone else and smiling. My stomach sinks further.

"*'Excelente'*? Hello, this is America? We say excellent," somebody behind me says.

Someone else laughs. "Spic." Another laugh. Huh? They're laughing at Miguel? I spin around to see if either one is that boy Pete, but there're too many kids who all look the same, all white arms and T-shirts and big flopping backpacks. A bell rings, and everybody starts going in the same direction, to six big glass doors under the sign, "Traverse City East

Middle School." Inside is louder than outside, lockers slamming, kids yelling. The faces blur, mean kids and strange kids and maybe friendly kids. So many.

"Lucy! Hey, Lucy!" I hear my name from across the hall.

There's Jared waving at me. Relief rushes in, pushing away both anger and fear.

"Hi."

"Hi." He shifts his backpack to his other shoulder. "Did you get your schedule?"

I nod, reaching into my pocket. They mailed it after I had orientation. "Math, Western Hemisphere Studies, gym, A lunch, Life Science, English, Digital Communications."

He looks at his. "I've got A lunch, too. And Digital Communications."

"Cool," I say. If I were at school with Graciela, I'd have someone all the time. But at least I'll know someone at lunch. That's the most important. Jared might not be cute, but he's not rude or mean. He's a friend.

Chapter 46
JANE

After Lucy's bus disappears over the ridge, I check Matt's room yet again, to be absolutely sure. I clear the folders and papers off the rolltop desk and poke into all the little compartments, open all the drawers. I drag it away from the wall, to check if something's slipped behind. There's an old baseball team photo from when Matt was about twelve and a dusty collection of pencils, rubber bands, and paper clips, but no gray velvet bag of jewelry.

Dropping onto Matt's bed, I close my eyes and retrace the events. The window broke in the storm. Juan brought the new glass to fix it. The new papers from Langley arrived. When I stored them in the desk, I must have subconsciously noticed the jewelry was missing. Then, waking from that nightmare a day or two later, discovering it really was missing.

But how could Juan have known the jewelry was there? Could he just have gone looking for valuables and concluded a desk was a likely place to keep them? Would he be that brazen? Who else has been in the house?

Lucy, of course, who even slept in there a few nights after the storm. Jared and Rebecca, on their workdays. Esperanza, the day she took Lucy to the movies.

Lucy doesn't even know I have the jewelry here. Jared isn't buying new cars and wedding rings. Nor is Rebecca. Esperanza has a vested interest. Maybe she was the one, after all. That day she took Lucy to the movies, she could have looked around while waiting for the bus.

But Miguel brought them here. He wouldn't bring thieves. Then again, how well does Miguel know Juan and Esperanza—or any of them, really? They just call him, the migrant health clinic, the Head Start office, or the farmers themselves when they need a liaison. Speaks Spanish, work connections all over Old Mission and Leelanau, and no family or personal commitments of his own, which makes him available nearly round the clock. Should I tell him about it?

There's no way to prove anything, though. If it was Juan and Esperanza, they've obviously sold it. All I'd do is make Miguel feel attacked or guilty. Gloria's jewelry is gone, and regardless of who actually took it, it's partly my fault for keeping it here, against Langley's advice.

Down the hall the phone rings. I roll off Matt's bed. The only saving grace is that Lucy didn't know about it to begin with.

"Robert Sears from the TCAPS food service office, returning your call," a male voice says, brusquely.

"Oh yes." I left the message almost two weeks ago. Nice of him to get around to calling back. "I called about becoming a vendor for the local lunch source program. Carol Montgomery gave me your name."

"You're a grower, then?" His voice softens a few degrees.

"I run a CSA on Old Mission."

"Are you farm-to-school certified?"

"Excuse me?"

"Farm-to-school certified. It's a USDA credential."

"Mrs. Montgomery didn't mention any credential."

"As a principal, she wouldn't be aware."

"I'm practically certified organic," I say.

"That's a good start. If you're organic, you're aware of all the hoops the bureaucrats make you jump, right?" Now he sounds chummy. And apparently didn't notice I said *practically.*

"Uh-huh." My stomach is sinking, thinking of the smug loan officer. Don't count your chickens, Jane. Or your bushels of apples or your new income stream.

"To work with schools, this is one. I can send you a link to the application on the Michigan Department of Education website—"

"How long does it take to get approved?"

"I'm new here, but it can't be worse than California." He laughs. "A few months. Three, four, I'd guess."

November or December. Not much growing around the forty-fifth parallel then. "I see. Well, thank you for calling back, Mr. Sears."

"Not a problem. So you think you'll be applying, then?"

"I'm not sure. I'd hoped to start sooner . . ."

"I understand. It's a pain. Just the way it is with government money. But I think it'd be well worth your time."

"Why's that?"

"I got hired to bring farm-to-school here. I'm looking to build a model for the state. Lots of work ahead. One reason I didn't call back sooner, on top of the new year starting."

Acknowledging that he was late mollifies me. "A model for the whole state?"

"Michigan's way behind. But these are win-win-win programs. Kids eat better, they do better in class. Schools support the local economy. Growers—who just happen to be parents and voters—put away a little in their pocket."

An evangelist, speaking the gospel of Plain Jane's.

"This area's a natural for it, the way farm-to-table's already taken off at restaurants. Wish I could wave a magic wand and make the red tape disappear, but I can't."

"Hmm." He's persuasive. But can I put my faith in him?

"There's one other thing. The district wants to expand employee wellness. The school board's approved offering a benefit starting first of the year."

"I'm not following."

"They'll give employees a lump sum, say a hundred bucks apiece, that they can spend on wellness. Gym memberships, personal training, CSA subscriptions."

A hundred dollars per employee? Times, what, several hundred, right? Do that math, Mr. Loan Officer. "Do you need any, um, credential for that?"

"Nope. There's an employee wellness expo coming up next month to kick it off, introduce employees to vendors. You could have a table. Bring some samples."

Chapter 47

LUCY

My toes curl inside my Hello Kitty high-tops as Mr. Abernathy hands me the grungy yellow pinny. The mesh material feels sticky, like it hasn't been washed since school started two weeks ago. Ick. But at least we don't have to pick teams. Pete, that mean kid from the bus, is in this class, but he doesn't get one. Hooray. After listening to him every day, I'm pretty sure he's the one who said Miguel should speak English.

"Yellow serves!" Mr. Abernathy blows his whistle and throws the volleyball to our side of the net.

Everyone else must already know how to play. A tall, pimply boy who's in my math class smacks the ball over to the other team. A girl hits it to another girl who hits it into the net.

"Off the net, off the net!" Pete yells, charging up from the back row, diving to the floor where the ball bounces.

"Yellow point!" Mr. Abernathy blows his whistle again, and then suddenly both the whistle and Pete's stomping to the back row are drowned out by a blaring alarm, louder than anything I ever heard before, louder than ambulance sirens or my window breaking during the thunderstorm or Sarge the first time he saw Lexie. Four times it buzzes, then pauses, and in the pause Mr. Abernathy yells.

"Fire drill! Everyone line up!" Buzz, buzz, buzz, buzz. "Line up!" He's pointing to the other side of the gym, behind Pete's team, where another teacher's opening double doors. Buzz, buzz, buzz, buzz. Beyond the other team I can see through the doors.

Grass. All grass.

Buzz, buzz, buzz, buzz. "Line up, everyone! Outside, walk away from the building to the football field. Walk, don't run." Mr. Abernathy herds us to the door, still blowing his whistle.

Walk to the football field? *Make her car crash.* I can't go out there. I can't. But where can I go? My stomach elevator dropping, I hang behind the pimply kid as I scan the gym. On the side wall, one section of the bleachers is pulled out. I could hide underneath, if Mr. Abernathy doesn't see me. Buzz, buzz, buzz, buzz. If he'd look away for even a couple of seconds, I could sneak—there! He's sticking his head out the door, talking to someone outside. I duck under the bleachers, peeking out through a crack. Did anybody see?

The last kid goes out. My stomach elevator stops, then lurches as Mr. Abernathy comes back. "Everybody out?" The sun casts his shadow long on the gym floor. He turns toward the bleachers. It feels like his shadow's pointing right at me, and then it swings away again, and he bangs the doors shut. A couple of seconds later, the buzzing finally stops. I exhale a shaky breath, clutching the cold metal edge of the bleachers, inhaling the stale sweat of the pinny.

Five minutes tick by on the clock covered with a cage. I did it. Pretty soon another bell will ring and everyone will come back inside. If I time it just right again, I can blend in when they come back, like I was there all along.

All of a sudden the doors fly open and Mr. Abernathy's shadow stabs at the bleachers again. "Ortiz! Lucy Ortiz! You still in here?"

I freeze, then drop down into a crouch. Kids start running in behind him.

"Lucy Ortiz! You in here?"

"Under the bleachers!" It's Pete, that big jerk. "I see her. Right there!"

Mr. Abernathy walks over to the bleachers and folds his arms when he sees me, a clipboard pinched under one elbow. He blows his whistle. "Rest of you. Back on the court! Back in your places. Yellow still serves." He turns back to me. "Come on out, Lucy."

Slowly I emerge from under the bleachers. I try to find something nice in his face, like how Miguel's cheeks crinkle when he smiles or Daddy's eyes would shine. I can't.

"You're new this year, right?"

I nod.

"But you had fire drills at your old school."

I nod again.

"Care to explain why you stayed inside?"

I shake my head.

"You know, we call these drills because it's practice. For the real thing. It's a matter of your safety."

I nod as I look at my shoes, curling my toes again, then flexing them. I'm starting to poke a hole in the right one.

"If this were a real fire, you'd be risking not only your life, but a firefighter's."

He's right, but if I walk on grass, who knows what else I'd risk? I can't tell him that, though.

Mr. Abernathy heaves a sigh. "You seem like a nice kid, but if you won't even talk to me, there's not much I can do." He starts scribbling on his clipboard. "Failure to evacuate during a fire drill is an automatic detention."

Detention? "But I have to take the bus after school!"

"Doesn't have to be today. You've got a week to figure out transportation and report, then it doubles." He rips a piece of paper off his clipboard. "Back out on the floor now."

Aunt Jane is going to be so mad.

It turns out I don't have to tell her, because she already knows. The school emailed her.

"Failure to evacuate for a fire drill. Let me guess, you would have had to walk on grass." Her hands are on her hips.

I shrug and nod at the same time, looking around for Lexie.

"I thought so. What are we going to do about this?"

"Just do the detention. What's the big deal?" It's the same argument we had the time she tried to take me to that therapist. Lexie wanders in, and I pick her up, a big, furry shield.

"That's not what I'm talking about."

"There's probably a late bus. Or the Livingstons could pick me up. Or Esperanza. So don't worry, you won't have to interrupt your work," I say.

"That's not what I'm talking about, either! Your grass phobia, that's the real problem here." Her voice is climbing, higher, louder. "You refuse to go to the therapist, refuse to even try to overcome it. What if there'd been a real fire? You could have been killed!"

She's almost shrieking, and the word vibrates, like it did when Mrs. Creighton told me about the car accident. Killed.

"It was just a drill," I start, but my throat closes up as my hands clutch Lexie tighter, her heartbeat delicate against my arm.

"You didn't know that!" Aunt Jane throws up her hands.

"Why would you even care!" I shout, wincing as Lexie's claws dig into my arm as she jumps away. I run upstairs, fling myself on the bed, and cry.

Chapter 48
JANE

Before breakfast I go out to retrieve yesterday's mail, forgotten in the fire-drill debacle. After I read the school's email, I berated myself all afternoon. I should have told the principal about the phobia when I enrolled Lucy. Should have made her go to therapy, keep that sod in her room, insisted on the exposure. What if it had been a real fire and she'd stayed in the burning building? The question both terrifies and taunts me.

Take care of our baby, Gloria's plea echoes. *You will, won't you?*

Amid the usual junk mail and bills, the thick, creamy envelope with the ornate cursive address stands out. It's also addressed to both me and Lucy. It looks like a wedding invitation, but I don't know anyone who would be getting married, let alone inviting both of us. Back inside I turn it around in my hands for a few minutes before I give in and rip it open.

LATINAS IN MEDIA USA

CORDIALLY INVITES YOU TO THE

2011 ANNUAL LEGACY DINNER AND AWARDS

FEATURING PRESENTATION OF THE INAUGURAL

Gloria Santiago-Ortiz Memorial Scholarship
Tuesday, October 25, 2011
Lotte New York Palace Hotel
Cocktails 6 p.m.
Dinner 7 p.m.
Awards program 8 p.m.

There's a number and an email to RSVP, and in the corner, a final punctuation: "Attire: Black Tie."

A light tread comes loping down the stairs, and I instinctively drop the invitation facedown. But it's only Lexie seeking breakfast. At least Lucy did have some creature comfort last night. When I followed her upstairs after her outburst, she refused to open the door. Did I over-react? She has to understand how serious this is!

"More trouble," I tell Lexie's patchwork back, frowning. Lucy will want to go, of course. But a midweek trip to New York City? Sentimental and laudable as a memorial scholarship is, it's out of the question, especially after yesterday's averted disaster.

With the progress she's made using the stepping stumps and running the farm stand and all, I thought she'd move on sooner rather than later. Wrong again. She's not acclimating to life here. Clearly I should have told Mrs. Montgomery about the phobia. In the detention email, the principal also asked to see Lucy's school records from last spring, to find out what recommendations the social worker made. The last place she should go is back where it all started. Not to mention the expense of flying both of us to New York, hotels, and black-tie attire, too. It's an annual event. She can go next year, when she's settled in.

Upstairs Lucy's door opens, then closes. Quickly I stuff the invitation back into the envelope and slip it into my CSA record book. She would never look through that.

After she's left for school, I email regrets. Lucy's school schedule, not wanting to disrupt new routines, I'm sure you understand. As I click "Send," doubt flickers. Should I check with Sarah Fischer? One of her friends would certainly host Lucy, eliminating the hotel expense. In my mind's eye I picture the school burning, with Lucy inside. No. Next year. She can go next year.

Saturday. Made it through the week, detention and all. Only one more Plain Jane's delivery left this season. Lucy's still asleep as I head outside with my coffee to take inventory. Tomatoes still holding their own. Potatoes. Onions and peppers. It'll be good to have a break, though the looming year-end accounting feels foreboding. Should I get some chickens? Eggs I could offer year-round. We could eat them, too. Or maybe this wellness program at the schools will—

"How could you!"

I drop my coffee cup, splashing hot liquid all over my jeans, as the side door slams against the house and Lucy's yell pierces the morning. She bounds toward me, taking the stepping stumps two at a time.

"How could I what?" My back winces as I stoop to pick up the cup, which didn't break, at least.

"Tell them I couldn't go to the dinner!" She's still in her pajamas and barefoot. Never been outside barefoot. Her face is flushed and she's fairly vibrating with fury.

"Tell who you—" Oh no. Gloria's memorial award dinner. Did I leave an email open? How could she have found out?

"How could you!" she says again, her fists clenched.

"Lots of reasons. It's in New York. On a school night. It would be expensive." I tick off the reasons on my fingers. The coffee has soaked through my jeans, making them clammy against my legs.

"I could stay with Phoebe!" My own rationalization, thrown back in my face.

"It's still on a school night."

"So what? This is more important!"

254

"I get to make that decision, actually." The real problem is she's not adapting here. A trip to New York isn't in her best interest right now. The day of the week doesn't matter.

"Stupid school! One day!"

"At least two days, to get there and back."

"Two days, then. What's the big deal?"

"That's exactly what you said about the detention, and that's the big deal. Your attitude. That nothing besides what you want matters. This reaction is why I didn't tell you about it."

Her lip is trembling and she's shivering in her thin pajamas. Am I really so sure? A flicker of resentment, like I felt in Paul's office, crackles alongside the doubt. This is exactly the kind of decision I didn't want in my life anymore. All this drama over one dinner. "It's important that you settle in here. This is where you live now." I step over the plants, heading back to the house for dry clothes.

"Oooh! Not because I want to! Not if I—" Lucy stops short as we walk to the house on our parallel paths.

"Not if you what?" I turn around to look at her, standing stock-still on the stump, her arms folded, tousled hair wild around her face. The memory of our first meeting, when her hair was pulled back in braids, surfaces. Why doesn't she wear it that way anymore?

"Nothing."

Nothing, my eye. But with her lips now clamped shut and her eyes telegraphing unmitigated hostility, she's certainly not telling me. I push open the side door, which feels far heavier than it should. Lucy follows me in and stalks upstairs, banging her door. A second later Lexie shoots downstairs and through the kitchen. Deserting again.

The kitchen computer is on and my email is open. I sit down to read. Lupe Hernandez, president of Latinas in Media, replied, suggesting that perhaps Lucy could join them via Skype for the awards.

A compromise. Hallelujah! I jog upstairs to present Lucy with the news.

"I want to be there!" She sits up on her bed.

"You've made that perfectly clear. But that's not an option. This is."

"It's for my mom. It's a big deal!"

I blanch at the hint of tears in her voice. Anger is easier to deal with.

"I understand. I do. And this is a way you can participate."

A wail, in between a sob and a snort, comes out of her throat. "It's not fair."

Maybe not. Nothing has been since April, why should it change now? But she's set my doubts smoldering again. What would Sarah have said?

"They said it's an annual award. Next year, after you're more settled into school and all . . ."

"Next year!" She makes that sob-snort noise again and flops back onto her pillow.

"Lucy . . ."

I reach for her shoulder, but she turns to the wall, away from my touch.

Chapter 49
LUCY

Jared's not at school Monday, so I don't have anyone to sit with at lunch. I've talked to a couple of other kids who seem OK, a girl with blue streaks in her hair who's in my Digital Communications class and another girl from Western Hemisphere Studies whose locker is near mine. But they don't have A lunch.

Pete does, though. From the corner of my eye, there he is, at his same table as far from the lunch monitors as possible, with the kid he gets on the bus with, one who's in our gym class, and two more I don't know. They're laughing and loud and obnoxious here, too, but you don't notice it so much in the cafeteria.

Is Jared sick? I pick at the soggy French fries and mealy apple on my tray, wondering. I kind of miss Aunt Jane's lunches now. They were weird, but at least they tasted good. What's the food like at Graciela's school? Mexican, naturally. Enchiladas, tacos, arroz, all *delicioso* like Daddy made or like Osorio's serves. And of course we'd sit together every day. If she was sick, I could take her lunch and eat with her, in our room. Which would be pretty and comfortable and safe, with no trees nearby to crash through the windows. Or any grass.

Every night would be like a sleepover, talking with flashlights under our covers and giggling. It would be sunny and warm all the time, even in winter. All the teachers would be nice and never give homework. We'd play soccer together—no, not soccer. Ride horses? I've never ridden a horse, but it sounds fun. Why wouldn't Aunt Bonita let me come? I wouldn't be any bother, especially since I'd be with Graciela, away at school most of the year. I could pay for myself, too, with the money Mr. Langley said is mine. If only I could talk to her, I know she would change her mind.

"Hola." Pete's voice punctures my daydream. But he says it wrong, like *hole-ah*. And mean. "Where's your boyfriend?"

"I don't have a boyfriend."

"Livingston."

Jared? "He's not my boyfriend."

"He hangs out with you all the time now." Pete puts his tray down.

I shrug.

"How come you didn't go out during the fire drill?"

"None of your business." My stomach elevator starts to creak.

"How come you're always talking to that new bus driver?"

"That's none of your business, either."

"I hear you guys talking in Spanish. Did you come from Mexico, too?"

I start to shake my head, but Pete keeps talking, leaning over his tray. I can see chocolate milk at the corner of his mouth. "You should go back there. In America, we don't want people who won't speak English and don't follow the rules."

The picture of Daddy and Mom and me in front of the Statue of Liberty rises in my head.

"Idiota." I stand up and sweep past him.

"Hey. What did you call me?"

"Figure it out!" I call over my shoulder, dumping my barely touched lunch onto the tray return. But Pete plus the daydream did plant an idea. *Go back there.* Why am I waiting? If I just went, Aunt Bonita would have to let me stay. Especially with a one-way ticket. My stomach elevator creaks louder, but now it's rising instead of falling. I could just go! Like I walked out of my old school that time. I just need a ticket. So how can I get $789? Or $732, since I have the farm-stand money.

Pawn, buy, sell. Best terms in TC! The ring Juan got Esperanza had one little diamond. Each piece of Mom's jewelry has lots of diamonds. So I could keep most of it, like she wanted. Practically all of it. Just sell one bracelet. Maybe a pair of earrings. I bet that would be enough. I could bring the jewelry to school one day and go to A-1 Buyers afterward. We pass the street on the bus; it's not far.

Chapter 50
JANE

"Good to see you again, Jane," Sarah says, gesturing toward a chair. I wonder if she's been expecting me to return all along, through some kind of therapist's sixth sense.

"Thanks for seeing me." Taking the UCLA envelope from my bag, I turn it over. I've practically memorized it, I've read it so often, but I still can't believe what she says.

"I found this letter from my sister about a month ago. Lucy's mother."

"Yes?" Sarah's eyes drop to the envelope.

"It got mixed up in her things. She dictated it in the ambulance, after the car accident, but before she died. She asks me to take care of Lucy for them." Pleads, really. *You will, won't you?*

"You hadn't already agreed to be her guardian?"

I shake my head. "It was a complete surprise. We grew apart. I did, anyway. Or I thought I did. She's really my half sister, and nine years younger."

"I see." Sarah is nodding, but confusion on her face belies her words.

"Sorry. I'm jumping around." I fill her in on our childhoods, the odd family quartet we made briefly, whittled to a trio when Esteban vanished, and then a de facto duo as Mom withdrew, foisting Gloria onto me. Jim's appearance as salvation and escape. Our good early years of marriage, taking on new assignments and Matt's birth.

"Then I got pregnant again," I say, suddenly noticing my chair is a rocker. How ironic.

Sarah removes her glasses, polishing them with the edge of her lacy blue shirt. The color recalls the bay outside my window earlier. It's turning my favorite shade, deep, serene blue. Gone are the bright, changeable aquas and pastels of summer. Now it's the autumn azure that I love, that abides instead of sparkles, steady and reassuring. The exact opposite of the memory replaying in my head.

"We were stationed in Alaska. It was tough, but it felt like an adventure together, too. Matt was almost three. I was thirty-six weeks. Everything seemed fine." I rock forward hard, giving the words, twenty years unspoken, momentum to emerge. "Then my daughter was stillborn."

Sarah's lips tighten, but she doesn't gape or let her face fall. "I'm so sorry."

"I had a hysterectomy, too. Emergency." I rock back.

"I'm so sorry," she repeats. "Two major losses, consecutively. How old were you?"

"Twenty-four." It seems astonishingly long ago. Matt will be twenty-four in February.

"Is this the first time you've talked about it in a therapy setting?" Sarah asks.

"The first time I've talked about it."

"Ever?" Sarah's voice climbs with incredulity.

"Since the first anniversary." Following Matt's tricycle, my mental stupor as thick as the Houston humidity.

"How does it feel? How do you feel?"

"I'm not sure."

"Fair enough." Sarah nods. "You know, there's a saying about grief. 'The only way out is through.'"

"Meaning?" I rock a little faster.

"You've buried those losses for so long. Tried to do what your husband wanted. But he was wrong. That's not healthy."

My hands clench the chair's arms tighter. "I know. And Matt was the one who suffered for it. His whole childhood, I felt like I was going through the motions. I—I denied him the mother he deserved because I couldn't get over her." There. I've confessed it all.

Sarah doesn't recoil, or even frown or grimace. She pushes over a box of tissues.

"People can only do as well as they can. You didn't get the help you needed," she says. "Grief needs to be expressed. We talked about this in terms of Lucy, if you remember."

"The exposure therapy," I say.

"Yes. While that's an effective technique to deal with symptoms like her grass fear, the underlying anxiety or grief also needs to be addressed. Same with you. I'm guessing Lucy's arrival stirred those feelings to the surface, but reflexively, you've clamped them down."

I pause my rocking, thinking. The high ten on the stepping stumps. Running the farm stand. The fire-drill detention scare. Her fury over the banquet invitation.

"Your son is grown. Gone from home?"

I nod, laying my head back, staring up at the ceiling.

"Now here comes another child, forcing you to confront all those memories of loss and guilt. Hard, conflicting feelings about what you needed, and what your husband wanted. A girl at that, struggling with her own grief. That's a hell of a lot."

I start rocking again.

"Gloria's letter brought you here. What else did she say?"

I finger the envelope again. "I didn't understand all of it, but it implied she was sorry we drifted apart." I hesitate. "And that I was a devoted mother, and they trusted me to take care of Lucy."

"How did it feel to read that?"

Now I don't hesitate. "Like a fraud."

"Because you're convinced that you fell short with your son."

I swallow hard. And that I will again. With Lucy.

"I'd encourage you to try and see it from Gloria's point of view. Possibly your son's, too. Ever talked to him about it?"

I shake my head, looking at the clock. We've gone well over the fifty minutes.

"You might consider it. Sometimes what we hang on to hardest, others have long let go of."

"I'm sorry to run over our time," I say.

"Not at all. So will you think about that?"

"I'll try." I stand to leave. Sarah does, too.

"May I ask her name?"

"Whose?"

"Your daughter's."

The hospital wanted one for the records. We hadn't settled on one, and Jim had taken Matt home. So I picked, arbitrarily, it seemed.

"Nina," I say, out loud for the first time in more than twenty years. "Her name was Nina."

Chapter 51
LUCY

"So quiet today, *niña*," Miguel says on the bus home.

"I'm picking out my outfit for tonight." Finally, it's the award banquet night! Esperanza texted me pictures of dresses that Raquel said I could borrow. Her daughters wore them to dances and stuff. Maybe even a *quinceañera*. Esperanza's bringing them over later and said she'd do my hair, too.

"Tonight?"

"The scholarship dinner!" I've only told him about it, like, a hundred times. I can't wait. It's all I've had to look forward to since the pawnshop wouldn't buy any of my jewelry. The red-haired lady said I had to be eighteen, and gave me a lecture, too.

"Honey, I remember you. And let me tell you, whatever you think you need to buy isn't as important as keeping this," she told me. Like she could possibly understand. I don't know how to get the money for the ticket now. But at least I have the jewelry to wear tonight.

"Isn't the dinner about being smart, not how you look?" Miguel says.

"For whoever gets the scholarship it is. Not me."

"*Tú también.*"

You, too. *"Inteligente y bonita,"* Daddy told me after we went to the bodega. Does he know what's going on with me right now? Can he and Mom see me, from heaven or wherever? Up there with the I-love-you stars? I know that I'm the best student in Digital Communications. I got a ninety-two on my last math quiz and a ninety-four on my Western Hemisphere Studies test. Mom would be proud of me for running the farm stand, too, I think. Being in charge of it, like she was on her show.

"Lucy?" We're at my stop.

"I know, I know. It's important to be smart. But tonight I want everyone to think I'm pretty."

"They will." Miguel smiles. "Have fun, *niña.*"

Like she has been since the detention, Aunt Jane is in the kitchen instead of outside. "How was school?"

"Fine."

"Homework?"

"A little."

"Better do it now, then. Later you—"

"I know, I know."

I'm glad I can see the driveway from my window. Over my math book I keep checking for Esperanza, but half an hour later it's the Livingstons' car that rolls in. The CSA is over. What are they doing here? Mrs. Livingston gets out by herself and carries in a shopping bag. I walk downstairs.

". . . as modest as I could . . ."

"What's going on?" I ask, interrupting Mrs. Livingston. Aunt Jane looks up, closing the bag quickly. Macy's. They have that here?

"What's in the bag?"

"A surprise from your aunt," Mrs. Livingston says.

Aunt Jane's last surprise was the high-speed Internet. I eye the bag. "What is it?"

"Go on, Jane." Mrs. Livingston sounds excited.

Aunt Jane hands me the Macy's bag. Underneath tissue paper is something soft—clothes—a dress?

I lift it all the way out. It has a black velvet top with short sleeves. At the neck is a heart made of rhinestones. The flouncy skirt is made of gauzy, tiered white ruffles. It looks like something a seven-year-old would wear to a Christmas party.

"I know how disappointed you were about not going to the banquet tonight," Aunt Jane says. "I thought you could at least dress up for the Skype part."

She wants me to wear this? To an elegant, formal banquet!?

"I asked Mrs. Livingston to pick out something, because, well, I'm not very good at gifts. Especially clothes," Aunt Jane says, suddenly breaking off. "What's that?"

I hear Juan and Esperanza's car before I see it, the opposite of the Livingstons' Prius. "It's Esperanza."

Aunt Jane's lips flatten. "Why is she here?"

"I invited her." What is Aunt Jane's problem with Esperanza? "To help me get ready."

"*¡Hola!*" Esperanza knocks on the door, coat hangers hooked over her shoulder and a big paper bag that smells delicious. Aunt Jane's face changes to a mask. Is she mad at me, at Esperanza, or both of us?

"Our own Latina banquet! From Osorio's," she says, dropping the paper bag on the table and looking from Aunt Jane to Mrs. Livingston to me. "*¡Otro vestido!*" she says, taking the black-and-white dress out of my hands. "*¡Qué hermoso!*"

"I want to see what you brought," I say.

Mrs. Livingston clears her throat. "Well, I'd better be on my way."

"Without seeing the dresses!" Esperanza tsks, shaking her head, handing me Aunt Jane's dress. "Try it on!"

"No, really, I don't want to intrude. You'll want to eat while everything's hot . . ." Mrs. Livingston says.

"Why don't you stay, too? There's plenty of food," Aunt Jane says as, reluctantly, I take the black-and-white dress to the bathroom. I have to try it on there since I don't have Mom's mirror in my room anymore. It looks better than I thought, but still little-girlish.

"*¡Qué bonita!*" Esperanza exclaims when I go back to the kitchen.

"You look just lovely, Lucy," Mrs. Livingston says, smiling.

Aunt Jane's pretending to be busy with the food, but really watching. "Very nice," she says, scooping salsa into a bowl. "What do you think?"

"It's OK, but—" I hesitate. "I want to try on the ones Esperanza brought."

Surprisingly, Aunt Jane nods.

There are three, one purple, one black and turquoise, and one a coral color. I like the purple one best, so I try it first. But the skinny straps are too long, and it falls too low. When I walk into the kitchen, Aunt Jane's eyes go kind of wide, like she's surprised, but she doesn't say anything.

"We could pin it," Esperanza says, lifting a strap off my shoulder and pinching it together. "No one would see."

"It's a beautiful color," Mrs. Livingston says.

The next one, with black and turquoise sequins, is also too big. It's strapless, and it has a bra sewn inside it. I look down at the cups that stick out, empty. Would it fit Phoebe? I'm not even going to show them.

The last one fits best, and the coral color is pretty, but it looks little-girly, too, the whole skirt made of ruffles.

"I like the purple one best," I announce to the kitchen, quiet except for Esperanza munching a chip. Mrs. Livingston looks at the floor.

"Then wear that one," Aunt Jane says, making my mouth fall open.

"Really?"

"I've got safety pins somewhere. Put it upstairs, and we'll adjust it after dinner."

A smile spreads across my face, the corners of my mouth lifting my stomach elevator, too. Even though she brought the other dress, Mrs. Livingston smiles back. So does Esperanza. I float up the stairs. Aunt Jane says something and I pause on the landing where the stairs turn.

". . . just like her mother," Aunt Jane says. "Gloria loved to play dress-up. Her dad always brought clothes home—he owned a dry cleaner's. Things people forgot to pick up. They became Gloria's costumes."

I never knew that. Either that my grandpa owned a dry-cleaning store or that Mom liked playing dress-up. I bet she was really cute. Maybe that's how she learned about clothes. *Can you bring down my navy-and-white spectator pumps? Find the scarf I bought on our trip to Majorca?*

"I remember pinning the straps, the hems so she wouldn't trip," Aunt Jane continues. Her voice sounds funny. Softer. It's weird to think of Aunt Jane knowing something about Mom that I don't. I'm torn between sinking into the cozy memory of Mom's closet and listening more.

"*¡Yo también!*" Esperanza says. "I have a little sister."

"In Mexico?" Mrs. Livingston asks.

"*Sí.* I miss her so much. She doesn't pretend anymore, but Rosa still loves to dress up. She makes most of our jewelry. I just sell it here."

"Really." Aunt Jane's voice changes again, sharper, like usual. "But you'll be seeing her soon, right?"

"*No creo.*" Esperanza's voice sounds sad.

"You don't think so? But it's October. The season's over."

There's a long pause. Mrs. Livingston coughs. "I'm starving. What's keeping Lucy?"

I run the rest of the way upstairs, throw the dress on the bed, and clatter back down to the kitchen, where all three of them are looking at their plates. I missed something, but I don't even know what to ask. And I can't decide if I'm glad I know about Mom and the dress-ups now or I feel bad that there's stuff I don't know about her.

After dinner, Mrs. Livingston and Aunt Jane say they'll clean up. In my room Esperanza plugs in a curling iron and pins up the straps on the purple dress. "Nails next," she says, taking out a bottle of purple polish.

How'd she know I'd pick the purple dress? I watch her paint my nails quickly, perfectly, no blobs or smears.

"Can you do my hair up?" I say.

"*Claro.* Something like this?" She gathers up my hair on top of my head and pulls a few strands down. "We curl these . . ."

"Yeah." I smile. Then Mom's dangly diamond earrings will show up really good.

It takes forever to get my hair fixed. I know it's almost eight, when I'm supposed to get the Skype call. I crane my head toward the clock and—*owww!*—the curling iron singes my neck.

"*¡Lo siento!* Oh dear." Esperanza looks stricken.

"It's OK. I'm OK," I say, standing up, even though my neck hurts. It's 7:54.

"*Hielo.*" She leaves.

"It's fine!" Ice will drip on my dress. I check the iPad's Internet connection. It's on. Wait, I forgot the earrings! I go to the drawer with my sweaters. I tuck the money back in the drawer and carefully slide the jewelry out on my dresser. The award dinner earrings have a diamond stud and three dangly diamond strands that catch the light when I move my head. I slide all the jewelry onto my dresser. There are three bracelets. I don't know which is the one Daddy bought when I was born, the Lucy-in-the-sky one, but I slide the one with the most diamonds onto my wrist. I wish I still had Mom's mirror! Maybe I can see my reflection in the window? As I peer at the glass, the door opens behind me.

"Here's the ice. Let me see," says Aunt Jane, entering in front of Esperanza.

"It's fine! I don't want to drip on my dress." 7:58.

"I brought a towel to hold it with. Here, just—oh my—oh my God." She drops the ice and towel.

"*¿Qué?* It's not that bad, is it?" Esperanza peers over her shoulder.

Aunt Jane stares at me. "Those earrings. Your mother's. Where did you get—" Except for her mouth, nothing is moving.

"The desk downstairs. In the bedroom." 7:59.

"And the bracelets. But how—" She's looking from me to Esperanza and then to my dresser, where I laid the gray velvet bag. Her cheeks are turning pink.

"I found them. After the storm." Why isn't anyone calling yet? My neck does hurt now. Downstairs, there's a knock.

"Juan. Time I go," Esperanza says, coming over to kiss my cheeks. "*Estás preciosa.*"

8:01. Officially late.

"Wait, I'll walk you out," Aunt Jane says. "Wrap up the leftovers."

"Keep them." Esperanza waves her hand. "We eat Osorio's three nights a week."

8:02. Finally, the Skype tones sound, but on the screen is a man in a black T-shirt with a headset. "Lucy Ortiz?"

"Yes?" Where is Lupe Hernandez? Where is the crowd? The beautiful banquet room? He glances at his watch. He's got a scruffy beard. No tux, no—

"I'm the production manager. They're running behind. When they're ready, I'll put you through."

"Oh." Duh. I feel silly. Of course, Lupe Hernandez wouldn't call herself. He disappears. My neck hurts again, and I pick up the fallen bag of ice and press it to my neck. 8:03. 8:04. 8:05.

"Still there?" The man in the black shirt is back. I drop the ice. It's 8:08. "They're ready. You're live in five. Four. Three." Then I see two fingers, then one, then he's gone, and the scene on the screen transforms into the elegant ballroom, with huge crystal chandeliers hanging over white-covered tables with giant flower arrangements. It's so fancy and beautiful. Then a woman is speaking, a lady who sounds like Mom, with perfect English accented just enough to make it seem like she's singing every word.

"*¡Bienvenida, Lucy! Me llamo Lupe Hernandez.* On behalf of Latinas in Media, we're so glad you could join us!" She's wearing a floor-length, blue sequined gown with one long sleeve and one bare arm.

"*Gracias,*" I say, smiling, and the room erupts in applause. They told me to prepare something, so I wrote a little speech. I take a deep breath.

"My mom's job was really important, and she was really good at it. She would be really proud to have an award named after her. So would my dad. And so am I."

"Beautifully said, Lucy!" Lupe Hernandez leads more applause. Then they play a highlight video of Mom. I didn't expect that. There she is on the set, in the chair I used to spin in. Her voice is her news voice, musical like Lupe Hernandez's, but confident and strong, too. On location in New Orleans for the hurricane, in front of courthouses, interviewing everybody from men in suits to J.Lo. It ends with the picture that was in the bus shelter ad, Mom standing with her arms crossed and her awards, Best Latina Anchor and all that, listed next to her. The picture stays up as they call up the scholarship winner, a girl named Carmen Delgado who says Mom was her mentor when she interned at the station.

"I'm going to the University of Michigan, so maybe we can meet someday," she says.

I nod, biting my lip. Hearing Mom's voice again has been really weird. If I try to say something back, I might cry. Actually, I'm glad I'm not there, in the huge, fancy room with Mom smiling at everyone from a giant screen. She belongs to me.

"*¡Qué mundo tan pequeño!*" Lupe Hernandez breaks in with her singsongy voice. "Lucy, we know it's a school night, so we'll say *buenas noches.*"

The screen goes dark. 8:17 p.m.

"Lucy?" Aunt Jane knocks and cracks open my door. "All done?"

"Uh-huh."

"That was quick. How did it go?" She steps into the room.

"Fine." I smooth the purple skirt. I can still see the picture, but with the words, plastered to the bus shelter. *¡No la pierdas!* Don't miss her!

But I do. I do, I do.

"I brought some more ice." She sits on the bed and hands me another Ziploc bag.

"It's OK now." I put my finger to the burn mark, and then the dangly strands of the earrings.

"I didn't realize that you had your mom's jewelry," Aunt Jane says. "We should probably keep it someplace safer—"

"I like having it here." It comes out louder than I meant.

"But—"

"I want to keep it in my room." She wasn't worried about safety when they were in the desk downstairs. The suit Mom was wearing in that picture was one of those that Deirdre abandoned at the dry cleaner's. Who's wearing it now?

Aunt Jane hesitates. "Well. I guess so." She stands up.

Suddenly I don't want to be alone. I even feel a little grateful she wouldn't let me go, because otherwise I would have been in that giant, fancy room. "Aunt Jane?"

"Hmmm?" She's taken two steps toward the door.

"My neck does hurt. A little."

"Here you go." She hands me the bag of ice and the towel from before off the floor.

"I, um, heard what you said. Before dinner. About my mom. Liking to dress up and stuff," I say as I settle the bag against the burn.

"That's right."

"Did, um, you, too?"

"Me? Heavens, no. Even back then, I was a plain Jane."

Plain Jane. Back in New York, the first day. She said the same thing. I didn't get it then. "But you still played with her and stuff."

"Gloria didn't really let people choose." But she's smiling as she says it. "She didn't take no for an answer."

"Daddy said that, too. That was why she was such a good reporter."

"I bet."

"They played a video of her. At the dinner. I heard her voice."

"Oh, Lucy." Aunt Jane has left the door and is sitting next to me on the bed again.

"Interviewing people. And stuff." The tears are coming back now, stronger. "I miss her."

"I know." Aunt Jane is stroking my hair, curling one of the loose pieces around her finger; then she takes the ice bag so I don't have to hold it, and I lean into her shoulder. It's funny, but both the cold ice on my neck and the hot tears falling make me feel a little bit better, the tears soaking right into Aunt Jane's soft green fleece vest without any tissue or anything, and she just holds and rocks me until my tears are gone and the ice cubes melt into water.

Chapter 52
JANE

I told Lucy to eat the Osorio's leftovers tonight while I'm at the school district wellness expo. It'll be good to get them out of the fridge. Esperanza's generosity stung my conscience all the more. Doesn't matter that she never knew. Borders aren't the only invisible, unforgiving boundaries, turns out. Assumptions and judgments are just as dangerous. *My* assumptions and judgments, or rather misjudgments, which are accumulating into a long list. Not telling the school about Lucy's phobia. Underestimating how important Gloria's award dinner would be to her. What happened to the jewelry.

"I feel so guilty," I confessed to Sarah at our next session.

"I think you're simply human. It's partly a function of our environment here up north. We are segregated, no two ways about that. Without personal experience, we can default to stereotypes or narratives we hear in the media."

"Then how do you stop it? I'm worried it's a pattern." Miguel, for instance. Misjudging his pride when I overpaid him last spring. Rebecca and her family, who, with some guidance, have turned out to be dedicated workers, not the greenwashed dilettantes I anticipated.

"The clearest pattern I see is you being hard on yourself. And let me ask you this. If it's really true that you've misjudged all those people, isn't it just as likely that you're misjudging yourself?"

Her suggestion was so novel it halted my rocking.

"The most important thing is to learn from misjudgments. Establish new patterns. And you are. Look how the banquet wound up compared to Lucy's birthday."

"She was in tears."

"But crying on your shoulder. Releasing grief and being comforted, instead of isolating herself and bottling up her emotions."

Good point. "Bottling's bad. I figured out that much," I say with a grimace.

"And again, very human. If we can convince ourselves everything's fine, *we're* fine, then nothing has to change," Sarah said, snapping her fingers. "Presto. We've enabled ourselves to avoid the pain and upheaval that comes with change."

I think about Gloria's letter. *Devoted mother.* Could that be just as true as what I've believed all these years? Memories blur—a snow-day morning, tucking in the blanket around Matt's shoulder. Blue knitted mittens. Piggyback rides, baseball games, cat rescues, stepping stumps, carrot cake with cream-cheese frosting. Presto, chango? Maybe so.

I turn the truck into the parking lot of the new high school, not the one Matt went to, where the wellness expo is being held. Like Lucy's school, it looks like a jail. If the school district's so keen on wellness, seems like one step in the right direction would be to stop building cinderblock fortresses and cooping up the staff for seven hours a day. Not to mention the students.

It takes three trips to haul in everything, including a bushel basket of apples to sample and another of fingerling potatoes, each handful bagged with my potato salad recipe. Robert Sears suggested that as a take-home reminder. I luck out with my assigned table, in between a

yoga studio and someone offering chair massages. The massage therapist is sure to get a line. While they wait, people can take an apple and
some information. I grab a schedule from the yoga studio. Sarah also
suggested trying a class, or meditation.

"Do the mourning you denied yourself," she tells me every appointment. "Regularly, so the grief is less likely to blindside you." With the
onset of the off-season, I picked mornings, after Lucy's left for school.
Morning mourning. The homophone reminds me, and the daylight
keeps it from turning to brooding. So far, I mostly just repeat her name.
Nina. Nina. Nina.

It's a start. *The only way out is through.* Which is true for Lucy, too.
The dam did seem to break after the award ceremony, the grown-up pre-
tense of the dress and that infernal jewelry vanished, and she huddled
into me like a—

I stop the thought, then swallow hard, considering. Yes.

Like a child would. *Una niña.*

It's five minutes before the official start time, but a woman has
stopped already. She's wearing reading glasses and a Traverse City West
Titans sweatshirt. A school ID dangles from a beaded lanyard. She holds
out one hand and takes an apple with the other.

"Plain Jane's! I used to buy your stuff at the farmers' market, but I
haven't seen you there in a while."

I push the picture of Lucy and me away. Focus, focus. "Since I
started the CSA, I cut back. You plan for your customer base, and not
much more."

"Supply and demand, right. I'm an econ teacher." She laughs.
"Well, count me in! Are you taking deposits tonight?"

"Um, not just yet. But I could let you know." I dig in my bag for a
notepad. The Extension people should see me now! The way it works,
the school district will reimburse each employee $150 for wellness
expenses. I was worried that wouldn't be enough incentive, since my
subscriptions start at $500. But an hour later the samples have dwindled

and the signup sheet of people ready to make deposits is onto a second page. Other people say they remember me from the farmers' market or stopping at the stand. It's a good feeling. Supply and demand, like the economics teacher said, and for once I'm on the right side of the equation. Never mind the worthless estate, *I* can take care of Lucy with Plain Jane's. The sensation is one of abundance, of deep satisfaction. From somewhere surfaces the memory of the pregnant Amish mother at the farmers' market. "Full of blessings," she'd described herself. Right now, I get that.

The glowy feeling lasts for the rest of the expo. It lasts through the conversation with the yoga teacher at the next table, who gives me coupons for two free classes. Maybe Lucy will try it with me. It lasts through loading up the truck, which only takes one trip, since all the apples and potatoes were taken. It lasts through town and the turn north up the peninsula, which itself glows in the water's reflection of the almost-full moon as I climb to the gateway view. It lasts until my cell phone rings, displaying a 212 area code.

New York City. Langley couldn't possibly have more bad news, could he? On the last ring before voice mail, I answer.

"Mrs. McArdle?" It's a woman's voice. "This is Barbara Solomon calling from New York. Lucy's friend Phoebe's mother?"

Dimly, I place her from the funeral. On the heavier side, dark hair, carrying a giant purse, accompanying Phoebe along with a nondescript husband.

"Yes. Yes, I remember. Of course. How are you?"

The connection's bad, and I can't make out her reply.

"I'm sorry, can you repeat that?"

Then there's her voice again, clear and high as the clouds that drift over the moon and the road that descends toward bays whose surfaces have gone black and flat. "We'd like to invite Lucy to come home for a visit in December, over her school holidays."

I learned my lesson with the banquet. I tell Lucy about the invitation at breakfast the next day.

"Oh yeah, Phoebe mentioned that a while ago." She fills up the cat dishes.

Oh. She sounds indifferent. "Well, do you want to go, then? Should I make arrangements?" I thought she'd be all excited.

"Sure." She shrugs, hoisting her backpack, heading for the door. "Bye."

She disappears down the stepping stumps, leaving me to puzzle out another misjudgment. Holidays are hard, so rife with memories and expectations. Is she bottling those up, like Sarah warned? Or with Gloria and Luis gone, maybe she thinks it doesn't matter where she goes.

I look around the house. A pair of fuzzy Hello Kitty slippers lie under her chair. Breakfast dishes in the sink. Lexie's curled up with Sarge in the sunny spot. I go to the window, in time to catch her stepping onto Miguel's bus. Time for morning mourning.

But instead of infant Nina, my mind fills up with Lucy.

"How did you celebrate Thanksgiving, Lucy?" Since the visit to the Solomons' will curtail Christmas celebrations, I decide to make an extra effort for Thanksgiving. Show Lucy she does matter.

"We watched the parade." Her eyes brighten as she scratches Lexie's ears.

"The big one on TV?"

She nods. "Not on TV, though."

"In person?"

She nods again. "Dad's friend always had a huge party. He lived on the fourth floor, above Sixth Avenue. Last year Phoebe came with us. We saw the balloons go right by." She smiles.

"What was his name?" I try to ask casually. I still haven't figured out who Nando is from Gloria's letter.

"Whose name?"

"The friend. Who had the party."

"Mr. Alvarado." She looks at me funny, but then she's back down memory lane. "There was a Hello Kitty one year, and . . ."

Some detective I am. And how can I compete with that? I used to like doing a big Thanksgiving dinner. It's one of the most ritualized days of the year, so it was easy to meet expectations. I cooked, Jim and Matt watched football all day, and then we sat down together to eat. Simple.

Then Jim dropped his dual divorce and Florida blows right before Thanksgiving. I donated the free-range turkey I'd ordered to the homeless shelter and didn't do anything to celebrate that year. Or the next, or the one after that. We could both use a new tradition, really.

"The parade party sounds like a lot of fun."

"No parades in Traverse City, probably."

"Nope. There's a turkey trot, though."

"A what?" She frowns.

"A turkey trot. It's a five-K run on Thanksgiving morning."

She makes a face. "That sounds terrible."

"I think so, too. I'd a whole lot rather sleep in." I pause. "So we know what we don't want to do. Can we think of something we'd both like to do?"

She looks at Lexie and shrugs. "Maybe."

"It sounds like you like parties. You liked going out for your birthday dinner, you said, right?"

"I guess." She looks up.

"What if we invited the Livingstons over for dinner? And Miguel?"

"OK," she says, shrugging yet again.

Not the most encouraging start, but I call Rebecca, who says they already have plans. Her sister's family and Paul's mother are both visiting.

"You and Lucy come, too. I'd love to have you, and so would Jared. My niece and nephew are three and five. Too young to be much fun."

279

I feel like we're intruding, but I promised Lucy a party.

"You're sure it's not too much trouble?"

"Absolutely."

"Then what can we bring?"

Snowflakes are whirling when the bus drops Lucy home the day before Thanksgiving. Thick, feathery flakes, the kind that drape everything in a perfect white coat. She comes up the stepping stump path slowly, her face lifted to the sky. With her purple jacket and the bright-green pom-pom on her hat, she's the only pinpoint of color from here to the horizon. She comes in smiling, snowflakes on her eyelashes and her hair.

"I never saw so much snow before!"

An elementary-age image of Matt in his snowsuit pops in my head. The first winter we moved here, probably, when wonder edges out delight. Delight requires anticipation, and you can't anticipate the majesty of your first real Old Mission snow. Next year she will, so this is a one-time-only experience.

"This is just the beginning. It's supposed to keep up all night. If it wasn't already vacation, they'd probably cancel school." Another memory surfaces, of snow-day mornings. When Matt emerged, yawning, I'd make pancakes or omelets, something we didn't have time for on school mornings. If the plows hadn't come through and Jim was still home, all three of us would hunker down together. It felt cozy, almost like that time we had the huge blizzard on Kodiak.

Watching Lucy stare out the window into the whitening world, it feels that way now. The toes of Lucy's shoes are soaked, and she's wearing thin, stretchy knit gloves, but she's oblivious, even to Lexie rubbing up against her leg.

"Did you know no two snowflakes are alike?" I ask, going to stand next to her, close enough that our arms touch, so maybe some of the wonder will brush off on me.

Chapter 53
LUCY

I'm still mostly asleep when I hear a roar outside. It sounds like a car, but it doesn't just fade away like the cars that pass. It's an engine and another scraping kind of noise. I pull up the window shade.

It's all white, a super bright kind of white, like a sequined dress Mom wore once to a charity dinner. I have to hold my hand over my eyes. A truck is going back and forth along the driveway, pushing a big pile of snow to the back of the house.

Lexie meows for me to pick her up. She bats at the window, which is frosted over, and her claws scratch some lines. I draw a peace sign, my fingertip melting the fuzzy frost.

Downstairs Lexie dives for her food dish. Aunt Jane is outside, talking to the man driving the plow, holding a shovel. He waves and backs up, heading down the road back to Traverse City. I open the door.

Everything is covered in white. The dull grass and the stepping stumps and the two bumpy gravel driveway strips all are gone. It looks thick and clean and beautiful, sparkling in the sun.

Aunt Jane turns around. "Lucy! Put on a coat."

The snow is so amazing I can't think or feel anything else, but I reach for the coat hooks. "Wow."

"At least ten inches, I'd say." Aunt Jane pauses. "Happy Thanksgiving."

"Happy Thanksgiving." I lean out the door to get a better look. My hair swings forward, and I push it out of my eyes.

"Your hair's gotten so long!" she says.

"I guess." I examine the ends.

"You know, um . . . it looked so nice in braids, but I don't see you wear it that way anymore."

I remember Phoebe's fingers, smoothing and tucking. "I can't do them myself."

"Oh." She pauses. "Would you like me to try?"

"Well . . . OK."

We go to Jared's at three o'clock. The snowstorm was so bad his aunt and uncle couldn't get here, or his grandma.

"So we've got plenty of food," Mrs. Livingston says. "I hope you're hungry."

It's weird being at Jared's house. He's watching a football game with his dad and brother and barely says hi. Aunt Jane and Mrs. Livingston disappear into the kitchen. I wander around. What's Phoebe doing? We haven't Skyped since my birthday, even though I'm going there at Christmas. How about Graciela? They don't have Thanksgiving in Mexico, so it's a regular Thursday. Since the pawnshop, I've run out of ideas to get a plane ticket. Jared talked about using his dad's miles that one time, but he's probably forgotten. I don't know if I want to go to either place anymore. Mom and Daddy won't be in New York, and it's just four days, anyway. I have to come back. And Mexico feels so far away and impossible.

Jared lives in a regular neighborhood, with other houses around. They're all drifted over with snow, too, the lights inside starting to glow as it gets darker. They look cozy. Across the street a minivan stops at a house that has a porch light on. Two little kids run up to the front door. One's a girl—I can see her pigtails bouncing. A lady opens the door and reaches down to hug her. Somebody else, a man, comes into the big rectangle of light from the open door and lifts up the other kid.

At the minivan another man is reaching into the back seat. The dad. He follows the kids up the walk now, carrying a baby car seat. Here comes the mom, with a dish. All seven of them stand there on the porch for a minute, hugging each other and smiling.

"Lucy?" Mrs. Livingston's voice. "You OK in here?"

Across the street the minivan family is going inside, the man who came to the door holding it open for everyone else. I turn away from the window. The "Stop" button on my stomach elevator isn't working. "Fine."

"Kind of a hard day, I bet."

I shrug, sitting down on the couch. It feels a little like a cave in here, with no lights on. I kind of like it dark, though.

"Well, this might not be much comfort. But when I think about what I'm thankful for this year, meeting you and your aunt is right at the top of the list."

"It is?" I look at her wearing a big apron with a turkey on the top. It's still got creases in it, like she just unfolded it from the package.

"Absolutely." She waves at the couch. "Can I join you?"

I shrug again, twirling the braid hanging over my shoulder. She notices.

"Your hair looks pretty in braids. I don't think I've seen it that way before."

"Aunt Jane did it."

"Nice." She settles down next to me. "She's done a lot for us, too. Being a part of Plain Jane's was a big deal for me. I'm so grateful for what your aunt's doing."

"Why?"

"She's helping people live better. Healthier, and smarter, too. It's so important to know where our food comes from."

"I always thought the grocery store."

"And now you know what comes before that, right? And so we know what we need to protect. No farms, no food."

I shrug. I saw that bumper sticker on their car.

She smiles. "That probably sounds a little esoteric to you. But we wouldn't have met you if it weren't for Plain Jane's, either. And I am really grateful for that. So's Jared."

"He is?"

"After you arrived, he stopped complaining about going out to Jane's so much."

"Oh." He did?

"And he's never been very interested in school, but now he talks about your Digital Communications projects all the time. That was his best grade, in fact."

We got our report cards last week. I got three Bs and two As, in Digital Communications and math. *Inteligente.* Or school's just easier here. Aunt Jane was happy, anyway.

"Two-minute warning, Rebecca!" Mr. Livingston appears in the doorway, shaking his head. "Lions are just about to make it official."

"Finally. I think our turkey's just about done." She stands up. "Mind giving me a hand, Lucy?"

She puts her arm around my shoulder as we walk away from the window, into the bright kitchen.

Dinner goes OK. They don't say grace or do anything weird. We barely eat any of the huge turkey sitting on a platter in the middle of the table.

"Well, we'll have lots of turkey sandwiches," Mrs. Livingston says.

"Let's do the wishbone!" Jared says. He picks up a skinny, brown upside-down Y-shaped thing from a paper towel.

"Is that from the turkey?" It looks gross.

"You've never done a wishbone?" Jared shakes his head. "We each hold an end and pull. Whoever gets the bigger end gets their wish."

Like a birthday. It's been three months since my birthday wish to go to Mexico. I could wish it again.

"Hang on, Jared. It needs to dry out for a few days first," Mrs. Livingston says, walking in with serving bowls. Aunt Jane's behind her with the turkey platter.

"Aw, come on. I was going to wish for a PS3," Jared grumbles.

"I think your parents would have much more to do with that than a wishbone," Mrs. Livingston says. "I'll save it for you two. Lucy can come over after school one day next week, if that's all right, Jane?"

"Sure," Aunt Jane says. "We need to return an invitation one of these days, too. Maybe Jared can come up to Old Mission."

"Yeah!" Jared puts it back on the paper towel. I look at the bone, then at Aunt Jane. That was nice of her.

Mr. Livingston comes in. "We were thinking about going sledding after we clean up a bit. Fight off the turkey coma. What do you say, bud?"

"Yeah!" Jared perks up. "Can Lucy come, too? She's never been sledding."

"We'll fix that tonight," his dad says.

"I'm afraid we don't have any snow pants or boots with us," Aunt Jane says.

"We've got plenty you can borrow," Mrs. Livingston says. "It's all in the basement. Jared, Jason, go look. Snow pants, jackets, mittens, hats. Paul, get the sleds down from the garage. Jane and I will finish up the dining room."

As soon as they all leave the kitchen, I eye the wishbone. Would I wish to go to Mexico again? If I don't, what would I wish for? From the dining room I can hear Aunt Jane and Mrs. Livingston.

"Your pies were delicious. Was that pumpkin from the CSA?"

"Libby's can," Aunt Jane says. "Shhhh."

Mrs. Livingston laughs.

"My son always liked it, so I figured, why mess with a good thing?"

285

"I didn't know you had a son."

"He's in the army. Stationed in Germany."

I didn't know he was there. Aunt Jane said Matt was in the army, but not where. That's far away. She hasn't said anything about him visiting for Christmas. I wonder if he can't, or doesn't want to? There's a long pause.

"I'm glad that you could come," Mrs. Livingston says. "Holidays can be so difficult, especially the first year."

Aunt Jane keeps stacking plates and doesn't seem to have heard her. Finally she says, "It was a wonderful meal. Thank you for having us."

"Do you have plans for Christmas?"

I move closer to the doorway, where I can see a little bit into the dining room.

"Lucy's going back to New York, to visit a friend from school. Flying out Christmas morning. She'll be back on the twenty-ninth."

"That'll be nice for her."

Aunt Jane nods.

"So you'll celebrate together Christmas Eve, then?"

Another long pause. "I expect so," Aunt Jane says.

"I'm sorry. I don't mean to pry." But Mrs. Livingston keeps standing there, waiting.

"It's fine. It's just, what you said about holidays being difficult." Aunt Jane looks up from the plates, off into the air. "My husband left me just before Thanksgiving five years ago. This is the first holiday I've truly celebrated since."

"My goodness. I didn't know. I'm sorry."

I didn't, either. Just that she was divorced. I can't imagine Daddy leaving Mom.

"Your son probably doesn't get many chances to come home, either."

Aunt Jane shakes her head. "I was looking forward to Christmas with Lucy, and then this invitation came up. After I denied her the award banquet, I felt like I couldn't say no to a trip to see a friend during vacation. You're right, of course, we can celebrate on Christmas Eve. It's not like she's expecting Santa Christmas morning, after all!" She digs in her pocket for a Kleenex and blows her nose. She hasn't been sick. Is she upset? I can't see her now. Looking at the wishbone again, twirling my braid, I wonder what Aunt Jane would wish for.

"But you had your expectations, too. You're entitled."

I can't hear what Aunt Jane says next, because Jared comes up to me. He's wearing these funny-looking black puffy overalls and is carrying another pair, blue. "Hey. You're going to New York over Christmas?"

"Yeah." I turn away from him, to hear what Aunt Jane is saying next.

"That's your chance!"

"My chance? For what?"

"To go to Mexico, duh!" Jared shoves the blue pants at me. "Here's your snow pants. Come on, let's go."

Chapter 54
JANE

Kitted out in our borrowed snow gear, we toss all the sleds into the back of my truck and head for the county civic center. Lucy's quiet as I turn into the complex, bathed in a pinkish glow from the streetlights reflecting off the snow. Does she understand that underneath it is grass? Sledding hill, ball fields, most of this whole property. Yesterday after school she stuck to the stepping stump path, but the ground wasn't completely covered yet, either. So far today we've been on sidewalks and streets, except to get into the truck at home, which I didn't see her do. Should I remind her? I decide not to ask for trouble.

I park next to the Livingstons' Prius. Jared is already grabbing sleds before I've turned off the engine.

"Come on, Lucy!" He hands her a sled that looks like a flattened piece of blue Styrofoam and runs up the hill with a purple plastic saucer.

"Come on, come on! Hurry up!" Jared's sitting on his sled at the top, waiting for Lucy. She lays hers next to his and sits down, crisscross applesauce. If she realizes only the snow separates her from the grass, she's not letting it stop her.

"On your mark, get set, go!" Jared pushes off only a second or two before Lucy does. They fly down the hill and then around the bowl-like rim, toward the culvert that drains the parking lot. Weeds grow tall around the opening. They're dead now, a yellowish gray, not green, but I hold my breath.

But she's OK! She sticks her boots out and halts the sled short of the weeds. Then she follows Jared up and down again. Again and again, switching onto his sled, which spins her even closer to the weeds, but not quite touching, and still she's OK. I exhale, fear and breath dissolving into the cold night.

Later Rebecca produces a thermos of hot chocolate. Drinking it feels familiar, yet distant. Kids whiz down on all different kinds of sleds. Saucers, tubes, toboggans. Some sit up, some lie on their stomachs. Jason's got a snowboard.

"I'll bet it's been almost ten years since I went sledding."

"How come?" Rebecca asks.

"Well, Matt outgrew it, and that was that."

"He's an only child, then."

I nod, waiting for the familiar pang that will tow me back two decades. Something stirs, but not so sharply. I don't feel disembodied, my mind reeled back to Alaska and the cruel mirror of the dark winter days. Instead the sledding scene sharpens: the laughter louder, snow crunching under boots, steam rising from my hot chocolate in curlicues, Rebecca talking while she pours two more cups.

"Excuse me?"

"I said that it's too bad, isn't it, that you need kids to give you permission to play?" She nods at Lucy and Jared, charging up the hill again. They take her cocoa cups and collapse, cheeks pink, mittens matted with snow.

"Look who's talking. Neither of you have gone down yet," Paul says, reaching for Rebecca's thermos.

"Oh, come on now, Paul." She backs away, shaking her head.

"Come on, nothing. You need permission to play, look. Plenty of sleds available." He manages to grab the thermos from her, then turns to me. "I'll hold your cup, Jane."

"What? No." Instinctively I shake my head. "My back—"

"Back, schmack. This'll do your soul a world of good. You can go together."

"Go on, Mom," Jared says, starting a chant. "Go, Mom. Go, Mom."

Lucy picks it up. "Go, Aunt Jane. Go, Aunt Jane."

Somehow he coaxes Rebecca and me onto the toboggan, their longest sled. "Room for one more," Paul says, looking at Lucy. "All the ladies?"

"OK!" Lucy swallows the last of her cocoa and stands up, no hesitation. She climbs on behind me, hands on my shoulders, and Paul pushes us off. It feels like we hang on the brink forever, but then gravity does the inevitable and we're flying down, Rebecca's scarf whipping in front of my eyes, Lucy's scream mixing with mine, half anticipation, half revelation, pure delight.

Triple loaded on the toboggan, we zoom straight down instead of careening around the edge of the bowl, plowing into fresh, untouched powder, which finally stops us.

"Whoo-hoo, Mom!" Jared has followed us down on another sled. "You went the farthest!"

I gaze at Lucy, laughing, exhilarated, traces of a cocoa mustache on her face, snow sparkling on the braids hanging below her hat, then at the sled tracks. Jared's almost right. It's Lucy and I who have come the furthest.

Chapter 55
LUCY

Christmas Day and the airport is deserted. Aunt Jane stares up at the monitors.

"Everything's on time."

Figures. I was kind of hoping a storm might keep the flight from taking off, like what happened to Jared's relatives at Thanksgiving. When I woke up, there was another layer of fresh snow, but not nearly enough to stop the flights. I picked up Lexie and held her tight against my chest. If only there were a way to take her. She has been my ambassador to Michigan. At first it was awful, but I've gotten used to it. Well, sort of.

Jared's face pops up. Miguel, Esperanza. Aunt Jane. My stomach elevator starts dropping. In Mexico, Graciela will be my ambassador, I remind myself.

Downstairs Aunt Jane was drinking coffee and making eggs. In the living room, the real Christmas tree she chopped down smelled so good! I plugged in the lights. Here at the airport, at the security station, they have a fake one, the kind you buy already decorated.

"Got your boarding passes? Your return flight info?" Aunt Jane says.

I nod, the eggs churning in my stomach. My boarding passes to Detroit and then New York, my return flight information plus my one-way ticket to Mexico, leaving the same day. This is it. Goodbye. *Adiós*, Michigan, Lexie, Aunt Jane. Forever. Aunt Jane hugs me, talking over my shoulder. "Have a nice visit with Phoebe. I'll see you in four days, OK?"

"OK," I manage to croak out. But it's not OK. I'm not OK. Why didn't I tell Jared to forget the whole Mexico idea?

She steps back and looks at me, then hugs me again. "I'll miss you, Lucy." She brushes hair out of her face—or is that a tear? I see a flash of silver at her wrist, the bracelet I got her for Christmas, one of Esperanza's. "Better get going, now. Don't want to miss your flight."

Somehow my feet walk me through the security line. Waiting for my carry-on to come through the scanner, I look back over the checkpoint. Aunt Jane is still watching. She waves and blows me a kiss. *Besos.* I feel both a sob and the eggs rise up, and just then the gray bin with my Hello Kitty bag bumps over the conveyor, and I hurry away to the gate without looking back.

"Lucy! Lucy! Over here!" Phoebe shrieks, running across the baggage claim area. She's wearing the same pom-pom hat that's on her Skype picture, and it bounces on top of her head. She throws her arms around me. "I can't believe you're really here!"

I can't, either. On the plane it felt like time was standing still. Plus it was cloudy when we landed, so I couldn't see the city. Except for Phoebe it feels like I could be anywhere. That's pretty weird, since New York is where I've lived my whole life. Well, practically my whole life.

"Lucy, darling!" Mrs. Solomon is beaming as she comes up behind Phoebe. "How lovely to see you!"

"Thank you," I say as Phoebe lets me go. "There's my suitcase." I can spot it from way off with the yellow ribbon Aunt Jane said to tie onto the handle.

"Just one?" Mrs. Solomon starts to take it from me.

"It's OK, I've got it." I pull out the handle extension so I can roll it. Inside I put some of the special photos, like the Disney World one and skating at Rockefeller Center, to take to Mexico. And a new one of me and Lexie. I wanted to put them in my Hello Kitty carry-on, like Mom's jewelry bag, but I was worried the frames would break. In the suitcase, I packed them in between some sweaters and flannel pj's.

"Mr. Solomon's waiting outside."

Outside it's so loud! Planes taking off, cars honking, cabstand men blowing whistles. Phoebe is talking, but I can't hear her at all. And the smell. Burning, yucky black smoke from the cars. Mr. Solomon is waving and smiling and talking, but I can't hear him, either, until the car doors slam and we're on our way to Phoebe's.

The car feels weird, too. So low, compared to Aunt Jane's truck. In the front seat Mrs. Solomon is talking, to me and Mr. Solomon at the same time: "How was your flight? Was there a long layover?" and "Did you see how the tunnel traffic was backed up on the other side, dear? Let's take the bridge this time" and "Lucy, you must be exhausted." Next to me Phoebe is texting, her face glowing in the phone-screen light, and it's all too much, so I tell Mrs. Solomon, yes, I am exhausted and close my eyes to shut it all away.

I must have dozed off, because I wake up when the noise changes again, the whoosh of the tires becoming a rattle. I sit up, and we're on the Queensboro Bridge into Manhattan. It's starting to get dark now, and the lights are on the bridge and the buildings shine and it's so beautiful and I feel so homesick and mixed-up. Because I'm homesick for Daddy and his smile and Mom and her dry-clean-only TV clothes and for Lexie, too, her warm body next to my feet at night. For Miguel and his *"hola"* every morning on the bus. For the beautiful soft white snow that sparkles in the sun when I look out my bedroom window and covers up all the grass.

The first time I saw it, I thought, *Step on snow.* The words that came into my head were *You can go.* So I did. And nothing bad happened, even after sledding down the hill, over and over again. So snow is good, and I know Aunt Jane will be upset when she finds out I've gone to Mexico. Thinking of her makes my stomach hurt. I remember her blowing kisses at the airport, letting me run the farm stand, baking the carrot cake that turned out to be good, and rescuing Lexie in the storm. Lexie! And Jared will probably get in trouble for helping me, buying the ticket with his dad's frequent-flier miles, and I'm sorry, so sorry, everybody, but I got the ticket and I'm just going.

The Solomons' building has underground parking. Phoebe is still texting as we walk to the elevator.

"Phoebe, put that away. Lucy's here. Who do you need to text?"

"Everyone, Mom! I have to tell them Lucy's here." She looks at me. "Everyone's so excited you're back. Rachel's having a party, and there's a flick and float at the Y, and ice-skating—"

"Don't forget the play. We're going to the *Wicked* matinee day after tomorrow," Mrs. Solomon says.

"How long is Lucy here?" Mr. Solomon asks, unlocking the door. "That's quite a schedule."

He swings the apartment door open. From the back I hear barking, getting louder.

"Ozzie, hush!" Mrs. Solomon commands as a little, shaggy white dog runs into the room, yapping, panting, and sniffing around my feet. I forgot they had a dog! "He'll remember you in a minute, Lucy. Just needs to get your scent."

I pull off my glove. Ozzie's nose and his tongue on my fingers are cold and wet. Gross. Lexie's soft and warm and cozy and quiet. Even Sarge is better. I wipe my hand on the edge of my coat. He starts barking again.

"Shush, Ozzie! Have you called your aunt yet to let her know you've arrived?"

"Um, no."

"Why don't you do that now, then," she says in an adult not-asking voice. "I'm sure she'd like to know that you're here safe and sound."

If I hear Aunt Jane's voice, I might just lose it all and start bawling. Mrs. Solomon's not going to let me out of it, so I pull my phone out and dial. Lexie's picture on the phone's screen makes me feel a tiny bit better.

One, two, three rings. "Hello, you've reached Plain Jane's CSA," Aunt Jane's voice says. "We can't get to the phone right now, but please leave a message."

Chapter 56
JANE

"Merry Christmas, Matt."

"Mom?" Surprise edges out sleep in his voice.

"Merry Christmas," I repeat. "It is still Christmas over there, right?"

"For another hour or so." He yawns.

"Sorry, did I call too late?" After prowling around the empty house all day with the cats, I couldn't stand the silence anymore.

"Nah, it's OK. It's just been kind of hectic here."

"The holidays," I say.

"Yeah. Lots of people on leave. Rest of us trying to cover. You know."

"Right. I remember, that's how it was with your dad, too." Jim always pulled holiday duty, even after we moved off base. I didn't mind. San Diego held few warm childhood memories. Wherever we went, first Mom, then Gloria sent the box of oranges and that was enough of home for the holidays.

"Hang on a sec, Mom." There's a snatch of muffled conversation, the other voice softer, higher than Matt's. A sound. A kiss? Then Matt's voice again.

"Allison's going to bed. She said to say thank you. She really likes the necklace."

It was Lucy's idea to add a gift for Allison to my Christmas package. We picked out one of Esperanza's pieces. For Matt, I got a pair of fleece pajama pants and made up some dry pancake mix. Snow-day morning stuff for an adult.

"Oh. Good. She's welcome." I contemplate my son and a woman, together in a tiny, boxy military apartment four thousand miles away. A woman I've not yet met who greets me through him, who kisses him good night.

"So I was planning to call you soon, too," Matt says. "Big news here."

"Yeah?"

"Allison's pregnant."

Pregnant? I'm dumbfounded, speechless. Jumbled memories collide: a three-year-old on Jim's shoulders; my hand-knitted blue hat and mittens; a red tricycle on a hot Houston sidewalk; grass-stained baseball uniforms; Boy Scout projects; a black graduation gown.

"It's all good. We moved into officer housing after she found out. The doctor says the baby's doing great."

"When is she due?" The words sound completely appropriate, the question completely impossible. Matt, my child, a father? Me, a grandmother?

"Around June 1."

So she's past the first trimester. Past the riskiest time. But not beyond it. No, never beyond risk when it comes to parenthood. "Do you know what it's going to be?"

"Nope. We're gonna have it be a surprise."

The understatement to beat all. I wander down the hall to Matt's room. I can see him here, curled underneath the plaid bedspread, doing homework at the desk in the corner. Will a grandchild ever visit?

"Well. Congratulations." To my ears the obligatory word sounds flat, inadequate, but Matt doesn't pick up on it.

"Thanks." His voice sounds easy. "Allison's really excited."

"Are you?" I blurt out the question, unable to keep anxiety out of my voice.

"Well, sure. I mean, I was a little surprised at first, but this is my kid. Another generation. Of course I'm excited."

"You're so young." I can't help saying it.

"Older than you and Dad were."

I do the math. "I guess so." I was twenty-two, Jim twenty-three, when Matt was born. He'll be twenty-four in February.

"And you did it. It's going to be cool." He yawns again. "So, got a lot of snow?"

You did it? End of story, now on to the weather? Is that really all there is to it for Matt? And Jim and I divorced. We did it, but we couldn't keep it up.

As much as the words, it's his tone that rings dissonant from my guilt-infused memories. Matter-of-fact, dismissive, even. Sarah's voice echoes. *Think of it from your son's point of view.*

"I really miss it. We've got a little, but nothing like home," Matt says. His voice actually sounds wistful.

Braced in the doorway of Matt's childhood room, I reel through the corridors of memory. *Nothing like home.* He means here. This house on Old Mission was where he grew up. With Jim and me. *A devoted mother.*

"Mom? Still there?"

"Mm-hm." Was Gloria right? Sarah, too? He's contradicting twenty years of regret and self-recrimination. What did he ask about? Snow?

"What does Lucy think? Must be way more than she ever saw in New York."

"Seems to like it. Got her first taste of sledding at Thanksgiving." The snow's been more like a godsend, somehow rendering Lucy's grass phobia dormant. Has she made it into New York yet? I hope she'll call and let me know.

"At the Civic Center hill?" The note of wistfulness is stronger. "That was great. I remember building jumps at the bottom."

"They still do."

"Good times." I feel like I can see a smile through the phone. It would be nice to see him. And Allison, and the grandchild. Could I make a visit?

What about Lucy? And a plane ticket to Germany? The Solomons bought Lucy's. It stung a bit to take their offer, but with money still so tight, it was the only way for Lucy to go. But next time I should try to Skype, at least. Lucy could help me set up an account, or use hers, or whatever. I walk back to the kitchen, looking for Lexie.

"Matt, maybe next time I'll call on Skype. I've got a high-speed Internet connection at home now."

"My mom, the technophobe, on Skype?" He laughs. "Having an eleven-year-old around is good for you."

"Twelve," I correct him, climbing the stairs to Lucy's domain. Lexie's curled up on the sill of the hall window. Her ears prick up as I approach, but she doesn't move.

"Twelve. Sure, we can Skype." He yawns again. "Listen, I'm on duty at oh six hundred."

"Oh. OK. Well. Tell Allison congratulations for me." This time the word comes easier. "I—I love you."

"I will. Love you, too. Night, Mom."

The cross-Atlantic connection cuts off. Lexie purrs and arches into my hand as I scratch behind her ears. The snap on her collar clanks against the silver bracelet Lucy gave me for Christmas, one of Esperanza's creations. I haven't worn any jewelry since I took off my wedding ring, but I put it on right away.

I gave Lucy a toboggan, like the Livingstons', and a jewelry box. After Thanksgiving the toboggan was an easy idea. I almost gave it to her early, since we went sledding in December, but held out. The jewelry box was harder. One weekend I happened to see a sign for a holiday bazaar at a church and stopped on a whim. An Amish man was selling beautiful small wood pieces—clocks, candlesticks, lamps—all handmade, dovetailed construction, sanded to a sheen. The jewelry box had a tray divided into velvet-lined compartments for individual pieces, which was inset over a bigger bottom compartment. The lid was inlaid with a mirror. It was perfect for Gloria's jewelry. When Lucy opened it, I got that full-of-blessings feeling again.

That was last night, so today I had nothing to unwrap. But Matt's words ring like a gift of absolution. I did it. I raised a child, well enough that he's ready to be a father himself.

Lexie's body is warm and vibrates with her purrs. Out the window, stars dot the inky sky that stretches down to meet the black depths of East Bay. I think of stargazers on another cold Christmas night, two thousand years ago, searching for a child. The window reflects my smile. In a few days, mine is coming home.

Chapter 57

LUCY

After I leave the voice mail, I stare at Lexie's picture. I might never see her again. I grit my teeth against the tears.

"Come on, let's go to my room." Phoebe pulls on my arm.

"I'll make you girls a snack," Mrs. Solomon calls after us. "Ozzie, stay here," she orders. He patters behind us a few steps but turns around when she calls him again. Phew.

In her room Phoebe turns on a light switch. "Ta-da!" In front of her window is a tabletop Christmas tree with white lights.

"Wait, you're Jewish!" It's one of those predecorated ones like at the airport. The star on top is crooked, and there're not many ornaments, but it's still a Christmas tree.

"Do you like it? Do you like it?" She bounces on her bed, and her boobs jiggle. Has she already grown bigger than in summer? "We got it for you. So you would feel more at home. Mom wanted to have it in the living room, but Ozzie kept knocking it over, so we moved it in here. He's not allowed to come in here." She flips onto her stomach, waving her feet in the air.

I nod, but my stomach is clenching with all the mix-ups. At the airport I saw signs for an international terminal, and I don't know if I should go there or stay in the domestic terminal, since I have to go to Dallas before Mexico City, and if I do have to go to the international terminal, how do I explain that when the Solomons drop me off? Now there're Christmas trees that don't belong at Phoebe's, and noisy dogs. Phoebe getting bigger while I'm still flat. Mrs. Solomon acting so nice, making snacks and buying theater tickets and stuff, but no snow out the window and no Lexie and Sarge curled up together on the couch with Aunt Jane in the kitchen, humming and puttering around.

"Rachel's party is going to be awesome. It's a night party," Phoebe says. "She's going to get a karaoke machine, and we'll sing and dance and probably play truth or dare."

I nod. I can't really remember what Rachel looks like.

"She and Eli are boyfriend and girlfriend now. And Veronika's dating Hunter." She rolls over onto her back, crossing her legs, jiggling her foot.

"Eli? Eli—" I can't remember his last name. The one from that day. The field trip.

"Eli Moore." Her foot is really close to the Christmas tree.

That was him. I can feel his knees poking my back. Now he's Rachel's boyfriend? "You mean they go places together? Like movies and stuff?"

"Sometimes. Mostly they just hang out together, you know, at lunch. After school."

"Everybody does that with their friends." Some of the ornaments are shaking.

Phoebe shrugs. "So, do you still hang out with the boy you told me about in the summer? Gerald, I think his name was?" She asks carefully, but I see she's stopped jiggling her foot.

"Jared," I say.

"Jared, right." She waits another few seconds. "So, do you?"

I shrug. "We hang out. It's no big deal." I think about sitting at lunch together, and Digital Communications class, and going sledding after Thanksgiving. Buying the plane ticket. We did it at lunch one day on his iPad, using his dad's frequent-flier miles. He even found an airline that let twelve-year-olds fly alone, so I didn't have to pay unaccompanied-minor fees and stuff. We do a lot of stuff together, I guess. Pete said he was my boyfriend, but he doesn't know anything. He's just Jared.

"Oh, good." She sighs and starts jiggling her foot again. "Sometimes I feel like everybody but me has a boyfriend."

"Girls, snack's ready." Mrs. Solomon pokes her head around the door. Ozzie starts barking again. "Ozzie! Lucy, dear, Phoebe's emptied a couple drawers for you to unpack your things."

If I unpack, Phoebe might see the photos and everything.

"I'm keeping everything in my suitcase. I'll just have to pack up again in a few days," I tell her as we get ready for bed. "Sorry you had to clean out your drawers."

"That's OK." She shrugs, yawning as she takes off a real bra, not one of the stretchy tank kinds. "I had so much old stuff that didn't fit anymore."

After Phoebe falls asleep I check the inside pocket of my bag. The gray velvet jewelry bag is still safely tucked away. The printout of the Mexico City ticket is inside my notebook. I kiss the phone picture of Lexie good night. After a second, I open up the photos folder and start scrolling.

There's Jared at the sledding hill—we went again the first day of vacation. There's Miguel, in the bus driver's seat. I took it on the last day of school before vacation. Lexie by the Christmas tree. Aunt Jane is in the background of that one, in the kitchen. I zoom in on her face. She's looking our way, smiling.

I swipe it closed, quickly, and scroll through more. Lots of Lexie in my room. The birthday party at Osorio's, with the slice of chocolate cake in front of me, and empty plates in front of Jared and his family, Miguel, and Aunt Jane. Her cake really was better. The last picture I see before I finally fall asleep is the one Jared took of me at the farm stand, beaming beneath the Plain Jane's sign.

Mr. Solomon is right about the busy schedule. It's so busy I can mostly forget about the extra ticket in my bag. We go to Rachel's party, where nobody is kissing or acting like boyfriend and girlfriend. Eli is there, but Joel Griffin isn't. We go to Broadway for the show and the Y for the flick and float. We don't go to my old street or to school or to Rockefeller Center to skate. We go to an Indian restaurant, because I haven't had dal or chapatis for months, and a deli and buy hot dogs from a stand. We ride the subway and buses and a hansom cab in Central Park, where the horses clip-clop past the John Lennon memorial and I try to imagine that I still live here, on Fifty-Sixth Street, but I can't. By the last day Ozzie stops barking when he sees me and I don't feel like a stranger in a noisy, smelly, gray city anymore. But I don't belong, either. I don't feel like anybody. Like if a teacher called my name in school, I wouldn't even know whether to answer. Maybe in Mexico I will.

Chapter 58

JANE

Rebecca's number pops up on the caller ID.

"Jane! Thank God you're home." She sounds breathless.

"What's going on?"

"Have you heard from Lucy since she left for New York?"

"Just a voice mail after she arrived. I'll pick her up tomorrow." I can't believe how empty the house feels without her, or how much I'm looking forward to her return. There's still a few days of Christmas break left. Maybe we can go sledding again. Today's perfect, not too cold or windy and that rarest of December gifts up north, sunshine. It feels like confirmation of the new light Matt shed on myself as a mother. Both he and Gloria, now. Double absolution. And now, entering a new year together, I resolve to let the past stay in the past. Lucy isn't Nina or Matt, and I'm not the same, either.

"You need to call her friend's family right away. I've got bad news— oh, I'm so sorry to have to tell you this, Jane! I can't believe this is happening, and Jared played a part—"

"Tell me what? What bad news?" My pulse quickens. Airline travel these days, so risky. But wait, she doesn't return until tomorrow. What could Jared know?

"Paul was in his Delta frequent-flier account today, booking some upcoming travel. The mileage balance was lower than he expected. It showed a ticket purchase about a month ago, one-way from New York to Mexico City, and he hasn't used the account since—"

"What does that have to do with Lucy?" I interrupt.

"Getting to that. He thought it was a mistake, so he called Delta. They said there was no mistake. Someone legitimately used his account to buy the ticket. Departing tomorrow."

"Tomorrow?" Fear freezes my bloodstream for a moment, then starts pumping double time. "LaGuardia?"

"Yes." Rebecca starts talking faster. "Jared sometimes uses Paul's iPad. The Delta account information is stored on it. And he's told us about Lucy's family in Mexico. So we asked him, do you know anything about it?"

Oh my God. She was in touch with her cousin on Facebook. Would she really go so far as to show up on their doorstep in Mexico?

Rebecca sniffles loudly. "Eventually he admitted it. He bought that ticket for Lucy. She's planning to use it tomorrow, instead of her return ticket to Traverse City."

My legs start trembling, and I slump onto the blue velvet couch.

"Paul's on the other line right now, cancelling it. There's no way she'll be able to use it, Jane, I swear. And I can't apologize enough for Jared's role in this."

A one-way ticket. Lucy wasn't planning to come back. She was running away. Memories tumble in my head. High-fiving on the stepping stump. Cleaning the farm stand. In my arms after the awards banquet. Braiding her hair. Sledding. Lexie jumps onto my lap, purring. Lucy's giant smile when I brought Lexie back the first time. And the second time. She was even going to leave her precious cat behind! I'm going to lose her. Another child. *Niña.*

The moving sidewalk at Detroit Metro is a mercy since my legs feel like they cannot function. I slide past neon signs and throngs of people.

Buddy's deep dish Detroit-style pizza has a line even at 10:30 a.m., Motown Bar and Grille, Motor City Shoeshine. The lines are longest at Starbucks, in all its green generic comfort. I wish for a cup but don't want to take the time to stop. Lucy's flight from New York is due at eleven.

It took me hours to reach the Solomons yesterday. They were "out on the town, celebrating Lucy's last night," Mrs. Solomon explained when I finally reached her. At first she was incredulous. The visit had been wonderful. Lucy had seemed fine, not nervous, uneasy, or unhappy. Planning to run away? Impossible.

Then she put Lucy on, who first insisted it was a mistake. When I told her Jared had fessed up, though, that did it. She started crying, which quickly turned to incoherence. Mrs. Solomon got back on and agreed either she or her husband would personally see that Lucy was escorted to the flight to Detroit today. I caught the first flight out of Traverse City down to Detroit to meet her and got a seat on her same connection back. The day-of ticket price was jarring, but I couldn't risk that she wouldn't concoct some plan B when she reached Detroit. I considered asking for a bereavement fare—after all, haven't I lost Lucy?—but just handed over my credit card.

Bewilderment at the plan, relief at intercepting it, and guilt that I could have avoided it all jostle in my head. Memories now stand out like red flags: Lucy bunkered in the truck the first day, unable to get out. Making a face at the rhubarb taste. Yelling at me over the banquet invitation.

The sign by the gate door is blinking: "Now arriving flight 2908, New York LaGuardia." Arriving physically, but what about her spirit? Will she be scared? Resentful and angry? If only I'd tried harder. If only I'd tried sooner. If only I can get a second chance.

Chapter 59
LUCY

I'm in the last row on the plane. One by one everybody files out the aisle silently, the same way people ride elevators. That's how it was last night, after Aunt Jane called. We had just seen a movie and were eating ice-cream sundaes.

"Jane!" Mrs. Solomon said. "Why yes, she's right here . . ." She looked over at me, smiling. Then her smile got smaller, and her teeth disappeared, then flatter and flatter, and her forehead wrinkled, and then she put her palm to her lips, and then she turned away and stood up, and I knew I wouldn't find out if Mexico felt like home.

Everything was really awkward at the airport this morning, too. Mrs. Solomon came to the airline counter and paid extra for the unaccompanied-minor fee, then gave me a hug. "Bye, Lucy. Happy New Year. We'll plan a visit for 2012. And Phoebe's bat mitzvah will be here before you know it."

"Bye, Lucy." Phoebe hugged me, too. "See you."

"OK." But I know I won't see her again. No way is Aunt Jane going to let me come back to New York, not even for a bat mitzvah. Probably she won't even let me Skype, she's going to be so mad. *Adiós, amiga.*

It's almost my turn. I check the inside pocket of my carry-on. The jewelry bag is still there, snug and safe. When I get to the front, the flight attendant, who watched me like I might crawl out on the wing, follows me.

"I can find her. You don't have to follow me," I say.

"Regulations. We have to check ID," he says.

Down the Jetway. It feels like a gangplank. Into the terminal. There she is, off to the side, her arms crossed over her green fleece vest. I see her before she sees me. When she does, her whole body sags, her arms falling to her sides, her face relaxing. I even see a tiny smile before she takes three long steps and pulls me into a hug. Wait, is she not mad?

"Jane McArdle? ID, please," the flight attendant says.

She holds me a second longer, then rummages for her wallet. She finds a tissue, too, and blows her nose.

"All set, then," he says, handing it back and folding up his papers. "Have a nice day, ladies."

"Well." Aunt Jane looks at me, and I see her body relax again. "You're safe and sound, at least. We've got a lot to talk about, huh?"

I look down, then up, over her shoulder, not meeting her eyes. Uh-oh.

"But let's find our gate first. And coffee."

The moving sidewalk is silent like the airplane aisle and elevator. It gives me time to think. Worry. What is she? Mad, or not mad? We step off at a Dunkin' Donuts.

"We're just a couple gates down, and we've got an hour. Are you hungry?"

I shake my head, heading to a table. She brings over a tray with a coffee, a bagel sandwich, and a blueberry muffin. "In case you change your mind," she says.

She still seems calm while she eats, but facing her, I can see she's trying hard to stay that way. She's acting, like she did in the parking lot of that social worker when it upset her that I wouldn't go in but she pretended it didn't. I'm in the seat facing out, toward the terminal. The restaurant's pretty full, and there're lots of people walking around. I guess Aunt Jane can't kill me here, with all of them around. I can't stand not talking about it anymore.

"I'm sorry," I say softly, looking at the little silver stand thing that has stacks of creams and sugar.

"I didn't catch that."

"I said I'm sorry." I look up at her quickly, then back at the packets. Nondairy and dairy. Yellow Splenda and white real sugar.

"For what, exactly?"

"For—" What do I say? For wanting to feel like I have a family again? "For making you worry."

"Worry?" She barks a laugh that sounds half like a sob. "Try terrified. If you had gotten on that other flight, if something had happened to you . . ." Her voice quavers for a second.

Her knuckles are white where she's gripping her coffee cup. If she was terrified, that means she cares, but—

"What was your plan? You had a ticket to Mexico City. And then what?" Her voice sounds sterner now.

"Visit Graciela and Aunt Bonita." I toy with the sugar packets, alternating them yellow and white. That's not a complete lie. It was just going to be a long visit. And is she mad at me or glad I'm back?

"Visit? Did they invite you?"

"Not exactly."

"Then what were you doing, exactly?" The quavering is gone, and her voice is a little bit angry now. "Did your Aunt Bonita even know?"

Slowly I shake my head.

"You were just going to show up there and hope she'd let you stay?"

I nod, then shrug. But she would have! Wouldn't she? "Well, we're family."

She stares at me. "So are we."

"But you don't act like it!" I burst out.

Her eyes go wide and her head jerks back like I hit her. I duck my head down, staring at the table.

"Whew." She blows her nose into her napkin. "I don't know what to say."

I don't, either, so I take a bite of the blueberry muffin. She thinks of something pretty fast.

"Using Jared's father's frequent-flier miles, that's basically stealing, you know."

"But it didn't cost anything."

"It did! It cost him the miles. If he doesn't have enough left, he'll have to pay the next time he needs a ticket."

"So we can pay him back."

"We?" Her eyebrows are up to the middle of her forehead. "A ticket to Mexico during the holidays has to be several hundred dollars."

Eight hundred fifty, actually. "You're supposed to be getting the payments from the estate soon," I shoot back. "There'll be plenty of money."

"Payments from the estate?" Aunt Jane looks shocked, banging her coffee cup on the table. "What are you talking about?"

"I heard Mr. Langley telling you about it. A long time ago, in New York," I say, feeling satisfaction at the shock on her face. "He said it would start coming in January."

Aunt Jane looks like she swallowed all her know-it-all words. I press my advantage. "I hate it here. You're always busy, working. That's why I did it." I push away the memories of the birthday party, sledding, and setting up the Christmas tree. "It's cold." Who cares if the snow's pretty and covers up the grass. "All I have is Lexie, and she doesn't even want to stay with me much." I shove aside thoughts of Jared and Miguel and Esperanza.

"Lucy." Aunt Jane is squeezing my arm on the table. "Lucy. You're shouting."

People are looking our way. So I'm making a scene. Like at the dry cleaner's with Deirdre, like with the real estate agent in our apartment. Like when Lexie escaped the first time. Scene after scene after scene, but I can't change the story. Mom and Daddy are still dead, I still stepped on the grass and made their car crash, and now I'm stuck back in Michigan.

Chapter 60

JANE

Gently I nudge Lucy's door open. She's asleep, Lexie curled up in the crook of her knees. I pull the blanket up over her shoulder. She stirs and twitches away from my touch. My heart feels like lead. Even involuntarily she retreats from me. I deluded myself these last few months. Yes, we had a few close moments. But I should have tried harder, sooner. She's not happy, and she deserves to be. I swallow hard. I have to call Bonita Ortiz.

Still I put it off for a week, hoping that Lucy gets a lift from returning to her school routine—Miguel driving the school bus, the ever-devoted Jared, whom I told the Livingstons to go easy on. It was Lucy's idea, after all, that he just helped execute. I putter around the house, trying to occupy myself with the usual Plain Jane's winter paperwork. But I keep returning to the folders in Matt's room, rereading Gloria's letter and Lucy's files, looking for clues I missed. One afternoon both Sarge and Lexie interrupt, rubbing against my legs, drawing my attention to their empty dishes. Lucy must have forgotten to fill them before school. Not like her. I reach underneath the sink for the cat-food bag. The water dishes are empty, too.

We're getting an early January thaw, the icicles dripping steadily, but Lucy seems frozen. The next day, I detect a smell from the mudroom. Opening the kitchen door, I close it just as fast. The litter box. First the food dishes, now this. She never forgets the cats.

She never forgot.

By the time Lucy gets home from school, the litter box stench is overpowering, but she doesn't seem to notice, kicking off her boots in the middle of the floor. "Lucy, the litter box is way overdue for cleaning."

"What?" She looks over at it and wrinkles her nose slightly. "Oh, OK."

"Yesterday I found their dishes empty, too. Both food and water."

"Oh." She looks at the floor, where the melting snow from her boots is already puddling. Deliberately I reach down and pick up the boots, putting them on the tray next to mine.

"The boots and water, we can clean that up. But the cats depend on you to remember."

"I know. I'll do it." But she makes no move to clean out the litter box, instead going the other way, into the kitchen, dragging her backpack, dragging my heart.

I have to call.

Miguel comes over for the phone call as interpreter backup. Bonita understands English but speaks less. She's stunned to find out about Lucy's runaway plan.

"She is very eager to meet you and her father's family," Miguel says.

"Meet us?" A sharp intake of breath, between a gasp and a sob. "*¿Mi sobrina?*"

"Let's be honest," I say. She needs the truth. "Lucy wants to move to Mexico." I steel my voice against the quaver.

She understands that, all right.

"Move? Live here? *¿En serio?*"

"Yes," I say.

"No." Her voice is just as steely as mine. "*No hay futuro en México.* Luis was trying to get us out. I think he was close to getting the papers, but then there was the accident." Her voice breaks. "He was the last of my family."

What is she talking about? Close to getting what papers? And what does she mean, the last of her family? "I thought you had another brother," I say, recalling the bio Langley shared. "A bit younger?"

"Fernando." Her voice hardens. "He's been dead to me for years."

Fernando. *Nando?* From Gloria's letter? Dead—to Bonita? What in the world does she mean?

"*Díganos, señora,*" Miguel says.

"When he joined the gang. Got mixed up with narcos."

"Drugs?" My grip tightens on the phone. *Watch out for Nando.*

"*Sí*, drugs. He wanted to go to *los Estados Unidos*, too. My parents told him he had to wait. After Luis graduated, they needed to save more money. Luis was trying to help, sending back practically all his paycheck."

Sending back all his paycheck. Next would come all his savings. The pieces are falling into place.

"But Nando got bored waiting. He didn't really want to go to school, anyway. He pretended he got a job, a legitimate one. He started giving my parents money. They were proud. Then we found out all the money was *sucio*."

"Dirty," Miguel whispers.

"My father told him to quit. Get out. But it was too late." The edge is gone from Bonita's voice. She only sounds sad now. "They owned him. And we all pay. *Mi padre*, they said it was a heart attack, but he died of a broken heart. I know."

We all pay. "Is that where Luis's money went?" I can't help asking her, looking to pin down another piece to the puzzle that's floated in my head since April. Of course Gloria and Luis would have wanted Lucy to stay in the US if his brother was a drug dealer. Cartels fighting each other, corrupt police and government, innocent bystanders victimized—I shudder, imagining Lucy in the middle of a newspaper headline.

"You know about that?"

"How did you spend it?" I have to know how Lucy became penniless. "More than three hundred thousand dollars in a year and a half."

"El dinero se nos va de las manos," she sighs.

"It goes like water," Miguel translates.

"First it was private school for my Graciela. To keep her away from the city. Away from her *tío*. Nando, he is smooth. Graciela is *joven*. Impressionable. So I needed to keep her away to keep her safe.

"Then Mama. All the stress is not healthy. She already had diabetes. Walking is difficult. Then her blood pressure, it goes so high. She needed medicine, dialysis. But treatments here are not good."

Miguel is shaking his head as he listens. Has he heard this story before?

"Luis wanted me to take her to Texas. But because of Nando, our family is on a government watch list. We cannot cross. That's why we couldn't come to the funeral, either." I hear a sniff.

"So he started working to get papers for all four of us. Mama, Enrique, *mi esposo*. Graciela. Me. To come live in America, too. *Y eso es muy caro.*"

And that explains how retirement accounts and a half-million-dollar second mortgage goes like water.

"*Mi madre*, she just died in November. Kidney failure," Bonita continues. "With Graciela away at school, it is just me and my husband *en casa*. It is not supposed to be that way. *La familia lo es todo.*"

Family is everything. I don't need Miguel to translate that. Finally, I understand Luis and Gloria's will. And her warning. But now what am I going to do about Lucy, whose dejection and isolation are as bad as they were in June?

I talk it over with Rebecca, who stops by with her CSA deposit while Lucy's at school.

She sighs. "The decisions don't get any easier, do they?"

"Well, the decision is actually pretty easy. She can't go, of course. It's making her understand why that's difficult." She'll probably think I'm just being mean old Aunt Jane again. But if it keeps her safe, I'll live with that.

"Could Bonita talk to her?"

"I suppose, but I think Lucy would still fantasize about Mexico as some promised land." Where her *familia* acts like family.

"Right." Rebecca drums her fingers. "She has to realize for herself that her future isn't down there." She hesitates. "Is a trip really out of the question?"

"Are you kidding?"

"Bonita said that Graciela went to a boarding school, right? Out in the country. What if they met there?"

"After everything I just told you, you really have to ask?"

"Lucy will. So you might as well practice the explanation on me."

She's right. OK, then. "It's not safe."

"Neither is driving a car. And you do that every day," she retorts.

"Driving a car is an acceptable, necessary risk. A trip to Mexico isn't." What if Bonita changed her mind when Lucy got down there?

"You're going to argue to Lucy, of all people, that driving a car is an acceptable risk?" Rebecca raises her eyebrows.

She's right again. But still. "This is an entirely different class. Drugs, gangs . . . there are State Department travel warnings, for God's sake. I looked it up online. US citizens should defer nonessential travel."

"This may well *be* essential travel. You thought so yourself, before."

"And now I have new information to factor in."

Rebecca's staring off into space. "Last summer. At Lucy's birthday dinner. Miguel talked about going home for his sister's *quinceañera*. In the spring sometime."

"March, I think. So what?"

Rebecca raises her eyebrows again and looks at me meaningfully. Unspoken, her idea dawns.

"What, you want him to take her down there? I couldn't ask him to do that."

"Do what? Invite three more people to the *quinceañera*. Lucy, Graciela, Bonita. What's the big deal?"

"Oh, come on, Rebecca. The responsibility . . ." And the possibility of Lucy falling in love with her Mexican *familia*. Wanting to stay.

"He's an adult. More important, he's an adult who loves Lucy and knows the lay of the land down there."

I hesitate.

"Just think about it, OK?"

The next day she calls.

"I checked, and the travel warnings are mostly restricted to a few border communities."

"Which she has to cross. Would have to, I mean."

"In an airport. With security all over the place. Where Miguel will be with her 24-7."

"Jeez, Rebecca. Whose side are you on?"

"Yours. And Lucy's. She's been good for you. Now she needs to realize you're good for her. Like I said, that starts with seeing that a future in Mexico is a dismal one."

But I can't be sure Lucy would conclude that. I shake my head, staring out the kitchen window. "Are you telling me that you'd let Jared go, if the situation was reversed?"

She pauses. "I can't say absolutely yes. Maybe that makes me a hypocrite."

"Maybe?"

"But the analogy doesn't work. I can't be you. Jared isn't Lucy. What I can say is I trust Miguel implicitly. He would protect Lucy like she was his own sister."

She's right about that. Am I trying to protect Lucy by keeping her home? Or myself? I draw a deep breath, trying to think clearly.

When Lucy gets home from school, her boots make it on the boot tray, at least.

"How was school?"

"What?" She stands there in her sock feet, looking almost like she did back when she arrived, alone and bereft. She lifts her hair off her neck and pulls it into a ponytail. Her face looks extra sharp. She's always been thin, but today the angles of her cheeks and her chin look starker than ever. Her skin looks pale against some dark circles under her eyes.

"How was school?"

She shrugs. "We got our report cards." She reaches into the backpack. "I know they'll email it, so I might as well just show you."

Her midterm card in November was pretty good, better than I expected from a kid at the front end of the middle of the pack, especially one with all the transitions Lucy faced last year. But this time the Digital Communications grade has dropped to a B and that's the best grade on it. Her GPA is listed at 2.3. There's a typed comment at the bottom. "Parent/guardian meeting advised. Please call to schedule."

Trepidation makes my hand tremble, and I dial the number wrong twice. Even though we discovered Lucy's plan before she got to Mexico, I knew that running away meant I'd probably already lost her. What other evidence do I need? Peaked, unfocused. Withdrawing from the cats, school.

Maybe the best I can do is help her move on.

Chapter 61
LUCY

It's freezing in Aunt Jane's truck. I wanted to ride the bus like I always do, but Aunt Jane said that doesn't make sense; she'll drive me to school since we meet with the counselor at eight thirty.

I miss Miguel. He's like Lexie, well, kind of. I don't have to worry about what he thinks. Sometimes we talk a lot; sometimes we don't. He's always in a good mood, but if I'm not, he doesn't seem to mind. And the bus is always warm when I get on.

Aunt Jane is, like, completely opposite. She's always waiting for a chance to say something, or wanting me to say something. And if I guess wrong, she's disappointed. I can feel her waiting right now, watching me out of the corner of her eye. I puff out a breath. I can still see it but only for a second. The truck's getting warmer finally. I pull off my gloves and hold my hands up to the heater. Aunt Jane clears her throat. Knew it!

"Is there anything that you want to tell me before we see the counselor?"

I shrug, keeping my eyes straight, staring out the dirty windshield at the gray sky.

"Are your classes too hard? Do you need extra help?"

"Uh-uh." I shake my head. We've had hardly any new snow since Christmas and the old snow and the cloudy sky blend into each other, both as dull and boring as this conversation.

"Then how do you explain how your grades slipped so much?"

"They're not *that* bad."

Aunt Jane sighs.

"They're not! I got Cs. That's average."

"But you're not an average student."

I didn't expect her to say that and can't help but look over at her.

"You weren't in New York, and you didn't start out that way here, either. Your midterm card was good."

I turn back to the window. We're passing the gas station in Mapleton, halfway down the peninsula.

"Now in two months your grade point has fallen a whole point. My concern is why." Aunt Jane takes a deep breath. "That was when you started planning to go to Mexico. Maybe that distracted you. Or you thought there was no point in working here anymore since you'd be living down there."

Hmmpf. I don't know. Maybe.

"And now you have the disappointment of being back here, and nothing else to look forward to. No reason to bother anymore. Am I right?"

I keep staring ahead.

"I talked to your Aunt Bonita."

What? Why didn't she tell me? "When?"

"About a week ago."

A whole week ago and she hasn't said anything?

"What did she say?"

"She's worried about you. Just like me." She pauses. "I can't say that you can go and live with her. That's her decision. But I can see you're not happy here, and it's getting worse. First you're neglecting school, now the cats."

"Lexie's *fine*!"

"So I want to propose a deal," Aunt Jane says.

Huh? I swerve my head to look at her.

"You bring your grades back up to a B average and"—she takes a deep breath—"you can go to Mexico."

"I can?" Suddenly, my stomach elevator is going up, up, up, climbing out of the basement. I thought it was broken and stuck forever.

"For a *visit*." She glances at me. "Miguel's going to his sister's *quinceañeara* in March, and he's willing to take you along. You can meet Bonita and Graciela. You can start there, and then we'll just"—her voice falters for a second—"just see what happens."

Now it's not only going up but feels like it's spinning, too. An elevator with a revolving door. It's crazy. She's going to let me go to Mexico? With Miguel? March is only a month and a half away! "Do you really mean it?"

"*If* you bring up your grades. That means do what the counselor says, whether it's extra homework or staying after school for help, whatever. And you keep up with your chores at home. No more empty cat dishes."

I can do that. The new semester just started, and I have Spanish this time. That's an easy A already.

"So—" Her voice falters again. "Do we have a deal, then?"

"Yeah." I nod as a little smile starts to spread over my face.

Chapter 62

JANE

Coatless, I step outside. A hot breeze, the kind that makes me want to head for shade, ruffles my hair, but there is no shade. The trees are leafless. Eerie, that's what it is. Just no other word to describe this in March. The two feet of heavy, wet snow we got the first week, the storm that downed the power lines again, gone within a week. Not melted into crusty piles or drifts, just simply gone, sucked into thirsty ground. The grass is still scrubby and brown, but warm enough for bare feet. In my beds the soil is in May-like condition, warmed and crumbly, a perfect cradle for the seeds it will nurture all growing season.

But there's the rub, right there. It's not the growing season. Not nearly. I can bide my time for a while. The orchards can't. Cherry and apple buds push forth every hour, aroused far too early. A day or two of seventy degrees we could survive. But since the day Miguel and Lucy left, temperatures have pushed eighty. Four days straight of pseudo-August weather. The tender green shoots swell from the branches, unaware of their imminent, indiscriminate peril. Frost.

May 24 is the average first frost-free day up here, more than two yawning, gaping months away. As climatically crazy as this heat wave is, escaping eight weeks without the temperature dipping below thirty-two is as fantastical as Lucy's runaway plan. Which I may have enabled, sending her to the *quinceañera*. Was that crazy, too?

Both weather and waiting for Lucy's return feel like another pair of deaths, in slow motion this time. With Lucy in Mexico, Martha's the only person I talk to. Her face is as ominous as an oncologist's as she sits in her car, elbow resting on the frame of the open window, waiting for me.

She hands me a small stack. Looks like a couple of subscriptions, ads, the Internet bill. I see the newspaper on the seat beside her. "Growers pessimistic," the headline reads, below the little weather icon of a full, mocking sun. Every day of sunny warmth the buds grow more vulnerable, the harvest more endangered. What about me and Lucy? Is every day with her Mexican *familia* endangering the fragile bond we forged?

"Been almost a week," Martha says. "Could even be worse than '02."

Spring frost killed the cherry crop in 2002, too. That was only a couple of years after I'd started Plain Jane's, so I wasn't as connected to the farm community. But I remember hearing about it as a fluke, once-in-a-lifetime event. Now here we go again, just ten years later.

"Worse? How?"

"This year's hotter, earlier." She sighs, pushing up the sleeves of her shirt past her elbows, as if just feeling it herself, before returning it to its window perch. "Sweets hung on back then, and apples. Not sure this time."

I nod. We all know Mother Nature doles out bad luck. Years when hail pulverized the fruit right before harvest. Wet years when disease ran rampant through orchards. Dry years when the crop was small. But those times felt within the boundaries of normal. And there were always people who fared better—the storm passed them over or they had a well-drained site or irrigation lines or something. An across-the-board, preemptory elimination of the second season in a decade is another thing altogether.

"Lucy and Miguel still gone?"

"They'll be back day after tomorrow."

She shakes her head again and starts the car. "Miguel won't believe it. Again."

It's that *again* that really makes this time worse. A recurrence, one that threatens life as I know it. No cherries and apples, no harvest. No harvest, no work. No work, no workers. People who've stayed, betting their futures like Juan and Esperanza, will leave. Most migrants won't come at all. Too much of a risk to travel without work waiting for you.

That threatens next season's harvest, too, because once bitten, twice shy. Without the picking workforce, even if growing conditions are perfect, fruit could rot on the tree. Then, after a couple of bad seasons in a row, farmers start to think again about trading in all the work and pain and suffering for that developer's offer. Instead of orchards sloping down to the bays, the view from my aerie could become condos, rows of soulless, twenty-eight-hundred-square-foot, two-story fortresses in three builder varieties.

It's almost physically painful to think about. Almost enough to make me forget what else threatens life as I know it, two thousand miles away at the *quinceañera*. Almost, but not quite.

Chapter 63
LUCY

Miguel's sister's gauzy pink dress is the poufiest I've ever seen. I don't know how she's going to get through the door. She has a jeweled tiara in her dark hair that's brushed shiny and fluffed out over her shoulders. She looks fancier than Mom when she went to the network awards nights, fancier than in her wedding picture, even. I look pretty fancy, too. Aunt Jane took the purple dress I borrowed for the banquet to a seamstress, who altered it to fit perfectly.

"Mija, tan hermosa," says Mrs. Esquivale, wiping her eyes as she comes into the bedroom where I'm sitting in a corner, watching Ana Maria and her friends get dressed. *Damas*, Miguel said they're called, the girls who are Ana Maria's best friends and all dressed up, too, but in white dresses, not pink.

Seeing Mrs. Esquivale cry reminds me of Aunt Jane when we left. "Listen to Miguel, now. He knows what he's doing down there," she said.

"I will."

"Only drink bottled water. Keep your passport with you at all times."

"OK. OK." She went on for a few more minutes, until Miguel said we really had to go. When she hugged me, I saw tears in her eyes.

The whole church service is full of crying. Way more than at Mom and Daddy's funeral, and this is supposed to be happy. Crying when Ana Maria walks in with her father. Crying when the priest blesses her. Crying during the communion. Crying when it's over and they all walk out in a big procession, Ana Maria and her *damas* and the priest, straight out the church door and outside, where the party is set up, right in the street, with a band playing and tables decorated with pink flowers and a delicious smell coming from under a white tent, where people are setting up big serving dishes. Finally, the fun part, and where I'm supposed to meet Aunt Bonita and Graciela. My heart is racing.

"Lucy? *¿Eres tú?* Lucy?" The voice is young, like one of Ana Maria's *damas*, but close by, when all of them are across the street, starting to dance. I turn, and there's the face I know from Facebook, the dark hair and skin like mine. Graciela, dressed up in a fancy turquoise dress. And behind her Aunt Bonita! Smiling and lifting up big sunglasses and crying just like Mrs. Esquivale. Then they're both hugging me, tight, and it feels so good, and I cry, too.

"Lucy." Aunt Bonita pushes her glasses on her head and wipes her eyes, then grips both my hands in hers. "You look like your father."

"I do?" Everyone always said I looked like Mom.

She nods. "I brought pictures to show you."

"Señora Ortiz?" Miguel's voice carries across the street, away from Ana Maria and the rest of the party. Aunt Bonita's eyes drift away from my face, and then she lets go of one hand, reaching out to shake Miguel's.

"*Sí. Llámame Bonita.* Thank you for bringing Lucy today."

"*De nada, de nada.* Was your trip"—Miguel hesitates—"all right?"

327

"Yes, *gracias a Dios*." She squeezes my hand. Why does she have to thank God?

"*¡Vamos a bailar!*" Graciela says, tugging my other hand, toward the dancers. "I've been in the car for hours and hours."

I hesitate. I want to stay and talk to Aunt Bonita and dance with Graciela, too.

"*Ve con Graciela, hermosa.*" Aunt Bonita pats my shoulder. "Have fun."

So I follow Graciela's dark hair and turquoise dress across the street. We dance a few songs, but then the music changes and everyone seems to kind of melt away until only Ana Maria and her father are left in the middle.

"*El baile padre-hija,*" Graciela says.

Ana Maria's father twirls her around the dance floor, looking very serious, like he's afraid he's going to forget the steps and mess up. Daddy wouldn't be worried about something like that. He'd know exactly how he was supposed to do it, and make it look easy, too. Wait, would he? Did he and Mom ever go dancing? They never talked about my *quinceañera*, not to me, anyway. Would I have had one? Would we have had a *padre-hija* dance?

"Only a year until mine," Graciela says into my ear. "I can't wait! You can be one of my *damas*."

"I can?"

"*¡Claro!*" Graciela sways to the music.

Of course. Her words stick as the father-daughter song ends and we all start dancing again. Who else would she pick but *familia*? And then Graciela will be one of my *damas*, in two and a half years. Maybe some friends from boarding school, too. I won't know nearly as many people, though. Will Miguel come to mine? Jared? Aunt Jane?

"*¡Tengo hambre!*" Graciela leads me to the food lines, and we carry our plates back to the tent with tables, where Aunt Bonita and

Miguel are sitting. Aunt Bonita's arm is stretched across the empty chair next to her, and when I sit down, she squeezes my shoulders, exactly like Mom or Daddy would have. I drain half my water bottle. It's so hot for March. My party will have to be inside, someplace air-conditioned.

"She looks well. It's such a relief to see her happy and healthy." Aunt Bonita is talking across me, to Miguel. "I am so grateful my niece has found a new home."

"Um. Aunt Bonita? I—"

"Perdón," says a voice behind me. Twisting around, I see Miguel's mother is back, with another girl in a fancy ruffled yellow dress. *"Lo siento.* I must claim my son," Mrs. Esquivale says. "So many friends and family he hasn't seen yet. You remember Rosa Alvarado, Miguel?"

"Rosita?" Miguel sits up straighter. "Not Esperanza's little sister?"

"Sí," the girl in the yellow dress says, smiling. She's wearing a bunch of the beaded bracelets like Esperanza's.

"Get Rosa a drink, *hijo,*" Mrs. Esquivale says, sitting down next to me. "Now Lucy, or Luisa, it is, *sí? Hábleme* about Traverse City. I miss it so."

"You do?" After she was deported?

"¡Sí! El L'agua limpia, las escuelas, las oportunidades . . ."

Clean water, schools, opportunity. So she's really talking about the United States, not Traverse City. I look at the bottled water. So what if I have to drink it this way. Schools? Graciela's boarding school will be fine.

"Oh, I never showed you the pictures of Luis. I'll go get them from the car," Aunt Bonita says, standing up suddenly, pulling her sunglasses over her eyes, even though it's evening now. *Wait!* I yell silently. I want to chase her, but Mrs. Esquivale is still talking.

"¿Cuántos años tiene?" Mrs. Esquivale asks.

"Twelve. I'm in seventh grade."

But no pets allowed, Graciela said. I'd have to leave Lexie. No boys, either. Jared's face pops to mind. We have two classes together this semester. No Miguel as bus driver, either.

A boy asks Graciela to dance. Now it's just me and Mrs. Esquivale at the table.

"And your *tía* has a farm that you help with, Miguel says," Mrs. Esquivale goes on.

Me, help with the farm? No way. Unless he told her about the farm stand. That's different. That was more like my own store, or business. Setting it up just right, talking with the customers. I didn't have time to get any of Esperanza's jewelry to sell last summer, but maybe this summer.

Wait. No, this summer I'll be here. Or not here, but in Mexico. At Aunt Bonita's house. Where did she go, anyway? Mrs. Esquivale finally leaves to talk to someone else. At last, I see Aunt Bonita coming back. Right away, she notices Graciela's empty chair.

"*¿A dónde va?*" Her eyes dart around the tent.

"To dance with someone. Aunt Bonita—"

"Someone? With who?" She starts walking toward the dance area, weaving around the tables fast.

"I don't know. A boy." I follow her as fast as I can. "Aunt Bonita, I really want to talk to you."

But now we're right on the edge of the dancers, and the music is loud, so loud we can't talk. Aunt Bonita has her arms crossed, and she's leaning forward, then to the side, then up on her tiptoes as she searches the crowd. It's like I'm not even there anymore.

The song ends and some of the dancers leave. There's Graciela, smiling up at a boy in a white shirt. He has his hands wrapped around her waist.

"There she is." I tap Aunt Bonita's arm and point. "Over there."

Graciela sees Aunt Bonita stalking across the floor, and her smile disappears. The boy drops his hands. Aunt Bonita pulls Graciela back over to me, whispering in her ear. Now Graciela crosses her arms and looks mad. When they get back to me, the music is starting again. Aunt Bonita pastes a smile on her face. "We came here to meet *su prima. Baila con Lucy.*"

Graciela takes my hand and pulls me out to dance, but I can tell it's only because she wants to get away from her mom.

"Mama makes me so mad!"

"What was his name?" I ask, looking where the boy disappeared.

Graciela shrugs. "He didn't say. He didn't even have a chance. It was just a dance. She never lets me do anything! I'm fourteen, after all. Look, here she comes." Graciela sighs angrily. Aunt Bonita's carrying her purse and has her sunglasses on again, even though it's nighttime, and a scarf over her hair.

"*Vámanos, Graciela,*" she says.

"*¿Ya? ¡Mamá, no!*"

"Already?" I say at the same time. I never got to talk to her!

"*Sí.* I'm sorry, Lucy. *Tenía miedo . . .* we can meet you *mañana.* For breakfast. I've arranged it with Miguel."

Miedo. Afraid. Afraid of what? But of course, I don't get a chance to ask her. She kisses my cheeks and swoops Graciela under her arm, and they're gone. She never showed me the pictures of Daddy, either.

That night when I fall asleep I dream about Aunt Bonita in her sunglasses and scarf, searching the dance floor, pacing all around, stretching up high, bending down low. Finally she sees what she's looking for, and her face gets all bright and excited as she rushes ahead, and then it's me who she sweeps up in her arms, not Graciela. For a long minute I hug her back, feeling so safe and happy. But when we pull apart and she takes off her sunglasses and scarf, the face isn't Aunt Bonita's, but Aunt Jane's.

I wake up by myself, on the floor at Miguel's parents' house. Automatically I reach down to pet Lexie, but my hand just brushes the blanket I kicked off in the night, since it was so hot. The *quinceañera* is over, and I only have one more chance.

Miguel and I meet them at a café. It's hot again, even before breakfast. Graciela smiles but still looks upset with Aunt Bonita, who's wearing another scarf and sunglasses. She shows me the pictures of Daddy, all from before I was born. He looks so young! I never saw him without a mustache. Aunt Bonita's in some of the pictures, too, but not the other man who was in the picture in Daddy's box.

As the waitress takes our orders, I work up my nerve. It's now or never.

"Aunt Bonita?"

"*¿Sí?*" She has taken off her sunglasses and is looking at the pictures with a sad, lost kind of look on her face.

"There's something I want to ask you."

"Of course."

I gulp a big breath, feeling Miguel watch me. "I . . . I'd really like to stay here in Mexico."

"And go to school with me," Graciela adds.

Even before Graciela has finished, Aunt Bonita is shaking her head, so fast it looks like a blur. "Lucy. I wish I could take you. Your father did so much for me, for us. But you are better off in the United States. He was so proud of you. *'Mi niña americana.'* He sent pictures." She pulls out another envelope and starts rifling through. I see the citizenship day photo at the Statue of Liberty, the Disney World photo with Mickey Mouse.

I look at my lap. My stomach feels like it did in Mrs. Creighton's office, after she told me about the car accident. The day I came to Traverse City, stuck in the hot truck with Lexie. In the ice-cream shop in New York, when Aunt Jane called Phoebe's mom.

"But you're my family."

"So is Jane, Lucy." Miguel interrupts. Aunt Bonita looks upset.

"Believe me, *linda*. If we could, I would. But it is not so easy. There are things you don't understand, things—"

"What? What don't I understand? Just tell me!" Mr. Langley said the same thing. It's been almost a year, and no one's explained it.

"Please, Mama. School is safe. You told me so," Graciela says.

"Graciela. Enough." Aunt Bonita speaks sharply as the waitress comes back with our food.

As soon as she leaves, Graciela starts talking. "I always wanted a little sister, too. *Por favor, mamá.*"

"Graciela, don't start. There are things you don't know, either."

"I do, too," Graciela snaps, folding her arms and sitting up straighter. "It's because of Uncle Fernando."

"What?" Aunt Bonita's face pales and she lifts up her sunglasses. "What do you know about your *tío*?"

"That he's a narco. Buys drugs, sells them, probably uses them. And he has enemies, dangerous enemies. People would use us to get to him."

My uncle is a narco? Dangerous enemies? I look around the table. Aunt Bonita's face is shocked, Graciela's is mad. Miguel's is sad, but not surprised. Did he know about it? Wait, Esperanza's story, about his family being deported, hiding behind locked hotel room windows and doors because Ciudad Juárez was not safe from the narcos.

"That's why we had to leave so early to come here, and drive so far, to lose his gang," Graciela continues.

Now Graciela's saying they might have been followed. They're not safe, either? Aunt Bonita still doesn't say anything, just gapes at Graciela.

"And that's why I go to boarding school. You're hiding me, or trying to." She slouches back in her chair, dropping her head so her hair curtains on both sides of her face, like she really is trying to hide.

Aunt Bonita is crying and kind of hiccupping as she tries to stop herself. "I know it's not fair. Uncle Luis was trying to get us out. To go live in *los Estados Unidos.*"

As I'm listening to them, an idea is growing in my head. A terrible, awful idea. If Daddy wanted to get them out of Mexico and Uncle Fernando needed them to stay—

"But even he could not do everything. It was slow. And expensive. And then"—her voice breaks—*"No tuvimos más tiempo."*

Then there was no more time? Or did someone cut it short?

Chapter 64

JANE

Miguel's face is grim through the bus doorway the Monday after they return. He manages a smile for Lucy, but it's gone as soon as she's past his driver's seat. He shakes his head at me, closing the door with a bang.

The bus pulls away, belching exhaust. My own breaths are puffs of white. So this is it, then. This is how a harvest dies. This, with the thermometer reading twenty-nine degrees, is the stage-four diagnosis. This, under clear blue skies, not even a wisp of a cloud that might trap some heat, is the *I'm sorry, chemo isn't an option now. There's nothing more we can do.*

But Lucy is home! Home to stay. It seems traitorous to Plain Jane's to feel so happy now, but it's the truth, as pure and simple as a fresh-picked apple. Nor has Bonita's refusal sent her down an emotional spiral, as I feared. She seems preoccupied since they got back Saturday, but not upset or angry. Maybe having a final answer, even if it's not the one she thought she wanted, was enough to put her on solid footing.

Later Miguel stops by in his truck with Lucy's suitcase, temporarily lost by the airlines. For the first time I can remember, his face is sober, not smiling. His step out of the truck is slow, not bounding. Under the brim of his cap, his eyes are dull.

"That bad?" I say, handing him a cup of coffee.

He nods, taking off his cap.

"When I got to the bus garage, I told myself not to worry. It would be OK out here. The water would protect them." He shakes his head. "But then, coming up Center Road, I knew I was wrong. I could see the frost, coating everything."

He bows his head, looking into his coffee cup. Hints of thinning hair startle me.

"Maybe things look better in Leelanau," I start, lamely. He knows it. *Growers pessimistic.*

"Even if they do, it's not even the first of April. Here I am, the April fool," he says bitterly.

"There's nothing you could have done."

"Not about the weather. But I could have been smarter. What's that you say, save for a rainy day?"

I nod.

"But here I was so confident. I could give Ana Maria her *quinceañera*. First it was just family. Then Mama asked me, can we invite a few friends? Sure, I said. Then it was that the church basement was too small. We needed to move it outside, rent tents, hire caterers. OK, Miguel? Sure, I said. Then it was that *abuela* and *abuelo* want to come, but they can't afford it. Can you buy them tickets, Miguel?"

El dinero se nos va de las manos.

"'Yes, Mama,' I told her. But no more, OK? *Nada más.*" He laughs. "When we get there, Jane? One hundred guests. A band. A banquet. Mama kept apologizing. 'I couldn't say no. I got carried away. My only daughter.' I used up all I had. If only I'd put my foot down."

If only. "Don't say that."

He continues like he didn't hear me. "The bills are still coming. Now this." He looks at me for the first time. "And the others. Juan and Esperanza, they are expecting a baby."

Niña or *niño*, I wonder automatically. So that's why they didn't leave after the season. Bad timing catching up to them, too.

"Raquel at Osorio's, they just had four or five relatives move up. They were going to open another location."

"They still could, couldn't they?" Work that's not dependent on the farms seems like the answer, actually.

He shrugs. "Mexicans are customers, too." Swallowing the last of his coffee, he scrapes his chair back wearily. "I have to go."

Next morning dawns frosty and cold, the thermometer again below thirty-two. Both the radio and the paper have long stories on the frost damage. The paper's got a close-up photo of a cherry bud covered with the deathly white crystals. There're quotes from farmers on both Old Mission and Leelanau rendering the same sentence: the 2012 cherry season is over before it started. Hope hasn't been completely abandoned for apples, but it will be touch-and-go for a while. Now I'm thankful for the USDA bureaucracy and the skeptical banker who denied me the loan for new trees. Anything newly planted would have been even more vulnerable.

Rebecca's number pops up on my caller ID.

"I saw the story in the paper." Her tone is serious. "It scares me, what we're doing to this planet."

I'm not surprised that Rebecca brings it up, but the bigger picture feels a lot less urgent when I recall Miguel's face yesterday.

"You just feel so helpless, as an individual, to do anything," she says. "I felt like joining Plain Jane's was one thing, especially the working share. Are you at risk, too?"

"Not the way the fruit growers and the migrants are. I've got time."

"The migrants?"

"They're the first ripple effect. No cherries or apples to pick, no work. It will keep a lot away. It's a pretty scary situation for those who stay, though."

"Can't they get other jobs?"

"Maybe some. But their skills don't exactly line up with what you see in the classifieds. Plus the language barrier, and the whole legal morass."

"Oh dear." Rebecca's quiet for a moment. "I just saw Esperanza. She's pregnant."

"I heard. Where did you see her?"

"At her house. Trailer, really. Paul got me a necklace and earrings for Christmas. I've been getting so many compliments I visited her to pick out some gifts. She's due in July. She was so excited."

That accident of birth north of a particular river changes everything. But July is almost four months away. How much can she sell a necklace for? A pair of earrings?

"I hope you bought a lot," I tell Rebecca.

Chapter 65
LUCY

Since we got back, I've been researching the narcos online, reading stories in Mexican newspapers, Wikipedia entries on gangs. Uncle Nando's gang is bad, really bad. I think it was his own gang that set up the car crash, not enemies. I'll bet Daddy knew everything, after all. He was going to get them out of Mexico. Then they would testify in a trial. The narcos would go to jail. Aunt Bonita and Uncle Enrique and Graciela could stay. Everybody would be safe. But if Daddy wasn't there to get them out of Mexico, well, then . . .

I'm telling Miguel on the bus today. He'll know what to do, how to start an investigation and stuff. And maybe then we could get Aunt Bonita and Graciela into the United States, after all! And Uncle Enrique.

But when I do, it seems like he's not paying attention.

"Nando's gang didn't set up the car accident, Lucy."

"How do you know?"

"Too risky, coming into the United States."

"Maybe it wasn't supposed to kill them. Just an accident. A warning."

"Plenty of ways to warn people in Mexico." He shakes his head. "You'd know it was them, too. Narcos rule by fear. They wouldn't leave you wondering."

"But—"

He's slowing down. "Look, the roads are icy. I need to pay attention to driving. Forget about it, OK?"

He sounds like every other grown-up. He's never talked to me like that before. I shrink down into my seat as he opens the door for the next bunch of kids, the cold blasting through the doorway and inside me, too. Maybe he was just in a bad mood? But I can't ask him again after school because I'm going to Jared's to work on a report for our Career Explorations class.

And the worst part is, if the narcos didn't cause the accident, then I still could have. *Step on the grass, make her car crash.*

"So what are your top three?" Jared asks.

We're in his room, at his computer. We're supposed to pick three jobs that interest us, and research the pros and cons of each.

"TV journalist, veterinarian, and FBI agent."

"FBI agent? Why do you want to be that?"

"So I can investigate people. It's kind of like a journalist, if you think about it. You just get to bring them to justice afterward." I can picture the headline: "Fernando Ortiz, convicted on hundreds of counts of drug trafficking, murder for hire, sentenced to life in prison."

"I think you have to go to a special school," Jared says. "Not just college."

"That's what I'll research for the report," I say. "What have you got?"

He looks at his screen. "Video-game designer."

"Is that really a job?"

"Somebody does it."

True. "OK. What else?"

"Pilot."

"That'd be cool. What's your third?"

He hesitates. "Don't laugh."

"I won't."

"OK. Well . . . farmer."

"Farmer?" I blink. "Like Aunt Jane?"

"Yeah."

"But . . . but you always complained about working there! Weeding, being hot, bored . . ."

"I know. It started out like that." He looks at his hands. "After a while I started to like it more. Being outside, and running the stand . . . I just changed my mind, I guess."

Huh. I stare at him.

"I thought we could do the stand again this summer. My mom signed us up for the work share and said maybe I can come out another day, too."

Just Jared coming out?

"People will remember us from last summer, so I bet we get even more customers this year," he says. "I thought we could make a Facebook page for Plain Jane's, you know, for advertising. And—"

"Wait a second." A Facebook page? Twice a week?

"What's the matter?"

"Nothing. It's just . . ." When did Jared make all these plans? He was the one helping me get to Mexico! Did he think I would fail?

The thing is, it does sound kind of fun. We could sell Esperanza's jewelry, like I thought of last summer. We could make maps to the lighthouse and wineries, and sell those, too. If we did it for a whole summer, we'd earn a lot from all the change people told us to keep. It feels really weird to be planning something at Aunt Jane's. I've wanted to get away for so long. What about Aunt Bonita and Graciela, still stuck in Mexico? What about the grass? The stepping stump path will still be there, but . . . it's so confusing.

"Lucy?" Jared waves his hand in front of my face. "Earth to Lucy?"

"I have to go to the bathroom," I say to escape.

The Livingstons have a big mirror that lets me see myself from the waist up. As I wash my hands, I turn to the side, trying to see if I'm growing at all. Maybe a little? Finally? I turn the other way. I didn't quite close the door, and shutting off the water, I hear Mrs. Livingston. She sounds really excited.

". . . been reading about it online."

"What makes you think a microloan could work?" Mr. Livingston's voice. He's not excited.

"Well, Ginny just loved the pieces I sent her, and everywhere I wear mine, I get compliments."

"You and your sister equal two customers. You didn't promise Esperanza anything, did you?"

Esperanza? I open the door a bit wider.

"Of course not. I wanted to talk to you first. But think of the possibilities we could open up for them, with a baby on the way."

Esperanza's having a baby?

"We? You want us to fund this personally? And just how micro are you talking?"

It was supposed to be a house first, then a baby. *Casa*, then *niño*.

"I'm not exactly sure yet, but—"

"How much, Rebecca?"

"A couple thousand. Five, if they were to develop an online store." Her voice is slower now.

"Five thousand dollars for beads and bracelets and earrings?"

"It's a loan, Paul. A *loan*. We loan Esperanza and her sister the money to buy the supplies. They make the jewelry and pay us back as they sell it."

"I'm familiar with how a loan works." He sighs. "What's the collateral?"

"They don't have any collateral." Mrs. Livingston sounds impatient now. "They're living in a migrant trailer, for heaven's sake."

"No collateral. No business experience. Uncertain market potential. If you were one of my clients, I'd tell you the risk ratio is about triple what's acceptable."

"I'm not your client, I'm your wife. We make these kinds of decisions together."

"What's taking so long? We still have to do the report, remember?" Jared's face appears in the gap of the door.

"Be right out." I shut the bathroom door and turn on the faucet again.

The house is empty when I get home. I go up to my room, to put on my birthday bracelets that Esperanza made. They are really pretty. I know people would buy them at the farm stand this summer. Could they sell more, enough to fill a whole store? Mr. Livingston doesn't want to help. And we don't have any money. If Jared and I ran the stand more, we could earn more.

Where is everybody? Lexie and Sarge are out mousing around somewhere. Aunt Jane's usually in the kitchen. I go back downstairs and look out the kitchen window. All the snow melted while Miguel and I were gone, so the stepping stumps are exposed again. I follow them out to the shed. She's busy with her shovels and rakes and stuff. Just like I thought.

"Hi."

"Lucy! I didn't know you were back." She puts a hand on her chest. "Did you finish your report?"

I nod.

"Just trying to get organized out here. This crazy weather, need to be getting ready soon. I didn't realize it was so late."

"Crazy weather?"

She looks surprised. "I guess this is your first spring here, isn't it? And you were away for most of the heat wave. Well, it's crazy, all right. Usually we still have knee-high snowbanks in March, and two months to go before we could hope to see eighty degrees."

I liked the snow, too, covering up all the grass. Aunt Jane goes on. "It's terrible for the fruit farmers. The whole cherry crop's already wiped out. Apples could be next."

"What do you mean?"

"I'll show you." She steps around her table, leading me out the door. But instead of turning down the stepping stump path to the house, she goes the other way, up the little hill behind it.

"Uh-uh." I shake my head when she turns around.

"Huh?"

I point to the ground.

She looks down at the stepping stump. "Oh." Her shoulders sag just for a second. "But it was OK all winter."

All winter it was covered with snow.

"Can you just give it a try?"

Graciela and Aunt Bonita are still in Mexico, trying to hide from Uncle Nando's gang. Now I have them to worry about. I shake my head.

She sighs. "All right. Let's just go back to the house, then."

She gets there first since I have to pick my way. The bark is rotting on the edges of most of the steps. One or two cracked right in half over the winter. In another spot there's a big gap where one is just gone, and I have to jump. Aunt Jane sticks her head back out the door.

"Could you get the mail? Martha was late today."

I nod. The path goes all the way to the mailbox. I pass the empty farm stand. If the weather has wiped out the cherry crop, maybe apples, too, what about the rest of the things Aunt Jane grows? Will we have anything to sell? I wish I could have followed her, to get the explanation.

The mailbox doesn't have much, some ads, a couple of envelopes. One is hand addressed and looks like a subscription. Aunt Jane will be happy. The other one is typed and upside down. I turn it over. It's addressed to me! Well, Estate of Lucy Ortiz, care of Jane McArdle. The return address says, "Law Offices of William E. Langley." What could he be writing about? I tear it open.

"Dear Ms. McArdle . . . in the matter of Hershey and Ortiz vs. NBC Telemundo, LAX Limousine, and Ronald James Prentiss, California DOT license no . . . in view of blood alcohol tests administered 4/13/11, deemed admissible by the court . . . to compensate for loss of affection and alienation on the part of minor child . . . settlement, less attorneys' fees . . ."

It goes on, but all I see are two things: *April 13, 2011.* The day of the car crash. And *loss of affection.* All of a sudden, I see Mom and Daddy more clearly than in months. Smiling. Laughing. Riding on Daddy's shoulders. Mom squeezing me in the mirror. Daddy singing, *"Abrázame muy fuerte,"* "Lucy in the Sky." Mom's face lighting up when we brought leftovers to her office on the weekend. Spinning in her anchor chair. Gone, all of it, forever. And the weight of it inside is like a hundred stomach elevators, pushing me down to my knees on the cold, damp stepping stump, where I crumple up the letter and sob until Aunt Jane comes running out, lifting me up, walking me to the house with her arm around me, asking *what's wrong,* over and over, *what's wrong, what happened,* and I can't answer, and we're finally in the house, bright against the darkening night, and I drop the balled-up letter and collapse on the couch.

I must have dozed off. There's a blanket over my legs, and Lexie curled up behind my knees. Aunt Jane is sitting at the computer. My throat is super dry, and I cough as I sit up. Aunt Jane swivels her head instantly. "You're awake."

She brings me a glass of water and sits down. Lexie meows and bounds away. After a few swallows my coughing stops. She smiles slightly.

"Well. Wrong day to send you for the mail." I see the letter, smoothed out but still wrinkly, next to the computer.

"What was that? What does it mean?"

"That you have money coming to you. A settlement for your parents' deaths."

A wave of despair rises up. "You mean somebody can just pay a fine, and—"

"Not just a fine. The driver of the limo is going to prison. He was drunk."

"For how long?"

"I'm not sure, but at least a year. I was doing some research about minimum sentences online." Aunt Jane waves at the computer.

A year. It's been almost a year since the accident. It feels both like forever and practically yesterday. I want prison to feel like forever to that driver.

"But the court believes you're due compensation, too," Aunt Jane says. "The settlement is from the limo service and the network."

"Huh?" It doesn't make sense.

"Because they hired a bad driver. This wasn't his first offense, turns out." She looks at me. "Time out for now. You need something to eat."

She heats up some beans and rice while I think. A drunk driver killed Mom and Daddy. I try to picture him, in prison. Someone who did it before. What happened the other time? If he had gone to prison then, maybe he wouldn't have been driving Mom and Daddy that day. Anger swells, but then something else dawns. If it was a drunk driver, it wasn't Uncle Nando and his gang. Miguel was right. Aunt Jane sets the bowl of beans and rice down. As I stir it, another idea occurs.

"It wasn't me, either." I don't realize I've spoken the words out loud until I hear Aunt Jane's voice, louder than usual, as she sits down next to me at the table.

"Lucy. Lucy. What do you mean, it wasn't you?"

"On the field trip." I can see myself back at the nature center, chasing Joel, tripping, the sickly sweet smell of the grass stains, the sticky green gunk under my fingernails. "Step on a crack, break your mother's back."

Aunt Jane's forehead looks like the letter, all wrinkled. "Field trip where? Step on a crack? What—"

"Step on the grass." I swallow hard. "Make her car crash."

"Make her car crash?" Aunt Jane says it like a question, then repeats it again like an order. Like how I always heard it in my head. "Make her car crash." She reaches for my hand. "You thought it was your fault? Oh my God—all this time—that's why—oh my God."

I look at our hands together. If she wasn't holding it, I feel like I might float away, I'm so drained inside. Maybe Aunt Jane realizes that, because she leans even closer and puts her other arm around me, squeezing my shoulders. "Why didn't you ever say anything?"

"I just . . ." I shrug. "I just couldn't."

"You thought you caused the car accident. All this time. My God . . ." She leans back, shaking her head. "But you realize now you didn't, right? That's what you just said."

I nod, then shrug again. "I guess."

"Don't guess. Know it. Believe it." She reaches for my hand again, sandwiching it between hers. "Some bad things just happen. As much as we want to explain them, they just happen. Not because of us, just to us."

"It's not fair."

She pauses. "Well. No. And yes. It's not fair that your parents died while you were so young. But unfair things, bad things, they happen. It's—how can I say this—universal."

My lip trembles. She squeezes my hand.

"I don't know—" I start to say.

"Let me show you. We can take that walk to the orchard now, right?"

Thinking of the grass, automatically, I hesitate.

"In the morning. Eat now. And then more sleep."

My clock says seven thirty. I rush downstairs. "I'm going to miss the bus!"

"I called in and said you were taking the morning off," Aunt Jane says calmly.

"You did?" Aunt If-There's-School-You're-Going? A plate with a muffin and a glass of juice sit on the table.

"I did. You'll learn plenty on our walk. Now how about some pancakes? Or an omelet?"

"Pancakes." I eat them in a daze, unable to take my eyes off the window. I'm finally going to walk on it.

"Ready?" Aunt Jane says when I've swabbed up the last of the syrup.

Lexie's waiting at the door, too. She bounds off like always. Standing on the concrete threshold, I watch her go up the little hill toward the barn, where I spent so much time last summer. It's not very green yet, which helps a little. It's a little bit cloudy. That helps, too. It doesn't feel like it's a big deal day. Just an ordinary day.

"Let's go," Aunt Jane says, heading off for the orchard up on the ridge behind the house.

So I follow her. On the stepping stumps at first, but when I get to the gap, I don't try to jump. I squeeze my eyes shut as my sneaker slaps the actual earth.

Holding the rest of my body stock-still, I bounce on my toes. It feels resilient, like the mats in gym class. I open my eyes to peer at my feet. They look the same as always. I scuff my toe into the grass, corkscrewing the blades. Stooping down I see I've smushed a little of it, releasing that sweet smell. I let my fingers brush the tips, then grip a handful and tug. Momentarily the earth resists me, hanging on, then yields possession. I look up and see Aunt Jane watching me. A breeze blows hair across my face as I stand up and let go, too, the green wisps scattering gently back down. Then my stomach elevator rises, up, up, up, and I run, my feet pounding hard and wild, fast and free, so weightless that it feels like I could take off, fly right up over the orchard, Lucy in the sky, up to Mom and Daddy in heaven.

But Aunt Jane is waiting and wants to show me something. She's waving and smiling, and now clapping, and she looks so happy. And I can see the farm stand from here, waiting for me and Jared, and the barn where Lexie is. I look up again, tip back my head, and kiss the air, *xoxox*, and then run over to Aunt Jane, who I think might be crying, but she wipes her eyes so quick I'm not sure.

"Well?" she says. "So far so good?"

I nod. It's quiet and still. No whispering voices, no elevators creaking. Just us and the trees.

"OK." She clears her throat. "Here we are." She swoops her arms out. "These are my apples. Like I said, they may be all right. They shouldn't look like this until May." She lifts a branch dotted with green leaves and tight, pinched buds. "But so far, we're lucky. It's another story over here."

She leads me farther away from the house, to another bunch of trees. They're a little smaller, and no leaves. Puckered greenish-brown buds dot the branches. Near the top some of them have opened into beautiful white flowers, but the edges of the petals are browning, too. Aunt Jane bends a branch down and pinches one of the buds. It's soft, not tight like the one on the apple tree. "That would have grown into a cherry. Except it got too hot, way too early. The tree got tricked. And then, when the normal weather returned . . ." She waves her hand. "Well. You see."

Going off in every direction are trees just like it, rows and rows, branches sparsely sprinkled with the browning blossoms and buds, covering the whole hillside.

"Miguel manages this orchard," Aunt Jane adds. "Hires the labor, like Juan, to spray it, tend it, pick it, prune it."

"So then, what does that mean?" I point at the branch.

She lifts her shoulders gently. "No work here this year."

"But—but, then how—" I think of Juan in the car. *This is a great country.* He and Esperanza, first a car, then a house, then a baby. That already didn't go right. Now this. Miguel's family, depending on him. "It's not fair."

"No." Aunt Jane is looking right at me. "Just like your mom and dad dying wasn't fair."

My breath catches. I look around. From up here, I can see the water on both sides. I feel something between my ankles and look down. There's Lexie, doing her figure eights.

"Sometimes bad things just happen," Aunt Jane says again. "And it's no one's fault."

I squat down to pet Lexie. "But that's . . ."

"Scary. You're right. But it's better than blaming yourself." She squats down, too, and squeezes my hand. "Believe me."

I run my fingers through Lexie's soft fur. I never took the bracelets off last night, and I spin them around my wrist again. I imagine Esperanza making them, choosing the colors, stringing each one. I think about her baby, and her and Juan wanting it to be born here. *Americano*, like Miguel. Like Daddy became. Like Aunt Bonita and Graciela wanted to be. I look up at Aunt Jane.

"I want to spend some of the settlement money."

She raises her eyebrows, but I rush on before she can say no. "To help Esperanza and Juan. They need money to stay here till their baby is born. Esperanza could make more jewelry if she had money for more beads and stuff. I heard Mrs. Livingston talking about it."

I hold up my wrist, jingling the bracelets. The sun glints off the beads, making them sparkle. Aunt Jane looks, but it doesn't seem like she sees them. She's looking past them, at me. It's completely quiet. She has to say it's OK.

"She wanted to help them, loan them money, but I don't think Mr. Livingston does. So I want to. I won't need the money for a long time, anyway." I take a deep breath. "They need five thousand dollars."

Another minute passes. She's still looking at me.

"Aunt Jane?"

"I think that's a fabulous idea. Finding work beyond the farms seemed like the best solution, but I didn't know what. And you're right, you won't need to access the money for a while, so there's time to make a loan." She looks at her watch. "We can call the bank as soon as we get back inside."

I exhale a gust of breath and grin. I pick up Lexie and rub my face against hers.

"It's very touching that you want to help Esperanza and Juan. Your parents would be proud of you," she says, reaching out to scratch behind Lexie's ears.

I swallow hard and look down at my feet, on the ground. Her hand moves to my shoulder and squeezes.

"I, uh, I'm very proud of you, too," she says.

Then her arms are all the way around me, and I feel myself lifted up, but it's not a stomach elevator; it's just her hug, *abrázame muy fuerte*. And I hold her very tight, too.

Chapter 66
JANE

Lucy can well afford the five-thousand-dollar loan. The settlement is for one million dollars, which doesn't seem like much for losing two parents. But it's more money than I've ever seen at once, and it secures Lucy's future a lot better than it had been.

I take the notification letter to the desk in Matt's room, where I've finally organized her files in the bottom drawer. It could be considered the start of a home office, in fact, since I'm gradually migrating in the CSA records. In it goes to the car-accident folder, the label typed by Langley's secretary so long ago. Mixed in are a few folders with labels I've handwritten, like the newest, *"Hermanas Hermosas,"* containing the loan papers from the bank. Beautiful Sisters, Esperanza named her jewelry business, since her sister, Rosa, is coming up from Mexico to help her.

Hermanas Hermosas drops in alphabetically behind the thinnest folder, its label also handwritten, bearing simply the letter *G*. I take out the notepaper filled with black and blue cursive.

> *They won't tell me about Luis. I think he's already dead.*
> *If I go, you get Lucy. I'm sorry. I should have told you. I*
> *couldn't. Take care of her. You will, won't you?*

You were such a devoted mother. I was afraid. I'm
sorry. Too late now. Forgive me. Just take care of our baby.
Watch out for Nando. His family must not—

Each time I read it, something else sticks out. First it was the devoted mother characterization. Then the warning about Nando. Tonight, the repetitions strike me, the regret and fear echoing. *I'm sorry. Take care of her. I'm sorry. Take care of our baby.*

Biologically we were half sisters, but emotionally we could have been identical twins. Regret and fear, fear and regret. The only difference is I have more time.

Opening another drawer, I turn to a fresh page in the notebook where I journal about Nina.

Dear Gloria—
I'll take care of Lucy. She's a kind, thoughtful, smart
girl. Don't be sorry. Be proud of her. Love her.
I know I do.

My hand stops, like my mind can't quite believe what it's written. Yet it's true. Somehow I've managed to outrun the regrets and fear to get here. It's not much, but it says it all. Carefully I tear the sheet from the notebook and slip it into the *G* folder.

I stand up, and my eyes fall on the desk calendar. *I have more time.* That lone difference is huge. I turn two pages ahead, to June. Matt said around June 1. I don't know about army leave policies, but it can't hurt to have another set of hands with a newborn.

What about Lucy? School won't be out quite yet. Rebecca would let her stay with them. But then, what about the cats? Find a house sitter? And all the to-dos for the start of the season? The new school wellness subscribers?

Finding work beyond the farms seems like the best solution. For a week or two, Esperanza and Juan could house-sit and manage the CSA. Lucy could start summer vacation a little early. She has another cousin to meet, after all.

It's time to silence the echoes of fear and regret. I pick up the phone to call my son.

ACKNOWLEDGMENTS

Writing a book is often likened to having a baby. My thanks to those who midwifed this work during almost four years of literary gestation. (That's twice as long as an elephant. Just sayin'.)

The Powerfingers: Mardi Link, Anne-Marie Oomen, Teresa Scollon, and Heather Shumaker. You guided me to the essence of this story.

The beta readers: Kandace Chapple, Patti Link, Barb McIntyre, Jennifer Pedroza, Sonja Somerville (again!), and Barb Wunsch. Their individual expertise on farming and CSAs, bereavement and grief, and Mexican-American family life helped authenticate Jane and Lucy and made their story a page-turner.

The Lake Union team: Miriam Juskowicz, Danielle Marshall, Chris Werner, Laura Petrella, Karen Parkin, and cover designer David Drummond.

Developmental editor Tiffany Yates Martin, who coaxed the best of Jane and Lucy out of the draft she read; Blanca Berger Sollod, who inspired Lucy's grass phobia; Rick Coates, whose coverage of deportations in northern Michigan inspired Miguel's character; the Leelanau chapter of the League of Women Voters for their work and studies on migrant labor issues; and Dan Hubbell, for walking me through the legal aspects of guardianship and custody. The Traverse Area District Library offered work space when home wasn't available. And at home, Mike, Owen, and Audrey rode out the highs and lows all along. *Gracias, familia.*

BOOK CLUB QUESTIONS

1. Lucy doesn't think Jane acts "motherish." What do you think of Jane as a mother? Did Gloria and Luis make the right choice when they selected her to be Lucy's guardian?

2. As she returns from meeting Lucy, Jane thinks: "Beginnings come from endings. All you can do is try to hang on to everything so it doesn't get lost along the way." Do you think we ever resolve grief, or does it continue to impact our lives? Is it possible to let go? How have grief experiences affected your life?

3. What do you think about Jane suspecting Juan and Esperanza as the jewelry thieves? Do unflattering stereotypes have a place in literature, if only for the sake of exposing them, or not?

4. Do you think Juan and Esperanza have a human or moral right to stay in the United States? Why or why not?

5. After talking to her son, Matt, at Christmas, Jane feels absolved of her maternal guilt. Do you think she is justified? Why is her recollection of Matt's childhood so different from his own? Whose is correct?

6. Had the Livingstons not discovered Lucy's runaway plan, do you think she would have boarded the plane for Mexico instead of returning to Traverse City?

7. Lucy's grass "phobia" is really a form of magical thinking. Have you ever developed an irrational belief like this? How did you overcome it?

8. Would Lucy have been happier with her Mexican relatives? What do you think happens to Bonita and Graciela?

9. When the spring frost hits, Jane thinks that "the bigger picture [of climate change] feels a lot less urgent" than the consequences of a season without work for the migrant community. Can short-term and long-term ramifications of our decisions ever be balanced?

ABOUT THE AUTHOR

Cari Noga is the author of *Sparrow Migrations* and *The Orphan Daughter*. She wrote the first drafts of both books during National Novel Writing Month (NaNoWriMo), which takes place every year in November. *Sparrow Migrations*, her debut novel, has been adapted into a five-part miniseries script. Cari earned a bachelor's degree in journalism from Marquette University in Milwaukee. In 1997, she landed in Traverse City, Michigan, for a summer job. For four years, she covered the region's evolving agriculture economy as a reporter for the *Traverse City Record-Eagle*. She and her husband live in Traverse City with their two children. Visit her at www.carinoga.com.